Tome II

Jonni Jordyn

The Untold Prophecy

*Dedicated to my granddaughter Lauren who showed me
both the good and the evil sides of a teenaged girl.*

Power corrupts
Absolute power corrupts absolutely

Lord Acton (1834-1902)

The Untold Prophecy

CHAPTER 1

Day zero

The world didn't realize it yet, but everything that everybody knew about everything just changed. The worlds of science and theology that had long been at odds with each other needed to redefine their places in society. Believers of both had traditionally allowed each to make sense by balancing the two; giving science domain of the physical and theology domain over the metaphysical. But there's a new player for them to contend with, and magic touches both the physical and metaphysical.

The events that occurred at the Boutin residence signaled the reawakening of magic in the world. The remote location of those events may have hidden them from view of anybody who wasn't already closely involved, but there were still

*others who knew, and the rest of the world was about to
learn about it.*

On most summer nights, the sweet perfume of honeysuckle would have mixed with the fetid musk of plant decay and assaulted the nostrils with a sweet and sour concoction that was the bayou. Tonight, however, the air was laced with the pungent stench of death and sulfur as the ash and smoke from the burning home, the charred remains, and the unnatural fire drifted ominously across the swamp.

Johnson was a blur in his camouflage fatigues as he crashed through the murky water, oblivious to the natural dangers the bayou presented. The moon cast slender beams through the cypress trees which barely illuminated the ground, but twinkled off the choppy water. He knew the gators were there, and he was no match for them in the water, but they didn't frighten him enough to stop running away from this place. Small patches of high ground presented them-selves to him as miniature islands of land jutting out of the swamp. When one plot ended, he jumped in and kept moving. The gators would have to catch him.

He saw another spot of dry land and leaped out of the water. His boots and socks were soaked. They squished beneath his weight as he ran blindly between the barely visible trees and plowed through the thorny brush.

What he had just seen was unnatural. They weren't human, and he wasn't one of them. They made fire and lightning out of thin air, with nothing but their hands. He didn't know what they were, but they couldn't be human. As a soldier, he was trained to face many enemies, but he wasn't prepared for this. She looked like a normal girl, pretty even, but she wasn't normal. She couldn't be. He emptied a full clip into her, or into something. His bullets found their mark and impacted upon the air around her as if she were shielded by bulletproof glass, but there was no glass. She was engulfed in flames and his bullets just burned up and fizzled out.

He was a tough guy. He had always been a fighter, and he thought he was brave. That's why he took jobs as a soldier for hire. He would fight anyone, anywhere, for the right price, but he couldn't fight this.

The land ended before him, and he jumped back into the water. He landed with a mighty splash and his boots sunk deep into the muck below. He struggled to suck his feet out of the mud and keep moving. The next plot was just ahead. He forced his way onward, swinging the weight of his weapon to help pull him forward. He reached the next island and climbed ashore, but when he plunged into a stand of cypress trees, he heard a splash behind him. Something or someone was following him.

He zig-zagged across the land, keeping as close to the large trunks as he could. Small twigs scratched against his face as he weaved his way through the trees. The distinct sound of boots stomping behind him echoed in his ears. That wasn't a gator.

His heart and his mind raced. Instincts and training took over. He stopped abruptly behind a large tree and planted his rifle against the trunk, aiming it directly behind him. His actions followed years of training, and he already regretted stopping even as he was still planting himself up against the tree. The moonlight flickered through the waving trees and glinted off the sight on the end of his rifle. His rifle was useless against them. He wondered if any weapon would have worked. Maybe, if he had armor piercing depleted uranium rounds, he could penetrate their shields. His mind was wandering now. He had to focus his thoughts and take control of his actions. The brush parted before him, and Gomez came crashing directly into his line of fire and ran right past him.

Johnson called out, "Gomez? Is that you?"

Gomez stopped ten meters past him and setup in similar fashion, aiming his rifle into the swamp from which they had just emerged.

The swamp was quiet. The water rippled and lapped up against the shore behind where they were standing. They could still see the glow of the fire in the distance, and they were still close enough to smell the smoke and ash, but there was little movement other than themselves.

Gomez scanned the area behind them and said, "I think it's just us. I don't think they are following us."

"How would we know?" Johnson asked. "I don't even know what they are, or what else they can do."

"I know," Gomez admitted. "I'm kind of sorry I ever teased Ray about being so superstitious."

"Yeah," Johnson said. "Me too."

The two men remained frozen, with their weapons trained on the path they had just taken. Their faces were painted with angular black and green patches, like their clothes. The whites of Johnson's eyes shone like beacons against his dark skin. They held their posts, rocking slightly against the trees as their chests expanded from the heavy gulps of air their lungs sucked in. Neither of them had ever known fear like this. They had no protocols to fall back upon. They were on their own and had to improvise.

Johnson broke the silence and said, "We should probably keep moving."

"Agreed," Gomez said. He felt childish for even thinking what he was about to say, but added, "Let's stick together."

Johnson was still staring down the barrel of his rifle when he heard his name shouted out, "JOHNSON!"

He shook his head and said, "Shhh."

"What?" Gomez asked.

Again, the voice reverberated in his head, "JOHNSON!"

"Knock it off Gomez!"

"What are you talking about?"

"Didn't you just yell my name?"

"Yell your name? Don't go wigging out on me now."

"This is no time for..."

"JOHNSON!"

This time he was looking directly at Gomez, and he knew it wasn't him. He snapped his head around, checking all angles for another person.

"JOHNSON!"

He swung his gun around, pointing it all over the bayou. "Where's it coming from? Can you tell?"

Gomez wasn't watching the swamp anymore. His eyes were on Johnson, and he was getting more than just a little concerned. His comrade was acting way out of character, and he had no doubt that what they just witnessed could have something to do with it. He didn't know how to respond, so he shrugged his shoulders.

"Are you telling me you don't hear it?"

"JOHNSON!"

Johnson dropped down on his belly and pointed the gun towards the fire. "There it was again," he said hoarsely.

"Look man," Gomez said. "I don't know what you're hearing, but I've seen enough crazy shit for one day and if it's them, I'm not sticking around for them to find us." He jumped back into the swamp and headed west, which he hoped would keep him clear of the small town where they started out.

"Johnson," the voice said without shouting this time. "I have a job for you."

Johnson put his head on the ground with his arms covering his ears, but the voice was in his head.

"I want you to go back to your vehicle and drive it up to Lafayette. When you get there, I'll have new instructions for you. If you fail to follow these instructions, your life will be forfeit and your mind will be overcome with madness. Do you doubt me?"

Johnson had thought that he could never be more scared than he was when he saw them shooting fire and lightning from their hands, but he was mistaken. This was in his head, and it was far more terrifying.

"Johnson," the voice said. "You must acknowledge your orders."

Johnson still had his head on the ground and was on the verge of a full breakdown, blubbering into the muck. "Affirmative," he replied. "I'll get the car and drive it to Lafayette and wait there for further orders."

Johnson remained trembling on the ground, afraid to look up when the voice barked in his head, "MOVE OUT!"

Johnson sprang up from the ground and took off, crashing through the thick brush and splashing full speed through the murky water towards the town.

The three librarians nodded and smiled over the successful implementation of phase one of their plan. They sat cross-legged in the middle of a small room with plain off-white walls which were void of any distracting decoration. They wore their formal grey robes with large hoods that covered their heads and hung low over their faces. The room was lit with a soft ambient glow that cast neither bright spots nor shadows. This was where they came together to meditate and cast those special spells that required two or more of them to work in unison to combine their powers. The room was built solely for the librarians. Outsiders were seldom permitted, but today, one other person was present in the room.

One of the librarians turned toward their guest and said, "Thank you for joining us, Mark. We have just begun the first part of our new plan and are pleased with our efforts so far. In our next phase, we will find a similar subject that we can use to launch a more direct attack for us as well, but as you know, our target is quite resilient."

"You mean the girl?" the guest asked.

"Yes," another librarian took over the conversation. "We mean the girl. She is unpredictable. You may still have a role to play should she slip past the traps we have set."

The third librarian said, "If she does not give up her plans to contact her mother, she will be going into a dream state in her mother's mind. Your task is to enter her dream world, as you have done before, and prevent her from reviving her mother. We would very much like it if you could convince her to give up and go into hiding instead."

"But," the first librarian said, "and we cannot stress this enough, you are NOT to kill her! Do not even attempt it!"

The second librarian said, "Repeat it. Tell us you know she is not to be killed."

Mark's cheeks flushed. He did try killing her on his last mission, and he thought he had succeeded, but his mission was only to prevent her from fulfilling her destiny. The librarians had to terminate his mission by yanking him from the dream world. "I understand," he said while nodding his head. "I am not to kill her. What about her mother?"

The three librarians put their heads together. Nothing was spoken aloud, but they nodded their heads inside their hoods and conversed telepathically.

"What about the mother?" the first librarian asked.

"She is of no consequence," said the second.

"But the girl would not take it well, and she would certainly retaliate," replied the first.

"Against whom?" asked the third. "Certainly not against us. She doesn't even know we exist."

"No," the first added. "Not against us, but against the others. Not entirely a bad thing, if you ask me."

"But," the second said, "we still do not want to risk exposure of our kind to humanity."

"True," admitted the first.

"What are we saying?" questioned the third. "This fool will fail. No matter what glamour he casts upon himself, she will still recognize him and kill him."

"An acceptable sacrifice," said the first.

"Yes," said the second, "but then she will be looking for us."

"Fine," said the third. "She may look for us, as long as she does not find us. Let us hope she will be distracted from her current goals."

"Let us not forget," added the first, "that even if she suspected our existence, she wouldn't know where to look."

"Nor when to look," said the third. "We can follow this course of action and still remain safe."

"Agreed," all three said together.

The librarians ended their private conference, and the first turned towards Mark and said, "The mother is of no concern to us. You may do what you want with her."

"And," added the second, "you may do what you will with anyone else who may join them."

"Except the boy," cautioned the third. "No harm is to fall upon either the girl or the boy. Not under any circumstances."

"Yes," said the first firmly. "You must even be willing to sacrifice yourself before you cause any harm to either the girl or the boy."

Mark swallowed hard. His eyes glassed over a bit at the suggestion that he may have to sacrifice himself, but he acknowledged them. "I understand. No harm to the girl or the boy. When will we know if I go in?"

"Soon," the first said, "but there is time enough that you may have a meal. Make it a good meal. We don't know how long you will be in there."

"It should not be long," said the third.

"Certainly not as long as your last mission," added the second.

"But you must be prepared, and you must have your strength, so eat a good hearty meal," said the first.

None of the librarians expressed their belief that this could well be his last meal. They simply bowed their heads and remained silent. Mark stared at them blankly, unprepared for the abrupt end of the conversation. The third librarian extended his arm and pointed towards the door. Mark knew he was dismissed.

"I will miss him," said the second.

"I won't," said the third. "He tried to kill her. Had he succeeded, it would have been all of our heads."

"Yes," agreed the second, nodding his head. "*HE* would have killed us for sure."

"Or worse," added the first.

Michelle kept a light grip on the throttle as she guided the small boat away from the blaze that had been their home since before Destiny was born. She wasn't quite sure what to make of the boy that sat between her and her granddaughter, but how was she supposed to tell a sixteen-year-old girl that the boy was trouble? She didn't trust him, but he *did* save them when they needed it most, and she was grateful.

Destiny twisted around in the front seat of the small boat and watched the flames receding behind them. A tear, too small even to be wiped, formed in her eye as she watched their home shrink from view. A deep melancholy began to supplant the vigorous adrenaline rush which she had sustained throughout the evening. "Nana?" she asked. "I'm sorry I burnt down the house."

"Hush Cherie, it warn't your fault. If daer be blame, it was dem men dat come wit' Blake here."

"Nana! You can't still be thinking Blake is one of them, can you?"

"No," Michelle sighed. "I reckon not." But she couldn't ignore her feelings.

The smoke was thick overhead, blotting out most of the light from the moon, but Michelle knew the way and could guide them back to the mainland in the dark if need be. She released the throttle and turned the boat for one last look at their home. Her white hair glowed faintly orange from the great fire that was consuming the structure and most of the small island where they had lived.

"I wish," she said, "there was time enough to grab up some of my special herbs and seeds before we lit out o' there so fast."

Another tear formed in Destiny's eye as she added, "And Martha, Claudia and Stick Master."

"Stick Master?" Blake asked.

"Ah yes," Michelle agreed, "the chickens too."

Michelle twisted the throttle and guided the boat back towards the edge of the swamp, and the civilization that lived just beyond the border. There was no use crying about it now. The smoke thinned as the home disappeared behind them, but the smell of ash stayed with them, saturating their clothes and hair. Worse still, was the smell of burning flesh that was etched indelibly in their memories.

"What do we do now?" Destiny asked.

Michelle answered, "We move on. We start over."

Destiny shook her head. "We can't move on like nothing happened. Those people are still out there."

Michelle stared intently at the back of Blake's head and said, "Those people is still right here with us."

Blake bowed his head remorsefully and said, "They may have raised me and taught me the things they know, but I was never one of them. I was always an outsider to them."

"You is an outsider to us too!" Michelle snapped back.

"Nana! That man was gonna fry me. I can still taste the electricity in my mouth from when he wrapped those coils of lightning around me. Blake rescued us. How can you still call him an outsider?"

"She's right," Blake said. "I'm not one of you. I'm not one of them. I don't know what I am."

"You're like me," Destiny said. "We have the power of both clans; the witches and the sorcerers."

"How dat be?" Michelle asked. "I been havin' the memories, visitin' the ancestors since I was a little girl, and they all said the power has been gone for near a thousand years. How come now, all of a sudden, you two gots the power?"

"Not just us," Destiny said. "Did you see that sorcerer? He was really powerful."

"Maybe," Blake said, "but he only just got his powers since we started looking for you."

"What about you?" Destiny asked. "How long have you had your powers?"

"Well," Blake answered, "I could always do some stuff, since I was twelve or thirteen, maybe, but I never done nothing this cool or this powerful until you started doing those things that you been doing."

Destiny cocked her head and asked, "What things have I been doing?"

Blake shrugged and replied, "I don't know what you do, but we all felt it."

"You all felt it?" Michelle asked. "There's more of you?"

"Yeah," Blake said. "Well, not more like me, but there are more of them. Brian's the only one that I know of who developed any power."

"And you of course," Michelle said, "plus Destiny makes three of you."

"What about you Nana? You put that voice in that soldier's head and nearly scared his soul right out of him. I heard it!"

"Yeah," Blake nodded his head. "I heard it too. That was pretty cool."

"Well," Michelle said sheepishly, "I don't rightly know what dat was."

The moon had fallen lower on the horizon and was unable to penetrate the thick canopy of the Cypress trees. The boat was surrounded by darkness and bumped it into a log, causing two gators to splash into the water. Michelle and Destiny had lived in the swamp long enough not to be too overly startled, but Blake was rattled. He held out his hand, palm up, and conjured a small orb of fire in his hand to illuminate the swamp where the log was.

Destiny leaned her head back and said, "They're just gators. You don't need to be so skittish."

"I know," Blake lied, "but there's more out there than just gators."

"What?" Destiny asked. "You mean those other two soldier boys? They're long gone. They high tailed it on foot then turned that-a-way," she pointed west, "because they're afraid of us and didn't want to be between us and the Bend."

Blake held his hand higher to watch the gators leave. They put a respectable, safe distance between themselves and the boat, then turned and faced the trio. Their eyes glowed red in the light of Blake's fire.

Michelle held her hand to her eyes and said, "Put dat fire out. I cain't see nothin' with you blindin' me like dat!"

Destiny snickered. "But Nana, I thought you always said you could find your way blindfolded."

"Hrumph," Michelle said. "It just be different wit' dis motor."

Blake tossed the ball of fire into the water, where it twisted and undulated like the glowing globs in a lava lamp. Destiny watched it fight for life. It spun and pulsated and just as it began to dim out; it shrunk into a tight ball and began to glow brighter. It grew into a brilliant point of light, then expanded until it filled her vision and all she saw was the bright light.

A blinding light blazed across the sky, bringing unimaginable heat that seared Destiny's skin and permeated her flesh. The wave of heat quickly washed through her and continued well past her. The molten hot light stretched out in every direction, dissipating and dimming as it stretched thinner and thinner until it faded out and Destiny could see the clear blue sky again.

The heat was followed by a terrible wind. It carried with it anything that wasn't fastened down and everything the blast was able to break loose. The wind roared in Destiny's ears as she was pelted with ash and debris that was caught up in the wake of the horrible explosion. She could see a column of smoke lift high into the sky. It was an immense pillar of soot, rubble, and disintegrated matter. It rose high into the sky until it reached the very top of the atmosphere and spread out at the edge of heaven into the cap of a mushroom.

Destiny had to do something. She knew this was the doing of the same people that tried to kill her on her nana's island and she wanted to strike back, but she was frozen. Not even her vision was under her control. She knew how to project her magic without the use of her hands, but she was unable to muster any kind of magical field. It felt like she was viewing one of her ancestral memories, but at the same time, she knew this was her own.

Immobilized as she was, she couldn't even cry. Though she was aware of her surroundings, she doubted her feelings. This could be a dream world, or it could be the real world, she couldn't tell. She tried to stretch out her feelings, but could sense nothing beyond the walls that surrounded her. She was in a bed, in a room. Why would she be in a bed if a war was being waged? How could she see and feel the great blast if she were in a room? She had many questions and no answers.

She heard a door open, followed by someone entering the room. Her stomach twisted into knots. She knew that feeling. It was the ancient cramp that witches and sorcerers felt when in each other's presence. But Destiny was different. They couldn't sense her that way. She was like them in some ways, but she was special, a hybrid of witch and sorcerer. She could do what they do and sense what the witches sense, but they could not sense her coming.

A sorcerer had entered the room, she could tell. He was there to kill her. That too, she could tell. She tried to summon a fireball to blast him back out of the room, but she could not. He approached the bed where she lay motionless. Her eyes were closed, and her hair was a blonde mat of tangles pressed against the pillow. He leaned close over her. A wicked smile formed across his face.

"Hello, little witch," he said into her face. His graveled voice was as foul as his breath. He pointed a finger and played with a few stray hairs that were stuck to her cheek. "I'm so sorry," he continued, "that you are unable to play. I was hoping for a more dramatic victory, but I will not allow this moment to pass just because you are not feeling yourself. I know that this isn't what you were hoping for, but it is time for your story to come to an end. You are not the chosen one, after all. You are merely the key to unlock the power that was destined to be mine all along. For that, I must thank you. I do hope you can hear me. I so hate being unappreciated for my efforts. Please, feel free to scream out as you feel your life slip away. I will try my best to bring enough pain to rouse you from your sleep."

For all the sorcerer's blustery talk, Destiny could tell it wasn't really him boasting. He was just a messenger. An avatar for a woman Destiny has yet to meet, but someone her future self, lying in the bed, knew all too well. The sorcerer puppet bowed his head and closed his eyes. He gathered his inner strength, then leaned back a half step, cocked his arms and blasted a terrifying pain throughout her body. Her whole body seized in agony, and she felt like her eyes sprung wide open, but her body lay there limp and unresponsive. She was screaming on the inside, but completely dead to the world on the outside.

She heard the door fling open again. Her mother entered the room and wrapped the sorcerer's mind in a field of terror and self-loathing. Her field terminated his connection to the woman pulling his strings. The pain in Destiny's body ended as the sorcerer fell to his knees and wept over all the wrong that he had done and all the wrong he might have done. He turned his magic upon himself and screamed mercilessly as he writhed on the floor and twisted like a worm until his being faded out, leaving only the stinking shell of a never quite human being on the floor.

Destiny wanted to cry out for her mother, but the vision popped from her sight, and she found herself staring at Blake's fireball as it sunk to the bottom of the swamp.

Blake's fireball sunk deeper into the water until it finally settled on the bottom and sizzled out.

Michelle eased her grip on the throttle and said, "You don't need to sass me none, little miss fancy pants. I knows my way in the dark just fine. It's just dat dis boat be a bit faster than your old nana goes with just pushin' the long pole."

The boat finally eased out of the thick swamp into an open area free of the oppressive trees dangling moss and vines from overhead. The low moon reflected green off the duckweed which covered the top of the water. Blake looked behind them and shuddered as he saw the red glow of two eyes peering out of the surface of the water. The horizon around them was dark, but the dock at Cricket Bend was illuminated by the gas station across the street. Michelle pointed the boat towards the dock but kept the throttle low.

Destiny knew that she had just had a vision. This vision included her mother, but more than that, her mother came for her and saved her. She didn't know why she was paralyzed in bed, and she didn't care. The most important element of her vision was that her mother had been freed from her mental disease and she needed her mother to save her. She chose to keep the vision to herself. There was no reason to worry her nana, but her future was clear: she needed to do something to save her mother.

"Nana?" she asked. "Where are we going?"

"We goin' to Cricket Bend, Cherie. You kin already see it ahead. Why would you ax such a silly question?"

"I know where we are going right now," she replied, "but what about after? Where are we going to go?"

"Well," Michelle said. "I been thinkin' on dat too. Could be we goes back to my daddy's farm where I grew up in Mississippi."

"Mississippi?" Destiny cried. "I don't want to be that far away from Mama!"

"Yeah, you right about dat. I guess I has a bit more thinkin' to do on how we gonna care for your mama if we goes back home."

Blake felt like even more of an outsider when they talked about family. He slunk his head down in his hands and wished he weren't smack dab in the middle of them.

Silence passed for a while, with only the low drone of the motor and the splash of the water in their ears, until the boat finally approached the dock and a pelican leapt off the end of the dock voicing his disapproval of their presence.

"Nana, you think maybe I could heal Mama? Then she can leave the hospital and just go with us without needing no special care."

Michelle loved her granddaughter's heart. "Dat be a wonderful sentiment, Cherie, but your mama ain't hurt like dat. I don't think you can heal a thing that ain't broke, and iffin you did, she would still be da same as before. Not learnin' her control of her gifts and goin' crazy all over agin. Then she be just like before and have to go right back to the hospital, only this time, she have us to blame for it."

"Still, I think I should try. If those other men come looking for us again, we might need her."

Michelle was torn. She didn't want to see Destiny disappointed, but she also didn't want to put her daughter through that kind of pain again. She sighed softly and said, "We'll sleep on it and see the way things be in the mornin'."

Dr. Richard Schaefer paced back and forth in his office, from the credenza near the door to the windows behind his desk. It was a nice office with a beautiful wooden desk and all the amenities, and he earned it, but he was going to miss it if things went wrong, and blame fell upon him. He wasn't a very powerful man; neither in physical strength, nor was he highly ranked within the organization's national or global presence, but he was the top dog at this facility. His hopes of gaining some national recognition if this operation was a success were slowly fading away. He kept one eye on his cell phone and the other on the weather. The weather didn't really concern him, per se, but he was watching for the sunrise. It may have been easier to monitor a clock. He had three of them in his office, but his main concern was with the start of business and when people would start arriving at their desks. He worried how long it would take Brian's office to wonder where he was. Checking his cell phone again showed no new texts. His last contact with Brian was over six hours ago when Brian texted him and said they couldn't ascertain the status of their operative and were going in to recon the situation. That was not good news, but neither was not hearing back from them after six hours.

Schaefer and Brian were both members of the sorcerer clan. For millennia, the sorcerers ruled the world. Find any king, emperor or even just a tribal chief, and he either was a sorcerer himself, or he had one by his side pulling his strings. They had only one enemy in the world: the witches. They hated the witches, and the witches hated them back. Wars were fought between the sorcerers and the witches and were usually won by the sorcerers. The last war, fought a thousand years ago, was a war of genocide. The sorcerers vowed to wipe the witches from the planet, and as the final hour neared, the witches produced a prophecy claiming that all magic would be lost from the world if the sorcerers persisted in this war. All magic would be lost until the day when a child born to both clans would come and reclaim it.

The sorcerers did not heed the witches' warning and proceeded with their plan to annihilate all witches until the first part of the prophecy came true and their powers were stripped from them. That made the sorcerers hate the witches even more, but they were powerless to use their abilities to kill the remaining witches and hatched a new plan. Instead of killing the last of them, they chose to use them to fulfill the second part of the prophecy.

Brian was higher up the corporate ladder than Richard. He was inducted into their inner circle and was given an upper management position as a regional director. He had the authority to work autonomously and mount an operation of this magnitude by himself. Schaefer was recruited by Brian to work on the project for him, overseeing the lab work and analysis to identify and locate the source of the disturbances that they called 'prophecy level events.'

He was instrumental in triangulating the location of the witches, although the truth was that it was really the boy that zeroed in on them. Schaefer's rank within the clan gave him access to the prophecies. He hadn't been aware, until Brian read him in, that their clan had been secretly conducting breeding experiments to cross the bloodlines, which is where the boy had come from. If something has happened to Brian, then what might have been a brilliant plan to return the sorcerers to their former glory would become an ill-conceived plan that risked their exposure, and Schaefer was not only aware of what Brian was doing, but he was now aware of secret programs that were above his pay grade.

He pressed the redial button on his cell phone, but like all his previous attempts, the call could not be completed. This didn't necessarily mean anything. Brian was in a remote location and could be out of range of the nearest cell tower, except that Richard thought Brian had a satellite phone which didn't require a cellular tower.

Richard bit his lip and looked out the window. A few scattered clouds high in the sky glowed brightly as the sun was about to peek over the foothills in the east. He wondered how long he could continue with business as usual before someone questioned him about Brian. He wondered how often the person who actually orchestrated a black op such as this actually went on it.

If Brian remained missing, there would be nobody in a position to cover it up and Richard could very well be the only one left to catch the flack.

The dock at Cricket Bend was not a huge structure. It was large enough to accommodate the inboard motorboats piloted by the wealthier residents, but the small boat that the trio rode was dwarfed by the main dock. Michelle steered the craft alongside the dock to a lower landing that was built for the tiny canoes and pirogues. The landing bobbed on floats, but Blake had no trouble climbing out and securing the bow line onto a free cleat. He reached down and offered a hand first to Destiny, then to Michelle, helping them out onto the platform.

The sun had not yet poked up over the eastern horizon, but the brightly lit gas station provided ample illumination to see three of the four main structures that comprised Cricket Bend.

A cool breeze blew across the three figures as they made their way down the dock to the mainland. The creaking sound of the wood was replaced with a crunching sound from the gravel that lined the shore and the highway. Directly across the road from them was the general store. Michelle crossed the road and peered in the windows of the general store. She knew it was too early to expect Henry to be up. She considered knocking but decided not to disturb him. Destiny tried the door, but it was locked.

"I got this," Blake said. He approached the door and reached inside with his mind and turned the tumblers to unlock it. He then reached out and easily opened the door.

"So," Michelle said, her voice dripping with disgust. "You're a thief too?"

"I'm not a thief," Blake defended himself, "but I had to learn how to improvise to survive. Besides, the men I came with rented a room overhead, so I have a right to be there. We can wait there till morning; maybe even catch a little sleep."

Michelle pulled the door closed and shook her head. "I been knowin' Mr. Henry too long now to be makin' him think he gots burglars in his store. Besides, I 'spect he gots himself some rock salt loaded in his shotgun and I don't want none o' that aimed at me. We can wait over in the diner."

Michelle considered checking the postbox, which was in the third structure that lined the highway, but there was nothing she was expecting, and she wouldn't know what to do with any mail she might get now, anyway. She led the other two down the steps and over to the gas station and the diner. Blake paused a moment when he saw the large barn hidden in the shadows on the other side of the gas station.

"That's the community center," Destiny said. "It's where..."

"I know," Blake interrupted. "I recognize it from the visions."

Michelle cocked an eyebrow when she heard that. She could tell that they shared a vision, and she was excluded. She frowned but shrugged it off and continued to the diner.

It was a small diner, barely large enough to host a handful of travelers that came through now and then on the bus. Most times, like now, it was empty, but remained open to service the truckers that came through sporadically.

A small bell on the door jamb rang as Michelle pushed the door open. Marie, their hostess, waitress, and cook, had been napping lightly and was surprised by the bell. She jumped up from her chair at the far end of the counter and greeted them from across the room, "Bon Jour, Bon Jour."

She straightened out her apron and her jet-black hair, then walked the length of the counter to greet them at the door. "I'm sorry," she said with an accent that mixed the customary Acadian with a slightly purer French, "but I am moving too slowly. I did not hear your car come in."

Michelle smiled at her warmly, unsure how she was going to ask if they could wait inside until the store next door opened. "Nonsense," she said. "We be sorry for wakin' you. A pretty young girl like you needs her beauty rest. You gots no need to apologize to a bunch o' vagabonds like us. Asides, we come by boat. You looks familiar to me, I'm sure we must have seen you at one of the Planchette's shin digs, but I don't believe we've ever been formally introduced. I'm Michelle Boutin, and I do regular business with Henry in the general store, but I'm sorry to say we never occasioned to come in here before."

"But," Destiny added, "I always wanted to come here for supper. My friend Gilbert told me you had a television here that he used to watch with his mama."

"Gilbert?" Marie asked. "Then you must know Madame Thibodeaux."

"Yes," Michelle said. "Ezora and I are well acquainted. This sassy young lady be my granddaughter Destiny, and that be her friend Blake."

Marie knew who Michelle was, but even though Michelle was Christian, her family had always shunned Michelle's practice of tonics and home remedies as non-Christian, so they had never allowed her to become friends. Marie had always abided by her family's wishes, but secretly wanted to know Michelle, because of the many things she had heard. Blake was about to plant a suggestion into Marie's head that she invite them in for breakfast when she volunteered, "Why don't you come in and find your seats? I'll go make some breakfast for us all."

Michelle was horrified, and patted her dress as if she had a pocketbook hidden somewhere in the folds. "But we have no..."

"Tutt tutt!" Marie interrupted her. "Do not insult me by trying to pay for what is my treat. I must apologize, mademoiselle, we do have ze TV, but this time of morning, they only show ze weather and farm reports."

Marie disappeared into the kitchen.

Destiny slid into a corner booth and Michelle sat next to her, with Blake on the opposite side of Destiny.

"She was sure nice," Blake said.

Destiny gave him a cold look and said, "You mean pretty, don't you?"

"No, I meant that she was really generous to offer us some food. I didn't have to push her or anything."

"Push her?" Michelle asked. "Is that somethin' you can do? Has you been pushin' us?"

"No ma'am, I never did that to either of you."

"Uh huh," Michelle's distrust grew a bit further, "but you done it before to people?"

"Sometimes," Blake admitted, "when times are desperate, I have helped people want to be more generous and considerate."

Michelle nodded slowly and said, "I was right before. You is a thief."

Blake started to speak but thought better of it and put his head down on the table. He wasn't going to win this battle.

Destiny was still giving him the same cold look. "So, you never answered me. Do you think she was pretty?"

"What?" Blake looked up at Destiny. "Her? No! I mean," he swallowed hard, "I suppose she is pretty if you go for that sort of look."

"That sort of look? You mean big, pretty eyes?"

Blake's voice weakened as he meekly replied, "Maybe..."

Destiny continued, "Or maybe you mean her pouty lips, or is it her creamy cocoa skin color?"

"Her skin color?" Blake saw no escape. "Your skin is a pretty color too! More pretty even!"

"So, you admit she was pretty."

"No! I mean...she...but you..."

Michelle softened a bit to see Blake caught in such a bind. "Boy," she said, "you best just quit now and put your head back down on the table like you was before."

Destiny cast the same icy gaze at her grandmother.

"Don't you be givin' me that look," Michelle said. "You gots to learn how to deal with this."

"Deal with this?" Destiny squealed. "I'm supposed to be okay with him looking at pretty girls?"

"Unless you plans to cast a spell on the whole world makin' all the other girls homely, or maybe a spell that makes him blind, I 'spect he'll be seeing other pretty girls."

"Blind?" Destiny asked. "Would that work?"

Blake popped his head up and softly said, "Destiny?"

Michelle shook her head and said, "Lord Almighty, what am I going to do with you?"

Marie returned with a platter of Beignets and Couche-Couche. She placed the platter on the table and said, "Bon Appetite!"

When Marie started to return back to the kitchen, Michelle asked, "But aren't you going to join us?"

"Oui! But first I have some Cafe au Lait to bring to ze table."

Blake had never sampled the local cuisine before, but wasted no time sinking his teeth into a Beignet. "Mmmm," he said, "it tastes like a donut." He was never terribly fond of mush, but cautiously tried the Couche-Couche and found it sweet and delectable.

Marie fetched the coffee and placed the mugs around the table, then sat down next to Blake, which earned him some more cold stares from Destiny.

Michelle and Destiny ate their meals, but watched Blake who was obviously tasting these foods for the first time. He sipped his coffee and puckered his face at the bitterness from the chicory. He reached for the sugar, but Marie slapped his hand and said, "No!" She picked up one of the Beignets, which were covered in powdered sugar, and showed him how they dip them into the coffee.

Destiny started to give Marie the evil stare, but Michelle elbowed her in the side and Destiny returned her attention to her own breakfast.

Marie nibbled the end off of her Beignet and dipped it into her Cafe au Lait while her guests devoured their Couche Couche. None of them had realized just how hungry they were until they had started eating.

"You know, Madame Boutin…"

"Please, call me Michelle."

"Oui, Michelle, my mother was always afraid of you. She saw the potions you sold at the general store, and we hear the stories that people say, but she said it wasn't Christian, and that you were a sorciere, a witch. I only ever heard good things about what you do, but my mama would not listen."

In the back of Michelle's mind, she thought the better approach, especially after the destruction of their home, was to admit nothing, but instead, she blurted out, "Your mama's right. And you be right too."

"And," Destiny added, "My nana is a good Christian too. We can be both."

"Mon Dieu! You too, mademoiselle?"

Destiny put her hand to her mouth and whispered, "Ooops."

Michelle smiled and said, "It's okay, Cherie. Marie is a friend now."

"Oui! Oui! I buy your lotion to soften my hair. It smells so good."

"Yeah," Destiny said, "but watch out for them bees. They might think your head is a flower."

Marie laughed and said, "But don't tell my mother. She would punish me if she knew."

Destiny nodded her head and glanced at her nana.

"A couple nights ago," Marie said, "I saw you gathering with your friends at ze Planchette's party. My mother calls them your court, or sometimes when she drinks too much, she calls them your coven. To me, it looks like just gossip, but at ze last party you left in a big hurry. Is everything alright? You looked so scared when you leave."

Michelle's better sense took over, and she said, "We just had some bad news, that's all."

Blake took one of his beignets and scraped the remains of his mush from the bowl. "I never had this before, but I sure do like it."

"Would you like some more?" Marie asked.

"No, ma'am, I wish I had more room. It was so good." Blake drained the remains of his Cafe au Lait.

Marie smiled and said, "Let me get some more coffee, at least."

"Jest some regular coffee, please," Michelle said.

"Oui," she said as she went to the kitchen and returned with a pot of coffee and four fresh mugs. She placed the mugs around the table and asked, "More Beignets anybody?"

Blake was tempted, but all three declined.

Marie sat down next to Blake again and sipped her coffee.

The sun was streaming in through the windows now. "Thank you," Michelle said. "You are a marvelous host, much too good for a bunch o' freeloaders like us, but we must be seeing Henry next door about the bus schedules."

"You are going somewhere?" Marie asked.

"We're gonna go see my mama," Destiny said. "She lives in… that is, she lives up north."

"I don't think I have ever met your mother."

Michelle shook her head and said, "She been gone since she was a teenager and don't visit us down here."

Michelle slid out of the booth and said, "You kids stay here and finish your coffee. I'll just go talk to Henry next door and come back for you."

Marie followed her to the door and said, "Hurry back. We can talk more. You are always welcome here."

Chapter 2

Day one.

The world still looked and sounded the same. The sun rose and the birds sang. Only the burned-out hulk of the Boutin residence and its smoky odor remained behind to tell the story, but the days of innocence were numbered. The genie was out of the bottle and there was no putting it back.

Michelle crossed the parking lot and climbed the steps to the general store's porch. She was mortified as a slight breeze swept across her face, and she could still smell the smoke from her hair. What must Marie be thinking, with the three of them smelling like ash?

The sun was warm and welcome. Even though it was still early in the morning, she could feel in her bones that it was going to be a nice day. It was too early, she knew, for Henry to have opened the store for business, but she thought he might be stocking his shelves for the coming day.

She peeked in through the window of the door and lightly rapped her knuckle against the glass. She still couldn't see or hear him and rapped again. Henry emerged from the cellar door and heard her knocking. He put the box he was carrying down on the counter and came to the door to tell the customer he wasn't open yet, but seeing Michelle at the door, he opened it and said, "Bon Joo Michelle, it be too soon for you to be makin' groceries. Did you forget somethin'?"

"No, Henry, I didn't forget nuthin. I apologize for disturbing you, but I'm in a jam. I gots to get myself, Destiny and her friend on da bus to Lafayette."

Henry knew about Destiny's mother, but he was too polite to say so. "Ah, you be needin' a bus schedule and some tickets then. Dat be no problem."

"Well," Michelle said, "that might be a problem. I got nothin'. No money, no goods to sell. Nothin' at all. I was hopin' maybe we could settle on the goods I left you last time."

"What is it, Cherie? Etes-vous en pris mal?"

Michelle had known Henry a long time, and regularly brought him potions and remedies which he sold to the tourists. Occasionally, Henry would arrange for her to mix up special potions for locals. She had never confided in him, but this was no time for her to stand on ceremony. "Yes, Henry, things is bad. We lost our home and everything in it."

"Co! No! What is it?"

"It burned to the ground."

Michelle hadn't really cried to this point, but she felt the tears bubbling up. Henry put his arms around his friend and said, "Mon Dieu! Comme c'est terrible! How?"

"How it happened don't matter, and you don't need to be gettin' involved."

Henry held her tighter. He was afraid of what he was thinking and asked, "Was it dose men?"

"What men?" she asked. "How did you know?"

"I put dem up over da sto. Dis is all my fault. I fix this. Whatever you needs, you just take."

"No Henry, I just needs to make a bill for my stuff and hopes it be enough to get us to Lafayette."

"It be enough. I make sure of it. If I spill da milk, den I pass da mop. I be da one dat make dis misere, so I pick it up and make it right."

Henry released Michelle and walked around the counter to the bus schedules. He filled out three tickets for Lafayette. "Da bus be here at ten, but it be late mostly."

Henry watched Michelle leave his store and walk over to the diner. His eyes narrowed when he saw Destiny and Blake meet her in the parking lot. He recognized Blake as one of those men.

It was five after ten when the bus arrived. It squealed and hissed as it pulled to a stop. The sweet scent of honeysuckle was overpowered by the acrid odor of diesel fumes as the bus sat in its place with the motor at a low grumble. The door opened to let the passengers off so they could use the facilities, grab snacks, and buy some genuine bayou souvenirs.

The driver busied himself counting the passengers who left the bus and reminding them to keep their ticket stub to get back on. Michelle was content to let him finish before showing him their tickets and boarding.

"Michelle! Michelle!" Marie ran out of the diner to catch her before she boarded the bus.

"Marie!" Michelle exclaimed. "What are you doing out here? You've got customers!"

"My time is over for today. My mother can care for them." Marie wrapped Michelle in a warm hug. "I want to say goodbye and give you this." She handed Michelle a bag full of sandwiches. "It's for your journey. I am only sorry I waited too long to finally meet you."

Michelle glanced over at the diner and asked, "But what about your mother? Won't she see you with me?"

"Oui, she might. If so, then I tell my mother I'm a big girl. I have my own friends."

"She still won't like it."

"If she does not like it, then maybe the day will come when I get on the bus too."

Michelle returned the warmth of Marie's hug and said, "I too be sorry we never met sooner."

Henry saw Marie hand a bag to Michelle and guessed it might be snacks, so he ran to the cooler and grabbed some sodas. "Excuse-moi," he said as he squeezed past the passengers that came in to browse his items. "I be bag here in two shakes." He ran from the store, down the steps, and out into the parking lot to give Michelle the drinks.

"Now Henry," she said, "what does you think you is you doin'? You already done too much."

"Nonsense, Cherie, I already miss you fierce." He leaned over and whispered in her ear, "You watch dat daer boy. He be one o' dem men."

Michelle nodded her head and said, "I knows. He turned agin them and helped us out when we needed it most, but I gots it in the back o' my mind that he still be trouble. You best gets back to your store now."

Henry returned to the store and Michelle saw the driver leaning up against the bus checking his watch and lighting a cigarette while he waited for the passengers to return. She approached him with her tickets held out in front of her.

He tipped his hat and said, "Morning ma'am." He accepted the tickets, tore off the ends and returned the stubs to her as he looked around for bags, but seeing none, returned to leaning against the bus and puffing on his smoke.

Michelle waved for Destiny and Blake to join her on the bus. She handed each of them their stubs and led them up the stairs.

The air on the bus smelled as stale and old as the bus was, which was not as bad as the sooty smell from their clothes. A newer bus might have offered better air, but she couldn't complain. She had nothing in her pockets, but they were still getting out of there, and probably would never return.

A few passengers had remained on the bus and Michelle nodded to them as she boarded, but they mostly ignored her. The few that did acknowledge her were quick to glance away, lest it lead to unwanted conversation or something. She walked down the aisle, checking right and left for some empty seats. The first few rows either had people still in the seats, or personal items, which she assumed were left by passengers visiting the diner and the store. Halfway back, she found a couple empty seats and said, "Here we goes. Destiny, Cherie, since you ain't road da bus dat much, why don't you go ahead and takes da window?"

Destiny was eager to have the view. The springs squeaked under the seat as she slid in. Michelle was quick to slide into the aisle seat next to her and said to Blake, "How 'bout you takes da seat in front of us?"

Michelle handed each of the kids their sodas and said, "Might as well drink these while they is cold. We got sandwiches for later. I reckon it be a pretty far piece to Lafayette."

Marie stood outside and waved at them. Michelle waved back. Blake started to wave but Destiny kicked the back of his seat to get his attention. He looked back at her and shrugged his shoulders and mouthed, "What?" Michelle could only close her eyes and shake her head.

The glare on the glass was hard for Destiny to see through. She wished she had worn a sweater with long sleeves so she could wipe the smudges off the window, but she only had on a t-shirt and shorts. If only she knew a spell that could clean the windows. She knew how to make fire and lightning, but she didn't know how to make soap.

The driver climbed on the bus and tooted the horn twice, then returned to his position outside the door and checked the stubs of the returning passengers as they slowly made their way back to the bus. When no more came, he climbed up the steps and counted heads from the front of the bus. The head count was short by one, but he could hear the last passenger snoring in the back of the bus. He climbed into his seat and closed the door.

"I hope you had a good rest, ladies, and gentlemen. Our next stop is Lafayette. The time now is ten fifty. We should arrive around one in the afternoon."

The brakes hissed, and the engine whined as the bus lurched forward and swung back around to the road. Destiny was glued to the window, watching the countryside fly by and the bayou disappear behind them. This wasn't her first time out of Cricket Bend. She used to go up to Anderton with her friend Anton and his mother. Anderton was only a half hour up the road and was their nearest town. Anton's mother would take them to the library or sometimes the mall. There was even a cinema in the mall, and on occasion, she would treat them to a movie.

Destiny had even been to Lafayette to visit her mother once. Michelle's cousin Louie had come for a visit and had driven them up there. He had been concerned about leaving Tempest so far away from the family at St. Austin Mercy hospital. He even offered to take her with him to their granddaddy's farm, but Michelle convinced him that Tempest was okay there, and that it was the best thing for her.

The bus seats were so far above the ground that Destiny felt like she was flying. She could hear the air rushing by the bus, making it easy to imagine she was a bird gliding alongside her nana.

As the hour pushed past noon, the temperature outside and inside warmed and windows were cracked open on the bus, but not much else had changed. The scenery rushing by was the same as it was an hour ago and the same as it would be in another hour until they reached the outskirts of Lafayette. Destiny leaned her head against the window and closed her eyes. She could hear the noise of the tires against the road through the metal frame of the bus. It throbbed and pulsated against her head and blended with her heart pounding in her ears. Shadows of the trees flashed against the smudges on the glass and flickered on her eyelids. Her heart fell into a soothing rhythm that was sympathetic with the road noise until she felt her whole head swooning to the hypnotic beat.

The sounds of the bus were replaced with the crackling of a fire. Destiny opened her eyes and found herself in a stone room dimly lit by only the fire. She was sitting on a large burlap sack filled with something soft but lumpy. In front of her was a large, cushioned chair that blocked most of the warmth emanating from the moderately large fireplace. Rings of smoke ascended from the chair, smacked into the ceiling, and faded into nothingness.

A deep elder man's voice said, "I trust all went well?"

She looked around but could see no one else in the room.

"Come now," he said. "You haven't come all this way to hide in the corner, have you?"

Again, she saw nobody else in the room.

"Why don't you come join me by the fire? It's rather nice here, and I doubt that sack of grain could be that comfortable."

She rose timidly and walked around to see who was in the chair. It was an elder man with long white hair and an even longer white beard. His skin was wrinkled, but his eyes were bright and young. "You!" she exclaimed, rather accusingly.

"Yes, my dear, tis I."

"Why didn't you tell me? Why all the little games?"

"Games?" he asked. "I played no games with you."

"No?" she said. "You should have told me who he was."

He put his pipe down on a table next to his chair and said, "I couldn't take that risk. Please, sit down and let us talk."

He motioned to the other chair, and she nestled into it.

"That's better," he said. "You were both in far too much danger for me to divulge his identity to you. I needed the two of you to discover each other. He had to save you, and you had to save him."

"Save him? I never did that. He may have saved me, but only barely. He was going to let me die!"

"But he didn't. And by saving you, he was saved."

"So, this was all about him, then? Because he is one of your grandchildren?"

The old man nodded his head and said, "Yes, but he is several generations removed, as are you."

"So, we are both from you? We're related to each other?"

"Bah!" he said. He picked up his pipe again and blew another smoke ring. He wiggled his fingers, and the ring changed into the shape of a heart. "When did you become such a prude? If you go back far enough, it is difficult to find any two people who don't share some lineage. The two of you are so many generations from me that you have nothing to fear. You come from Nimisen and me, while his blood took a somewhat different path."

Destiny was shocked. "Does Nimisen know?"

A woman's voice behind Destiny said, "She does."

Destiny jumped up and turned to see her. She had only seen her once before. In fact, Destiny was her, reliving one of her memories, and she was very young at the time, but Destiny still recognized her. She ran up and wrapped her arms around Nimisen. The old woman chuckled and said, "Well, it's certainly nice to see you too."

Destiny released her grip and said, "I'm sorry. I'm not quite sure why I did that."

"It's quite alright. It is healthy to love oneself, even if one isn't one's self at the time."

Destiny didn't understand.

The old man chuckled and said, "Now dear, you make it sound like a riddle."

"Love is a riddle," she said. "It always has been."

Destiny was confused. She looked at Nimisen, then at Marvalaine, then again at Nimisen, hoping for a clue.

Nimisen ushered her back to the chair and said, "It's only confusing because we have the ability to know each other. Some souls find their peace in the vast eternity of the afterlife, while others are more content to journey through life over and over. When that happens, many lives will share the same soul."

Destiny's eyes popped open and her jaw dropped, shaping the word, "Oh," which escaped from her lips as a whisper. "You mean we are the same soul?"

Nimisen smiled warmly and nodded her head.

Destiny momentarily returned the affectionate smile, but the expression faded from her face.

"What is wrong?" Marvalaine asked.

"Well, knowing this kind of complicates things between Blake and myself. I assume that Blake shares your..."

Marvalaine nodded.

Destiny closed her eyes and continued, "And there was Billy and Diane…"

Marvalaine nodded again and said, "But fear not. You shall not remember this when you return. You might feel it, we all do, but it won't be clear to you when you are in your world."

Destiny sunk back into the plump cushions of her chair and said, "As if going back and forth in time and visiting ancestors weren't confusing enough."

Marvalaine's face turned somber. "We would like to caution you, however. Grave dangers still loom ahead of you. You are about to embark upon a very perilous journey. You must be very careful, especially when you visit the past. Take extreme care if you change what has been, or you may not have a home when you return."

"But we already lost our home."

Nimisen sat on the arm of the chair next to Destiny and pulled her close. "Not that home," she said. "We mean the time where you go when you are yourself."

"Oh," Destiny said, though she still did not fully understand.

"That's okay," Nimisen said. "All will become clear. You are always welcome to come visit us. Maybe next time, you can come see me before my face resembled a prune and we can talk and do girl stuff together. Always remember, if you ever have any questions, you need only ask us."

"Well," Destiny said. "I do have one question."

"Go ahead," Nimisen said. "You can ask us anything."

Destiny brushed a stray hair from her face and looked up at Nimisen, asking, "If Blake is not yours, then whose is he?"

Nimisen shot an accusing look over at Marvalaine, and asked with a whimsical song quality to her voice, "Yes, dear, why don't you tell her whose blood young Blake springs from?"

Marvalaine found that he would much rather examine the intricate teeth marks on his pipe than answer the question.

"Dear?" Nimisen asked. "If we tell her she can ask anything, then we must be willing to answer anything."

He shrugged his shoulders, then turned his head away from them and mumbled, "Phble."

"What was that?" Nimisen asked, clearly enjoying the embarrassment it brought her husband. "We couldn't hear you."

"Phoebe."

Destiny knew Phoebe and even had a hand in getting them together. She would have grilled him about their encounters, but the dream world faded away and was replaced with the sensation of her flying like a bird, skimming majestically over the treetops.

Richard still paced back and forth in his office. He stopped occasionally to drink some coffee and spent much time refilling his cup. He was concerned about Brian, but he was even more concerned about his own skin. The whole night had passed with no word from Brian, and fortunately for Richard, no questions about Brian's whereabouts. His fatigue grew overwhelming, and with it, his need to do something beyond wearing tracks in the rug.

He sat down at his desk and pulled up his contact list on the computer. He copied down two numbers onto a small strip of paper. One was for the little shop in Cricket Bend where he knew Brian was staying with the mercenaries, and the other was for the bar outside of Mobile where he had first contacted the mercenaries when he had sent them to meet up with Richard. After writing down the numbers, he deleted them from his contact list.

He carefully folded the small piece of paper and slid it into a pack of gum, which he returned to his shirt pocket. His knees shook and his heart pounded in his ears as he tried to nonchalantly stand and leave his office. He put his coat on and told his secretary he'd be back in a few, then proceeded to walk wobbly legged through the office and out of the building. He drove for three and a half miles to a bus station, one of the few places where he knew he could still find pay phones.

He fished a handful of quarters from his pocket and dialed the number for the bar near Mobile. When the mechanical operator instructed, he started feeding more quarters into the phone. The phone rang several times before it was picked up, but nobody answered.

Richard cleared his throat and said, "I was just wondering, that is, a couple days ago, I placed an order for some friends to go on a hunting trip with another friend of mine and I was wondering if you've heard back from them?"

Silence followed.

"I've lost contact with them, and I'm just trying to find out if something's happened."

"We ain't heard nothing." The phone clicked, and the call was over. This did nothing to quell Richard's fears. He fed some more quarters into the phone and dialed Cricket Bend. Again, the mechanical operator instructed him to feed more quarters into the phone.

"Bon joo."

"Hello," Richard said. "This is... I'm the guy that sent the package for my friends who were renting a room from you. Did they get it okay?"

Silence followed. Richard wondered why everybody answered the phone with silence. He did not like the feeling that nobody was willing to cooperate with him.

"Hello? Hello? Can you hear me?"

Richard thought he could hear breathing on the other end, but nobody spoke.

"I haven't heard from my friends in a long while. If you see them, can you have them call me?"

Henry broke his silence and said, "If dose friends shows daer faces here, den I be sures to guts 'em like da swine dey is. Den I feeds 'em to da bayou and I be wishin' the cocodril a bon appétit." The line went dead and Richard's face drained to white.

He got back in his car and stared at his dashboard. Henry's words echoed in his head. The first time he had contacted Henry a couple of days ago, Richard thought he was almost impossible to understand. He strained to catch enough familiar words amidst Henry's French and Cajun accent to piece together what he was saying. He thought Henry must be quite a character and told Brian so. This time, however, he had absolutely no problem understanding Henry. His message was loud and clear.

Richard reached stiffly for the ignition and started the car. His vision was narrow, and he was barely aware that he was driving as he returned to his work. He drove automatically and pulled into his reserved parking place and automatically shut off the car. The doctors come and went from the asylum that he managed as he just sat there a moment and watched. He wondered if he would be better off, right now, as a patient, rather than an administrator. As his mind began to regain some focus, he wondered if maybe he shouldn't have returned at all. Maybe he should just try to disappear.

In spite of his fears, he left the car and started walking back to his office. His knees wobbled as much as they did when he had left, only this time he was intensely aware of his heart beating in his chest.

His secretary was on the phone and seemed a bit frazzled when he returned. "Here he is now," she said into the phone, then covered the mouthpiece and said, "It's Dr. Logan on line one."

"Thank you, Marcy."

Richard returned to his chair and tried to relax. His body was trembling. He drew a deep breath, picked up the phone and said, "Hello Frank, what can I do for you?"

"You can tell me what Grupp is up to and where I can find him. I'm told he's on a field trip, but nobody can reach him. I hear that you might know something about it."

"Yes sir. He is in the field, but he wanted to keep it quiet until he completed the mission."

"Mission?" Logan asked. "Please explain."

"Well, sir, he was investigating the unusual disturbances of the past couple of weeks. He was convinced that they represented some kind of prophecy level event. I was brought in when he ordered me to do some research to help him triangulate the epicenter of the events. He went in with a team to locate and possibly neutralize the source."

"So, the two of you cooked up a scheme to go in without notifying anybody?"

"Well sir, Brian made that call, and he does outrank me." There it was. Richard's heart was playing drum solos in his head while perspiration streaked down the sides of his face. The elders were looking for someone to pin this on and he just threw Brian under the bus.

"Hmm," Logan said. "We'll deal with that later. Have you heard from him?"

The trembling in Schaefer's limbs migrated to his throat, and he stammered, "No sir, not since last night. I tried contacting his last known location, but the locals were hostile to me on the phone."

"Hostile?" Logan asked. "We better send another team in. Now tell me about this so-called prophecy level event."

"Well sir, it started with the inmates running around screaming about burning. We thought it was some kind of crazy localized thing until we discovered that the event occurred at all our locations, and I was able to compare the time of the event to compute an approximate location. The second event was a day or two later when our people experienced an increase in static charges all at the same time."

"You mean last week?" Logan interrupted. "I had a static spark that scrambled my computer last week. You think that was related?"

"Yes sir. It appears that magic is returning. Brian said he was getting the old powers back, and they grew stronger by the hour. He was convinced that they would find a witch at the center of the events. He planned to find out how they got the power back and then terminate the witches. The last word I had from him was that they had positively identified the witches and that he was going in."

"So," Logan said, "some witches got their power, and that fool went in to face them alone?"

"He wasn't alone, sir; he had a team of mercs with him and a boy."

"A boy?"

"The boy was one of us. Some kind of secret training I gather. Brian thought the boy would be able to help pinpoint the witches' location. I wish I could be more specific. He said he would tell me more about the boy when the mission was over, but that it was above my clearance for now."

"A boy..." Logan repeated. "And did he? Did the boy help find the witches?"

"Yes, sir, apparently so. I told them where I thought the epicenter was, and he was already there. The boy had led them there. I assume that means the boy was getting his powers back, too. Brian said the boy also located another place, a mental hospital not far from the witches, but it wasn't one of our facilities. I have it somewhere here in my notes."

Logan could hear Richard shuffling through his papers and said, "Send me both locations, A.S.A.P.. I'll send teams to both."

"Right away, sir." Richard waited for Logan to hang up. He felt like he had just endured the inquisition, but he wasn't sure if he had survived it yet since Logan was still on the line.

"Is there anything else," Logan asked, "that Grupp had you do for him?"

"Yes sir, I..."

"Put it in a report and send it to me. Do you believe him? Is the magic back?"

"Well, sir, the witches certainly did something, and it was very powerful. Brian said he was able to make fire. He wanted me to check with the training facilities and see if there has been any improvement. He also wanted me to start retesting our elders."

"Hmm. Keep that discreet. We don't want to start any rumors, unless it turns out to be true."

"Yes, sir."

"I look forward to your reports, Schiffer."

"Schaefer," Richard said, but it was too late. Logan had already disconnected.

The days approaching Blake's arrival on their island were filled with wondrous discoveries where he learned to control fire, lightning, and moving things around with his mind. He never dreamed it could get better than that until his first night on the island where they put him up in their smokehouse. His dreams were more vivid and more real than anything he had ever dreamed in his life. They were also more terrifying and threatening, but they brought him to her. Destiny saved him from the dreams that were trying to kill him.

And still, everything that had happened to him up to that point was nothing compared to what he was about to experience. Destiny showed him the marvels of reaching back through the memories of his ancestors and reliving moments from their lives. He saw firsthand how magic used to affect the world. He saw both the horror and the beauty of it.

Something quite special had come back with him. He didn't return with special abilities like Destiny had done, but for the first time in his life, he felt an attachment to someone else. He never had that bond with his mother. She loved him like any mother would love her child, but deep down, she believed he was a monster. He was the product of a great and terrible experiment forced into her womb by the most evil men she could ever know. She loved him as if she were the mother of a serial killer. It was a tenuous relationship that never fully gelled.

In his ancestral memories, he lived the lives of ancestors in love. He felt the passion they felt. Destiny was with him through each of those romances because the target of his affection was her ancestor, too. They were swept through time together, finding and rediscovering each other in the forms of new ancestors in love. The memories ended while they were still locked in a passionate embrace.

Now, sitting on the rambling bus, he could think of nothing more beneficial than using this time to find more examples of that passion. He closed his eyes and imagined he was staring into Destiny's candle. A rush swept over his face as the bus faded out and left him floating in the void. He focused on and searched for the passion he had felt. He recalled not only the thoughts running through his mind, but the warmth in his heart and the image of Destiny before him.

His mind spun slightly and the void was replaced with a white room. Destiny was sleeping on a bed centered against the wall. He wanted to rush to her, but it was someone else's memory, and he could only see and feel what they did.

His host rushed to her side and took her hand as Blake had wanted. He slathered kisses on her hand and cried, "Destiny, come back!"

The voice Blake heard was his own. This had never happened before. Destiny remained still. She wasn't cold to his touch, but neither did she move nor respond.

An explosion outside drew his attention to the window. From there, he could see violent fighting just a block away. He had seen something like this before. Sorcerers formed a large circle around the block and pelted it with all manner of fire and lightning. Witches inside the perimeter created a bubble that protected the entire block. Fireballs crashed into the bubble and burst into magnificent fireworks, then fell to the ground as glowing embers. Buildings outside the protective bubble were reduced to ruins.

Each explosion against the bubble took its toll and required more and more energy from the witches, but their energy was eroding, and the bubble was shrinking.

A woman burst into the room and Blake spun around and struck an offensive pose, ready to fire upon the intruder.

"Why are you here?" screamed the raven-haired woman. "Go now! Get the orb and bring it to me!"

"But," Blake cried, "I can't leave her."

"She will leave you," the woman cried back, "whether you like it or not. She will leave you and she will leave me, and she will leave all of us. Maybe she won't mean to, but they will take her from us. Bring me the orb! Without it, all is lost! Without it, she will perish! We *ALL* will perish. Hurry!"

Blake nodded his head and rushed out the door, but instead of being in the hospital's hallway, he was back on the bus watching the endless procession of trees flying by.

Michelle was as tired as the kids. She saw each of them close their eyes and fall off, so she tried remaining vigilant lest they be unprotected while they slept, but she couldn't resist the drooping eyelids and finally succumbed. Her sleep was rocked with the image of

Destiny, gripped by the sorcerer's threads of electricity. She could see the blue filaments coil around Destiny's torso, but tied to the chair with her own hands tied behind her, she was unable to do anything. The truth was, and she knew it, that even were her hands free, she could not have combatted the man. Only Destiny was able to wage war against him, which she had done and which she lost.

Michelle tried guiding her unconscious thought away from the horrific scene, but when she did that, she only rewound slightly to the moment when she planted a commanding voice in the mercenaries' heads, and that moment terrified her as much as the dream. She didn't know where that voice had come from or how she had summoned it, just like nobody on Earth had summoned lightning or fire in centuries until Destiny had started recalling her ancestral memories.

The worst part for Michelle was that right after she had used the voice, the sorcerer had gripped Destiny in his electric tentacles, and that was the scene she was trying to escape, and the very scene her nightmares landed on following the voice.

Blake was shaken by his dream. He saw Destiny trapped in a bed, probably in a coma; possibly dying. Then there was the woman who demanded he go get some orb. He didn't know who she was, but she certainly was frantic. Destiny must have been dying.

An old man in front of Blake turned around and looked into his eyes. His face was marked with years of wrinkles and covered with a scraggly red and grey beard. He wrinkled his nose and sniffed, then shook his head slightly. "It can all be avoided," he said. His voice was worn hoarse from years of tobacco abuse. His teeth were brown and crooked. He didn't smile, but continued staring at Blake with sad eyes. "She rushes in and brings it upon herself," he continued. "Stop her. Only you can stop her."

The old man turned around and leaned his head against the window. Blake looked behind him to see if Michelle or Destiny had heard him, but each of them had their eyes closed. A shiver wracked Blake's spine. He turned back to the window and watched the scenery fly by, but a darkness had settled into his heart. He didn't know what it all meant yet. How could he? He would have to wait for it to reveal itself.

"Will he listen?" asked the first librarian.

"How could he not?" replied the second librarian. "We had his attention. He heard the words."

"Yes," said the third, "and if he hasn't had the visions already, he soon will."

The first librarian hung his head. The large grey hood swung right and left as he shook his head. "But that's not what I am asking. Will he heed our warning?"

The second librarian pulled his hood back and hung it off his shoulders. He had heavy dark bags under his bloodshot eyes. "Even if he does, can he stop her? She is headstrong and not easily influenced."

"Can we guide him to gain such influence?" asked the third. "I do not believe he can stop her by force."

The fire in the center of their circle died down to glowing embers. Without the three of them staring into it and focusing their power on their task, it had only its own fuel to burn. It crackled and sent a solitary spark into the air.

The first librarian pulled his hood off and ran his fingers through his damp hair. "I will pretend you did not say that. If you seriously plan to offer him advice in his relationship with her, or meddle in his thinking in any way, you can count me out."

"Yes," the second agreed. "You would be on your own."

"Fine," the third said. "We have orders to stop what comes at all costs, but you don't think he wants us to try everything we might to accomplish it?"

"We have our orders," the second replied, "and I feel our master's desperation, but when he says to stop her at all costs, I believe he means all other costs."

"I agree," the first librarian said. "We must tread carefully where the boy is concerned."

The bus squealed and hissed as it finally slowed and jerked to a stop, waking all three. Michelle was thrilled to be free of her nightmares, while Blake wanted to hold on to the feeling of energy that had sprung from his core. Destiny was the most refreshed of the three. After visiting with Marvalaine and Nimisen, she had drifted around viewing old memories. She was just a voyeur in these, which was more relaxing than visiting the past as an active participant.

Michelle rose first and led the youngsters off the bus. The bus station was dark and grimy. The sun was still high in the sky, but the station was a large, covered garage with sooty windows. They were surrounded with running bus engines that rumbled and belched out diesel clouds, filling the space with obnoxious fumes. They needed no further prodding to exit the place and find fresh air.

Several lines of commuters led from the different buses to ramps and stairs that took them down to the first floor where the exits were.

Michelle fell in behind the passengers, who had already gathered their luggage, and followed them down a ramp that led them under the bus terminal. A brightly lit door down a long corridor to the left led them outside, where the air was at least somewhat more breathable.

Once outside, Michelle waved her hand in front of her face to fan the air around and took a deep breath. "Well," she said, "we still gots us a long walk to the hospital. It be a good thing we still has these sandwiches to eat." The outside of the building was just as grimy as the inside, and it smelled of urine. Across the street was a rundown hotel advertising cheap rooms rented by the week. Signs further down the potholed street marked the train depot in the adjacent block. This was not the kind of neighborhood that felt safe enough to hang around.

Michelle started walking and said, "There's a park not too far up here and it's on the way to the hospital. We can stop there for a spell to eat."

"You know," Blake said looking up towards the sun, "It's probably already kind of late for visiting hours. Even if we get there by three, it will be dark before we leave. Maybe we should find a room for the night at that hotel and start out in the morning."

"How is we gonna get a hotel when we be flat broke?"

Blake shrugged his shoulders and timidly said, "It doesn't look very expensive, and I could always..."

"If you says you can push them, then the answer be NO. I don't know about you, but me and Destiny ain't no thieves."

"Fine then," Blake said, "but I thought it would be easier than arriving late at the hospital and pushing the orderlies to let us stay after hours."

Destiny saw where this was going and took a couple of steps back, preferring to keep out of it.

Michelle stopped walking and looked around her at the weather, then she looked at Blake and said, "It looks like it's going to be a pleasant night. We can just rest up for the night in the park and then, like you said, start out in the morning."

"Whatever you say," Blake answered, "but they don't like vagrants hanging out in the parks at night, but I suppose I could always push the police so they don't bother us."

Michelle's temper was showing as she barked, "Is that your answer for everything? You has to push this or push that? Cain't you just get by like normal people does?"

"We aren't normal people. Smart people make their living being smart. Strong people make their living doing strong things. Witches make their living doing magic. We were born this way. It's what we are, and it's who I am."

"And regular folks burns witches at stakes. Didn't dey teach you nothin' about your heritage?"

"Those witches couldn't do half of what we can do. We're not the ones who should be afraid."

Destiny had stayed out of the argument long enough. She walked to Blake and looped her arm around his. "But we are afraid. I'm afraid. It's not just the regular people, though they are going to have a pretty hard time with what we are. It's also them, the people who raised you. They tried to kill me. If they know where we are, they will try again. I think we should keep a low profile until we get a few more things figured out."

Blake's first instinct was to continue arguing, but she was right. He nodded his head jond said, "But, they still don't like people sleeping in the park, and this time of year, it could burst into rain for no reason."

Michelle knew he was right about that and said, "We'll just cross that bridge when we comes to it."

She turned back up the street and continued leading them to the park.

Logan didn't like being out of the loop. Brian was technically within his rights to mount his own investigation, but for him to keep it secret could only mean that Brian wanted Logan's job. Logan couldn't blame him for that. Someone else had the job before Logan took it. But Logan didn't know what Brian may have discovered, so he devised multiple plans to cover at least the most likely scenarios. In this case, he prepared himself for two eventualities. If it was true, that Brian had discovered active witches and terminated them, Logan would take credit. If it wasn't true, or if Brian failed, then Logan would blame it all on him and spin the outcome in his favor.

He couldn't enact either plan until he learned the truth, so he dispatched two teams to learn what happened. They would share a private jet to Lafayette and split up from there. The teams were hand-picked by Logan from some of the top up-and-coming members of the organization. He didn't know what kind of controversy they were going to land in, so he picked a couple of his top legal minds to lead the teams. Regardless of what they might discover, he was certain that he would need their expertise when dealing with the psychiatric hospital.

Once the teams were assembled and underway, his active role would be done. He need only sit back and wait for the reports.

Simon Tangiers was already aboard the Gulfstream with his lone associate when Nathan Vanderlew arrived with a team of three. They had met before at various functions and didn't really know each other well, but they didn't like each other at all. They were each briefed on both missions, but only Simon paid any attention. Nathan didn't need to know anything about Simon's job to fulfill his assignment. Simon nodded to Nathan, taking a quick appraisal of his expensive suit, manicured nails and Ken doll hair, then turned his attention back to his own team, making sure to arrange his left arm on the armrest so the jacket sleeve fell enough to display the silver Rolex on his wrist.

Nathan nodded to Simon and ignored his watch. Since Simon had already settled in at the front of the jet, he directed his team to a section over the wing.

Logan wouldn't send them out without at least one hostess to serve them, and being a typical misogynist, he was prone to hiring young and beautiful female attendants. She brought a tray of glasses with a bottle of scotch and a bowl of ice. Nathan flashed her a smile, revealing his dimples and blue eyes. Women loved his dimples and blue eyes. She returned the smile, delivered the drinks, and returned to her station to prepare for takeoff.

Simon may not have known Vanderlew personally, they ran in different circles, but he knew his reputation. Simon worked his way through law school while Nathan had a free ride provided by mommy and daddy. There was no doubt in Simon's mind that Nathan's father greased the wheels to get him accepted by Harvard. Simon had the grades and test scores to earn an invitation to Yale, but he couldn't come up with enough loans or scholarship money to make it happen, so he attended a lesser-known university, but still was just as much a lawyer as Vanderlew, probably more so. He rose through the ranks and made partner in his fourth year. Vanderlew was only a junior partner in his father's law firm.

The plane lurched forward with the engines at full throttle and vaulted down the runway. It pitched its nose up and rocketed into the heavens. Simon reviewed the notes he was given for the assignment. After landing, he would be driving down to some backwater town called Cricket Bend. He'll probably be swatting flies and mosquitos while Vanderlew is lounging around the pool, tossing back mai tais.

Nathan didn't give Simon a second thought. His eyes were focused on the long-legged stewardess. In his mind, it wasn't a matter of if, but when she would be his. He could press for an on-board mile high romance, or lure her back to the suite he reserved in Lafayette.

When the plane had leveled off, she brought him a fresh round of drinks. He barely raised his hand to reach for the drinks, forcing her to lean over further to reach him. This allowed him to further appreciate the ample cleavage of her low-cut blouse, and the name tag on her bosom. He looked up into her eyes and flashed her a big, perfect smile. "Thank you, Jennifer." He accepted the drink from her and pulled a Cuban from his jacket pocket, but she said, "I'm sorry, but there's no smoking on-board. Is there anything else that you require?"

He returned the cigar to his breast pocket and said, "I was hoping for something a little sweet before we land."

"We don't have any food on-board, but I can bring you a soda if you like."

"No, thank you," he said, "but I was thinking of something more... say, those are really beautiful earrings, quite exquisite. You like diamonds? I love diamonds. There is no stone on earth as pretty as a nice big diamond. I especially like buying diamonds. The more expensive the diamond is, the bigger the rush. And I can't think of anything more spectacular than the look on a girl's face when she receives a new diamond gift."

She was weary of his attention, but forced a practiced smile on her face and asked, "Did you want that soda, sir?"

"No," he said. "I was thinking of something more... more brunette, actually."

The smile evaporated from her face. She quickly turned to his companions and asked them, "How about you?"

They restrained from snickering and shook their heads no, so she returned to her station. As she passed Simon, he muttered, "He's always been a jerk." She almost stopped to talk with him, but chose to continue on to her seat instead.

***

The park was farther than Michelle had remembered. The sun beat down upon them with every step, and by the time the park was in sight, Michelle's hair was soaked and firmly matted to her head. Even without the glaring sun, her aging legs were ready for a break, and seeing the trees ahead brought a wave of relief to her tired body.

She didn't have to announce the park. Destiny was already pointing and asking, "Is that it? It's beautiful."

It wasn't overly large, but it was a nice-looking park. A dog bone shaped pond was in the center of the park, surrounded by a jogging path and grass. Trees dotted the perimeter, giving the illusion of privacy from the urban world without completely hiding the interior from the outside. It was enough privacy for picnic goers without providing the kind of seclusion sought out by drug dealers and other nefarious denizens of the night.

A bridge crossed the narrow center of the pond and led to a playground with a wooden fort complete with slides and swings to the left of the bridge, and picnic tables with barbecue stoves to the right.

Michelle led the trio across the bridge and pointed to either side. "If it be cold tonight," she said, "we just starts a fire in the barbecue, and if it rains, we can hide under the play fort behind da shoot-da-chute."

Blake was puzzled until he saw Michelle pointing to a slide.

Destiny grabbed the bag of sandwiches from her grandmother and ran to a picnic table. She leapt onto the bench facing the pond and said, "Sounds great. Let's eat."

Blake said, "Yeah. I'm starving." He followed Destiny to the picnic table and sat across from her.

Michelle went to the bridge and peered into the water.

"Aren't you hungry Nana?"

"Yeah, you know I am, but dat tain't much food for supper and dinner. I was just wonderin' if daer be any mudbugs in dis lake."

"Mudbugs?" Blake asked. "Your nana eats bugs?"

Destiny hit him with the wrapper from her sandwich and said, "No, silly, but we eat crayfish, you know!"

Michelle knelt down at the edge of the pond and reached into the water but came up empty. She splashed around repeatedly with equally unsatisfying results.

Blake turned around to see what she was doing and asked, "What's a crayfish?"

Destiny shrugged and said, "It's a... crayfish. We mostly call them mudbugs. What do you call them?"

Blake got up from the bench and went to look over Michelle's shoulder. "I don't know," he said. "What is it? What does it look like?"

Destiny followed him to the bridge and looked into the water. They tried seeing into the water, but they couldn't see through the ripples Michelle was stirring up.

"Dang it," Michelle said. "I thinks I scared dem all away."

Destiny giggled and said, "Here, let me try." She closed her eyes and reached her senses into the water. She could feel them down there, looking up at the trio. Her nana was right. The commotion up top had scared them. Destiny inhaled deeply, then exhaled out slowly. Her heart slowed and she exuded calmness into the water. She could feel the effects on the crayfish below. She filled them with a sense of well-being, and then she filled them with a new curiosity. It was a simple suggestion by her that something yummy might await them up top. One by one, they ventured up to the edge of the beach.

Blake pointed into the water from the bridge and said, "Look! Lobsters!"

Destiny chuckled and said, "They ain't lobsters. They're mud-bugs."

Michelle reached in and easily plucked them out of the water. She collected them in the folds of her blouse and carried them up to the barbecue, saying, "I don't know when I'll ever gets used to dis. You simply amazes me, Cherie. Where in the world did you learn that?"

Destiny followed behind Michelle and said, "Mala taught me, only she used rattle snakes."

"What?" Michelle nearly screamed. "She had you luring rattle snakes to you?"

"No, she set the snakes almost on me and had me calm them so they wouldn't bite."

Blake leaned in close to Destiny and whispered, "You pushed them."

"I didn't force them to come to us. I just made it seem like something they would want to do."

"Uhuh," Blake said, "like they wanted to jump out of the water and be food for us."

"Dey is mudbugs," Michelle said definitively. "Dey ain't hotel clerks and dey certainly ain't the police."

"Yeah?" Blake asked. "Well, I wasn't going to kill or eat anyone."

Michelle winced at the memory of him killing the sorcerer, Brian. She didn't hold it against him. He had to do it, or they would be dead. She laid the crawdads out on the table and Destiny said, "Now what? I sure wish we had a pot to boil them in."

Blake laughed and said, "Maybe you just should have boiled the whole pond."

Destiny blanched and said, "Eeeww."

"Well," Michelle said, "I wish we had some cayenne and filet too, but at least we gots us a fire pit."

"What's filet?" Blake asked.

"It's a flavoring my Nana uses in her gumbo, but we don't have any stock neither, so I guess we just grill them."

Blake went to the pit and said, "Here, let me start the fire."

Michelle snapped her head towards him but didn't say anything. She didn't have to. Blake saw the look and remembered the last fire he started and said to Destiny, "Maybe you can start the fire."

Blake searched under the trees and found some branches blown down from a storm. He gathered a few and broke them into smaller pieces that would fit in the pit. After stacking them, he bowed to Destiny, and she reached in, looking around to be sure no strangers were watching, and ignited the wood with flames from her fingertips.

The sun was dipping below the tree line. If anyone thought they shouldn't be there, the fire would provide a beacon to find them.

Michelle grilled the crayfish until the shell turned a blackened red. She used two sticks to turn them until all sides were done. She placed them on a large leaf that Destiny had picked by the bridge and took them to the table where Destiny and Michelle broke off the tails and pulled out the meat. Blake just watched, slightly disgusted until his hunger overcame his aversion to something called a mudbug. It needed seasonings, but as hungry as everyone was, nobody really cared.

The skies were clear, and it looked like it would continue to be a clear night, but Michelle chose to camp out under the children's fort, anyway. It was practically a little room with two and a half sides. Chalk marks on one of the walls looked like a refrigerator, and another wall had a TV drawn on it. She picked a corner of the little playhouse and tried to get comfortable, a task she soon realized would be nearly impossible. Destiny chose to join her and leaned in against her nana. At the very least, they could keep each other warm.

Michelle turned slightly, to ease the pain of the hard ground against her hips. A moan escaped her lips and Destiny touched her thigh, releasing healing waves to numb the pain. Healing was her first gift, and she was glad to offer it. Michelle asked herself why she didn't let Blake arrange a room for the night.

Blake sat outside with his back against the same wall Michelle leaned against. He was on the opposite side, facing away from the lake and the jogging path, and hoped he would be hidden from view should anyone actually pass by.

The night cooled but didn't turn cold for them. Destiny's healing waves also brought Michelle more peaceful dreams than she had on the bus. Destiny dreamed of Mala. Even though their time together had been tumultuous, she had fond memories of her mentor, and dreamed of saving her. Michelle thought Destiny was crazy for wanting to save Mala. She died over twenty-five thousand years ago. But Destiny was there, in Mala's dream world, when she died.

Mala sacrificed her life to save Destiny, and Destiny believed there must be some way to save her, but first, they would save her mother.

Blake didn't know if he could sleep. Between the slight chill and the uncomfortable surroundings, it would have been a difficult task during the best of times, but this was not the best of times. He had just killed two men. They were bad men, but he couldn't shake the anxiety he felt from ending their lives. He also couldn't shake the feeling that something bad was coming. He didn't know when or where, but he felt something up ahead of them and he didn't like it.

Worry or not, he eventually drifted off to sleep. When he opened his eyes, his vision was filled with an old man's face staring back at his. The old man was close enough for Blake to smell the flecks of pipe tobacco in his beard. He had the smooth complexion of a pampered man, but it was covered with a wild white beard that grew untamed like a vagabond's. His smile was warm and reassuring and his bright blue eyes darted about under long white eyebrows. "Yes," the old man said. "I know who you are, and I know what you seek, but I don't know if you are ready."

"Ready?" Blake asked. "It's not for me, it's for her. I'm only the courier."

The old man backed away, giving Blake a chance to see the rest of the room. A fire roared in the fireplace and bathed the hearth and the two chairs facing it with light, but barely flickered upon the walls of the small room. The old man selected a poker which hung on the fireplace and stoked the logs. He could have simply waved his hands to raise the fire, but he enjoyed the simple things. "I know," he said, "that you are only here to transport it, but it is very powerful, and it can be very seductive. You must know the full meaning of its power and the cost of misusing it and the toll it demands for just possessing it, even if only for a little while. I don't think you are prepared yet."

Blake pushed himself up in the chair and looked around the room. He hoped to find someone else there for support, but he was alone with the stubborn old man. "I have no time for this," he said. "She lies near death already and while we waste time arguing about it, they close in to finish her. She is all that matters."

"No," the old man said. "She matters, for sure, but she is not all that matters. Her future relies on another's, so she also matters."

"You confuse me," Blake said. "She needs the orb to save Destiny, and Destiny is required to save everyone else."

"Yes," the old man said, "but you forget that Destiny must first save her mother. Her mother requires the orb so she can, in turn, save Destiny. Destiny requires the orb to save the future, and the future has a role to play in allowing all this to fall into place."

Blake closed his eyes and said, "My head is spinning."

"That is understanding seeping in. All events rely on each other and lead back to themselves, creating a circle. The circle is what will save us all. That is her destiny. Do not lose sight of this circle of magic. The orb is at the center of the circle. The ancients called this kind of magic distinak. It is the strongest kind of magic we know about. If you do not keep all parts of the circle in your mind, you may forget yourself and break the circle."

Blake nodded his head.

The old man smiled and said, "Good. I think perhaps you are ready."

CHAPTER 3

Day two.

Even the most innocent undertakings can unintentionally trigger disastrous results. The ecosystem of nature balances actions against reactions. Any game that has a winner must also have a loser. The game of life has long been a struggle between good and evil. If that balance is ever upset, and a winner is declared, then the game will end.

Future historians will look upon this day as the day which started the calamitous chain of events that ultimately led the world into chaos, but the world is not there yet.

The crickets chirped softly throughout the night while a handful of frogs bellowed out their locations under the bridge that crossed the pond. Except for a slight chill from a mild breeze, the night remained warm and inside the little wooden fort was cozy, if not quite comfortable.

The early birds sprang into song with the first ray of sunrise. Blake would be the first to wake. His spot outside the small shelter was less inviting than the girl's location inside the fort, but the night had neither rained upon him nor layered him with dew, for which he was grateful. A sliver of sun peeked through the swing set and glanced upon his eyes, bringing his attention to the rousing world around him. He yawned, stretched and walked a few paces towards the pond when he became intensely aware that he had a few morning necessities that required his attention before the girls woke up. He wasn't sure how they were going to deal with their morning requirements.

He left the play area and walked to the bridge, hoping he could scout out a suitably large tree. Daylight brought an entirely new dimension to the park. It wasn't as large as it had seemed at twilight, and judging from the sizes of the trees, it wasn't terribly old. He saw a diner up the street and considered getting breakfast for them. If he hurried, he could get it before Michelle gave him her look about using his powers to influence people, but his focus on the diner was derailed when he saw restrooms just beyond the half-court basketball hoops. They would probably be locked, but he doubted Michelle would scold him for unlocking a couple of restroom doors.

Michelle and Destiny woke while Blake was still gone.

Michelle got up first and stretched, then, seeing Blake was not around, asked, "Now where in da world is that boy?"

Destiny got up and left the tiny enclosure. She rubbed the sleep from her eyes and shrugged her shoulders.

"Blake," Michelle growled, with her irritation evident in the tenor of her voice. "If you up an' left us here, I'm gonna..."

She didn't finish her statement before she heard Blake reply, "Alright, alright, I just had to go to the bathroom. You don't have to yell."

Michelle and Destiny both looked around, but Blake was nowhere in sight.

"Where is you?" Michelle asked.

"I told you, I had to go to the bathroom."

"How is it," Michelle thought her words instead of speaking them, "how is it that you can hear me?"

"How could I not hear you?" he thought back. "You're practically thundering in my head!"

"Sorry," she thought. "So, is you holed up behind some tree or sumpin?"

"No," he replied. "Follow the path past the big end of the pond. You'll see the bathrooms on the other side of the basketball court."

Destiny didn't waste a moment wondering how they heard him. She heard his directions loud and clear and sprinted down the path. Michelle wished she could still walk so fast, but she kept her gait slow and steady, preferring not to shake up her insides any.

Blake washed his hands and exited the lavatory. Destiny was nowhere in sight, but Michelle was still approaching. He pointed to the ladies' door so she could cut the corner and shorten her trip. He waited outside for them and returned his attention to the diner.

Destiny snuck up behind him and poked his ribs while shouting, "Boo!"

His eyes were riveted on the diner. She sidled up alongside him, hooked her arms around one of his and followed his gaze across the park. Seeing the diner, she nodded her head and stared at it alongside him. The more she looked, the hungrier she got, until she couldn't hold it in and blurted out, "I sure am hungry."

"I know," he said. "Me too. Do you think your nana will let me push them just a little bit so we don't starve?"

"No," Michelle said from behind them. "She will not."

Blake turned to face her and asked, "Are you sure? You must be hungry, too."

"I is, but it be a cold day in hell before I steals."

"Not even food?"

She shook her head and said, "Not even food."

Destiny's attention was still on the diner. She cocked her head to the side and pointed towards the diner, saying, "Look at that!"

Someone was running toward them. It was a girl with long black hair, carrying a bag. Blake had barely turned to see where Destiny was pointing, but Destiny had already started walking towards the girl. Blake and Michelle followed.

"Hey there," the girl said. "I ain't never had no order like this before. I wasn't even sure if you would be here, but there you is, just like he said you would be."

Michelle shot Blake an accusing look and said, "What did you do?"

Blake reached both hands for the sky and said, "Nothing! I didn't have anything to do with this."

The girl slowed as she reached them and said, "It's still hot. We got some Andouille scramble. My grandpa likes to call it a quiche, but it's just scrambled eggs and sausage. I added some lunch cartons of milk and juice and some biscuits."

Destiny reached the girl first and accepted the bag.

"Give that back," Michelle said. "We ain't takin' charity. I'm sorry miss, but you was deceived. We cain't pay you for this."

Destiny gave the bag back to the girl, heartbroken.

"Thank you, miss," Michelle said. "I'm sorry for your trouble."

"But it's all paid for," the girl said. "If you don't take it, it will just end up in the trash."

"I'm sorry," Michelle said. "I'm sure you think you was paid, but..."

"I tell you I didn't do this!" Blake objected. He went to the girl and took the bag, saying, "Thank you, miss. That was very kind of you."

The girl was glad someone there was being sensible enough to take the food and gave him a friendly smile before backing away.

Michelle would have argued more, but the girl turned and ran back towards the diner.

"We ain't through with this," Michelle said to Blake.

Before he could respond, Destiny hit him on the shoulder.

"What was that for?" he shouted.

Michelle gave into her hunger and took the bag, then started walking in a straight line to the nearest picnic table.

Destiny looked piercingly into Blake's eyes. Her eyebrows were scrunched down in anger.

"What?" Blake asked.

"Like you don't know," she replied, her voice laced with sass.

"I don't."

She turned to follow her nana and said over her shoulder to him, "Are you telling me that you automatically flirt with every pretty girl from every diner and that it means nothing to you?"

"Oh, Lordy!" Michelle said while shaking her head. "Here we goes agin."

Blake hung his head and followed behind, still rubbing his shoulder.

The black Gulfstream landed in Lafayette Regional Airport on time, per its flight plan. It rolled along the taxiway at the maximum permissible speed and went directly to a private section of the airport restricted to the privileged few who could afford such personal luxuries. It slowed and pulled to a stop inside a private hangar where two other vehicles waited.

Jennifer opened the door and deployed the stairs at the bottom of the door. She stepped to the side of the door where she could execute her last duty and wish the departing passengers well. She braced herself for Nathan's last assault.

Nathan let his associates retrieve the briefcases they brought on board and walked directly towards Jennifer. He stretched his lips into a well-practiced smile. It was a warm, inviting smile that showed both his kind inner self and his perfect veneered teeth. He stopped at the top of the stairs and said, "I think we may have gotten off on the wrong foot. I wouldn't want you to get the wrong idea, first impressions can be quite lasting as I'm sure mine will be of you. Perhaps you and I can..."

Simon pretended to talk to his associate as he blundered into Nathan and shoved him down the stairs. "Oh, I'm sorry Nathan, I didn't see you standing there." Simon winked at Jennifer, and she giggled softly while returning his wink.

Simon descended the stairs and stared at the two vehicles from the bottom step. He directed his gaze first to Nathan's car, then his, then back to Nathan's, then his again. He sighed audibly and drooped his shoulders.

Nathan would have retaliated and made one more attempt to woo Jennifer, but seeing Simon's obvious displeasure with their vehicles, he chose to forget her and walked arrogantly to the white stretch limo that waited for him. The driver held the door for him. He turned to give Simon a half smile and an insincere shrug of his shoulders, then slid into the all-white vehicle. He was followed by his associates while the driver loaded their luggage into the trunk. When all were seated, the driver settled in behind the wheel and the car departed for their five star accommodations atop the Hilton.

Simon watched him leave, shook his head and muttered, "Putz."

He then proceeded to his own vehicle, a dirty old Jeep with a rag top and plastic windows in the rear. He piled his luggage and his associates into the back of the Jeep. The man standing with the vehicle handed Simon the keys and said, "She's all yours. Have a safe trip."

Simon considered handing the keys to his assistant, but she was as tired as he was, so he went ahead and slid behind the wheel.

Jennifer ran down the stairs to the Jeep and said to Simon, "I think you dropped this."

Simon looked puzzled, but accepted the slip of paper from her and returned her smile as she ran back to the jet and disappeared inside. He unfolded the slip and found her name and number. He smiled and snickered at Nathan's expense, then folded the slip and tucked it into his breast pocket.

Michelle didn't wait for the kids. She sat down at the picnic table, handed out the styrofoam boxes she found in the bag, and opened the box she placed before herself. The aroma was magnificent. It could have been full of stale potato chips and she would have devoured it, anyway. She dug her plastic fork into the scramble and shared the fabulous spices with her taste buds.

Destiny sat down and opened her box. She grabbed her fork and forgot why she was mad at Blake. He of was grateful for the truce and dug into his own breakfast.

They were all too hungry to savor the moment. Breakfast was done in a twinkling, and they were on their way.

"How far is the hospital from here, Nana?"

"Not much farther," Michelle said as she pointed up the road past the diner.

As they passed the diner, the girl inside waved at them. Blake's hand involuntarily twitched upwards to return the wave, but he stopped himself when he felt Destiny's glare upon the back of his neck. He tried hiding his reaction to her wave by raising his hand to shield his eyes so he could look into the sun. "It's pretty early in the morning," he said. "What time do you think the hospital opens?"

"It be early," Michelle answered, "that's for sure, but I'll talk with 'em and see if I kin talk our way in to see my daughter."

The walk to the hospital was farther than Michelle thought it would be. Her pace wasn't as brisk as the kids' might have been, but they didn't complain. They held on to each other with their heads pressed together and talked privately about everything and nothing.

The road to St. Austin Mercy was unremarkable. They passed through a small suburban complex with a grade school that was just waking up. The play yards were filled with the sound of children whose parents dropped them off during their early commutes to work. Volunteer parents patrolled the yards and the crossings.

Michelle didn't remember the school being there, and it certainly looked new. She thought it odd that a school would be built so close to a psychiatric hospital, but when they arrived at the hospital, she saw that it had undergone some transformations of its own. Gone were the open hedges that gave the sprawling lawns such an inviting and calming feel. In their place she found wrought iron fencing with spear like pointy tops. The building had bars on the windows, something else Michelle did not remember.

She pressed the button on the intercom at the gate. There was no answer. A camera across from the intercom swooped around, swinging its aim from the street to the intercom. She pressed the button twice more.

A voice from the intercom snarled, "I thought I told you kids to stop playing around here!" The camera completed its arc to the intercom, and the same voice said, "Oh, I'm sorry ma'am, I thought it was them brats from up the road again. Did you need something?"

Michelle leaned in close to the speaker and said, "I was hoping I could see my daughter, she's a patient in there."

"More like an inmate," Destiny whispered to Blake.

"I'm sorry, ma'am, but visiting hours aren't until ten. "

"I understands that," she said, "but we be on foot here, and has no place to go to wait."

Silence.

"It embarrasses me to admit," Michelle continued, "but I had to sleep in a public park. Couldn't you jest let us wait inside?"

More silence followed then the gate swung open admitting them.

Once inside, as they put more distance between them and the fence, Michelle thought some of the grounds felt more familiar to her, but the building still looked far less inviting than she remembered. They were met at the top of the steps by a young man in white pants and a yellow shirt.

"This way," he said. "We have a couch and some chairs where you can wait. It's still a quarter to eight, you have quite a wait ahead of you."

"Thank you," Michelle said. "Perhaps there is someone in charge who could make an exception if he knew we were here."

The young man really didn't want to let his superiors know that he allowed them in.

"He doesn't want to let them know we are here," Blake whispered into Michelle's ear.

"I know," Michelle said. "I heard him."

She turned her attention back to the young orderly and said, "Hector, we really appreciates you allowin' us to wait inside, and we certainly don't want you to get in no trouble if someone sees us here. It might be best for you if you lets them know we is here."

The young man was perplexed. Dr. Weinhart was warm-hearted and would have seen to their needs, but Dr. Emery was a stickler for the rules, and Dr. Emery would be the first to arrive.

"Does Dr. Emery use this entrance?" Michelle asked.

"No, ma'am, he usually uses the side door near his office."

"But," she continued, "isn't today the day he brings bagels, and doesn't he usually bring them to the reception area?"

"How do you know that?" he asked.

"Maybe," Michelle suggested, "you should let us wait in Dr. Weinhart's office. We'll keep nice and quiet there until she arrives."

The orderly nodded and led them to her office, which was in the opposite corridor from Dr. Emery's office. Blake and Destiny gave each other quizzical looks, wondering what was going on with her nana.

The jeep rumbled down the highway. The knobby tires vibrated against the road and a draft whistled through the cabin. Tangiers was certain that the jeep was everything that Nathan's luxurious limousine was not. The road from Lafayette turned into an endless nondescript lane of black top surrounded by a seemingly infinite swamp and jungle. It reminded him of the everglades in Florida. He didn't see as much marsh as the everglades, but he had no doubt it would be just as depressing if they had to walk through it. The great outdoors had always made him feel very small and overwhelmed. He didn't like the feeling and hoped the Jeep was more reliable than it appeared.

He didn't know what to expect once he eventually arrived in Cricket Bend, but he was reasonably certain that the shabby appearance of the jeep and his less ostentatious wardrobe would be a better fit than if he had arrived with the style of Vanderlew.

He glanced over at his associate. She wore earbuds and had her eyes closed. Simon wondered if she were trying to avoid seeing where they were or if she was just enjoying her music.

Dr. Weinhart's office was a magnitude beyond cozy. While there was a large walnut desk with an office chair and a bookcase filled with technical manuals detailing the diagnosis and treatment of various psychiatric ailments, the rest of the office was wall to wall comfort. A thick shag covered the floor. A large cushy sofa dominated one wall while three book cases filled with self-help and holistic books by a myriad of authors ran the length of the opposite wall. Even the guest chairs in front of the desk were soft and inviting.

Michelle plopped herself down in the overstuffed chesterfield, while Destiny gravitated behind the desk to the only exposed wall in the room. It was covered with framed pictures and a few obligatory licenses and diplomas. She found dozens of pictures of a pretty young woman hugging children and old people from various countries around the world. She didn't recognize most of the places, and assumed they were places that hadn't existed yet when her old geography and history books were printed. A grin crept across her face as she realized that all her old home school textbooks were lost in the fire.

Michelle chuckled and said, "Don't you worry Missy, I'm sure we kin find some new school books for you when we gets to my daddy's farm."

Destiny frowned and returned to the couch where she settled into the opposite end from her nana, taking one of the throw pillows and hugging it against her chest. Blake turned one of the doctor's guest chairs around to face the center of the room instead of her desk, and made himself at home in it.

Vanderlew was reasonably certain that the hospital administrator would not be an early bird, and even if he was, there was no need to stage a meeting at the crack of dawn, so he took his time starting his mission. He had already prepared the papers he planned on using to intimidate the hospital. They were legitimate enough, though he had no real intention of filing them with any court. His main goal was to flush out the girl in the report. He didn't see why she would try to contact her retarded mother, but he was ordered to stake her out on the thin chance that she did show. It wouldn't be the first time he was given stupid orders. His secondary goal, which he used as an excuse for being there, was to try questioning the mother. He had no clue what her condition would be and hoped she wasn't some kind of a raving drooling lunatic.

For now though, he nestled back into the comfortable chair of the living room in his suite at the Hilton. He saw no reason why his being stuck in the sticks like this should mean he couldn't live the lifestyle to which he was accustomed.

He had already ordered room service and now had the time to flick on the news and see what was happening out in the real world.

Dr. Weinhart was surprised to find guests waiting for her when she arrived, but it was never in her nature to be inhospitable. "Good morning," she said as she dropped her things on her desk. "Was I expecting you?"

Michelle rose from the couch and said, "No. I apologize for dropping in on you like this. I am Michelle Boutin. My daughter Tempest be a patient here. I don't believe we ever met before. Dr. Kerrigan was her regular doctor on my previous visits."

Dr. Weinhart shook Michelle's hand and said, "Pleased to meet you. You know, Dr. Kerrigan has been gone for quite some time."

"I didn't know that. We don't get out this way near enough. It is a long hard trip for us, but here we be now. Tempest's daughter over there..."

Destiny waved from her place on the couch.

"...was hopin' to see her mama. She was born here. Did ya know that?"

"I see," Dr. Weinhart said, "but I don't understand why you are here to see me."

"Oh," Michelle said as she turned towards the center of the room nodding her head this way and that. "Well, the truth be that we is here in your office just so's we kin avoid Dr. Emery."

"Ahhh," Dr. Weinhart laughed. "That explains everything. Why don't you just make yourself comfortable and I'll go see if I can bring Tempest here..."

The door, which Dr. Weinhart had closed behind her, swung open. A stern gentleman in a white coat filled the doorway and bellowed out, "Judith?"

The mirth faded from Dr. Weinhart's expression as she responded, "Have you forgotten how to knock Dr. Emery?"

His already serious expression only worsened. "I will not have vagrants roaming around in my hospital!"

Dr. Weinhart's face, which was not prone to look unpleasant, darkened. "And I," she barked, "will not have you bursting into my office when I might be with a patient."

"These aren't patients," he said. "They are the intruders I was looking for."

Dr. Weinhart walked up to Dr. Emery and placed her hand against his chest, pushing him towards the door. "They may not be patients, but they have a family member here and I was consulting with them on her status, for which they are guaranteed the same rights to privacy as is given to a patient!" She pushed again, but he resisted.

"Let me remind you," he said, "that I am the hospital administrator here, not you. I set the hours within which we operate, and we are not open for visitors of any kind at this time in the morning."

Michelle wriggled her way between them and said, "I be truly sorry, Dr. Weinhart, I never meant to bring dis kind o' trouble down onto you. We kin wait outside."

Dr. Weinhart's expression immediately softened. "No need, Michelle. You just relax on the sofa, and I'll take care of this."

Dr. Emery's irritation was evident. "You'll take care of this?" he whined. "Perhaps you would like me to add some notes to your file detailing your insubordination?"

"You are out of line," she said. "These are my friends, and they have come to visit one of our patients. I…"

"Your friends?" he interrupted. "Do you really expect me to believe that these filthy country bumpkins are your friends?"

"That's enough!" Michelle bellowed. Her voice originated in his head like the voice of God. "I come to see my daughter and you is not standing in my way!"

His pupils shrunk and perspiration sprouted on his temples. He wanted to run, but his knees shook too much for him to leave the room, so he merely pointed to the hallway and said in an empty shaken voice, "Yes, ma'am, she's that way."

"Don't you go anywhere," Dr. Weinhart said. "You relax here, and I'll get her."

She walked to the doorway and saw an orderly just outside. "Hector," she said, "escort Dr. Emery back to his office and wait with him. Make sure he's okay."

Nathan couldn't put it off forever. He put his suit coat on and checked his hair and tie in the mirror. Satisfied that everything looked perfect, he grabbed his briefcase and left the suite for the elevator. He told the team to wait for him by the car at nine, and it was a quarter past now, so they should be ready.

He ignored the annoyed glances and silent grumbling from his team and slid into the back of the limo.

They were an odd-looking group. His co-counsel was dressed in a business suit, but the other two wore drab camouflage shirts and pants with army boots. The only missing detail was the greasepaint on their faces.

Nathan didn't chat with them during the trip. He pulled out his computer tablet and read the journal. The driver knew where to go, and it was a short trip.

Dr. Weinhart would have preferred some warning that Tempest was to have guests. She could have tapered off some of her medications so she could be slightly more responsive during their visit. It was early enough that she could delay her morning medication before they saw her, but she would still be considerably sedated for several more hours.

Tempest's life ran on a rigid schedule. Orderlies would help her from her bed to a wheelchair, then they would take her to the common room where a nurse would bring a paper cup with her pills and a glass of water with a straw. She wasn't a complete vegetable. She made eye contact, and she could take the pills and swallow them, but she didn't engage in conversation and never initiated any actions of her own. They even scheduled her bathroom visits, where she obliged but never walked or wheeled herself there on her own accord.

Dr. Weinhart exited the elevator on the second floor and turned towards Tempest's room. As she passed the nurses' station, she signaled one of the orderlies and said, "Max, come with me." Then she turned to the nurse and said, hold Ms. Boutin's morning meds for now. I'm taking her downstairs for an interview."

The halls were still empty. By midday, they would be filled with wandering patients and busy staff. The floors were clean and polished, and they squeaked under Dr. Weinhart's sensible shoes. Max followed her to Tempest's room. Most patients had pictures of family and drawings that they had made on the walls, but Tempest's room had no such personality. The walls and furniture were bare.

"Good morning, Tempest."

She opened her eyes and looked at Dr. Weinhart. Her face revealed a question. She knew this was not the normal routine.

"You have some special visitors this morning. I'm going to take you down to my office so you can have a private visit with them."

Tempest sat up in the bed, but Max had to help her into the chair. There was nothing wrong with her legs, but she didn't exercise enough to walk on her own and confined herself to the chair.

"Thank you, Max, I'll take her from here."

"Yes, doctor."

This was definitely out of her normal routine. It might have been thrilling if it weren't so mysterious and frightening. Tempest tried one of her rare vocalizations, but it came out, "Wahh wah woo." Her medications deeply affected her ability to communicate. She was trapped in the chair and had no choice but to trust her physician.

The limo drove past the hospital, then circled the block. They could see that the fence completely surrounded the block and the only way in or out was the front.

Nathan pointed to two different positions within the compound and said, "I want the two of you to set up there and there."

"Seriously?" one of them asked. "Do you really think you are giving us operational instructions? Driver! Take us around the next corner, then pull over and pop the trunk."

The limo passed the gates once more, then pulled around the corner and rolled up to the curb. The two mercenaries slipped out of the car and went to the trunk. They each pulled out a suitcase, then closed the trunk and returned to the rear door of the vehicle.

"Here," one of the snipers said. "Hold on to these for me." He handed Nathan his billfold and a letter to his family. The other sniper did the same, then shut the door and slapped the roof of the limo twice. The driver pulled away from the curb for one more trip around the block to the front. Nathan stuffed their personal belongings in the small storage on the back of the seat in front of him.

They took their cases into a thick stand of bushes and assembled their rifles. They put radio headsets on, but had little need to communicate. When ready, they hand signaled and one of them entered deeper into the bushes and scaled the fence. He chose a position in one of the older trees, which gave him a vantage over the front steps of the hospital. The other slipped across the street and onto the roof of a grocery store on the corner. He had a clear line of sight to the front gate. He could see into the compound as far as the circular drive in front of the main doors, but his view of the hospital and the front steps was blocked by trees. He could see the limo approach from around the far corner. He lifted his gun and could see Nathan in his sights. His finger twitched.

The car pulled up to the gate, and the driver spoke into the intercom. The gates opened, and they were inside. Both snipers followed the car down the drive to the front of the hospital. Nathan left the vehicle and headed for the doors, while the driver waited out front for his return.

The road from Lafayette was tediously monotonous and Simon was greatly relieved when he saw the sign announcing Cricket Bend. Ten more miles and he would be there. Just knowing he was close helped relieve the tedium in his back while the jeep plodded along the desolate highway. As the minutes went by, he wondered if he had misread the sign. There were no signs of a town anywhere on the horizon. He and his assistant, Melissa, kept checking the side of the road for exits until they reached a point where there was only water on her side of the car. He could see lights ahead and said, "That must be it ahead." But as he arrived at the lights, he saw that it was only a gas station; a truck stop with a diner. He drove straight through, wondering where in the world Cricket Bend was.

Melissa turned in her seat to give the gas station and general store a good look and said, "I think maybe that was it."

Simon looked in the rear-view mirror at the shrinking gas station and general store. There was nothing ahead of them, so he pulled the jeep over to the side of the road and check his location on his GPS. She was right. That must have been it. He turned the car around and returned, pulling the car into the gas station parking lot in front of the diner, next to a sheriff's squad car.

He looked at the diner, then at the general store, then back at the diner and asked, "You hungry?"

She smiled back and said, "Sure." She didn't care how small Cricket Bend was. She was thrilled to be on a field trip and saw it all as an adventure.

Once inside, he saw a small crowd congregated around the sheriff at the far end of the diner, and had to wait for a waitress to come seat him. The waitress had to drag herself away from everyone to direct them to a booth by the front door.

The vinyl seats were cool against Melissa's bare legs. Once they were seated and handed menus, Simon asked, "What's going on?"

"We have ze fire a day ago," the waitress said. "It burned a house to ze ground. It was cas fortuit, ze act of God, if you ask me."

Marie was seated at a nearby booth in the corner, quietly crying about her new friend's misfortune. Henry had shared with her what Michelle had told him, that they had lost their home, but hearing the details of the ruins had brought tears to her eyes, and hearing her mother's callus remarks was more than she could bear. "How can you be so cruel, mother? Zey lost their home and all you can be is bitter?"

Marie's mother's face clouded with embarrassment, not for what she had said, but for being reprimanded by her own daughter in public. She stormed off to the kitchen, leaving Simon and Lisa with menus but nobody to take their order.

Marie came to their table and said, "I'm sorry. My mother has ze primitive notions about them and she can be a bit harsh on some people she doesn't like. Whenever you are ready, I will take your order."

"Just coffee," Simon said, "and a sandwich. Do you have ham and cheese?"

"Monsieur, we may not be New Orleans, but we do serve ze finest Muffuletta in town." Marie waited for some reaction and getting none, snickered and repeated, "In town...you get? No? Is a small town. I make ze joke. Is a little joke, but a really big sandwich."

Simon smiled and nodded his head. "I'll have one of those, with the coffee."

"Me too," Lisa said. "I saw one of those on TV once."

"I'll bring one for you to share. Zey are too big for just one person."

Tempest hadn't been on the first floor since Destiny was born. She was a lifer in the institution and, except for rare excursions to the outer grounds, had spent Destiny's entire life on the second floor. Visits were normally in the common room upstairs, and even trips to the grounds outside were curtailed years ago. This was highly unusual in any case, but for someone so locked into a routine, it was also slightly terrifying. She was still heavily sedated, but her eyes rolled around watching the lights in the elevator and the doors they passed as Dr. Weinhart wheeled her through the reception area and down the corridor to her waiting family.

Destiny waited almost patiently on the couch. She repeatedly adjusted the hair that framed her face. She had wanted this moment for a very long time and now that it was here, her knees shook and her heart thumped audibly in her ears. She bit her lip anxiously when she heard the click of the doorknob turning. She hugged the throw pillow tightly to her bosom and held her breath.

Dr. Weinhart wheeled Tempest in, and Destiny leapt out of the sofa and screamed, "Mama!"

Tempest rolled her eyes around but offered little clues as to whether she recognized anyone in the room.

Blake's mouth fell open and his mind spun at the sight of the raven haired woman.

"Mama?" The smile slowly eroded from Destiny's face as she asked, "What's wrong with her?"

"I was afraid of this," Dr. Weinhart said. "Her medications are very powerful and until they wear off, she may not know who you are."

Destiny fell to her knees beside her mother and took her hand and rubbed it. "It's me, Mama. It's Destiny."

Tempest rolled her eyes to rest on Destiny, but showed no sign of understanding.

"Give her some time," Dr. Weinhart said. "She hasn't had her morning medications, and she should be able to respond to you in a few hours."

"A few hours?" Destiny cried. "Isn't there anything you can do for her? Something you can give her?"

"I'm sorry, no. She just needs some time to work last night's medications out of her system. She'll still be sedated then, but she should be able to respond to you. We can give her some water; that can sometimes help speed up the process. Why don't you just sit with her like that while I go get her a glass with a straw so you can give it to her?"

Dr. Weinhart left the room and closed the door behind her.

Destiny turned to Michelle and asked, "Nana? Can I try?"

Michelle knew what she meant and nodded her head.

Destiny got up off her knees and rolled her mother closer to the couch. She sat on the edge of the cushions and held her mother's hands while she closed her eyes and tried to bring up the healing waves into her hands. Nothing happened. She tried again, this time gritting her teeth while she tried to force up the healing, but again, nothing happened. She remembered what Mala had taught her. Her mother wasn't hurt in the hand, so holding it might not work. She reached up and held her hand to her mother's forehead. She used her hand to feel what might be wrong, but she sensed nothing.

"I'm sorry, Cherie, but I don't think she's broken like that. You cain't fix what's not broke."

Destiny wasn't ready to quit. She held her mother's hands by the fingertips and focused deep inside herself, focusing on a warm, happy part of her own mind, then projected her thought into her mother's mind. She knew her mother was in there somewhere, she only had to find her. A silence fell around her as her natural senses were replaced with her extended senses.

"Mama?" she asked.

"Who's there?" she heard her mother say before she was abruptly aware once again of the sounds of the office.

"What are you doing?" Dr. Weinhart asked from the doorway.

Destiny quickly released her mother's fingers and pulled her hands back to her lap. She looked around wild-eyed, afraid she was caught doing something wrong.

Michelle said, "She was just trying to reach her mother; on the inside. It's something she can do. I don't think there's any harm in it."

Dr. Weinhart's pulse quickened. She had always believed there was more to the human mind than what science could prove. She had to keep her beliefs bottled up while she was in medical school, but she had shelves full of books about people with special abilities. She wanted them to be true, and she wanted this to be true. She had heard the voice before, when Michelle had told Dr. Emery she wanted to see her daughter, but convinced herself she imagined it. Now she wasn't so sure. "Okay," she said timidly, "but I'd like to watch, and if I think there is anything wrong with what you are doing, I'll call a stop to it."

Michelle and Destiny agreed. Dr. Weinhart closed the door to her office and sat down in the second guest chair, which Blake had turned around for her.

Destiny took Tempest's hands into hers again. She had no intention of trying the healing magic again and went directly to entering her mind. She learned how to do this when she was attacked by witches who thought she was a spy. Sit was like so many other magical things that she had learned. She was like a tape recorder that could record magic and play it back.

She closed her eyes and ventured into her mother's mind. Even though everyone in the room sat and watched silently, Destiny could hear the room sound around her change, and she knew she was there. She opened her eyes and found herself in a long, white corridor. The walls, floor, and ceiling were glossy white and looked like the same material to her. The hallway was brightly lit but she could not see any lights in the ceiling. She looked both ways and saw no doors or other distinguishing features. This was certainly not what she expected.

Neither direction seemed better than the other, so she simply shrugged her shoulders and chose to take the hall on the right. The corridor did not extend indefinitely as she had originally thought, but as she walked, she could see a corner where it turned to the left. When she turned the corner, she saw another hallway. Something moved at the other end of the corridor. She only saw it for a moment and could make out no more than a grey blur that disappeared around the next corner.

Destiny ran down the barren hallway and swiftly turned the corner. She was close enough now to recognize a grey-robed figure running away from her. It could be her mother. Destiny ran faster. The robed figure turned another corner, but she was catching it.

As Destiny rounded the next corner, the robed figure darted through a doorway on the right. Odd, but she hadn't seen any doorways before. This time, however, it was lined with doorways on the left, but only the single doorway on the right. As she reached it and began to turn right, something tugged at her from her left. She heard a woman moan behind one of the doors. "Mama?" she asked. "Is that you?"

She walked to the first door on her left and turned the knob. The doors were common office style doors with frosted glass panes. She tried pushing it open, but it didn't give. She pulled instead, and the door opened out into the hallway, revealing a solid brick wall blocking the way. The second and third door were the same, but when she opened the fourth door, the brick wall wasn't complete and only filled the lower three feet of the doorway. She looked in the top half and saw a figure disappear through a door on the opposite side. She scaled the wall and ran to the other side and through the door, revealing three corridors, front, right, and left.

Destiny closed her eyes and stretched out her senses. This wasn't like the real world, and it was different from the dream worlds she had experienced during her training. All she felt was an emptiness, and again she had to choose a direction at random. She chose the middle hall in front of her. There were no doors in the walls, but she thought she could see a door at the far end, straight in front of her. It was a long corridor. She picked up her pace. The hallway seemed to stretch in front of her, with the doorway at the end slipping further away. She broke into a run and was catching it. All she had to do was keep up the pace and she would reach the door. The hallway abruptly stopped stretching, and she found herself facing the door.

She reached out and wrapped her hand around the cold metal doorknob. It resisted slightly as she turned it, but clicked and opened to reveal a small square room. There was no furniture in the room, only a woman huddled in the corner with her hands over her head and her arms blocking her ears.

Destiny approached the woman. All she could see was tangled black hair splayed out over a hospital gown. When she reached the corner, she knelt down and parted the woman's hair to see her face.

"Mama?"

The woman barely turned her head, but her eyes darted up and to the side so she could see Destiny.

Destiny reached out with both hands, offering the woman a hug and asked again, "Mama? Is it you?"

The woman locked her eyes on Destiny's and gave her a quick, short, jerky nod.

Destiny leaned forward to embrace her mother, but the shivering woman shied away.

"Oh, Mama, let me help you."

The woman looked away from Destiny. She took her hands down from covering her ears and wrapped them around her knees. She rocked slightly and her eyes darted wildly around the room, but never rested on Destiny.

Destiny didn't know what to do. She found her mother, but she couldn't help her. She was only inches away and she couldn't reach her. Tears pushed their way out of Destiny's eyes and down her cheeks. The woman in front of her was like a wild animal unaccustomed to human interaction. Destiny's tears were now accompanied by mild sobs and uneven breathing. She reached out and tried to use her healing magic on her mother, but she shrieked and blocked Destiny's hand with her arm.

Now the sobs came more freely. Destiny fell backwards against the wall and let it out. She wiped her tears from her face with the back of her arm. She was so sure she could have helped, but she was useless. Falling over on her side, she curled up and wept for her mother. She closed her eyes to shut out the bright white room and cried herself to sleep.

Tempest watched. She saw her child crying, and it moved her more than her fear. Reaching out to brush the bangs from Destiny's face, she lay down in front of her daughter and curled up in a similar position, but touched their foreheads together.

Nathan approached the reception desk with his briefcase in his hand and a practiced smile on his face. "Good morning," he said. "I'd like to speak to your hospital administrator, if I may."

The nurse looked him over suspiciously and asked, "May I tell him what this is regarding?"

He handed her a card and said, "My name is Jonathan Tidwell. I am an attorney representing Titus Shaw. Mr. Shaw would like to bequeath an endowment to your facility."

The nurse tilted her head and arched her penciled eyebrows as she asked, "The Titus Shaw?"

"Yes," Nathan said. "*The* billionaire philanthropist."

The nurse didn't have to get Dr. Emery on the phone, he had recovered sufficiently from his earlier confrontation with Michelle to be standing off to the side listening. "I'm Dr. Emery, what was that you were you saying about an endowment?"

Nathan approached him with his hand extended. "How do you do? As I said, my name is Jonathan Tidwell, and I am here on behalf of the billionaire Titus Shaw. It has come to our attention that you have one of his long-lost cousins staying here and Mr. Shaw would like to oversee her ongoing care. He has, of course, arranged a very generous and appreciative donation for the care you have shown her thus far."

Emery heard billionaire and appreciative in the same breath and gladly shook the stranger's hand. "That's wonderful news. You said he has a cousin here? Would you happen to know his name?"

"Boutin, her last name is Boutin. We're not sure what first name she was listed under."

"Tempest?" Emery asked. "Frankly, I've never even been sure that was her real first name, anyway." He turned to Hector, who was at his side, and said, "Why don't you go get Ms. Boutin and bring her to my office?"

Hector nodded and trotted off.

Emery held his hand out to indicate his office door and said, "Why don't you come with me and wait in my office? Tell me, what kind of arrangement did Mr. Shaw have in mind? Did he want to arrange a private room for her?"

Nathan followed Emery's directions to his office door and said, "Mr. Shaw would like to transfer her to his home for private care."

"I see," Emery said. "How soon did you want to arrange her transfer?"

"Immediately," Nathan replied. "I have all the paperwork with me, including a sizable check for your hospital."

Hector arrived in the common room, and Tempest wasn't there. He ran to her bedroom, but she wasn't there either. He asked one of the nurses, but Max was the only one who knew Dr. Weinhart had taken her and he was in the dispensary. Hector ran back down to Dr. Emery's office. He stood just inside the doorway, breathing heavily.

Nathan was showing Dr. Emery the papers outlining the guardianship ordered for Tempest, naming his firm as conservators when Hector arrived in his office. Emery looked up and asked, "Where is she?"

Hector shrugged and said, "I don't know. She wasn't upstairs."

Emery frowned until he remembered Dr. Weinhart's guests. He got up and said, "Follow me. I think I know where she may be."

Marie carried two plates from the kitchen and placed them on the table in front of Simon and Lisa. Each plate held half a Muffuletta, which was piled over two inches high with slices of Italian ham, salami, and cheese. A thick layer of olive salad oozed out the sides and dripped onto the plate, mixing with the small portion of coleslaw.

Lisa took one look at the enormous sandwiches and whistled, saying, "You weren't kidding. Those are huge."

Marie smiled and said, "Oui. Enjoy your lunch."

She turned to return to her booth, but Simon gently grabbed her arm and said, "If you don't mind, I'd like to ask you a few questions."

"Moi?" Marie asked, surprised.

"Yes. I couldn't help noticing how moved you were over this morning's tragedy. I assume you were friends with the victims?"

"Victims? You mean Mademoiselle Destiny and Michelle? Oui. I think I am their friend."

"If you don't mind, can you sit a moment and talk?"

Marie nodded and slid into the booth next to Lisa.

"When was the last time you saw them?"

"Zey were here yesterday morning. We had breakfast before zey left."

"Ahh," Simon said. "So, they are okay? That is certainly a relief."

"Zey are unharmed, but without a home."

"Do you know where they went?"

Marie thought that it was a little strange that Simon would be more curious about her new friends than about the fire. She studied him and Lisa then asked, "Why is it that you do not sound like ze other reporters? You don't sound so interested in the fire."

Simon understood her confusion. "I'm not a reporter. I didn't even know about the fire. My employer learned that some men we are investigating planned to hurt someone in this area. I was sent here to try to prevent it. We don't even know who we are supposed to protect, but when I heard about the fire, I thought maybe I was too late. I'm glad to hear they escaped, but I'd still like to warn them."

Marie leaned back in her seat and looked at the man across from her. She cocked her head and squinted her eye trying to measure him up. "What kind of man would learn these things? Are you police?"

"No, miss, I'm not with the police. I'm an attorney. Sometimes we learn privileged things that we are not allowed to divulge, kind of like something a priest might learn in the confessional."

"And you learned this way zat someone wanted to hurt Michelle and Destiny? Why would someone want to hurt them?"

Simon saw his opportunity open before him. If he played coy enough, he could probably draw his suspicions out of Marie. "I really can't say too much, but these people believed that your friends weren't like you or me. They thought your friends were different, and that they were somehow dangerous. I don't know how much you know about your friends, and I certainly wouldn't want to start any rumors. In fact, I think that maybe I've said too much already. Please forgive me, but I can't actually tell you what these people thought your friends were."

Maria intended to remain silent and just listen, but she was caught up in the intrigue and blurted out, "You mean that zey were witches?"

"You knew?" Simon asked.

"Everybody knows. Madame Michelle and Mademoiselle Destiny are wonderful people, but zey help others with their problems sometimes."

"Is that why your mother disliked them?"

"Oui. She thought zey were not Christian, but zey were."

"So, you've actually seen the things they can do?"

"No, not in person, but she has." Marie pointed to the woman in the center of the throng of people with the sheriff. "That is Mrs. Pinet. She went to visit Michelle this morning and discovered the burned down home."

"Thank you. You've been very helpful. We will do whatever we can to protect your friends."

"Merci," Marie said as she stood up. "Enjoy your lunch."

Destiny released her mother's hands and cried softly, saying, "She's scared. She's like a wild woman and couldn't even talk. I don't think she even recognized me."

Dr. Weinhart had shelves full of eyewitness accounts of aboriginal psychic practices and ancient folklore. She thought there was more than just a grain of truth to them and found it easy to believe that she had just witnessed something remarkable. She felt like she should be the authority here and it was her place to say something, but in reality, she was little more than a voyeur and didn't know how to respond.

Michelle said, "Your mama been here a long time, Cherie. And you never seen her before she was put here. She heard da voices when she was jest a teet little girl and they drove her mad."

"She was hiding," Destiny continued. "I had to find her, but she kept trying to get away from me. There was someone else in there trying to lead me away from her, but I could hear her and didn't follow him. It was the strangest place you could ever imagine. There were walls between us everywhere I looked. Even the doors had walls behind them!"

Dr. Weinhart surprised even herself when she responded, "That could be the drugs. We keep her mind heavily sedated."

"I finally found her and tried to help her," Destiny continued, "but she pulled away."

Dr. Emery burst into the room, took one suspicious look at Michelle, then glanced at Tempest and exclaimed, "There you are! What a relief! We were afraid you were lost."

Dr. Weinhart jumped out of her seat and yelled, "Didn't we already discuss my patient's privacy when my door is closed?"

"But," Dr. Emery said, "she is no longer your patient. I just transferred her into the care of her new guardian."

Nathan entered the room and tried smiling, as he was accustomed to doing, but seeing Destiny there, he quickly put two and two together and never quite managed the warm expression he intended.

Michelle rose slowly from her seat. An intense anger boiled inside her. "Who the ..."

Nathan's stomach twisted in a knot as his eyes fell on Michelle and he saw the animosity on her face. He still was unable to manage any kind of smile.

Destiny rose slowly from her seat. She was ready to reveal exactly who and what she was when Dr. Weinhart jumped in and quickly intercepted Nathan. She tried unsuccessfully to push him out of her office.

Dr. Emery pleaded, "People! People! There is no need for this. Mr. Tidwell here is a lawyer, and he represents Michelle's cousin, a famous billionaire who has offered to take care of her. It's all quite legal, and the papers have already been signed.

"Like hell he's gonna take care of my lil girl," Michelle said. "She's my daughter and I don't know nuthin' about no billionaire cousin. He be lying and daer be nuthin' at all legal about dis."

Destiny could already feel the heat building in her hands. She lowered her head and looked up at him through her eyebrows, saying, "You ain't taking my mama."

Dr. Weinhart undid a button and fanned herself as she felt a palpable jump in the room temperature.

Michelle stepped towards Nathan and like before, her voice bellowed in everyone's head, "You kin just take yourself out of here afore it be the last place you ever sees!"

Dr. Emery's limbs trembled, and he stumbled as he retreated to his office and fell into his chair, content to hide there and shudder.

The knot in Nathan's stomach grew unbearable. He raised his hands up to grab on to someone before he doubled over onto the floor, and for the first time in his life, he released a small bolt of electricity which found a target in Dr. Weinhart, who fell faint onto the floor.

Destiny was quick to hit him with a bolt of her own, except her bolt was large enough to eject him from the room and slam him into the wall opposite the hallway. His stomach still twisted, but the fear in his heart helped him rise and stumble down the hall towards the exit.

Michelle and Destiny followed him. Destiny kept her arm cocked so every time he looked back, he knew what he would get should he turn around. Outside the building, the driver waited courteously by the limo.

The sniper in the tree had his sight trained on the steps, waiting for his target to emerge. He saw Nathan back out of the building and fall down the steps. Destiny followed him with her hand held in a curiously offensive manner like she planned to throw a stone. He took aim at her heart but before he pulled the trigger, he felt a sting in his shoulder and the rifle drooped, firing a round into Nathan's leg.

Blake helped Dr. Weinhart recover and together, they pushed Tempest out of the office and down the hall. Dr. Weinhart paused at the nurse's station to offer some instructions, then continued escorting Tempest out of the building.

The sniper fell from the tree. Blood oozed from a bullet hole in his shoulder and his ribs hurt when he hit the ground, but he was able to crawl through the bushes and struggle over the wall until he was off the grounds.

The driver tried running around the car to get in and escape, but bullets started spraying into the ground in front of him. He raised his arms and backed away.

Michelle saw Dr. Weinhart with Tempest and asked, "Are you okay?"

"I'm fine," she replied, "but I'm not quite sure what happened."

Michelle pointed to Nathan and lied, "Dat dare man hit you with his fist and you fainted."

"Was that gunfire I heard?" Weinhart asked?

"Sure was," Michelle said, "but we don't know who it be."

"Whoever it was," Blake said, "they seemed to be helping us."

"Here," Dr. Weinhart said. "Take Tempest with you."

"How?" Michelle asked.

Weinhart shrugged and said, "Take their car."

Michelle was horrified. She couldn't drive.

Blake heard her fear and said, "I can drive."

Michelle turned to Nathan and his driver, and this time knowing she would use the voice, commanded, "Give him da keys. And don't neither of you never tell nobody dat dis here car been stolen. You just forget about da car and you forget all about us. You ain't never seen none of us."

The driver tossed the keys to Blake. Destiny and Dr. Weinhart helped Tempest into the back of the limo.

Michelle started getting into the limo when one of the nurses came running out of the entrance waving a small bag and Dr. Weinhart said, "Wait! I have something for you." The nurse gave her the bag and Dr. Weinhart checked the contents then gave it to Michelle saying, "There are two bottles in here. Give her one pill in the morning every day. Use the big pills first. It's easy to tell them apart. After they're finished, give her the small pills. That should help keep her from getting sick while she comes off her medications. She's probably going to start hearing her voices again. I hope you plan to find her another doctor wherever you end up. Otherwise, I don't know how she will cope with the voices."

Michelle hugged Dr. Weinhart, saying, "I don't know how I kin ever repay you."

Dr. Weinhart smiled and hugged back, saying, "You already have given me more than you'll ever know."

CHAPTER 4

Destiny and Michelle sat in the back of the Limo with Tempest between them. Tempest slumped over to the side slightly, and Destiny was happy to offer a shoulder for her to lean on. She looked at her mother's blank face and stroked her hand, wondering when the drugs would start to wear off so she could communicate with her. She wondered if her mother was even aware of who she was or that they were together now. Michelle saw Destiny's concern and felt for her, but was even more worried that her daughter would be completely unmanageable when the drugs finally wore off. She remembered how wild her daughter was following the rape when Destiny was conceived. Tempest was like a feral animal during that period. She was unable to talk or care for herself. Reason eventually returned, but it led her back to alcohol, the only thing she knew to quiet the voices and the thing that lured her to her rape. She ran away from home and discovered how easy it was for a pretty girl to get alcohol, but a young girl on the streets can't hide forever. She was eventually caught and taken to a psychiatric hospital, where she finally found real tranquility in psychotropic drugs prescribed by the doctors. Michelle caught Destiny watching her expression and knew she couldn't hide her feelings, so she quickly searched for a new thought to occupy her mind.

Blake turned the key and started the car. His heart raced as he wrapped his fingers around the steering wheel and gave it a squeeze. He told Michelle he could drive, but in truth, he not only didn't have a license, but he had absolutely no actual experience behind the wheel. Everything he knew about driving, he had stolen while invading the mind of the commandant at the camp where he was raised. There were more than a few things he had learned while living vicariously in other people's minds. When he thought about it, it was not so different from Destiny's education except that she had learned her craft from the memories of people who had died hundreds or even thousands of years ago.

He focused on the dashboard and familiarized himself with the speedometer and gas gauge, which he figured were the two most important gauges for him to know. He grabbed the shifter and was ready to put it into drive, but wasn't sure where to go.

Michelle said, "Mississippi. We be goin' to my daddy's farm. I don't rightly know how to get there. I recall that Daddy's farm is somewhere between Hattiesburg and Gulfport, but I don't know if we be close enough to see a sign for them or not. Might be we sees a sign for Jackson, though. It be a pretty big city, but I don't think it was all that close. Could be we heads towards Jackson until we finds a sign to Hattiesburg, or maybe we just goes east until we finds a sign to Gulfport."

Michelle's directions were anything but definitive, but she never said South or West, so Blake put the car in drive and pulled it out of the compound and headed east. He was pretty sure that was the general direction to Mississippi.

The sniper held his bloody shoulder and remained hidden in the bushes where his camouflage kept him comfortably invisible. He saw the limo pull out of the gate and down the street, but already knew it had been commandeered by the mission objectives. He looked up to the roof of the grocer and saw the silhouette of a man with a rifle, but it was not his partner, so he remained hidden deep within the bushes and slinked off in the opposite direction until he could turn the corner and head up the block, out of view, and hopefully, out of range.

Simon waited for the commotion to die down and for the sheriff to leave before he approached Mrs. Pinet.

She looked suspiciously at the stranger, but ultimately decided that her fame could sustain one more interview.

"Mrs. Pinet?" Simon asked.

"Yes?" Mrs. Pinet let her answer trail off like a question and waited for the stranger to introduce himself.

"My name is Simon Tangiers. I am an attorney, and I was sent here when my firm learned of a threat to the Boutin family. I understand you may have actually witnessed something, and I may be too late to warn them."

"All I know is what I saw. The house was burned to the ground. I only ventured barely onto their property. I called out for Michelle, but heard nothing coming back. The sheriff seems to think I should have looked further, but there were smoldering fires all over the grounds and many piles of ash. I was not going to start poking around in all the ash looking for my friends. I called for them and either they were not there, or," she swallowed hard, then continued, "or, they were not there."

Simon took her hand and patted the back, which brought a gasp to her lips until he said, "I can see you care deeply for your friends and fear for their safety. They escaped. When we are done here, you should go talk to Marie about what she knows, but first, I have a more delicate question for you." He removed his hand and looked around, more as a pretense than an actual concern that anyone would be listening. He leaned closer across the table and said in a low voice, "Did you know that your friends are witches?"

She pulled her hand back to her side of the table and looked slightly alarmed, not sure if he was actually here to warn them or to hunt them."

"We already know about them," Simon continued, "but I'm trying to determine how open they were about what they could do."

"Michelle had her gifts, but she never made claims. It was Zeline who always claimed she was a witch and tried bragging about it but most everyone knew she was a fraud."

"But," Simon said, "everyone must have known that Michelle was genuine."

"Most everyone. Not everyone liked it, but most of us accepted it. She never done nothing bad. She was always a hit at the parties when she would read the bones..." Mrs. Pinet shrunk down in her seat and mumbled, "Except last time."

"Last time?" Simon repeated.

"About a week ago, the bones told her that a stranger was coming and someone close to her was going to die. Then this morning, when I saw that her place was burned down..."

Simon nodded. "I understand. So, you knew that when she read the bones, it was genuine."

"Yes."

"Have you ever seen her do anything else? What other kinds of powers did she have?"

"She made potions and tonics. Mrs. Thibodeaux would go to her to have curses removed, but most of them was in her head, I think."

"What about the young one, Destiny?"

Mrs. Pinet shrugged her shoulders and asked, "What about her? She's Michelle's granddaughter."

"Did you know she was a witch too?"

"She's just a girl."

He nodded to Lisa and said, "Let's go talk to the store owner. Thank you for your time, Mrs. Pinet."

Tempest's eyes were open, but blank. Michelle found cold bottles of water in a small fridge behind the front seat and used them to wet her daughter's lips. Occasionally Tempest would take a deep breath and sigh, but still didn't display any sign that she was regaining any true sense of consciousness.

While Michelle tended to her physical needs, Destiny tried again to reach inside her mother's mind. She held her head against Tempest's and channeled her thoughts. The world around her dissolved and once again she found herself in the long white corridor, but this time there were no doors. She walked down the hallway which was long but not endless. At the end of the hall, it turned left, and she faced another hallway, again with no doors. She followed this hall and the next. It brought her back to where she started. It was a square shaped hallway with no entrance or exit.

She placed her hands on the inner wall and walked around the hall again, tracing the wall with her fingers, hoping to sense some weakness that would let her in, but she found none and returned to the car.

"Now there aren't even any doors," Destiny cried. "It's like she is a prisoner trapped inside a room with no windows or doors."

Michelle wetted Tempest's lips again and handed another bottle to Destiny. "Maybe," she said, "your mama ain't in no prison. Maybe she's in a fort, hiding from you."

"But I want to see her, to help her."

"Could be she don't want you to see her like this."

Destiny started to respond again, but sat back and pouted instead. "There must be some way to get inside. Maybe I just need some help."

She closed her eyes and reached back in time. She followed the trail of memories through her ancestors and sought out her old friend Marvalaine. When she opened her eyes, she was in a magnificent courtyard. The shade trees were bigger than she remembered, but she recognized the pond and the benches and knew exactly where she was.

She barely had time to take a breath when someone or something tackled her from behind, with her arms and legs wrapped and pinned against her body. The weight of her attacker pressed down again with hot breath exhaling on the back of her neck and the distinct slobber of a large beast upon her back. She twisted her head around to see what had attacked her and heard the squeals of three little voices screaming, "Aunt Destiny! Aunt Destiny! Mama! Mama! Aunt Destiny has come to visit."

Again the beast pressed her head to the ground and slavered his tongue against the back of her ear until she heard Nimisen enter the court yelling, "Chauncey! Get off of her you big oaf!"

With the beast removed, she was able to rollover and face the remaining attackers. Nimisen came to her rescue and offered her both hands to raise her from the ground.

As certain as Destiny was about where she was, she was equally uncertain about when she had arrived.

"I can see from your expression," Nimisen said, "that you are a bit caught off guard. Children! Line up for Aunt Destiny and introduce yourselves."

First was the oldest, a slender boy of ten years. "This feels silly. Aunt Destiny already knows us."

"You may know her already, but look how young she is! She hasn't met you yet."

The boy bowed at the waist and said, "I am Bertrand, and this is my younger brother Phillip, and the girl at the end is Destine. She was named after you."

Phillip bowed and Destine curtsied in turn.

Nimisen took Destiny by the arm and started walking her towards the main exit which led to the market square. "I'm so glad you came to visit. Perhaps now we can have some of that girl time we always planned, but never seem to have time."

"Uhmm," Destiny squirmed. "I was actually looking for Marvalaine. I'm having a problem with my mother."

Nimisen nodded knowingly and said, "We all have problems with our mothers at your age, but why would you seek his advice? Wouldn't another woman be more knowing in this case?"

"It's not that kind of problem. She's sick and I'm trying to help her."

Nimisen directed her to a marble bench that sat before a small pond. "She's sick? Can you not heal her? I'm not sure how my husband can help you with that, he was never that talented in the healing arts."

Destiny leaned forward on the bench and rested her chin on her hands with her elbows on her knees. She wasn't sure what kind of help she wanted or how to ask for it. "She's not that kind of sick. Her problem is in her head. Nana says it's because she wouldn't accept her gifts when the time came and the voices drove her crazy. All I know, is that the first time I entered into her mind, she was running away from me like she was afraid of me. But the last time I went in, I couldn't get to her at all. She was locked inside a room with no doors and no windows."

"Ah," Nimisen said. "It sounds like she has locked herself in a dream world and she doesn't want you in."

"But, she doesn't know what she wants. The drugs they gave her to silence the voices have turned her into a vegetable."

"A vegetable?"

"Well, that's what we call it when someone sits all day and doesn't talk or do anything."

"I see," Nimisen said. She paused a moment to smooth some wrinkles out of her dress then continued, "If your mother has indeed built her dream world to keep you out, yet you still wish to pass her barriers, then again, Marvalaine may not be your best adviser. You already know one of the greatest dream world architects who ever lived."

"Who is that?"

"Your mentor, Mala, of course."

Destiny sighed. "Mala is dead."

"Of course she is dead. Even to me, she has been dead many thousand years. You need only go visit her when she is not dead."

"You don't understand," Destiny cried. "I saw her die. She died to save me."

"Then you must visit her before she died. She is your best advisor in this."

Destiny closed her eyes and entered the void that is the gateway to ancestral memories from the past. Voices floated past her like smoke being carried by the wind. She focused her mind and listened for the sound of Mala's voice. When Mala was her teacher, she would call out for Destiny leaving an easy trail for her to follow, but now, she heard nothing.

She pulled herself forward, deeper into the past. Random voices bobbed around her, but not the one she sought. If she could not locate Mala's voice, perhaps she could find someone near her. She came upon a cluster of voices and thought she heard the familiar tone of Ishun, Mala's mentor. As she pulled closer to hear the voice, a barrier prevented her from getting any nearer. She strained to hear what was inside and recognized enough to understand. This was the moment in time when Destiny was almost killed and Mala sacrificed her own life to save her pupil's. Destiny could not enter this memory again, but beyond it, she reasoned, she should be able to find a younger, still living, Mala.

She ventured around the shielded memory but found many more barriers in her way. She could not see the barriers, but she could sense an emptiness, a void within the void where she heard no voices at all. If she focused enough, she could follow the silent emptiness of the walls which separated her from Mala's voice as well as she ever could have followed anyone's voice. She did not know what kind of magic created these obstacles or who put them in her way, but she was determined to get around them. If it was some kind of a test, then it was a test she would pass. If it was a warning, she would ignore it, and if it was to keep her out, she would defeat it.

The string of barriers led her deeper back in time until she could finally sense the silence of the walls narrow to a point where they finally ended. Success was within her grasp as she aimed herself at the spot where the obstacles seemed to end. She listened keenly for Mala's voice and even tried calling for Mala, but all she heard back was a baby's cry.

She peeked into the memory and knew that she had not won at all. This was worse than failure; this was defeat. She found Mala, but she was still a baby clinging to her mother's breast.

The general store was exactly what Simon expected, from the wide wooden steps to the covered porch and wicker chairs. Inside, he found a variety of items from the souvenirs you would expect to see at any trading post to the grocery items you find at the corner store.

Henry wasn't expecting customers just yet. His local regulars usually came in on weekends and his other customers were tourists that came with the bus. There was no bus scheduled to arrive for a while. He was in the storeroom putting away the seasonal winter items when he heard the bell on the door. He poked his head out of the cellar door and was surprised to see two strangers just inside the shop.

"Bon Joo," he yelled. "You make your groceries while I pick up my extra rain wear bag daer. I be bag wit' you in a jiffy."

Before Simon could squeeze a word in, Henry was gone. He looked at Lisa and asked, "What did he say?"

She just shrugged and seeing nothing to do but wait, he began browsing through the hunting isle while Lisa gravitated to the clothing.

Henry put the last box of galoshes and hats on the top shelf then returned to his customers. "Tanks for the waiting. What you do now?"

Simon approached Henry with his arm extended and said, "We came here to warn Michelle Boutin that she might be in some trouble, but I guess we're too late."

Henry looked at him warily and asked, "How be it dat you knows Michelle?"

"To be honest," Simon said, "I don't actually know her, but my employer learned of a plot to cause some trouble and we came to warn her."

Henry still wasn't comfortable with the stranger. "Who would put da hurt on dose nice ones?"

"I'm not at liberty to say who they were, but ..."

"You not be at liberty?" Henry's suspicion was taking a turn towards anger. "Den how you know dis?"

"I work for a law firm," Simon replied, "and sometimes we learn things that the law forbids us to divulge."

"The law!" Henry spat on the floor and asked, "So, why you here if your law forbids you?"

"The law forbids us to share what we are told in confidence, like with a priest in confession, but it does not always forbid us to do the right thing about what we learned."

Henry was a devout Catholic, and hearing Simon compare his information to the confessional soothed Henry's suspicions considerably, but it did nothing to calm his seething anger over what had transpired. "Oui," Henry said, "but why? Maudit! Dose salauds be strange to dese parts. Dey got no reason to hate some here."

"They were witches, weren't they? These men that plotted against her needed no more reason than that."

"Oui," Henry said, thinking of Marie's mother. "Daer be some what need no more reason than dat."

"Thank you," Simon said. "I should probably move along. I may still have a chance to catch them."

As Simon was opening the door to leave, Henry added, "If I sees dose men agin, you won't be needin' to catch dem no more."

"Wait," Simon said. "Did you see them?"

"Oui. And I seen da teet one wit Michelle when she leaved."

Nimisen watched intently as Destiny returned to the courtyard garden. She waited for Destiny to speak, but she couldn't wait forever.

"Well?" Nimisen prodded. "Did you find Mala? What did she say?"

Tears gathered in Destiny's eyes. She leaned her head on Nimisen's shoulder and Nimisen responded with an arm wrapped around Destiny's waist.

"Mala was there," Destiny cried in a voice so soft that Nimisen could barely hear it, "but she was shielded from me. I could not get to her. I tried going around the shield, but by the time I found the end of it, all I found was Mala as a baby. Who could do that? Why does this keep happening to me?"

Nimisen had no good answers for her. "Magic is not always easy. Sometimes what we want to do defies all the laws of nature or even the laws of magic. Our magic is a gift. We don't know why we were given such a gift, so it can be difficult for us to know what we were meant to do with it. How we use it may not always be our choice. We cannot deny that it is a gift just because it suits us."

"But I need my mother. I have seen it. She saves me, so I must be able to save her yet my way is blocked at every turn."

"If you have truly seen this," Nimisen said, "then it must not be against the laws of magic. Sometimes, I have found that I am not strong enough on my own, and I need a little help, just a little extra magic behind me."

Destiny looked up and asked, "Does Marvalaine help you, then?"

"On occasion, but I was thinking of an object that can help amplify your power." Nimisen went to a shelf against the wall. She passed her hands over a small chest and unlocked the magical barrier, then opened it and pulled out an amulet with a long gold chain. She handed it to Destiny and said, "This talisman has served me well over the years. Take it and see if it can help you pierce the shields that block you."

Destiny accepted it and put it on. "Wish me luck," she said as she closed her eyes and started to picture the void.

"Wait!" Nimisen almost shouted. "It is not ready for you. You must put it on and wear it close to your heart so it can absorb some of your energy. You will know when the time is right. I should caution you to take care with the amulet. Use it when it is necessary, but try to use it sparingly. Its use can come with a cost. Now, since you have some time to spend, perhaps we can browse the marketplace?"

Destiny wiped the tears from her eyes and bobbed her head up and down. They exited through the main doors to the village and the many stalls and vendors that waited to share their wares.

Richard sat in his office watching his coworkers arrive from his window, wondering how much longer he would have before it all came crashing down around him. He didn't dare destroy any evidence of what he had done for Brian. It was too late for that. He kept his notes locked in the bottom drawer of his desk and waited for further instructions. That was all he could do now. What had looked like a promising career ready to rise up the ladder just a few days ago, now turned into him doing Logan's bidding and keeping his name below the radar. The phone rang, and he saw that it was Logan.

He tried sounding unconcerned as he answered, "Yes, Logan, what can I do for you?"

"I want you to come to my office and take notes."

"Yes, sir."

Richard hung up the phone. He had gone from the head of one of their asylums working on a leading-edge project to a humiliated secretary now. He grabbed a notepad and pen and hustled to Logan's office. It wasn't even Logan's real office, Logan didn't work out of this facility, but he was important enough that when he snapped his fingers, a conference room was immediately converted to an office and made available for him. He sat behind a desk larger and more opulent than Richard's, with a window looking out over the best view available. Richard entered the office and scanned the room, seeing an assortment of three very different-looking men arrayed around the room. One of them looked like he might be important, judging by his finely tailored suit, the second had a nice suit but something about it looked more like a uniform while the third one looked like a man of action, including the sling that held his arm.

"Close the door," Logan said. He pointed to the man with the sling and said, "Tell us again what you saw."

"Well, sir, when they came out of the hospital, the girl held her hand in the air like she was going to throw a grenade or something. I was about to shoot her when someone shot me in the shoulder."

Logan nodded his head, then pointed at the other two gentlemen and asked, "And what about these two?"

"Well," the mercenary continued, "the fancy one in the suit had his hands in the air and fell over backwards keeping away from the girl like he was afraid of her, and the driver tried getting into the car to escape, but the same loco bastard that shot me fired a bunch of rounds into the ground until he retreated. That's when the old one stepped forward and said something to them. I couldn't hear what she said, but the two of them became all docile and handed them the keys. They practically waved at them when the car drove off."

Logan pointed at Nathan and asked, "What did the old one look like?"

Nathan shrugged and said, "What old one? I don't know what any of this is about."

"And what about you?" Nathan asked while he pointed at the driver. "Who did you give the keys to?"

The driver looked blankly at Nathan, then back at Logan and asked, "What keys?"

Nathan nodded to the sniper and said, "Tell us who he gave the keys to."

"It was a boy. Same age as the girl, I'd say, but the boy never done nothing suspicious. He just took the keys and drove them off."

"Thank you, you're dismissed." Logan motioned for Richard to stay. Once they had left and closed the door behind them, he asked, "What do you think?"

"Well, sir, Brian was investigating the possible threat of witches fulfilling the prophecy and regaining their magic back. It sounds to me like we have two very active witches on our hands with all of their old-time powers back."

Logan nodded his head and said, "Yes. I agree. But why them? Why would they get their powers back and nobody else?"

Richard thought for a moment. The more he knew about Brian's mission, the deeper he was involved in the whole mess. He wished his memory were wiped, like the driver's, but he wasn't going to start lying now. "Well, sir," he said, "Brian swore he was getting his old powers back too. He asked me to quietly check with our training facilities and with some of our veterans to see if all of our people were getting their powers back."

"And?" Logan asked. "What did you learn?"

"Nothing sir. Except for the events, there have been no reports of increased extra normal activity."

Logan paused for a moment, chewing over the last thought. He swiveled his chair to look out the window at the Utah mountains. Spring was returning to the immediate area, but snow still capped the mountains on the horizon. "We still have one other team," he said. "They are in the field investigating Brian's disappearance. I want you to touch base with them and report back to me when you learn something."

"Yes, sir." Richard stood and made his way to the door.

"One more thing," Logan said. "Brian should have brought this to my attention instead of going out on his own like he did. I don't want you to make the same mistake he made."

"Understood." Richard left the office and breathed a sigh of relief. He may survive this fiasco yet.

Logan knew that Brian was perfectly within his rights to investigate the events as he had. Logan had done the same when his asylum had been affected, but he didn't like the fact that Brian had succeeded in locating the witches and he had not. He especially didn't like the report that Brian was getting his powers back. He didn't want Richard getting ahead of him in this. Witches apparently had their powers back, and he wanted his.

The three librarians sat cross-legged in a circle. They still stared into the flames in the center of the circle as they came out of their trances. The smoke lifted gently from the flames and left the room through vents in the ceiling, leaving only a pleasant hint of their scent behind. Without being stoked by their mental energy, the flames died back until they were little more than glowing coals.

"The mother is free," said the first.

"But she is not with the others," said the second.

"And the girl lives," added the third.

"But they are together! The mother has been rescued," said the first, "and she is with her daughter. He won't be happy."

"The girl is with her mother," said the third, "but they are not yet together."

"Yes," said the second. "The mother still lies beyond her reach."

"Nothing is beyond her reach," growled the first. "We are not yet done here."

Together, the three librarians nodded their heads in agreement and stared back into the coals to finish what they had started. The embers brightened, and the flames burst forth again as they re-entered their trances.

Richard returned to his office. As head of the institution, his was the best office available, but it was small and drab compared to Logan's converted conference room. He grabbed a candy from his candy dish and sat down at his computer. The witches made a fatal mistake if they thought they could mess with a couple of lackey's memories and get away in their car. All their limousines had anti-theft devices that would let him track the witches.

He fired off a memo to their transportation department. It was ironic that witches had all the mental powers, but they weren't known for their brains. They didn't have the technical skills to hack computers. All the hackers belonged to his clan. He was confident that no matter how many memories they may have scrambled, he could still locate records for the limo that was used and track its location.

If this worked, he might be able to score some sorely needed points with Logan.

━━━━━━━━━━━━

Destiny opened her eyes, and she was back in the Limo. She looked out the window and saw that they were on a narrow, raised highway with a swamp below them. There were no houses or buildings to see, just trees and swamp. "Where are we?"

"On the highway," Blake said, "heading east. We passed Baton Rouge a little while ago, but still have a ways to go before we cross the border into Mississippi. The good news is that there have been signs for Gulfport, and it turns out it was only about a three-hour drive to get there, and we have plenty of gas."

Destiny looked at her mother, who now leaned her head on her nana, but still had the same blank expression. "I guess we still got some time before the drugs wear off."

"I ain't so sure," Michelle said. "I gots a feeling that even without the drugs, she may be doing this to herself."

Destiny's stomach growled. Michelle heard it and said, "I'm kinda hungry, too. Maybe we should stop for a quick bite."

Blake pulled off the highway and said, "You don't have to tell me twice."

"But what about money?" Destiny asked. "Are you going to let Blake push them now?"

"She doesn't need me to," Blake said. "I think she can push them herself now."

"I'll do no such thing!" Michelle protested. She showed Destiny the billfolds she found in the back of the seat and said, "Those fine men was kind enough to leave us some money."

Blake mumbled, "And you called me a thief!"

Michelle ignored him and Destiny's stomach growled again. She reached to pat her stomach and felt something cold between her breasts. She slid her hand up and felt the amulet still hanging around her neck.

Michelle saw what she did, but didn't ask about it. She just smiled and shook her head in amazement.

Simon crossed the street and walked part way out onto the dock. It was a mildly warm day. A gentle breeze blew in from the bayou and swept pleasantly across his face as he peered out across the water to the thick trees that contained the Boutin property.

He checked his phone and still had enough bars to place the call. He dialed the number Logan had provided, but was routed over to Richard's office instead.

"Schaefer here."

"Schaefer? I was calling for Logan."

Richard didn't know Simon and Simon didn't know Richard, but Richard was expecting his report. "Is this Tangiers?"

"Yes," Simon answered cautiously. His assignment was still top secret, and he wasn't going to be the one to make it public.

Richard was equally careful in his wording. "Logan asked me to take point on the Bend report. Do you have something?"

Simon was satisfied that Richard must already know something about his assignment and asked, "How well has Logan briefed you on this job?"

"I worked with the initial team that went in to investigate the first disturbances. What have you learned?"

Simon looked around to make sure nobody except Lisa was in earshot. "I've confirmed that they were witches."

Richard frowned and said, "We knew that."

"Everyone here knew they were witches, but it sounded to me like they only did the usual stuff like reading tea leaves. One witness specifically recalled her reading the bones at a recent party, where she predicted that a stranger would come to her and someone near her would die. That was about a week ago, and now something has happened. Their home was burned down, but they escaped to Lafayette and there are no reports of fatalities yet."

Richard knew that if the prediction was a week ago, then it was before Brian and his team went in. "I don't like it," he said. "Our first team went in, pretty much as she predicted, and now they are missing, and the witches came out unharmed. Can you and your team investigate the property and check for any remains?"

Simon looked at the swamp and at the little boats tied to the dock, then replied, "No, sir, I don't think so. First of all, I'm just a lawyer. And my team is just me and my lovely assistant. I'm no Davy Crockett. Even if I tried, there is no way for me to secretly cross the swamp to reach the scene, and that's assuming I could find it without getting lost. On top of that, the sheriff is already involved, and it may have been classified a crime scene by now."

"Understood. Find some place to stay for now. I'll see if we can find someone to send who can lend you a hand and maybe get you a peek at the scene."

Gulfport was still an hour away when they started seeing exit signs for highway fifty-nine that would take them north to Hattiesburg. Michelle didn't recognize any of this. She was just a child the last time she visited, but something told her to take the turnoff, and she was feeling a newfound confidence in her instincts.

"Let's take that exit," she said. "After a spell, we can look for another highway heading east again."

Blake looked at Michelle in the rear-view mirror and said, "But you told me to head for Gulfport."

"And now I'm telling you to head to Hattiesburg."

"But I thought your daddy's farm was between Gulfport and Hattiesburg."

"It is," Michelle said. "Didn't I just say to turn east halfway up?"

"But we could miss it! Why don't we just go to Gulfport and then turn up to Hattiesburg?"

"This be a shortcut."

"A shortcut?" Blake yelled. "Who cares if it's a shortcut? We still end up at the same place, except you might get us lost going this way."

Michelle raised her voice to match his. "I might get us lost? Just who here knows where we be going anyway?"

"Yeah?" Blake slammed back. "Well, who here knows how to drive?"

Destiny held her mother's head against her shoulder while she swung her own head back and forth, following the argument. At first, she thought it was amusing, but the yelling between them was becoming anything but funny.

"How hard can it be?" Michelle snapped back. "Driving a car? If a young punk like you kin do it on da first try, I don't see no reason why nobody else here cain't pick it up."

"FINE!" Blake yelled at the top of his lungs. He jerked the car to the right lane and exited the highway. As fortune would have it, he pulled directly into a rest stop. He pulled the limo into a marked parking place. The wheels hit the curb, and the car was crooked, but he didn't care. He shut the car off and flew out the door, leaving the keys hanging from the ignition.

"Has you ever?" Michelle asked to nobody in particular. "Whatever do you s'pose got into dat boy? We is better off without him."

Destiny couldn't help the astonished look on her face and directed it at her nana.

"What?" Michelle asked. "You think it was me?"

Destiny leaned her mother back onto Michelle's shoulder and left to check on Blake.

She found him standing in front of a large map. He pretended to be intensely interested in the map, but he wasn't really looking at it.

"Blake?" Destiny asked in the softest voice she could muster. "What's going on?"

Anger was visible in his eyes as he turned his head to look at her, but then he turned back to feigning interest in the map.

She tried again and asked, "What was that about?"

"What do you mean?" he asked. "You heard her. She's completely unreasonable."

"She is the only one of us who knows this area at all."

Blake turned to face her again. "But she's going to get us lost."

"So? Why do you care? Why are you so angry?"

In truth, Blake didn't care. He was driving, and he didn't care where they went or how boring it might be on the way. He hung his head and looked at his feet, which he scraped around on the ground. "I don't know," he said as he shrugged his shoulders. "It just bugged me."

A highway patrol car pulled into the lot and stopped. The driver opened the door and stood outside the car with a radio microphone in his hand. "Ladies and gentlemen," he said, using the car's megaphone. "If I could have your attention for a moment?" He waited for people to either gather around or at least stop what they were doing long enough to listen. "There's been a chemical spill on interstate ten, closing the freeway until sometime tomorrow. Anyone heading to Gulfport or Biloxi is being rerouted south along the coast. Some of you may choose to take fifty-nine north to twenty-six. If you need any help with directions, I'll be over by the large map to help everyone find their destinations. Meanwhile, traffic stuck on ten will be rerouted back to fifty-nine, so if you want to avoid the traffic jam, you might want to get an early start."

"Oh great," Blake said. "Now there will be absolutely no living with her."

Destiny just giggled and walked back to the car with him.

The librarians came out of their trance and took a deep breath. The hoods of their grey robes hung over their heads, heaving up and down with each breath.

The second librarian pulled his hood back from his head and let it hang off the back of his shoulders. His dark hair glistened with perspiration and stuck, matted against his head. He looked at his brethren, still breathing heavily, and said, "Well, that was just fantastic."

The other two pulled their hoods back and turned to look at each other. Nobody was smiling.

"That girl must live under a lucky star," the third said.

"You know it has nothing to do with luck," said the first.

"He won't be happy," said the third.

"No," the first replied, "but he is never happy. He told us the boy would be hard to influence. It was a long shot at best."

"Perhaps," the second added, "but maybe we should have closed both highways."

"That would have been too conspicuous," said the third. "We don't want to give ourselves away."

"She knows nothing about us," said the second. "We definitely should have closed all the highways."

"No," the first replied. "She's met one of our agents before, and she saw him again in her mother's mind. She would figure it out if we were to be so obvious."

Richard gathered his thoughts and dialed the number to Logan's temporary office.

"Logan."

"I spoke to Tangiers. He says that not only were our witches there, but everyone in the area was aware that they were witches. He also said that one of the witches predicted that a stranger was coming and someone was going to die. That was maybe a week ago, right before Brian went in with his team."

Logan put his hand over the phone and said something Richard couldn't hear, then asked, "You think the witches killed Brian?"

"Well sir, something happened. The witches' home was burned down, and they came out, but Brian didn't, or at least he hasn't surfaced yet."

"Excuse me," Logan said. Again, he covered the phone with his hand and Richard could only hear him say, "Thank you," before removing his hand. "Did Tangiers investigate the home?"

"No sir, apparently, their home is deep in the swamp. Tangiers can't get to it without arousing suspicion. He also mentioned concern that it may have been classified a crime scene already."

"When you speak with him again, I want you to tell him that we're sending a team in to investigate. I'm also going to arrange a job for him with the local prosecuting office. Maybe we can turn our witches into criminals and fugitives and get the police to help us apprehend them."

"We may not need the police, sir. I've been tracking the limo. They left Louisiana and entered Mississippi."

"Do we know where they are going?"

"No, sir, but we'll know that when they stop."

"Good work Schaefer. When you learn their destination, draw up a plan to intercept. As a backup, I'll move forward with the plan to apprehend and prosecute them too, as plan B."

Highway fifty-nine north looked the same as ten east, only a bit smaller and a bit more crowded. More than just a few travelers heeded the patrolman's advice and hit the road early, before the crush of cars being rerouted off of ten arrived.

"So," Blake asked, "how far north do you think we should go?"

Michelle shrugged her shoulders and said, "I dunno. I'm hopin' I recognize somethin' on the way."

"The patrolman was routing people to twenty-six. If we don't see something by then, you want me to take it?"

"Yeah sure," Michelle said. "Actually, now dat you mention it, twenty-six does ring a bell. I tink it's da one we want."

"Aye aye captain."

The road rushed by with little in the way of landmarks. There were some homes and businesses at the interchanges, but the road quickly delved back into wilderness until they crossed a small draw bridge and found themselves back in civilization. It wasn't the big city, but there were pockets of communities built around small towns that followed the highway.

Destiny leaned her head against the glass. She needed to try and reach Mala again, and her eyes glassed over a bit, but she wasn't comfortable enough to leave Blake and her nana alone like that.

"There!" Michelle exclaimed while pointing out the window. "Take that exit."

"But," Blake said, "I thought you said twenty-six sounded right to you. It's still another fifteen miles ahead."

"Take that exit," Michelle repeated.

Blake pulled the car over to the right lane and pulled off the highway onto a much smaller road heading east. "Great," Blake said. "You got us on Sleepy Hollow. Maybe we should lock the doors."

Michelle snickered and said, "It be Steephollow. Follow it to da end and take a left."

The road shrunk down to a single lane each way, but at least it was still paved. As instructed, he followed the road which wound around past farmhouses and ranches and finally came to an end six miles later. He made the sharp left and Michelle was already pointing ahead.

"Turn right up there."

The next road on their journey was still paved, but it was barely a divided road. It had a faded yellow line running down the middle, but the lanes were skinny, and the shoulder of the road occasionally encroached into the lane where the asphalt had fallen off.

More farmhouses and ranches lined the road at well-spaced intervals. Some of the farms had old wooden fences with peeling paint, while others were adorned with intricate white picket fences covered in a fresh glossy coat of paint. Wild brush lined the road and here and there they could spot a pond. Eventually the yellow center line disappeared entirely, and the road narrowed to a single lane strip of blacktop. Against all of Blake's hopes, the road degraded further until it was a dusty dirt and gravel road.

The dirt road seemed like it would go on forever. Blake half expected it to turn into a hiking trail, but instead, the pavement returned, and they came to a stop at a crossroad. On the other side of the intersection, the yellow center line returned and a bit further the pavement was fresh and smooth. A sign on the road indicated that the road they were on had just turned into Old Highway twenty-six. Michelle sat back and smirked. Blake remained silent.

Simon knew there was nothing on the road behind them to Lafayette, so he took the jeep further down the road. He came across a small cottage style motel and paused the jeep. Each of the cottages appeared run down and Simon had no doubt that the creep factor would double after sunset. He glanced over at Lisa, and she quickly shook her head and said, "It smells like a serial killer." Simon knew they had seen too many horror films but put the car in gear anyway and found another motel thirty miles up the road where it crossed with another interstate. It wasn't a chain motel, but it was a damn sight cheerier than the cottages.

He handed Lisa a key to her room and said, "Sorry kid, I can't offer you much night life here, but let me know when you are ready for dinner, and we'll hit the road again and see what we can find."

She accepted the key and carried a large bag of books into her room and said, "That's fine. I can catch up on my studies, anyway."

Old highway twenty-six was as much of a blessing to their backsides as it was to the car. It was smooth and quiet and very relaxing.

Destiny ran her fingers through her mother's hair and thought the road was finally smooth enough that she could try again to reach Mala, this time with the amulet. Unfortunately, their time on old highway twenty-six was all too short before Michelle shouted, "Turn there! We're here."

Blake left the highway and found himself on a private road with a fenced pasture on the right side and plowed fields on the left. He hadn't gone very far down the road when a large pickup pulled in front of them and blocked their way. Destiny's stomach knotted up, which she had come to learn could indicate the presence of sorcerers. Two men jumped out of the back of the pickup, and a third from behind the wheel. All of them wore the same overalls, hats, unpleasant expressions and, most importantly, shotguns.

"Tha's far enough," the leader shouted as he pointed the gun directly at Blake's head.

Blake put the car in park and raised his hands so they could see them through the windshield.

Michelle pushed her door open and stepped out of the limo. The pungent odor of fresh manure and the ancient scent of the earth filled the car. Destiny scanned the scene outside for signs of the sorcerer clan, but detected none. One of the three men quickly pointed his weapon at Michelle and stepped to the side so he would have a better angle around the car.

Destiny didn't like the guns pointing at her nana and jumped out of the car ready to rain fire on them, but she was overcome with an unexpected wooziness and leaned on the car, content to stare down the gunmen.

Michelle was the only one who detected Destiny's dizziness, but she had no time to deal with Destiny while she had guns pointed at her. "Put dat down," she said. "Is zat any way to welcome your own cousin Michelle from Louisiana?"

The man kept his shotgun trained on her and said, "Well, maybe you is my cousin and maybe you ain't."

"Point dat ting away from me!" she said, using the voice.

He buckled at the knees and pointed the gun at the ground, barely able to remain standing on his trembling legs. The third gunman tried pointing his gun at her but she gave him a sharp look and he shied away.

"You too!" she commanded the leader, again with the voice.

He haltingly lowered his gun to the ground.

"Now then," she said, "since you all be too young to recollect my last visit, why don't you take me to Cousin Zeb so we kin be properly introduced."

The leader removed his hat from his head and placed it over his heart. "I'm sorry Ma'am," he said, "but Zeb ain't gonna be able to do that."

Michelle's heart sunk. "You means cousin Zeb has passed? That cain't be. I woulda felt it."

"No, Ma'am, he still lives and his body is strong enough, but he ain't been right for a while now and he cain't talk to nobody."

"Who be runnin' the farm, then?" she asked.

A woman stepped out of the truck and said, "That would be me." Abilene Boutin stepped out from behind the truck door and said, "Hello Michelle. I cain't rightly say that you is welcome here."

Michelle scowled and said, "Fair enough. I wouldn't expect no welcome from the likes of you, no how."

Abilene scowled and said, "You might as well come in, but don't get too cozy. Say your piece to Zeb and move on in the mornin'."

"Same old Abilene, I sees."

"And you ain't changed a bit neithers, sister. You and your mama always had the best gifts, and neither never wasted a minute waitin' to show them off. The both of you always had to be the queen bees around here, but then you had to leave. The both of you run off and leave Zeb with everything."

"That's right sister. Mah daddy bedded a McAlister bitch and brought her and his bastard whelp home to be raised on da farm. You and your mama was always itchin' for a showdown, even though you knows you was gonna lose. We didn't want your blood on our hands, so we left before it come to that."

"And now," Abilene said, "you comes waltzin' in here all eagers to show off your latest tricks. Well, you might find that I has some new tricks of my own and it's just too late for you, dear sister. Nobody cares about what you kin do now. So, you kin go ahead and pay your respects to Zeb and move on to wherever it is you is goin' come morning."

Michelle spat on the ground and said, "Once a McAlister, always a McAlister."

"Oh no, dear sister, Daddy give me his name. I is a Boutin now through and through."

Michelle gave a sly, knowing smile and said, "Well dear sister, just so you knows. After we pays our respects to Cousin Zeb, this is exactly where we be goin'."

"Like hell it is."

"And, dear sister, as far as your reign as queen bee around here goes, I ain't the one you gonna be bowin' to." Michelle turned to the car and said loud enough for everyone to hear, "Destiny, Cherie, come out from behind that door and say hello to your great aunt Abilene."

Lisa exhaled loudly as she fell backwards onto the bed in Tangiers' room. She tried studying in her room but couldn't focus on her books. Being here in the field was too exciting to waste with her nose in her books, yet she was bored to tears and sitting around bored was not how she had pictured her new assignment.

Tangiers alternated between tapping a pencil and drumming his fingers. There was no television reception, and he couldn't focus on his books either.

"I thought you would have gone for a swim," Simon said.

"Me too, but the water's green." Lisa spun around and hung her head off the edge of the bed. "I don't think I've been this bored since I was a kid."

A shadow blocked the light from the open motel door. Lisa turned her head and saw an upside-down giant looming in the doorway.

"Excuse me," the large man said, "I'm looking for Simon Tangiers."

Simon jumped up and said, "You found him. How can I help you?"

"My name is Gerald Polin. I'm an arson investigator from Lafayette. Mr. Logan asked me to lend a hand."

Simon grabbed the big man's mitts and shook them vigorously. "Come in, please. That is my usually upright legal assistant on the bed."

Lisa waved from her upside-down position and timidly said, "Hi."

Polin remained standing and said, "I hope I'm not intruding, but if you don't mind, it's already after two and I was hoping we could get out to see the crime scene before it got dark."

Lisa turned back around to sit up and reassess the large man with the handle-bar mustache.

"Sure thing," Simon said. "Let's go see the general store about a boat."

"No need," Polin said. "I brought my fan boat."

"Perfect," Simon said. "Why don't you just follow us out to the dock?"

Lisa stepped up alongside the tall, fit man and said, "Maybe I should ride with him in case we get separated."

Tangiers saw through her ruse, but simply nodded his assent.

***

Cricket Bend didn't have an elaborate boat launch. The larger boats that came to the Bend were regulars and tied to the dock, never even coming out of the water. Most of the other boats here were small pirogues that could be simply carried in and out of the water.

A small access road dipped into the water and served as a launch ramp. It was covered with cobblestones and crushed clam shells. Polin backed the trailer halfway into the water and parked his truck.

Lisa jumped out of the truck and walked down the dock to watch him launch the boat.

Polin released a couple clamps and loosened the straps which held the boat to the trailer then jumped into the water and guided the flat-bottomed boat into the swamp.

Tangiers joined Lisa and stared out into the water wondering what manner of deadly creatures might inhabit these waters.

Polin waded through the water and guided his boat to the dock. He tossed the bow line up to Simon and pointed at a dock cleat saying, "Here. Tie this rope to that while I park the truck."

He pulled the truck across the street to the diner and parked it next to Tangiers' jeep.

The three librarians reassembled in their customary circle in the center of their meditation room. They had taken a meal and reported their failures to their leader.

"He took that well," the first said. "Though it is kind of hard to judge when we don't actually speak directly to him."

"Perhaps," said the second, "but he knows best."

"Never the less," said the third, "it was like he was expecting the news of our failure."

The second gripped his hood on both sides and flung it forward over his head. "Are we not supposed to succeed?"

"I don't know," the first replied. "Perhaps we are only here, in a sense, to make noise and flush them out."

The third nodded his head and said, "True. Who knows his plans?"

"I agree," the second said, "and only he seems to know their plans."

A knock on the door brought the second librarian to his feet. He opened the door and was handed a small slip of paper. He returned to the circle and said, "It's as if he listens to us."

"As if?" asked the first. "You don't think he does?"

The second passed the note around the circle and said, "He wishes us to find some converts in New Orleans. We are to lay in wait there for the others to arrive."

The third looked at the note and asked, "Why didn't he just tell us when we made our report?"

The first put his hood on and asked, "Why must you question one who cannot be questioned?"

"Shhh," the third said. "Do not speak that so loud."

The second took a deep breath and said, "Let us begin."

CHAPTER 5

A bilene didn't wait to meet Destiny out on the farm road. She and her boys jumped back into the truck and stormed back to the compound without even waiting for the limo to follow them. She returned to her office and watched for them from the window. Her feelings towards Michelle were clear to everyone who was present at the entrance. News of their arrival would spread, as would word of her disposition, but, even though the rest of the family had come to fear her reprisals, she knew they would still make their guests feel welcome, and she was not going to stop them yet.

Blake pulled the limo into the compound and parked it next to the truck Abilene had used.

People had already begun to gather around the car, and as soon as Michelle and Destiny stepped out of the car, they were quickly surrounded with family eager to greet them and show them around. Abilene's youngest daughter, Honey, would have joined her mother and treated their guests with equal disdain if it weren't for the boy that drove the limo.

Abilene remained hidden behind her office curtains and watched Destiny warily, looking for any clue that would explain Michelle's ominous warning. There was nothing in the world that was going to make Abilene bow to one of Michelle's bastard children, not after the way she felt she was treated as a child, and certainly not after what Michelle had just said to her. Her mind was so full of jealousy and hatred for Michelle, that there was little room for the truth even in her memory. She remembered a vastly different childhood from what Michelle remembered.

Women and children gathered from all directions. The sun had not begun to fall in the West yet and there were still plenty of chores to be done before the day was over. The men were in the fields, and the boys that drove Abilene out to meet Michelle returned to join the men leaving only the women and children to greet the guests.

Blake stepped out of the car and Honey headed straight for him. She unbuttoned her top two buttons with a slick practiced move and revealed a tan braless cleavage. Her dark black hair flowed around her shoulders and undulated from side to side as she swayed her hips seductively during her approach. "Hey cousin," she said. "My name is Honey 'cause I'm sweet and yummy, like you."

"Hey," Blake said uncomfortably, "but, I don't think I'm your cousin."

"No," she said. "I don't 'spec you is, but it don't matter neither way." She took one of his hands in hers and walked backwards towards the house, still swaying her hips in an exaggerated and hypnotic rhythm. "All the menfolk are still workin', so you just gonna have to let me show you to your bed."

Destiny took a step towards Blake, but a young girl with fiery red hair tugged at Destiny's wrist and said, "Hey! My name is Ashlin and you can bunk with me."

The young red head felt Destiny pull towards Blake and said, "Don't worry about him. Honey can show him to the men's rooms. She knows where all the boys sleep."

Panic set in Destiny's heart as she saw the slender vixen toy with Blake. She moved toward Blake again and pulled the little girl with her. The little girl held onto her hand and followed hesitantly behind her but kept turning back to look at the limo. Destiny followed the crowd. She followed Blake and the scene in front of her blurred except for Blake and Honey. The little redhead said, "You ain't told me your name yet."

"My name? It's Destiny, and that boy is Blake. He don't know it yet, but he's gonna be in so much trouble. That over there is my nana."

Destiny practically dragged the little girl who was still looking over her shoulder at the car. Blake and Honey were getting further away and Destiny asked, "Are you coming?"

"I don't know," the girl said. "Did you forget something?"

Destiny saw her looking back at the car and screamed, "Oh my god! We gotta help my Mama." She ran back to the car and took her mother's hand. Tempest made brief momentary eye contact with Destiny. "Mama? Are you feeling better? Can you get down from there okay?"

Tempest was not feeling better, but her fear for this place had forced just enough of her to the surface so she could be aware of what was going on. She placed first one foot, then the other, outside the car but was unable to stand on her own.

Ashlin took one hand and said, "Come on, we'll help get you to a room."

One of the older women joined them and said, "Here, let me help. I been tendin' Zeb long enough now that I knows what to do." She crouched by the car and slung Tempest's arm over her shoulder then gently heaved her up out of the car. A second woman, also familiar with caring for Zeb, quickly took the other side and together they guided Tempest to the living quarters.

Ashlin stepped back so they could pass. She led Destiny towards the main house and asked, "What's wrong with your Mama? Is she like Zeb?"

"I doubt it," Destiny said. "I don't know Zeb or what ails him, but my mama been like this since she had me. In fact, they had her locked up in a hospital my whole life, up until this morning."

"That's sad," Ashlin said. "I guess you never got to know your mama."

"But I will," Destiny said, "when she's better."

"I wish Grandpa Zeb were better. I liked things a lot more when he was in charge."

"How long has he been sick?"

Ashlin pointed up to a second-story window on the main house and said, "That's Grandpa Zeb in the window. He only been like that for a few weeks now."

Destiny couldn't tell if he was watching them or just staring out the window into nothingness. As she watched him through the window, she saw two images as if she were looking through a reflection in the glass. One image was a decrepit old man with grey hair and a scraggy grey beard. Black empty eyes stared out from under grey bushy eyebrows. The other image wasn't any younger, but it was clean shaven and had bright eyes peering at them from thick trim eyebrows. Neither image acknowledged her presence, but both of them seemed in dire need of help.

"Well," Destiny said. "I'm gonna make my mama better. Maybe I can help Zeb too."

"How you gonna do that?"

Destiny put her finger to her lips and said, "Shhh. You'll see, but it'll be our secret. Okay?"

Ashlin felt like she were in on a very great secret and eagerly nodded.

Simon and Lisa climbed aboard Polin's boat and sat in the wide double seat which was positioned in front of Polin's higher pilot's seat. Polin untied the rope to the dock and climbed up the roll cage into his seat. He gripped the joystick with his right hand and pressed the ignition with his left. The motor sprang to life.

Polin pressed forward on the joystick and the clutches engaged the fan pushing the boat forward. He had a small map taped to the back of the double wide seat which guided him to the property.

The hairs on Lisa's arm and neck prickled with excitement. She raised her face to the sky and felt the wind whip against her cheeks. She reached out with her hand and sampled the cool spray of the water. This was exactly the kind of adventure she was hoping to have.

Cricket Bend shrunk behind them as the fan boat rapidly crossed the expanse to the Cypress lined edge of the swamp where the Boutin's had lived. He slowed the boat down as they entered the dark Cypress swamp. The boat could easily overcome sandbars and thick growths of hyacinth, but trees were obstacles to be avoided. The hull thumped against debris that floated in the stagnant waters.

A dank, earthy musk clung to the dark interior of the swamp. The thick canopy overhead allowed only slivers of light to reach the surface. The foul water brewed a putrid combination of decaying debris which fell from above and the fungus and microorganisms that thrive in the dark.

Polin carefully zigzagged the craft though the trees. He followed the map he had prepared, but it was their noses that confirmed it was the correct route. The smell of burnt wood permeated the swamp, with a hint of sulphur that mixed with the smoke and fetid swamp aroma.

"Sulphur," Simon said. "Did they use that to spread the fire?"

"Unlikely," Polin said. "Sulphur requires an extremely high temperature to ignite. It's probably a byproduct of something else that burned."

The thick cypress opened up before them and the sky was visible again. Polin pushed on the joystick and accelerated the craft up to the small island which was the Boutin home. The boat skidded easily up onto the shore and afforded everyone a simple dismount to dry land.

Polin and Tangiers climbed out and hiked towards the center of the small plot of land. Lisa followed behind with pad and pencil at the ready.

The smell of burnt wood was unmistakable. A greasy black soot coated some of the leaves of the bushes which grew near the edge of the shore. As they climbed up the embankment to the small plateau, they found the island littered with small round pits of scorched earth. The pits ranged from a foot in diameter to a full three feet wide. The scent of sulphur was strong in the burned depressions.

Polin held a wand in his right hand which was wired to a meter in his left, and a camera strapped around his neck. He took pictures of each depression and inserted the wand into the center of the holes measuring the temperature inside. He bore a new twinkle in his eye and a spring in his step. As an arson investigator, this was the find of a lifetime. As Logan's man, it smelled like exciting times ahead.

The main structure was flattened. There were a few blackened posts sticking out of the ground, and Tangiers could identify the metal coils of mattress springs and a box that was the fridge, but the home was reduced to a pile of grey and black soot. Polin stepped gingerly inside the ash of the home and found the charred remains of at least two people. One of the remains had the twisted metal remnants of an automatic rifle and a pistol. The magazines of each weapon were open and warped. Polin assumed the ammunition may have exploded. He took a pen from his pocket and carefully lifted each weapon and placed them in large plastic bags. He sifted through the remains looking for any other evidence that might make the scene look like self-defense. With the weapons removed, he returned to the yard and the burned pits outside the home.

He drew a map and marked on the map all the different places where he found burned pits. He turned to Simon and Lisa and said, "There's more here than I could have expected. It will probably take me a couple days to complete my measurements. I'll take you back to the hotel. You can tell Logan he was right. I'll draw up two reports. One will include what we know about these fires, and what we suspect about how they were created. The other report will exclude all the indications of magic and will contain just the stuff we let regular people know about them."

Lisa showed him the notes she was keeping and said, "You kind of read the temperatures out loud, so I wrote them all down. I can come back with you and record everything you see."

Simon didn't care anymore what Lisa's motive might be. He wanted the best records he could get if they intended to use this in court. He looked up at the sky and at the swamp surrounding them and said, "There's still some daylight left. If you would like to make use of it, I don't have a problem waiting by the boat. Maybe I'll just take a walk around the perimeter."

Polin grunted and said, "Sure, I guess you know enough about preserving evidence not to disturb it. Shout out if you find anything unusual. In fact, make yourself useful and see if you can see any partial remains in the water."

"Partial remains?" Simon asked.

"Yeah," Polin said. "Something the gators might have dragged out of here."

At the center of the farm was a grand old house standing two stories tall with well-maintained white paint and a green roof. It was the biggest house Destiny had ever seen, even bigger that the Planchette mansion back home. Zeb, Abilene and Honey lived in the main house. Everyone else had rooms in one of the three dormitories to the North.

As they neared the house, Ashlin pulled Destiny to the side, but Honey was directing Blake into the main house until she saw her mama watching through the window screen. She veered him off to the men's dorm which was also on the North side.

Up until recently, the dorms were reserved for migrant workers. The main house was large enough to fit the family, but Abilene changed all that when Zeb took ill and moved everyone out to the dorms. She kept Zeb where she could keep an eye on him and gave a room to her daughter.

Fortunately for the family, this had been a pretty good year on the farm and the dorms weren't the most depressing spots on earth. During lean years, the dorms would decay into squalor and weren't fit for company.

Ashlin's spirits sunk when she realized that the women had taken Tempest into the first cabin while she was leading Destiny into the second where her room was. She stopped on the porch outside and said, "It's okay. I know you wanna be with your mama."

Destiny could feel the twinge in the young girl's heart and said, "Don't be silly. She's with people that know how to take good care of her now. I'll have plenty of time with her after she's all better.

Besides, you already knows one of my secrets. That makes us like a club."

Ashlin took hold of both of Destiny's hands and jumped up and down exclaiming, "We can be like sisters! We can be like sisters!"

Destiny pulled her close and wrapped her arms around the young girl. "Sure," she said. "We can be just like sisters, except, not like my nana and Aunt Abilene. In fact, I can already feel it. I feel like I known you all our lives. You feel exactly like you was my real sister."

Ashlin couldn't contain her excitement and burst into her room spinning and dancing all around.

Honey led Blake into the men's dorms and to one of the empty bunks. She smiled broadly and traced her finger down his chest, saying, "I guess this is your bed, with all the other boys. My bed is in the house, upstairs. I got my own room. It's real private, if you know what I mean."

A round little boy burst into the room yelling, "Has anyone seen the new kid that just come in?" He skidded to a halt and almost dropped the large frog he was carrying. "Oh, hi Honey. I didn't see you..."

He started to back out of the room until Blake shouted, "Hey! Is that a bullfrog? He sure is big. Can he jump?" Blake didn't really care about the frog, but he squirted out of Honey's clutches and zipped out the door yelling, "Let's go see how far he can jump!"

Richard went to Logan's office to deliver the news personally. The door was open and Logan was on the phone when he arrived, so he waited in the doorway and knocked lightly on the doorjamb to get Logan's attention.

Richard could see Logan nodding his head and talking animatedly into the phone. Logan raised his arm and flicked his wrist to invite Richard in while he finished his call. Richard entered the office, but remained standing.

"Yes Sir," Logan said into the phone. "As soon as I know something, you'll be the first I call."

He didn't look entirely happy as he hung up the phone, but he put on a braver face for Richard who was somewhat comforted to learn that he wasn't the only who had to report to disappointed superiors. Logan motioned for Richard to sit and said, "I hope you have good news."

Richard nodded his head and said, "We have a location. They're in a rural area in Mississippi. It looks like some kind of a farm. Here are some satellite images."

Richard handed the photos to Logan and continued, "Would you like me to assemble a recon team to go in for a better look?"

Logan looked at the photos. His expression was impossible for Richard to read. He flipped between the three different images Richard had given him and asked, "Do you have a map showing the location?"

"Yes, sir." Richard handed him the rest of the data he brought with him which included a street and highway map of the area.

Logan nodded his head yes, then shook it no, then yes again. "We won't be needing a recon team. I know this place and we have an asset there already."

This was not something Richard was expecting to hear. "I was assuming they were meeting up with other witches. What is this place?"

Logan looked up from the map and nodded his head. "They're witches alright. We've been fortunate enough to get one of our people into the family. They're nothing special, just an old witch family like so many others."

"Well," Richard said. "They might be special now. If the witches we've been tracking teach them how to unlock their powers, they'll be special alright."

Logan nodded his head and said, "Assemble a team in New Orleans, but not for a recon mission. I'll get word to our asset and find out what's going on before we decide how we're going to handle it."

Richard got up to leave but stopped at the door and asked, "What about our other team? The lawyers? They're still looking into the fire."

"Tell them to stay put. They are still our fall-back plan."

Ashlin danced around the room until she had finally burned off enough excitement to settle down. "We still gots time before supper. Whatcha want to do till then?"

Destiny wasn't quite sure how much she wanted to confide in Ashlin. She was learning to trust her instincts and something inside was encouraging her to go ahead and open up with the young girl, but she didn't know why. She was an adorable little girl and for some reason the whole sisterhood thing between them felt inexplicably real.

Ashlin went to the window and stared up at the house. Zeb was in his usual window watching over them, although, in his vegetative state, he was unable to interact with anyone anymore. While she watched him in his window, his caretakers slid him over to one side and someone else joined him in the window. "Hey look!" Ashlin said. "They moved your mama into the window with Grandpa Zeb."

"I know," Destiny said. "It will be easier for them to care for both Zeb and my mama together."

Ashlin looked quizzically at Destiny, then back out the window towards Zeb, then again at Destiny. "How'd you know they moved her? You been here with me the whole time!"

Destiny went to the window next to Ashlin and looked up at Tempest and Zeb. Again, she felt the tug to confide in the little redhead. She put her arm around the young girl's shoulders and said, "Sometimes I just feel stuff like that."

"Wow," Ashlin exclaimed. "I wish I could feel things that way. You think I can learn?"

"Sure," Destiny said. "Anything is possible."

Ashlin smiled. Her new sister was going to teach her a lot of neat stuff. "I think it's real nice that they moved your mama with Grandpa Zeb, but I never would have thought Abilene would let them do that. She really hates your nana and all the rest of you too I guess."

"Abilene don't know they did it. It was my nana's idea."

"How do you know... oh right, you feel stuff."

The librarians sat in their usual circle in the meditation room. Bags under their red streaked eyes told of the many sleepless nights where they tried controlling the fate of the world.

Librarian number one had just rejoined the circle after checking outside. Number two didn't have to speak or even think his question, he only had to arch his eyebrows.

"No," number one said. "We still have much work to do. So far, our attempts to prevent the evil one from awakening have failed, as have our attempts to keep the chosen one and the evil one apart. He thinks, and these are his words, 'if we cannot keep her from meeting with their leader, we should at least keep their leader from meeting with her.'"

"That's pretty vague," number two said, "even for him."

Number three shook his head and said, "I wish we had never tried meddling with time. What makes him think this will work?"

"He is desperate," number one said, "as is the world. We can't make things any worse, only different."

There was nothing more to say and the three of them bowed their heads and entered the void to search out the one they called leader.

Logan was in the airport waiting for his flight to Gulfport. He was early and found a table with power to set up his laptop. He planned to send an email to Richard outlining his itinerary, but when he opened his browser, a news item caught his attention.

"Local authorities were quick to call for Federal help after the first explosion. But, what first looked like a terrorist attack turned into something completely new when this man, Frank Logan, walked out of the wall of flames surrounding the university and took credit for the bombing. Eyewitness reports claim he walked straight up to the police and said he was the new world leader and it would be best for them to just surrender. When they tried to cuff him, he burst into flames and laughed at them."

Frank was mesmerized by the account. It must be a joke. He clicked the link to see the video that accompanied the report and saw a shaky image of himself laughing at the police and bursting into flames."

Logan stared into the flames and the world around him melted away. He found himself standing in front of the petrified police. They couldn't place him in custody while he was a human torch. He decided to give them a demonstration and pointed at one of their cruisers. Flames leapt from his arm and engulfed the car until it exploded.

The police opened fire. Bullets flew into him from all directions, but he didn't care. The closer the bullets got the hotter and softer they became until they were like puff balls bouncing off his flesh.

One by one he pointed at the police and incinerated them. He was surrounded with burning police and vehicles. Two men dressed in grey robes walked out of the police flames. He pointed at them and said, "That's not a very good idea." He doused them in red hot flames, but they simply walked out of it.

"Do you think," one of them said, "that you are the first human who has discovered this ability? Look around you. This never happened. For centuries, men like you have come forward and believed they would be the emperor of the planet, and yet, you have never heard of any of them, have you?"

"We," the second one said, "are your masters. We know where you are going and where this happens. Sadly, your airplane will never land and you will meet a very untimely end. We give you this time to put your affairs in order."

The video ended and Frank was staring at a blank laptop screen. He wanted to scoff at it. It couldn't have been real, but the panic that gripped his heart was very real. He went back to the ticketing agent and bought ten tickets to different locations. He then went to another airline and bought ten more tickets. They can wait for him all they want, he won't be there.

Ashlin went to the small vanity that faced away from the window. She sat down and used a key that hung around her neck to open the center drawer, then removed and opened her journal. She watched Destiny in the mirror as she recorded all the events surrounding the arrival of her new sister.

Destiny remained in the window watching her mother when she felt the weight of the chain around her neck and the pendant began to throb between her breasts. Nimisen said she would know when the pendant was charged and the time was right.

Destiny quietly stepped to one of the beds and sat down in the center cross legged. She closed her eyes and imagined the candles she used to use when she entered her trances. The room shrunk around her and was replaced with an inky black void. She drifted through the void passing small clouds of voices. Ancestral memories surrounded her like nebulae in the universe. She had no time for idle memories and focused on finding Mala.

She reached out and felt for the same hole in the voices where she had found Mala before. A dark veil separated her from Mala's memories. She drifted towards it, but it pushed her away. She wrapped her fingers around the pendant. It was warm to her touch. She drifted towards it again and reached out with her left hand to feel the barrier. It wasn't hard or sharp or electric feeling as she had expected. It was soft and rubbery like gelatin. She pressed her ear against it, straining to hear what was on the other side, but all she heard was the muffled tones of Mala's voice teaching her how to charm a snake. She remembered that lesson. It was too recent, so she worked her way down the barrier, backwards in Mala's life until she found a time before they met. She heard Ishun, Mala's mentor, telling her she should prepare for a new student from another world. He was talking about Destiny's training. This would be a good time to enlist her help.

She pushed her hand into the barrier. It retreated slightly from her touch and resisted as she penetrated the thick gooey wall, but when she was in about wrist deep, it flowed around her hand and ran up her arm while gripping her hand. She pulled to get free, but the grip was too tight. She squeezed the amulet and released an electric flow into the wall.

The barrier opened around her hand, not like it was retreating from pain, but like oil is repelled by soap. It floated above her skin without touching her. She focused on her hand and created an electric bubble around it. The amulet warmed as she felt the energy flowing from it into her hand. She enlarged the bubble until it was a gaping hole wide enough for her to slip through. Once through the hole, she was able to latch onto the memory of Mala and Ishun.

The world was forming around her with brilliant blue skies and clean unspoiled air. She stood on a hill looking down at the huts when a warm blast gripped her in the side and flung her out of the memory. She landed back in Ashlin's room and was thrown off the bed onto the floor.

Startled by the crash, Ashlin spun around and saw Destiny on the floor. An orange glow surrounded her and was gone in a blink so fast that Ashlin wasn't sure she actually saw it. "Oh, my God!" she exclaimed as she leapt to the floor to help Destiny get up. "Are you okay?"

"Yeah," Destiny said. "I'm fine." She got up from the floor, rubbing her tailbone, but the room spun around her. Her vision narrowed and floated in front of her. She leaned against the wall to keep from fainting and rubbed the sweat off her forehead with the back of her arm. "That was pretty clumsy of me," she said, "falling off the bed like that."

Blake burst into the room screaming, "Is everyone okay?"

"She fell off the bed."

Destiny stopped rubbing her butt and adjusted his collar. "What are you so worked up over?"

Blake wiped the perspiration that was dripping down from her temple and thought she felt hot, but simply nodded his head towards Ashlin and said, "Me? Nothing. What were you doing?"

Destiny kept her mouth shut as she silently thought to him, "I was trying to reach Mala. I almost made it but something really powerful ejected me back to here and I landed on the floor."

"Are you okay?" he thought back. "You're all sweaty and you feel like you're hot to me."

"I don't know," she thought. "I feel kinda funny, but I think I'm just tired."

Blake thought, "Would you like me to help you try again?"

"I might have to," she thought. "Even with the amulet, I was overpowered."

"Okay," he thought. "Let's go find someplace private, away from little eyes."

Destiny looked at Ashlin and bit her lip. Ashlin had been watching them and wondering why they were so silent.

"Ashlin's okay," Destiny said. "Can't you tell? She's my new sister. I'd like to go back in and find Mala, but I need to recharge this thing before we try again."

Blake nodded and took another look at Ashlin before leaving.

"Is he your boyfriend?" Ashlin asked.

Destiny nodded her head and smiled.

Ashlin watched Blake through the window and said, "He's cute, even Honey think's so, but he's kind of strange if you ask me."

The smile evaporated from Destiny's face at the mention of Honey.

Ashlin hugged Destiny and said, "Don't worry about Honey. He's totally into you. I can tell."

Abilene saw the change in everyone's behavior starting the moment Michelle had arrived. She wished she could know what they were thinking, but that wasn't one of her gifts and she could only guess what was in their heads. It hadn't been very long since she had gained control of the compound and now she felt like she was losing it already.

She watched Destiny when she entered the compound from her window and saw her go into Ashlin's room. She looked like just another stupid teenager to Abilene. Why did Michelle think she would be so special? What was it Michelle had said? Something about the end of Abilene's reign as queen bee and her bowin' to this brat. Probably, Michelle was just trying to plant the idea in her head. Michelle had always had it in for Abilene since the moment Michelle's daddy had brought Abilene and her mama home to the farm and now she finally thought she was strong enough to do something about it. "Well," Abilene thought, "I gots a few surprises for you dear sister."

She picked up the phone and dialed a number she never thought she would have to use. The man who had given her the number was on the creepy side and he scared her, but he knew private things about her and told her to keep the number in case she ever needed it. He had just called her recently and seemed especially interested in the events that started a few weeks earlier when things changed for Honey and her. He even encouraged her to make some changes around the farm, that she should be the one in charge.

She listened to the phone ringing on the other end, unsure how she would begin the conversation.

"Hello?" a woman answered.

"This is Abilene. I need to talk to Frank."

"He's not here."

"When do you expect him?"

"I can't say. He's out of town on business right now."

Abilene frowned. She never really wanted to call him, and now, when she did, he wasn't there. "Can you tell him that Abilene called? It's urgent. He left me his card and said to call if something happened."

"I'll tell him you called. Would you like me to tell him what happened?"

"Just tell him I got visitors and they concern me. I wondered if he knew anything about them."

"Got it. Was there anything else?"

"No," Abilene said. "That's all."

***

Dirt was the accessory de rigueur in the grimy tavern where the bikers knew to steer clear of the soldiers of fortune that frequented the back room looking for work. The juke box still functioned, but the music was as old and stale as the air. A pool table still stood in the corner, but the felt was ripped and the sticks were held together with duct tape. Nobody came here to relax or unwind, and the decor offered no pretense that this would be a nice place for a drink. This bar was for men that wanted to stir up shit or tell stories about the shit they already stirred up.

Outside the small establishment was a storm canal and a small bridge that led into New Orleans. Bikes lined the canal and the front of the bar. Trucks crossed the bridge and passed through without stopping here. The French Quarter and the Mississippi river were in sight, but may as well have been as far away from here as the Grand Canyon. Few people ever stopped here by accident and nobody did that twice.

Mercenaries gathered in the back room. A call went out for soldiers of fortune, and a few heard the call and responded. Two of those gathered were imposters. They were well known and recognized by many, but they weren't themselves. The librarians sat cross-legged in their room of meditation, but two of them were firmly implanted in the imposter's minds.

"One, two," a silver-haired man with a limp counted heads, "eight, nine. Good. Someone close the door."

Sensing the meeting was about to begin, the crowd came to order, which was surprisingly ruly for such a rough and tumble assembly.

"Okay, boys. We got a new job for you, and it's close by. There are three targets, an old lady and a teenage girl and boy. They're up the road a couple hours into Mississippi."

A big guy with a mangled nose snickered and said, "An old broad and a couple teenagers? We don't need a whole squad for that."

"Maybe not," the old man said, "but they already escaped three guns, and we don't know how."

"Must have been rookies. What did they say happened?"

"They're still missing and their files don't look like they was green. I don't have much details about the encounter, but I'm told that fire was involved. Our benefactor doesn't want any more mistakes. He would like to be quite sure that the objective is neutralized this time, and he's willing to pay for the added insurance."

***

Destiny felt the now familiar throbbing of the amulet against her heart. It beat out a rhythm which matched the wobbling of the room caused by the dizziness that had been warping her mind all day. She reached under her blouse and wrapped her hand around the jewel. The amulet was slightly warm to the touch and her skin was also warm and damp. The amulet was charged again and Ashlin had been conveniently called away to do some small chore for dinner leaving Destiny alone in the room this time.

She took a pillow from the bed and placed it on the floor. She sat cross-legged on the pillow and closed her eyes. Sucking in a deep breath, she thought to Blake, "Okay. I'm going in now. I don't know when Ashlin will be back, so do you think you can find a secluded spot to join me from where you are?"

"I think so," Blake thought back.

She let go of this world and entered into the void. She floated freely allowing the memories to brush past her until she felt Blake's presence.

He called to her, "Destiny, are you there?"

"I'm here," she said. "Come to my voice."

He moved towards her and said, "Marco..."

"Huh?" she asked, "Marco?"

"Never mind," he said. "It's a game kids play in swimming pools where they try to find each other blindfolded."

"Oh," she snickered. "I guess they don't got no gators in their swimmin' holes."

"Nope," he said. "I'm here. Lead the way."

She moved through the void to the emptiness. When she arrived at the barrier, she slid down to the point where she thought she had been the last time, where she heard Ishun's voice.

"Why are you stopping?" Blake asked. "Why aren't you going into the memory?"

Destiny gripped the amulet with her right hand and reached out to touch the spongy barrier with her left. "You don't sense the wall between the memory and me?"

Blake moved forward between Destiny and Mala's memory and said, "I don't see anything else out here."

She was still testing the soft barrier with her left hand when Blake reached out and took hold of her hand and easily pulled her through. He held her hand and guided her into the memory. They were standing atop the hill, looking down on Ishun's hut, when Blake threw Destiny to the ground and yelled, "Look out!"

He then turned and started firing lightning and fireballs off into the west.

Destiny took a position down the hill opposite of the direction where Blake was aiming.

"We're not alone. Someone out there was trying to hit us with something."

Destiny crept up to peek over the crest of the hill, and Blake pointed to some rocks on a neighboring hill and said, "There, behind those rocks."

Destiny reared back and fired some fireballs up into the air. They arced across the valley between the hills and showered down on the hill around the rock, bursting into massive explosions when they hit.

"What's the meaning of this?" Ishun commanded from behind them.

Destiny turned and saw that Blake was already frozen by Ishun as she was when she completed her turn. "Ishun," she said. "It's good to see you again."

"I don't believe we've ever met."

"No," she said, "not yet, but we will. I came to enlist Mala's help."

Ishun looked deep into Destiny's memory and soul. He was satisfied they were not foes and released them. "Come with me," he said. He led them down to his hut.

Inside the hut, they found several woven mats arranged in a circle around a small crackling fire.

"Please," Ishun said. "Sit down. Mala! Come join us."

Destiny and Blake took seats to Ishun's left, and each sat cross-legged facing the fire. Mala came out from behind a curtain and sat to Ishun's right. Blake had never met Mala before and was surprised when he saw that she was barely ten years old.

"Oops," Destiny said. "I guess I came too far back."

Ishun nodded and said, "I suspected as much. When are you from?"

"We are from far in the future, after magic is gone from the world."

"Magic is gone?" Ishun asked. "Yet you are here?"

"It's just starting to return." Destiny said.

"She's just being modest," Blake said. "She brings magic back. They call her the chosen one."

"Shhh!" Destiny said as she slapped Blake on the thigh.

"She is right," Ishun said. "You probably shouldn't say too much. So, without revealing the future, what brings you here?"

"I need to heal my mama, but I need Mala's help. She..."

Ishun held his hand up to stop her and said, "Mala, perhaps you can go outside and play while we talk."

Mala sprang out the door and they could hear her laughing and romping around.

Destiny continued, "Mala was my teacher. After magic was destroyed, there were no teachers left in my time."

Ishun noticed the past tense used by Destiny. "Why did you come when she was so young? Do you need a lesson on how to find the correct time?"

"No," Destiny said. "Well, yes actually. Finding the correct time is still difficult, but that's not why I'm here. Someone was trying to stop me. They created a barrier around Mala's life that kept me out. I needed this amulet just to get through, but someone attacked me and ejected me from the memory when I came through the first time."

"And," Blake added, "I'll bet it was the same guys who attacked us from behind those rocks."

"When I was outside the barrier," Destiny said, "I had to guess when to come through."

"I see." Ishun stroked his beard and said, "You may return home. I shall send Mala to contact you when she is older. You might want to use a glamour so she does not recognize you later when she is your teacher."

"There is one more thing," Destiny said, "about Mala..."

"No!" Ishun said. "I must not know. She must not know. I grieve for your loss as I grieve for my loss. But our fate must always end the same."

Tears fell from Destiny's eyes. "But it was my fault."

"I do not believe this," Ishun said. "Your tears tell the story of one blaming herself unjustly. You can never tell or warn Mala about what happens."

"But..."

"Never," he repeated. "We are but shadows of other shadows in your life. You cannot alter us."

Destiny continued crying for a moment longer, then bowed and said, "Thank you, Ishun. Come on Blake, let's go back now."

Blake's mind reeled from the intrigue. Someone very powerful tried to keep Destiny away from Mala. Someone else had warned him to stop Destiny from doing something. Was he supposed to stop her from coming here? "No," he reminded himself. She was trying to save her mother, and he needed her mother to save her.

They shimmered out of the memory and Destiny was sitting, once again, on the pillow in Ashlin's room.

CHAPTER 6

Farm operations usually extended from dark to dark, but the news of Michelle's arrival had spread throughout the workers. Word spread not only of the guests' arrival, but of the animosity between Abilene and Michelle. Some said they smelled fear in the air, and if there was gonna be fireworks, nobody wanted to miss it. It started with just one of the men quitting early, then two, then finally all the men followed suit and came in for the evening. Abilene saw the men arriving hours earlier than usual, but she was as anxious to get it over with as everyone else was to meet them.

Everyone knew that Abilene had already decreed that the guests were only staying a single night, so the women who took turns working in the kitchen agreed to work together to prepare a special feast for the evening meal. Abilene had few friends among the family members and the possibility of a showdown was the most anticipated of all the whispered rumors.

The dining table at the Boutin farm was as long as it was old. It was built by Ansel Boutin when he first settled this area and built the farm. Abilene was seated at one end of the table and Zeb was at the other. Zeb was not at the end of the table out of respect. He was a vegetable now and Abilene didn't want him anywhere near her. Tempest was placed next to Zeb, for the same reason, with their caregivers on opposite sides of the table near the family so they could care for both Zeb and Tempest. Destiny was placed across from Tempest next to Blake while Michelle was next to Tempest directly across from Blake. They were very far away from Abilene. Michelle had no doubt that was by Abilene's own hand. Honey pined to be next to Blake but her mother had already had words with her about her obvious infatuation, so she was placed next to her mother, but she stared at him from her seat which earned him an elbow in the side from Destiny whose vantage point gave her a perfect view of the dark-haired vixen.

Before everyone was seated and the meal was served, Michelle leaned over the table and spoke quietly to Destiny and Blake, "Listen you two, I don't know what she be plannin', but I knows Abilene will be pushing all our buttons trying to make us pick a fight. I know the two of you could probably end any fight in a heartbeat, but I don't want you two showin' off your special powers. You hear me?"

"Yes, Nana."

"But," Blake asked, "what if she gets crazy and brings in guns or something?"

"These people be my family. I need to coax 'em on my side. I don't want them all turned into piles of ash."

"But," Blake continued, "what if we need to defend ourselves? We can't just do nothing?"

"If it come to that, don't let them kill us neithers. I just don't what dis to be a bloody massacre. We don't need to advertise everything we kin do, at least not just yet."

Blake nodded. He would refrain from any overt offensive magic, but if things turn hostile, he might enter some minds and turn their hostility against themselves.

"Maybe you ain't hearin' me," Michelle said directly to him. "I don't want them all dead, and that includes you making them shoot each other."

"No fair," Blake complained. "You are spending way too much time listening to our thoughts."

Destiny pressed her head against his and said, "You practically said it out loud. Some of them might have heard you think it."

Blake blushed bright red at the notion that he couldn't control his own thoughts.

Honey seethed in her chair at the sight of Blake having such an intimate moment with Destiny. She gripped the tablecloth in both fists and squeezed so hard she thought she would catch the table on fire until Abilene placed her hand on Honey's arm and said, "Honey, sweetie, I told you to behave. We're gonna feed them and send them on their way in the morning."

"Yes'm."

Michelle leaned in closer to Destiny and asked, "Cherie, is you feelin' okay? You look a bit flushed."

"It's nothing," Destiny said. "I think I'm just tired or something. I've been feeling a bit dizzy most of today. Might be I caught a cold sleeping in the park."

Little Ashlin wanted to be next to her new sister, but she was happy enough to sit next to Michelle where she could wave at Destiny across the table and they could still talk. As more of the family was seated down the length of the table, Ashlin would announce their names and sometimes squeeze in a little tidbit about them.

When everyone had found their places, Abilene stood and clanged her knife against her glass. When everyone had settled down and given Abilene their full attention, she put on a fake smile and scanned the length of the table giving each of her guests a slight nod of the head. "Well," she finally said. "Don't we all just look our very best this afternoon?"

She directed her gaze to the middle of the table and said, "I don't believe I've ever seen you bathe for dinner before Hank."

Hank's cheeks colored as he squirmed uncomfortably in his chair.

Abilene shifted her focus across the table and said, "And look at you Monique. Is that your Sunday dress?"

Monique shrunk down in her seat, as did the rest of the table.

Abilene exhaled loudly and shook her head. "I don't know what y'all been gossipin' about, but this ain't no social." She pointed down the length of the table and said, "That be my no-account sister Michelle from Louisiana. She and her mama left here in disgrace when she was little."

Destiny tensed in her seat and set her jaw. Michelle silently planted the thought, "Easy Cherie, let her have her talk."

"And now," Abilene continued, "she come crawling back here with her bastard brood and she's still the same disgrace she was when she left afore. This ain't no festival. We don't celebrate our family skeletons. Now, because the menfolk came in from the fields earlier than they should have, they'll have to put a couple extra hours in the field to make up for today." She paused to let it sink in. "And the rest of y'all will have to skip a meal to make up for all this extra food!"

Blake looked at Michelle and silently asked, "How long do you intend to let this go on?"

"Just let her rant on," Michelle thought to him. "She be a filthy jay screaming outside the window, but she ain't no threat to us."

"Now," Abilene said, "I ain't no monster. I have a heart and I'm not turning away family in their time of need. I see cousin Tempest there next to Zeb. She certainly deserves our pity, and I pray for her well-being. I don't know them young ones what came in with my sister, but I can certainly imagine what kind of rotted fruit has sprung from her poisonous loins."

"Not yet," Michelle thought to both Destiny and Blake.

"But," Abilene went on, "what's done is done. Let us eat this meal and when we be done, my sister can pay her respects to Zeb, then in the morning they can move along and we'll all go back to normal around here."

Michelle rose slowly from her seat and said, "Well, sister, I see that you still be prone to your tantrums."

Abilene started to object, but Michelle used the voice and said, "No, sister, you just listen. It's my turn to speak."

Honey was shocked. She heard the voice and saw her mother stand there dumbfounded by Michelle's command.

Michelle turned to her family and said, "I am truly sorry that you all had to witness that. I feels the embarrassment from all around the table, and I don't think we needs any more of that. As Abilene said, what's done is done. She always been one to flap her gums and she think it makes her look all smart, but I'm willing to let her words go. Water under the bridge, I say." She smiled broadly and continued, "The food looks and smells absolutely wonderful. Let us eat this splendid meal. Afterwards, if Abilene wishes, I can continue putting her in her place. We gonna have lots of time for me to show her what's what since I be staying here now."

Honey's jaw dropped when she saw her mother sit down and start scooping mashed potatoes onto her plate.

Even Honey's hound, Remus, knew something was different about her. He usually curled up behind Honey's chair and waited for scraps, but tonight he went to Abilene and laid his chin on her lap. She reached down and absently scratched his head.

Ashlin couldn't contain her excitement. "Wow!" she exclaimed. "What was that?"

Destiny put her finger to her lips and thought, "Shhh! For now, let's keep that our secret too."

"But," Ashlin said, "everybody else heard it too."

"Shhh," Destiny thought to her. "I know everyone heard it, but we don't have to talk about it out loud."

Ashlin's eyes widened, and she thought, "Can you hear me?"

Destiny nodded.

"Oh, my God!" Ashlin thought. "My mama told me it used to be like that in the olden days way before she was born, but I never thought nobody could still do it!"

"Our secret," Destiny thought to her. "Remember?"

Michelle saw enough of the back-and-forth looks between Destiny and Ashlin to suspect what was going on and eavesdrop on their thoughts. "I see," she thought to them, "that we been sharing some of our secrets."

Ashlin was wrong when she thought that she couldn't be more excited. "You too?" she thought, then turned towards Blake and thought, "What about you? Can you hear me too?"

Blake smiled and winked at her.

"Don't worry," Michelle thought. "We'll let the secret out soon enough. I can tell you must be ready to bust."

"I won't tell," Ashlin thought, "cross my heart."

The mood around the table lightened some when Abilene started filling her plate. All around the table, food was served onto plates and then passed along.

Honey split her attention during the meal between her mother's odd behavior and Blake. She played with her food seductively, but was unable to distract him from Destiny or little Ashlin. Something was going on at the other end of the table. The four of them ate in silence, but laughed and smiled as if someone said something funny. She wondered if there was something wrong with Blake. Getting a boy's attention had never been this much trouble before. She narrowed her focus onto Destiny and decided that she must be the problem.

With the meal complete, she pushed herself away from the table. Cobbler and ice cream were being dished out, but she had other ideas. She kept her eyes glued to Blake while she swished her hips around the room. Remus looked pleadingly up at Abilene then followed behind Honey. Blake barely glanced up at Honey before he returned his attention to Ashlin and Destiny. Honey frowned but continued until she reached him and said, "I'm gonna go get me something a bit stronger than ice cream. You wanna join me? Or is you gonna stay with the children?"

"No," Destiny said. "We're fine."

Honey looked down her nose at Destiny and said, "I wasn't talking to you."

Ashlin thought privately to Destiny, "She's rude to everybody. Some people think she might be crazy too."

"Lordy," Michelle said. "If you ain't every bit like your mama."

"Oh?" Destiny asked, "Is her mama a tramp too?"

Honey dropped the sultry attitude and snarled, "Bitch! What did you say?"

Michelle stepped between Honey and Destiny saying, "Maybe you should back off and go sit with your mama before you bites off more than you can chew."

"And maybe you should back off before I feed you to my hound! Remus!"

Remus jumped to attention and snarled menacingly at Michelle. Destiny quickly focused waves of calmness and peace over the hound. Remus stopped growling and sat down looking from Michelle to Honey and back. With Remus now calm and confused, Destiny planted a suggestion in his mind that he would find some sausage in Honey's pockets. Remus turned and went straight to her pockets, sniffing and slobbering, but he couldn't smell the sausage.

Honey pushed him away and yelled, "Get down off me you mangy mutt!"

Remus bared his teeth and growled at Honey.

Destiny took a slice of beef from a platter that hadn't been cleared yet and said, "Remus!"

The hound came to Destiny and sat with his tail flopping in all directions.

Destiny gave him the scrap of food and said to Honey, "You need to stop threatening us. Why don't you just go back to your seat and enjoy some cobbler with your mother."

Honey was furious and was prepared to attack Destiny, but Remus turned his attention back to her and bared his teeth again. "This ain't over between us," she said. She glanced at Blake but he was laughing at her. She stormed off to the other end of the table and sat back down with her mother. Remus curled up behind Destiny.

Michelle remained standing and addressed the table one more time. "Before we retire for the evening, I wants to introduce you to my granddaughter Destiny. Those of you who have spent time reviewing the memories may remember what it used to be like. Some of you may even have learned about a ancient prophecy predictin' how magic would disappear from the world. Well, that certainly come true enough, but there was another prophecy."

"Nana?" Destiny thought. "Not now. There's a spy at the table. I don't know who, but I can feel them in my gut."

Michelle nodded to Destiny and continued, "The war between our people nearly put an end to us. Sadly, this war continues today. The second prophecy says that one day, a chosen one will return the power to our people. Think about it. The chosen one could be sitting right here at this table. Look around you at your neighbors. Is he or she the chosen one? Will the person sitting next to you return magic to the world? Or is dey a spy sent here from da sorcerers. Is you sitting next to someone who ain't a witch at all, but is here to steal our power when the chosen one rises up and fulfills the final prophecy?"

Family members now looked around the table trying to tell friend from foe.

"Who here," Michelle continued, "doesn't have da gifts? Does someone next to you not commune with their ancestors? You don't have to say it out loud. Just think it, cause, if dey don't got da gifts, then dey won't hear you."

"I seen it," Hank thought. "I seen the lightning come from her hands."

"Who?" Angelica thought.

"That don't mean nothing," Monique thought. "I seen the prophecy and it says the chosen one can do the lightning and fire that the others could do."

"Ain't no way that Abilene is the chosen one," Hank thought, "and I seen her do their kind of magic."

Angelica added, "Now that I think on it, I ain't never seen Abilene read the memories."

"Fear not," Michelle thought. "Abilene is not the chosen one. I want everyone who hears me and believes me to get up and come stand behind me to meet Destiny."

One by one, the guests at the table rose and congregated behind Michelle leaving only Abilene and Honey at the other end.

"Well, well, well," Michelle said out loud. "It would appear that we has TWO spies in the family. I tell you what, sister. I gives you two choices. Come morning, the two of you kin go pack your belongings and leave dis family, or you kin stay and do something very unwise and most likely leave dis world. It be your choice."

Abilene rose and said, "I don't know what you and this sack o' shit family is up to, but idle threats ain't gonna scare me none. Maybe it's about time I shows you what I learnt." She held her arms out at her sides and blue filaments of electricity arched over her head from one hand to the other.

Michelle clapped her hands and said, "Very pretty! But you still be a minor leaguer at dis table."

Blake stood and held out his hand producing a fireball in his palm.

Honey sneered at him and said, "You call that a fireball?" She stood and produced a larger fireball in her hand.

Blake conjured another fireball in his other hand then put them together to create one larger than Honey's.

Honey sucked in her breath and blew on her fireball until it was larger than his.

Destiny stood and stepped away from the table saying, "If you two are done playing around, I'll show you some real fire." She started with a protective shield that clung to her skin, then turned her whole body into a full size fireball. The dizziness and slight stumble were only observed by Michelle and Blake. Destiny held the flaming fireball around her turning her into a human torch. The room spun violently around her, but she held her stance.

Michelle looked down the table and said, "I suggest that the two of you don't actually use those here. Tain't nothing you kin do dat my Destiny cain't top. So you kin just put your little tricks away and go. I'll let you spend the night, but it be your last night here. I expect you to be gone in the morning."

Rage burned in Abilene's eyes, but there was nothing she could do to top Destiny's full body flame. She withdrew her lightning and said, "Come on Honey, let's go. We'll deal with this another time."

Destiny extinguished the flame and flopped down into her chair.

Michelle thought privately to her, "What da hell is goin' on wit you Cherie? And don't bother tellin' me you is just tired."

Destiny didn't know what was wrong, and when she looked at her nana to respond, a tear involuntarily collected in her eye. "I don't know, but it's been like this ever since we got here."

Librarians one and two remained vigilant while their hosts rode with the squad from the small bar outside of New Orleans up to the farm in Mississippi. The sun was finally reaching the horizon, and the colors were fading from the world. It was still warm and humid, but as the sun fell towards the west, the breeze that licked the land was able to pull some heat off faster than the sun was able to replace it.

The third librarian returned to the meditation room after delivering the news that they had failed to keep Destiny out of Mala's memories which, apparently, was no surprise to their leader. He joined his fellows in the circle and entered his trance. He located his operative and said, "Johnson?"

Johnson had come to expect their visits, but he still hated it when they got in his head and spoke to him out of the blue. He was perched halfway up a tree and grateful that he had secured himself to the trunk with a rope, or the sudden intrusion of the librarian's voice might have knocked him to the ground. His vantage afforded him a view over most of the farm including the road coming in from the highway.

"Johnson," the librarian said. "They should be arriving any moment. Are you in position?"

"They're here now," Johnson said. "They have taken up positions surrounding the place already, but it looks like they're waiting for something."

"Very good," the librarian said. "We want you to look out for the two operatives with the bright orange bandanas around their necks. They're with us."

Johnson shook his head. What kind of idiot would wear bright orange into combat?

"The kind of idiot," the librarian said, "that we want you to easily identify and not attack."

Johnson winced and vowed to more carefully monitor his thoughts.

"One more thing," the librarian said, "although we don't particularly care if the soldiers live or die, we do not want the girl to be blamed should bodies be discovered. While she is still there, we'd prefer to keep the deaths to a minimum."

"Roger that," Johnson thought back to him.

<hr>

Polin went from one pit to the next with Lisa following behind writing down what he dictated. He measured the temperature inside the pit as well as its width and depth. He took small scoops of ash and collected them in small bottles which he labeled to match the locations marked on the map he made first.

"That's my last evidence jar," he said. "We'll definitely have to come back tomorrow with more jars. I can take more temperature readings tomorrow too. Maybe we can get some idea how quickly these cool."

Simon had just finished a lap around the island and said, "Does that mean you're done for the day?"

"Yeah," Polin replied. "We should get back before it gets dark anyway."

"What about the bodies?" Lisa asked. "Don't you need to measure their temperatures too?"

"Not me, I leave that for the coroner. I'm only interested in what started the fire. Speaking of which, where is he? The medical examiner usually gets first crack at the crime scene."

"The witness only reported the fire," Simon said, "and we have other reports putting the residents on a bus. I don't think anyone knew there were bodies until we arrived. I'll call in an order for a pathologist when we get back."

Polin played with his mustache and asked, "The residents left town? That sounds kind of suspicious."

"Look at the place," Simon said. "They sure can't stay here. Someone said they have family in Lafayette."

"A mother," Lisa added.

"Still," Polin said, "they left town and there are two unidentified bodies in the fire."

"Don't forget why we are here. Those are probably our bodies and the reports are that one of them has been playing with fire. We might need to cover this up before suspicion falls on us."

"I know why we are here," Polin sounded annoyed. "It's not enough to cover up our involvement with the fire. Logan told me to make sure the evidence and all related suspicion points to the witches."

The sun had nearly reached the western horizon, but the farm was still bathed in light. The only trees on the farm were those that lined some of the fields to shelter against the wind and those that surrounded the houses. Visibility on the farm was largely unobstructed and Johnson could see almost everything that went on.

He saw the mercs arrive and spread out around the farm. He made mental notes of all their locations, especially the orange bandanas who were far too easy to spot.

When the mercs had settled into their locations, Johnson shimmied down the tree and worked his way counterclockwise around the farm. His first target was a big guy that took up position behind a brick corner post that stood at the end of the driveway nearest the home. Lethal force would have been easier and a lot safer, but he crept in as requested and snuck up behind the big guy's position. He wished he had some chloroform for this one but swung his arm around the big man's neck and gripped his hands together on the other side to double the strength of his choke hold. He twisted and pulled the larger man to the ground with his own weight crashing on top of him. If the choke weren't enough, landing on the ground knocked the wind out of his opponent and the man blacked out.

In retrospect, Johnson thought he may have been lucky with this guy. Johnson had special training, but he wasn't Special Forces. He was just a soldier and the encounter could have gone against him. He tie strapped the man's hands behind him and gagged his mouth then moved on to find the next target.

The family that had heard Michelle's thoughts and congregated behind her were thrilled to see Abilene shown up and forced to leave, but they still gravitated away from Destiny and Blake. Many of them had the sight and some of them had seen enough of their ancestral memories to know that fire was not a natural gift for their kind.

Ashlin stood strong at Michelle's side and said, "What's wrong with all of you? Can't you tell they are here to help us?"

"You're too young to understand this," one of the adults said, "but our people can't do fire like that."

"So?" Ashlin retorted. "That doesn't mean anything. I can hear their thoughts and I trust them."

"We all heard their thoughts," the same adult replied, "but that doesn't mean we can believe them."

"Why not?" another adult asked. "The others can't share their thoughts with us or hear ours. We all saw that Abilene and Honey didn't hear any of us."

"Yes," the first adult admitted, "and none of us could share our thoughts amongst ourselves so easily before they came."

"That," Michelle said, "is because magic is back. My Destiny brought it back."

"But," several said together, "she brought back black magic."

"No," Michelle replied. "At first, she came back able to heal. She fixed my burnt arm. The other stuff came later. We can't always explain the gifts we get."

"Yeah, I can," Destiny said, "and I'm not the only one. Maybe some of you have traveled in the memories and met a wizard called The Great One?"

An elder woman said, "I never met him, but I heard of him, though I doubt he likes being called a wizard."

"No," Destiny said. "He told me himself that he wanted to be his grandfather's court wizard. It was just a name the people used during that time. When he was little, they called us faeries."

"What do you mean, he told you? Memories can't actually talk to you."

Destiny smiled and said, "There are a lot of things that have been kept from our people for a long time. Those days are over. I can talk with him. I can visit our people in the past. In fact, the point I wanted to make was that Blake and I are both descended from him.

His powers and our powers are all linked up with some crossed blood from the others."

Ashlin asked, "Can you teach us?"

Destiny shrugged and said, "I can demonstrate, but I don't know if all of you can learn."

The crowd collected back around Destiny and Michelle again.

"And don't forget," Ashlin said. "You were going to heal Grandpa Zeb."

Laura, the adult who had spoken out before, said, "Now that I think about it, I'll bet it was that witch Abilene what hurt Zeb in the first place."

General agreement was spoken in the crowd, but Michelle said, "Except, that it would appear that my half-sister warn't no witch at all."

"Maybe so," Laura said, "but I think maybe I'll go keep an eye on Abilene and that no account brat of hers."

"I'll go with you," one of the men said.

"Be careful," Michelle said. "She's one of them, and apparently, she knows how to do some bad things. You know how to keep in contact with us now."

Laura winked and thought, "Don't worry, I'll keep in constant contact."

"And I'm getting my shotgun," the man with her said, "and I won't be packin' rock salt this time."

Johnson continued circling around counterclockwise and found the next soldier. This one wore an orange bandana. Johnson wasn't wearing any distinguishable colors and hoped these guys knew how to recognize him. The merc lay prone on the ground with his rifle just under a white fence rail. He had a clear view of the compound, but he was watching his companions at the various positions they took to his right.

The ground was crunchy with twigs and debris. Johnson couldn't approach quietly and didn't want to spook the armed man, so he gently tossed a pebble at him. The man was fast. He turned and leveled his gun to Johnson's left and Johnson held his finger to his lips and said, "Shhh."

The man nodded. He recognized Johnson. Johnson signaled, walking to the next post with his fingers. They found the next guy in a position up a tree. Johnson gave the orange bandanna guy a phone and mimed that the call was for the guy in the tree. Johnson circled around the other side of the tree while the other guy said, "Psst" and held up the phone.

The guy in the tree wanted him to throw the phone, but he shook his head no, forcing him to come down to answer it. When he did, Johnson swung his arm around the smaller man's neck to choke him, but the bandana guy was less patient and slugged him in the head knocking him out.

Two down, five to go.

Logan was in his office drawing up plans to take over the farm. There was something special about that farm. It wasn't new to him, but the fact that the limo led them there was a surprise. It was also fortuitous, since he already had two assets placed on the farm and they were showing signs of the old magic, but Abilene and Honey were two of the most unreliable people he could imagine. He needed to get better people in there to find the source of the power so they could harness it and hopefully bottle it up and distribute it.

The farm had been under his surveillance for years, and if he ever had any doubts about the place, they were erased when the witches fled directly there. As he mulled that thought over in his mind, the doubts returned. Why would the witches leave their home in the bayou when the power they developed there was much greater than what they had recorded on the farm? Even the few sketchy reports that remained from Brian's attempt to capture the witches indicated that his power was returning as he approached their home.

Maps covered the top of Logan's desk. He had geologic maps showing the fault lines running under North America, and he had maps showing the magnetic variations over the globe. Mostly, he had maps of ley lines. He had modern and ancient maps of ley lines. He even had maps of Indian sacred sites which followed the same ley lines. They all showed one thing to him. The bayou home that the witches abandoned was near an intersection of ley lines. It was directly under one of the ley lines where it intersected a magnetic line. The farm was under a ley line, but with no intersection nearby and no magnetic lines, it should be much less powerful than the home they left behind.

The phone rang. "Hello, this is Logan."

"Simon here. We found corpses inside the witches' home. We'll need a medical examiner to look at them before we'll know if we can identify them."

"You'll have one in the morning," Logan said.

"We don't have enough evidence," Simon said, "to force a conviction. The place burned down and there were fires all over the property. But with two bodies and them fleeing the scene, we can mount enough of a case based on suspicion to hold them."

"Excellent," Logan said. "I was just looking at the maps and wondering why they would have left their home. That explains it very nicely. We have the farm, where they went, surrounded and should have them in custody very soon, assuming, that is, that something very bad doesn't happen to them during the night. I hear it is a very dangerous location, and it is possible that something may happen to them before they can be arrested."

Logan hung up the phone and Simon's imagination filled in the maniacal laughter that so often accompanied such proclamations from evil geniuses, or at least that's how Hollywood portrayed them.

Zeb and Tempest remained near the end of the table where everyone had gathered around Michelle and Destiny. Nobody knew how much they could hear or understand about what had gone on, but Destiny wanted to find out.

Destiny sat down at the table across from Zeb and said, "I'm going to go into Zeb's mind and see if I can help him. It's very similar to going into a trance, like you do when you go into the memories."

Ashlin grabbed a short fat candle from a drawer and placed it in front of Destiny, then sat down in a chair next to her, glued to her side.

"Thank you, Ashlin. I don't actually use the candles no more, but I will this once, just as a demonstration."

One of the men fumbled with some matches, trying to light the candle, but his hands were shaking so much the flame kept puffing out.

"Here," Destiny said. "Let me get that for you." She reached across the table and brought her forefinger and thumb together around the wick. The candle burst into flame.

"I'll stay behind," Blake said, "in case Abilene returns. I'm not a healer, anyway."

Destiny nodded. She turned to the candle and stared into the flame. It was reminiscent of her first time, which was only a few weeks ago but seemed much longer. The flame filled her vision, and the room dissolved around her. She was in the void. She focused her mind on Zeb but heard a call from Mala. Mala didn't call her by name, but Destiny could still hear her voice. Ishun didn't want Mala to recognize Destiny, so she took on the appearance of little Ashlin. She reached out for the voice and found her sitting in her hut.

"Hello Mala."

Mala looked up at her and said, "This be a very strange request. My master made promise for me to come to you since I was very young. Here I am."

"Thank you. I am a healer like yourself, but I need help with healing people's minds. Nobody in my time knows how it is done."

"Ah," Mala said, "so you are not from my time."

"No," Destiny replied, "and so I must not reveal too much."

"This is good..." Mala stopped mid-sentence. She looked beside Destiny and said, "This is strange magic. Why you do this?"

Destiny was confused and followed Mala's gaze to find young Ashlin sitting by her side. "What are you doing here?"

"Hey!" Ashlin exclaimed, "You're me!"

"Argghh," Destiny said with her head in her hands. "I apologize, Mala, but Ishun asked me to disguise myself in case we ever met in your future, so I selected a particularly precocious little imp to impersonate."

She turned back to Ashlin and asked again, "What are you doing here? And how did someone of your age manage to get herself here?"

"Ach!" Mala interrupted. "What age have to do with anything?"

Destiny was surprised by the question. "She's so young. She couldn't have even reached her womanhood yet."

"What strange times you come from," Mala said. "You think you need to reach your womanhood to be trained?"

"That's when I was trained," Destiny replied. "That's when the gifts arrive."

"Bah," Mala spat. "How you train boys when they never is blooded like girls?"

Destiny could only shrug her shoulders.

"I'm sorry," Ashlin said, "but I was only looking in the flame and listening to what you said. The next thing I knew, I was here with you both."

A big smile spread across Mala's face. "She is good student. You will teach her."

"Great," Destiny said. "I'm just learning myself."

"You are strong," Mala said. "I see it. Ishun sees it. We are here now. How I help you?"

"We have two patients," Destiny said. "I already been in my mama's mind. She's been sick since I was born, but her mind is a maze and I think her mind is keeping me out of the inner parts. Grandpa Zeb only got sick recently, so I thought you might show me how to help him first."

"Good," Mala said. "You lead, I follow."

Destiny closed her eyes and focused on Zeb's mind. The hut faded around them and they were in an alien wasteland surrounded by tall rock spires. The sky was a dark cloudless blue with forks of lightning streaking across, then arcing down and striking the top of one of the many pinnacles. Beneath the forest of rock, fires would flame up out of the ground and burn out. There was a dim light far off on the horizon, but the only light around them came from the fires and the flashes of lightning.

Ashlin clung to Destiny's side and asked, "Where are we?"

"I don't know," Destiny said. "Is this Zeb's mind?"

"Dis is his fear," Mala said. "His mind is lost in dis nightmare."

A flame burst next to the trio. Destiny screamed and jumped aside, covering Ashlin and shielding her from the heat.

Mala held out her hands and healed the ground where the flames erupted. "He is in much pain. Come, we heal him together."

Destiny stepped next to Mala and extended her hands. "Is it real pain, or is it just fear like you said before?"

"Pain is real. Fear come from pain. Close eyes and tell what you feel."

Destiny closed her eyes and let her senses reach out. She turned slowly in a circle, then stopped and said, "Over there. It's different. I can taste metal in my mouth."

"Good," Mala said. "We go that way."

They zigzagged between the spires and came to a spot where the ground was hot and glowed an iridescent blue. Destiny's hands tingled as she released the healing waves. The glow dimmed, and the ground cooled.

"Did you hear that?" Ashlin shouted. "Grandpa Zeb?"

She ran off toward the sound she heard, with Destiny and Mala trailing behind.

When they caught her, she was with Zeb. He was curled up on his side like a baby.

Destiny fell to her knees and ran her hands over his head. She couldn't find the source of his pain.

"It is good you try," Mala said, "but his fear is too much here. We must lead him out of dis place."

Mala reached down and lifted Zeb to his feet. Destiny reached for his opposite arm, but Mala said, "I help him. You heal fire and lightning dat come for us."

Ashlin held Zeb's hand and Mala said, "It is good he has someone he knows."

The horizon was far off, and it seemed like they would never reach it. Destiny thought it receded from them, even as they approached it. Lightning struck all around them. It would usually hit the spires above them, but would occasionally land on the ground next to them. Destiny healed the strikes and the fires that seemed to pop up beneath their feet.

She tried erecting a protective shield to keep the lightning out, but Mala snickered and said, "It nice you try to protect us, but shield not work on fear. Only healing."

Destiny tried releasing the healing waves in all directions, but Mala said, "Another good try. You are strong, but not that strong."

She reached under her shirt and gripped the amulet with one hand while releasing the healing waves with the other. The lightning receded, the sky lightened, and the spires seemed to melt down into the ground around them.

Mala looked at Destiny, but all she saw was a copy of Ashlin gripping at her chest. "Ach!" she exclaimed. "Why you not say you have the talisman?"

Destiny shrugged.

"Now," Mala said, "we heal him."

She laid Zeb down on the ground and pointed at Ashlin, saying, "You here. Put head on lap." She then knelt at his left and motioned for Destiny to position herself on the other side.

Mala placed one hand on top of his head and one under his chin and said, "Do like me."

Destiny mimicked her with one hand on the side of his head and the other on his forehead. Not wanting to be excluded, Ashlin, whose lap now served as a pillow, slipped her hands under his head next to her lap.

Mala and Destiny released the healing forces. There were no tastes in her mouth this time, only the familiar tingling of her hands. Zeb's cheeks pinked up a bit, and he opened his eyes.

"Grandpa Zeb," Ashlin shouted.

He looked up at her through his bushy eyebrows and smiled. He tried to speak, but his mouth was dry.

"No speak," Mala said. "We get you home first."

He looked at Mala and didn't know who she was, but when he looked at Destiny and saw Ashlin again, terror set in his mind. Instead of lightning and fire, the ground shook. The spires sprung back up from the ground then cracked and fell over, showering them with dust and rock debris.

"No!" Mala said. "No do that. We help you." She released waves of calmness into his brain. The ground steadied, but shook slightly, then calmed again like the throbbing that accompanies a fever or injury.

Mala and Ashlin lifted him up again and guided him towards the light. Destiny followed behind; afraid her glamour might cause worse quakes.

It wasn't far, now. As they approached the light, the light seemed to approach them. The ground shook occasionally, but only enough to remind them to hurry.

When they reached the light, the field of pinnacles ended, and they stood before a broad meadow that extended off into the horizon. A large brass bed stood far enough from the rock spires to be surrounded with pink and blue flowers. They led him into the meadow and laid him down on the bed.

"You sleep," Mala said. She turned to Destiny and said, "You do good. Your apprentice is also good. You go help mother. I think you don't need me now, but maybe we meet again."

"Yes," Destiny said. "We will meet again, but you won't know me."

"Ishun would say this is how it must be."

Mala bowed her head and shimmered out.

Destiny took Ashlin's hand. Together they shimmered out, leaving Zeb asleep on the bed to wake on his own.

When they opened their eyes, the candle still burned before them. Ashlin's mother had been wiping her head with a wet cloth and now turned to Destiny and cried, "How could you take her with you?"

Destiny shrugged and Ashlin said, "Mama, she didn't do it. It was me, and Grandpa needed me there. It's okay."

Mother and daughter hugged. Then Zeb sucked in a big breath of air and the whole family followed suit.

Zeb's caretakers asked, "Zeb! Is you okay?"

Zeb opened his eyes, but still couldn't speak until someone placed a glass of water in his hands. He sipped at first, then guzzled until someone said, "Slowly, Zeb. They always say to drink slowly."

Zeb put the glass down and said only one word, a name, "Abilene."

Logan called the number for the man he hired to lead the charge on the farm, but nobody answered, and he assumed the assault was probably underway.

But the assault on the farm wasn't quite underway yet. Johnson had the man locked in a choke hold. The ringer was off, but Johnson could feel the phone rattling against his arm as he squeezed the breath out of the man. When he finally felt the body go limp in his arms, he pulled the phone from the breast pocket and tossed it into a horse trough.

Logan tried again, but this time the call went immediately to voice mail. He didn't care whether the man just refused to take his call or was simply unable. Something was wrong. Logan was no longer in control of the events on the farm.

His next call was to the troopers he had on standby. He would go with plan *B*.

It was an uneasy night all around the farm. Most of the family celebrated Zeb's return and were too happy to sleep, but Abilene and Honey were too afraid. Abilene went directly to her room, but Honey went to the parlor and released a massive fireball, filled with her frustration, into the fireplace, igniting the logs stacked on the hearth.

Abilene knew she couldn't confront Destiny and Blake head on, but she believed there might be a more devious scheme that she could use to overcome them.

Abilene was throwing clothes into her luggage when Honey stormed into her room.

Honey screeched when she saw her mother packing her bags. "What are you doing? We can't give in to these people!"

"You saw them," Abilene said. "We can't take them on."

"So, you're just leaving?"

"No," Abilene said, "not exactly. I'm just pretending to leave. I cain't ever leave this place. All my power is here."

"All our power," Honey corrected her mother.

"Yeah, yeah, that's what I meant."

"Wait a minute," Honey said. "You were going to leave without me?"

Abilene stopped packing long enough to turn toward her daughter and say, "No, of course not. I told you I wasn't really leaving."

"But you were going to leave me with them while you snuck around outside."

"What are you afraid of?" Abilene asked. "The rest o' the Boutin's are pathetic. They gots no power. They cain't do nothing to you."

"The newcomers can. You was leaving me to fend against the two of them by myself."

"I told you I wasn't really leaving."

Honey couldn't help it. Anger and fear flowed through her veins, and distrust and abandonment settled into her heart. Fireballs appeared in her palms completely on their own.

Abilene produced tendrils of lightning, just as a warning, and asked, "What do you plan to do with those?"

"Mama," Honey cried. "Was you using me as bait? Or maybe I was just a diversion for you?"

"No!" Abilene objected. "It warn't nothing like that."

"Then you explain to me why you was leaving without me!"

"I keep tellin' ya, I ain't leaving. You knows that I went to show my lightning to that Logan feller, but it fizzled out when I got to him."

"You told me."

"And I also told you it come back when he brung me home. My power is tied to this farm. I'm tied to this farm. I warn't leaving you. I just wanted them to believe I was gone, so we'd have the advantage. Don't you see that?"

"Yeah," Honey said. "I sees it all right. They think you is gone and then you sneak back behind them after they kills me. Maybe you even hope I takes one of them out before they finish me. That's what I see. But I gots other plans."

Honey ran out of the room even more scared than when she arrived.

Abilene continued packing her bags. What she told her daughter was true. She planned to make a big show of leaving, but she never planned to stay gone. This is where her power was. She couldn't leave the farm.

Honey also thought she could scheme her way out of this situation, but her mind was more one dimensional and offered up a vastly different approach. Fortunately for her, she wouldn't need her mother's help to implement her plans. She thought she could improve her odds by recruiting Blake. Then she wouldn't be one against two, but two against one. And she could decide later whether to let her mother back in.

Neither Abilene nor Honey were aware that Destiny was awakening the power within the rest of the family, so the family was completely discounted as any kind of a threat. The Boutins had always been weak and pathetic in their eyes.

Blake's day had started out with them spending the night homeless in a park. The morning improved when he was able to sit behind the wheel and drive them out of Louisiana, but that had dragged on too long to remain fun. In the end, Blake was just too tired to stay up with the rejoicing family. It was time for some sleep. He left the revelers behind in the dining room and returned to the room they had given him. Lazily, he pulled his shirt over his head without bothering to turn the lights on, and instead, flicked his finger to produce a small flame to find his bed, but was surprised by the reflection of two eyes shining on the bed. He increased the light and saw Honey sprawled out on top of the bed.

"What are you doing here?" he asked.

"What do you think?" she replied. "You're not gay, are you?"

"No," he said defensively, "but I'm tired. I just want to go to bed."

"That's all I want too," she flirted. "You should have told me you had powers. You're even more interesting than I thought."

"Yeah? Well, you didn't exactly come out and tell us what you could do, either."

"So, we all have our secrets," she said as she patted the bed for him to join her.

"Look, I'm really tired, do you mind?"

She flattened her shoulders to the bed and arched her back, thrusting her braless breasts against the thin material of her shirt, stretching out on the bed like a big cat. "I don't mind," she purred. "Climb in. It's real easy."

"Nothing is that easy."

She pulled her t-shirt up over her head and tossed it on the floor. She cocked her head to the side and said, "I am."

He couldn't say that he wasn't tempted. She was gorgeous with or without her clothes. He also couldn't deny the change in his pulse or the sweat on his skin. His body was reacting on instinct. He couldn't tear his eyes from her any more than he could lie about his reactions.

She locked her eyes on the now obvious bulge throbbing in his pants and smiled. "You certainly don't look like you're gay. What's the problem?"

"I can't do this," he said hoarsely.

"Why not? Is it that girl? She don't have to know. Like I said before, we all have our little secrets."

"What secret?" he asked. "You haven't exactly been very subtle."

"This ain't no time to be subtle," she said as she reached for his pants, but he backed away.

"No," he said. "You have to go."

Honey wasn't used to being spurned like this. She was losing interest, but she didn't know how to back down. She stood defiantly, making no effort to cover her bare breasts. "You're crazy. She's just a little girl, while I'm full grown and I know how to do things. You and me could be real special together. We share the same gifts. You know this."

The anger in her voice helped Blake tremendously. "She is special," he said with a trembling voice, "and you're pretty, real pretty, but you're not very special."

"Arrrggghhh!" she screamed. She produced a fireball in her hand and waved it before him, unsure what she would do with it.

Blake simply produced a fireball in one hand and a ball of electricity in the other. "Don't," he threatened her. "Just leave."

She ran out the door without bothering to even pick up her shirt. One of the mothers in the yard pulled her little boy close to her and wrapped her apron around his head when he saw the half-naked Honey run out of Blake's room. Honey was already humiliated by Blake's rejection and crossed her arms over her chest, hoping to avoid any further humiliation as she ran across the yard to the main house.

"Blake," he thought to himself, "you have got to be the dumbest man on the face of the Earth."

Destiny stroked her mother's hair and said, "Soon, Mama. I'm going to help you too, real soon."

Tempest sat alone in the window while Zeb's caretakers were fussing over by his bed.

His eyes rolled around the room wildly. "No!" he thought. "I do not want to go to bed. I been asleep long enough."

"But that's just it," Gladys said to him. "You ain't been sleeping. And now that you is mostly healed, you needs some sleep to finish getting better."

Zeb tried arguing, but his words came out garbled. "You see?" he thought. "You couldn't have heard me! I can't even say my words!"

"Yes," Gladys said. "Don't talk now. You need to meet Cousin Michelle's granddaughter. She's da one what helped you and she been teachin' us a thing or two. Destiny? Come on over and meet your Cousin Zeb proper like."

Destiny didn't respond. Her eyes were glued outside where she saw Honey leaving Blake's room with her arms crossed over her clearly naked breasts.

"Destiny?"

"I can't now," Destiny said as she sprang from the window. "I need to take care of something."

Michelle entered the room and shouted, "Destiny! Don't be rude. Say hello to my Cousin Zeb."

"I can't Nana."

The image she saw flashed in Michelle's mind. "Lordy," Michelle said. "Now what?"

Destiny sprinted down the stairs and met Honey at the back door just as she opened the screen. Her hair lifted into the air as if in a breeze. "Just what the hell do you think you are doing?"

Honey was still gathering her thoughts to reply when Destiny thrust her hands forward and hit Honey with a force wave that shoved her backwards off the porch and left her sprawling, half naked, on the ground outside.

"Don't you think you're in enough trouble already?" Destiny screamed. "Do you really want to make it personal?"

"Personal?" Honey yelled back. "Maybe it is personal and it just ain't none of your business!"

Destiny stepped out onto the back porch and yelled back, "Maybe it is my business."

A crowd started to gather around the yard. Young boys pointed at Honey and snickered about her titties. The men had seen them before and were more amused by the ass kicking that seemed eminent.

Everyone at dinner had heard the warning. Honey and Abilene had to go. The men weren't really going to miss her, but didn't care so much one way or the other. The women, on the other hand, were considerably more enthusiastic to see her leave.

Honey climbed back up on her feet and brushed the dust off her. She flinched for a moment as if to cover herself again, but then decided it was too late and she didn't really care. "Fine," she said. "He's all yours. I'm done with him, anyway."

The ground throughout the farm began to quake, but for Destiny, the world wobbled in her head, far worse than the quake, which was bad enough. "What do you mean," Destiny screamed, "you're done with him?"

A glow from Destiny's chest caught Honey's eyes. "I mean," she said, "that I only needed him for ten minutes." The ground shook harder, and the glow between Destiny's breasts grew brighter. Honey smiled wickedly and added, "Well, maybe it was twenty minutes, which is a heck of a lot better than the thirty seconds I get from most of the men around here." The crowd gasped and Honey added, "Especially the married ones." The ground shook again, and Destiny lost her balance slightly, which looked to everyone like a result of the earthquake, but was really the spinning of her mind.

The trembling ground was joined by large claps of thunder from the dark clouds gathering overhead. Honey's eyes were locked on Destiny's chest.

"No!" Destiny cried. "You're lying!"

"Whatever," Honey said. "He's all yours."

"You're lying!" Destiny repeated. She cocked her arm aggressively and yelled, "Get out! Now! I ain't giving you till morning!"

"Well," Honey said coyly. "Are you at least going to let me get some clothes?"

"No!" Destiny yelled back. "You can leave here like the harlot everyone knows you are."

Destiny's sentiment was echoed unspoken around the yard by the other women.

"Well, maybe I don't want to leave," Honey said. "Maybe the menfolk don't want me to leave neither."

Destiny swung her arms towards Honey and buried fire and lightning into the ground around and below her. She bounced up into the air and landed backwards, off her feet. A large fork of lightning cracked down from the sky and struck the ground between Honey's legs. Dust burst up into the air and the ground glowed hot as quartz and sand melted into crystalline spider webs in the sand. The smell of electricity filled the yard and the family members who had formed a ring around Destiny and Honey took a step backwards. All eyes were on Honey, except her's. Honey's eyes were locked on the light, which was positively glowing between Destiny's breasts.

Destiny looked around the yard and said, "Look around you. Do you really think the men don't want you to leave? Cause I don't see no men folk coming to your aid now, do you?"

Honey stood up again and said, "You bitch! What do you know about men? You're just a pathetic little girl who ain't never been with a real man. You wouldn't even know what to do with one if you had him. Maybe you don't even like men. I done you a service by breaking in your little boyfriend."

Destiny had never been so angry. She reared back and flexed her fist, ready to cut Honey in two, when she impulsively closed the gap between them and slapped her hard across the face.

Honey's face stung, but she ignored it and said, "I was right, wasn't I? You don't even like men. I wonder who you're really jealous of. Is it the boy?" She reached forward and wrapped her hands around Destiny's breasts. Destiny was frozen, unprepared for such an attack. She tried pulling away, but her head was spinning and she nearly fell forward into Honey's grasp. Honey squeezed and mashed the mounds beneath her palms and asked, "Or are you really jealous of me?" Destiny's mouth fell open when quick as lightning, Honey reached under her shirt and yanked the amulet off her neck. She turned and ran out of the yard and onto the entrance road, wishing she had given more thought to her escape.

Destiny's mind went blank as the spinning in her mind nearly rolled her eyes backwards in her head. She stumbled backwards and fell onto the ground. The quakes had subsided and now she just wanted the dizziness to pass before she got up again, but she had to get her amulet back.

CHAPTER 7

Blake didn't know what to do. He didn't know how to handle Honey when she offered herself to him, and he didn't know how to handle the aftermath after he turned her away. Nothing in his experience prepared him for this. He was simply too young, and she was far too aggressive for him to deal with. He had even less idea how he was going to explain it to Destiny, and he had no doubt that she would eventually learn about Honey running half naked out of his room. When he heard the ruckus which immediately followed her departure, he knew he was in trouble.

He watched the scene develop through the window, admittedly afraid to face Destiny, but when he saw Honey snatch the amulet and run off, he took off after her without ever giving it a second thought.

Blake wasn't an athletic guy, but he was fairly certain he could catch a half-naked girl. He found that thought mildly amusing, since he wouldn't be chasing her if he hadn't sent her away in the first place.

"You did?" Destiny asked. She was right behind him.

"Yes, she threw herself at me, but I kicked her out," he thought back to her.

"Dummy," she teased.

Blake may have been able to catch her, but Destiny was still struggling with a light head and the running was too much for her. He heard her crash to the ground behind him. When he returned to help her, she tried urging him to continue chasing Honey; the amulet was more important, but a pickup sped by them and picked up Honey ending any hope that he would actually catch her on foot. Honey jumped into the cab and the truck peeled out in a cloud of dust and rocks.

Destiny was sitting on the ground, while Blake was doubled over at the waist, trying to catch his breath.

"Now what?" he asked.

Another car pulled up beside them and the driver yelled, "Get in!"

It was an older car with bench style seats. They slid into the front seat and the car roared to life. Its engine let out a deep throaty roar as it pressed them against the seat backs and propelled them down the road.

"Nice car," Blake said.

"Thanks. I restored her myself. I'm Ralph. We sorta met before, briefly. I guess we're cousins."

"Hi. I'm Blake. She's your cousin, actually."

"Hi," Destiny said weakly.

"So," Blake said. "You restore cars? Do you race them too? This one sure is fast."

Ralph patted the car on the dash and said, "You hear that, Honey? He likes you. She's definitely the fastest vehicle we have and when I saw that bitch Abilene steal Zeb's truck, I jumped straight into Honey and took off after her."

"Honey?" Destiny asked. "You named your car Honey?"

"Honey's Revenge, actually."

Destiny smiled and said, "Wow, it's almost as if it were written in the stars."

"Stars?" Ralph asked. "No. Honey and I had a thing since we were kids, until a couple years ago when she discovered that she could sleep with every man on the farm. That's when I renamed my car. I figured it was the only thing faster than her."

Blake snickered.

"But," Ralph added, "there ain't nothing easier than her."

Destiny giggled at that remark.

Abilene saw Blake when she sped past him and stopped to pick up her daughter. She planned on putting as much distance between them as she could, but stopped when she reached the end of the road, which was blocked by police cars.

A patrolman walked up to the truck and aimed his flashlight inside, and compared Abilene's face to the image he held in his hand. She clearly was not the young girl they were looking for so he moved the beam over to the passenger seat and fell upon the topless form of Honey where he held up the image in his hand as if he were comparing them, but his eyes and the beam actually fell to her naked breasts where they lingered longer than he should have. Honey, not only made no attempt to cover herself, she thrust her chest out slightly and asked, "Is there a problem, officer?"

The officer's sergeant was approaching from the other side, and he quickly pulled the beam away, cleared his throat, and said, "Move along. You can go."

Abilene wasted no time hanging around and quickly pulled the truck away and back onto the road. At the end of the drive, she swung the truck around to the right and headed south on old twenty-six.

"What the hell's wrong with you?" Abilene yelled. "Ain't you got no shame? You're damn lucky that cop you flashed your titties at didn't pull you out and bend you over the front fender!"

"How's that lucky?" she asked. "Seems more like not getting lucky if you asks me."

Abilene looked at her daughter, hoping she would see the embarrassment on her face, but she couldn't keep looking at her nakedness. "Look behind the seat," she said, "and find something to put on. I can't talk to you like this."

Honey took her breasts in her hands, squeezed slightly and asked, "What? You mean these? It's not like you don't have a pair of your own, although they may not be as firm and perky as mine. Is that it? Are yours..."

Abilene returned her attention to the road and said, "You really are a sick little girl, you know that? How the hell did you ever become so wicked?"

Honey laughed sinisterly, but looked behind the seat for a t-shirt anyway, preferably one with the thinnest material and the lowest neckline that she could find.

The truck was out of sight by the time Ralph had stopped to pick them up, but they had it in view as they approached the end of the road.

"What the hell?" Ralph exclaimed.

The junction to old twenty-six was filled with the familiar flashing lights of police vehicles. The truck had been stopped by the roadblock, but as they pulled up to it, the truck pulled out and took off.

Ralph stopped the car and hopped out, yelling, "Stop them! They stole that truck!"

Troopers quickly descended upon him and said, "Sir, please remain in the vehicle."

Another officer added, "I need to see your hands. Show us your hands!"

While the first two troopers concentrated on Ralph, the sergeant on the scene went to the passenger window and looked inside comparing Blake and Destiny to a picture in her hand. She clicked the mic on her shoulder and said, "It's her."

Two more troopers joined her on the passenger side with their hands on their side arms. "Miss, can you please step out of the vehicle?"

After the sergeant had identified Destiny, the first two troopers decided to keep Ralph out of the car to search him.

"What about them?" Ralph complained. "They stole my grandpa's truck and you're just letting them get away!"

As soon as Destiny had climbed out of the car, a trooper turned her around and handcuffed her wrists behind her back, adding confusion to her already woozy mind.

"We can get out of this," Blake thought to her.

"No," she thought back. "This may be my vision of the trial. We knew it would come to this."

Blake could tell there was more to it than just that. He sensed the turmoil in her mind as the world reeled around her.

"It's okay," she thought to him. "I think I'm feeling better already."

Ralph was livid. He sprang away from the trooper and yelled, "What the hell are you doing? You let the stolen truck go right through your blockade and now you're hassling her?"

The trooper that had searched him now spun him around and slapped handcuffs on him.

"What's that for?" Ralph demanded.

"Resisting arrest for starters. Then there's aiding and abetting."

Ralph nodded to Blake, who had remained calmly in the car and asked, "What about him? Are you done with him?"

The troopers looked at each other and at the sergeant and shrugged their shoulders. "Yeah," one said. "I guess so."

"Take the car," Ralph yelled out as they dragged him away.

"No," Blake yelled back, looking straight at Destiny. "I can't leave her."

"Go!" Destiny yelled. "Get the amulet back. I need it to save my mother!"

That triggered something in the back of Blake's mind. They must save her mother.

Destiny was pushed into a squad car and Ralph pleaded with Blake, "Take the car and chase that bitch down!"

Blake slid into the driver's seat. The brake, gas and steering wheel were the same as the limo, but that's where the similarity ended. It had clusters of gauges that were added onto the dash and were unfamiliar to him. "Here goes," Blake said to himself.

The car rocketed out onto the road in a spray of rocks and dust. It was less a show of indifference to the police, as it was Blake's unfamiliarity with this much raw power. Ordinarily, such a show of speed directly in front of so many patrol cars would lead to a quick end to his story, but they had their quarry and weren't interested in writing up a mundane traffic citation. Just beyond the roadblock was old highway twenty-six, the same road which had brought them here.

Blake didn't see which way the truck went but he knew there was nothing to the right where they had come from getting here, so he squealed the car around to the left and launched it down the road.

Johnson and the two orange bandana cloaked librarians completed their counter clockwise circle of the farm's perimeter. Their attention was duly set on the commandos, and they completely missed the excitement between Destiny and Honey, but after they subdued the last soldier, they saw the lights at the end of the road.

The third librarian sat in the meditation room with his friends and saw the smiles erode from their faces. He closed his eyes and said to Johnson, "What happened? I thought it was going so well."

"Just a second," Johnson thought back.

He tried hiding behind the fence, but it wasn't much of a fence. White wooden rails on sunken posts did not provide them much cover, but at least it was getting dark. Johnson crouched down below the fence's height and crept along the road on the farm side of the fence. He wished he had scouted what was in the pastures and hoped it wasn't some crazy bull.

As he neared the collection of police vehicles, he held up his hand in a fist, indicating that they should stop. The second librarian ran into him, anyway.

"Well?" the third librarian asked Johnson. "What's going on?"

"It's the police," Johnson thought. "We eliminated the mercenary threat, but the police have taken a girl and a boy into custody."

"Is it them?" the librarian asked.

"I can see them through the window. The girl looks about the same age; blonde hair and... wait, she's turning her head this way. It's her. I recognize her now."

"Excellent," the third librarian said. "Our master will be pleased."

The second librarian crept to the fence and started to rise above for a better look when Johnson pulled him back down and yanked on the orange bandana while shaking his head no. The librarian removed his bandana and peeked over the fence for a better look, and saw the patrol car leave with Destiny and Ralph inside.

"Was it them?" the first librarian whispered.

"Yes," the second said. "I also recognize her, too."

The third librarian thought to Johnson, "You're done here. Your next objective is in Gulfport. You'll have to hurry. They are already ahead of you."

"All of us?" Johnson thought back.

"No, they have another rendezvous."

The road outside was dark. The truck's headlights were old and weak and dimly illuminated the center line dividing the two lanes, but Abilene wasn't letting off the old truck's gas pedal.

"I shoulda grabbed a faster car," Abilene said.

"Yeah," Honey said snidely. "There's a reason why you never hear about getaway trucks!"

Abilene didn't want to leave the farm. Her power was strongest at the farm, but she needed to regroup somewhere. She reached the turnoff to Gulfport and left twenty-six behind. Highway Forty-nine was bigger and faster, and she knew she could find some place to lay low in Gulfport. She took one hand off the wheel and snapped her fingers, sending little forks of lightning out from her hand.

"Hey, watch that!" Honey screamed when one zapped her in the arm.

"Sorry, just wanted to do that one last time before we gets too far away from home. What's that you got there?"

Honey was spinning the amulet around by the chain and staring into the gem. "I dunno," she said, "but that blonde bitch was wearing it and it glowed for her. I think she used it to make the ground shake, leastwise, that seemed to be when it glowed the most."

"Here," Abilene said. "Let me see it." She reached over to grab it, but Honey pulled it away.

"Hell no," Honey snapped at her mother. "It's mine now."

She looked at the ends of the chain. The chain had snapped when she yanked it off of Destiny's neck. She tied the chains together and slipped the chain over her head, then slid the amulet down into the low neckline of her shirt.

"I'll just wear it until I figure out how to use it. If this is what gave that bitch her power, then I'm just gonna let it do the same for me."

Blake couldn't bring himself to call the car Honey, and he certainly wasn't going to talk to the car or pet the dashboard. The asphalt wasn't as smooth or fresh as it was when they first crossed onto the old highway, but it still maintained a faded double yellow line down the middle. The soft shoulder of the road sometimes fell off into brush and open fields, leaving the lanes narrower in spots.

Just a mile down the road, the two-lane highway narrowed and plunged into a forest. The yellow line faded away, and the shoulders were lined with thick stands of trees which stretched up overhead and disappeared into the inky night. In the dark, the trees made the road feel like a tunnel. Blake kept his foot on the pedal and went as fast as he dared, but as the road roughened, the expanse of his dare softened.

He wished he could have a sign that he was going in the right direction. He thought about pulling over and trying to search out Honey's mind, but he was afraid she would get further away if he did.

Destiny closed her eyes and fought through the fogginess in her brain. "Nana?" she thought.

Michelle had been discussing Zeb's condition with his caretakers. She was particularly interested in how and when he had been struck down. She felt lightheaded, for a moment, as her heart was filled with panic. "Cherie?" she asked. "Is you okay? I heard you was in a fight and run off. Where is you?"

Ashlin ran into the room and tugged on Michelle's sleeve to get her attention.

"Just a second, darling," Michelle said to Ashlin.

"We have a problem," Destiny thought. "I'm okay, I think, but I've been arrested by the police."

Ashlin said, "Something's wrong. I'm scared."

"Just a second," Michelle said. "Arrested?" she thought. "What on earth for?"

"I dunno exactly. They didn't say, but it might be like my visions. Do you suppose it could be for killing those men in the fire already?"

Ashlin sucked in her breath and covered her mouth with her hands.

"What?" Michelle thought. "You ain't even the one that done that! Is Blake with you?"

"No, I'm with Cousin Ralph. They arrested him too. Blake is in Ralph's car trying to get my amulet back."

Ashlin tried tugging Michelle's hand while she said, "We need to tell Auntie Laura."

"Oh Lordy," Michelle thought. "Where is they takin' you? I'll get someone to drive me."

Ralph had been watching Destiny's expression and asked, "Are you okay?"

Destiny said, "Just a second," and thought to her nana, "The car they put us in has Hattiesburg on the sides, but I think they mean to send me back to Cricket Bend."

"All right, we'll come up and see if we can straighten this out. I'm sure Cousin Ralph will need a ride back, at least."

"Come on," Ashlin said urgently, still tugging on Michelle's hand. "Auntie Laura needs to know."

Librarian's one and two collected the mercenaries from around the farm and herded them into the same van they arrived in. They returned the men to somewhere near the small hovel where they had started the operation. They locked the van and tossed the keys under the van. One of them would escape eventually, or someone will find them. They climbed into their own car and left for their next destination in Utah.

The tunnel created by the trees curved around to the right and took Blake on a long sweeping arc that ended in a junction with a dirt road on the left and a barely paved road on the right. He turned right and followed the paved road for another mile until he came to yet another road. The sign said it was Old Highway twenty-six.

"Damn it!" he thought to himself. "I thought I was on twenty-six."

He turned right and followed the road until he came to a familiar split.

"I've seen this before."

He took the left split this time and plunged into another tunnel created by the trees overhead. It shot straight across a corner of the forest and emerged out the other side, a mere two miles further. The road turned west, and a faded yellow line returned. The trees still lined the right-hand side but across the other side of the street were empty fields, invisible in the dark, but Blake could see solitary mailboxes set on posts at intervals and telephone poles along the way. Occasionally, he could see his headlights reflect off the wires that stretched between the tall log poles.

He accelerated slightly, hoping to catch sight of the truck's taillights ahead, but he had yet to see any other vehicles on the road. He now wished the car could drive itself. If it could, he would even talk to it and stroke the console if it were able to guide itself down the road. No doubt, it would know the way and be much faster than he was.

***

Michelle's mind was spinning. Ashlin led her out of the main house and she was blindly following, not sure what she should do.

"Auntie Laura will know what to do," Ashlin said.

Michelle asked, "How old is you? You sure is an amazing young woman."

"I'm twelve, but my mama says I has an old soul."

"I think maybe your mama is right," Michelle said. "You reminds me so much of my Destiny."

Ashlin smiled and said, "Destiny and I are sisters now. She's tellin' me her secrets..." She stopped suddenly and put her hands on her mouth. "Oops," she said. "That was a secret."

"Dass okay," Michelle said. "I knows her secrets pretty good too. It sounds to me like she be doin' a bit more than just tellin' you her secrets and you be learnin' a bit much for you age; purty fast too, if you asks me."

Ashlin continued showing Michelle the way to Laura and said, "I always been a fast learner."

"Destiny too. Mebbe you is like sisters. So, where is it that you be takin' me?"

"Auntie Laura is Cousin Ralph's mama. He don't have no daddy, so she had to teach him about cars and stuff her own self. She fixes cars for the Poplarville police. I don't think they like Hattiesburg too much, leastways, not when they gets together at picnics and such. I'm sure she'll know what to do."

Michelle shook her head in amazement and followed the young redhead. *Old soul indeed.*

Destiny reached out again and said, "Blake?"

Blake jerked the car over the center line a bit but righted himself back in his lane and said, "I'm here, but I'm lost."

"I'm okay, you don't have to worry about me. Just get the amulet back."

Blake continued to rocket down the empty road. Trees roared by on the right with occasional signs of civilization on the left. "They're gone," he screamed out in frustration. "I don't know where they have gone or even where I am going."

"I feel you," she said.

"Thank you," he said, "but that doesn't help."

"No," she said softly. "I feel you. I can sense where you are and point my finger to you."

"I thought about pulling over and getting into Honey's head to find them."

"NO!" she yelled into his mind. "I don't want you getting into any part of her! I mean..."

She stopped abruptly, and he said, "It's okay, I know what you mean, besides, I'm afraid it will take too long and they will just get farther away from me."

"I was talking about us," she said. "I can feel you. Can't you feel me?"

"You want me to pull over and sense where you are? How is that going to help?"

"Don't stop the car," she sighed. "I was just hoping that part of you always told you where I was, like a compass."

The police caravan with Destiny and Ralph turned north from highway twenty-six to forty-nine north.

"Did you just turn?" Blake asked.

"Yes!" Destiny exclaimed. "You CAN feel me."

"I still don't see how that's going to help me. I doubt they are taking the same road."

"Search that feeling. The amulet she took from me has some of my power stored up in it. I was hoping maybe you could sense it too."

Blake calmed his breathing but felt nothing new for Destiny. "Nope," he said. "I can only sense you."

Destiny sighed and said, "Oh well. You keep going. I'm stuck in the back of the car here. I might as well try to reach some ancestors and see if they can help."

***

Ashlin led Michelle down the stairs and out across the yard to one of the dormitories. Inside, she walked her to a bedroom door and knocked.

When the door opened, Ashlin said, "Auntie Laura, Cousin Michelle has something to tell you, Ralph's in trouble."

"Ashlin?" Michelle said sternly. "Allow me?"

Laura stepped out and walked into the yard looking around. "Where's my boy? What happened?"

"He's okay," Michelle said. "He went with my Destiny to follow Abilene and Honey. I think he wanted to help Destiny get back the necklace Honey stole from her, but they was arrested at the end of the road."

"Arrested?" Laura asked. "Why would he be arrested?"

"That's a longer story," Michelle said, "but I think Ralph was arrested just for being with Destiny, or mebbe he tried standing up for her. She thinks they is taking them to Hattiesburg."

Laura went back to her room, grabbed her keys off the dresser and said, "Let's go get them." She led them across the compound to the garage where her tow truck was parked.

Ashlin started climbing in jond Michelle complained, "Just where do you think you be goin' little lady?"

"She's my sister now. I gots to see that she's alright."

Michelle was ready to bark out no when Laura said, "Let her go. We'll watch her."

"Then we should tell her mama."

"I just did," Laura said. "That's a pretty neat trick you brung with you, sharing our thoughts."

Ashlin climbed into the middle and Michelle followed behind her.

Laura started up the truck and headed out to the road. She picked up the mic on her radio and said, "This is unit 91, unit 91, dispatch? Come back."

"This is dispatch. Laura? It's Katie. What's up?"

"Sounds like my boy got himself in some trouble with Hattiesburg. Can someone find out what's up with them?"

"Sure thing. I'll get this over to Ned."

"Thanks Katie, he had a cousin with him. Her name is Destiny. I'm on the road heading up there now. Lemme know what you find out."

"You bet. Ten-four."

At the end of the drive, Laura turned onto old twenty-six and asked, "So why don't you start that long story?"

Michelle said, "After Destiny brung back her powers, four men came to our home in the Bayou. Three of them had rifles and machine guns, but the fourth had the fire and lightning. He was a hunert times worse that what I seen from Abilene. They came to kill us. Destiny fought back and two of them escaped, but two of them never left."

Laura waited for more and after a long pause, Michelle said, "I guess it tain't such a long story after all."

"So," Laura said. "You killt two men and fled the scene? No wonder they is after you."

"They burnt down our home," Michelle answered. "We had nowhere to go. And besides, how was we gonna explain dose bodies dat were not more than a pile of ashes?"

"Yeah," Laura nodded. "I see what you mean. Let's hope if we can't explain it, neither can they."

Abilene was distracted. She could have been distracted because her whole world just turned upside down, again, but that wasn't it. Her world had just undergone a complete transformation when she had suddenly discovered her powers just a few weeks ago. Then it changed again when she managed to subdue and incapacitate Zeb so she could take over the farm. Everything was perfect until Michelle strolled in. But, all of that was tucked away in the back of her mind. Right now, her mind was occupied with thoughts about the bauble that was currently tucked away in Honey's shirt.

She kept the truck speeding down the road, but her eyes kept pulling off the road and wandering over to the amulet. Honey was sleeping with her head leaning against the window. Abilene reached over with her right hand and tried to delicately slip two fingers into the gap between Honey's breasts, but Honey slapped her mother's hand away and said, "Now who's the pervert here?"

Abilene put her hand back on the wheel and muttered, "Little bitch."

"I heard that, Mama."

Highway twenty six was still only one lane each direction with a broken yellow line between them, but Blake had emerged from the forested area and was now driving through businesses and homes with mowed grass lining the road. Some of the homes sported white picket fences or white railed fences with pasture land for horses while most of the businesses had cyclone fencing with an array of trucks parked inside. Most of the homes still had wide open yards with no fencing and only wilderness for a backyard.

The number of businesses grew denser and the remaining forest receded away. Gas stations became more plentiful as Blake approached highway forty-nine which could either take him to Hattiesburg or Gulfport. Destiny was heading to Hattiesburg. He could feel her tug at him from the North. He had no idea what remained east of here, but forty-nine appeared to be two lanes moving much faster than twenty-six and his instincts told him that's where Abilene and Honey would flee. He took the south exit heading to Gulfport wishing he could have a better sign that this was the right direction.

Forty-nine wasn't just wider than twenty-six. It had sprawling lanes that were wide and comfortable. A large grassy depression separated the North and South bound lanes and an equally wide shoulder lined the road. The roadway was lit at crossroads, but even without street lamps, there was no forest to block out the moon which illuminated the highway. There was also more traffic. He was no longer alone on this road. He pulled over into the left-hand lane and passed one semi after another. If he was going to catch them, he would have to weave around trucks and travelers. The road wasn't fresh black top, but it was smooth enough and for him to catch the old truck that they stole, if they were even going in this direction. He stepped on the accelerator and Honey responded. Blake winced slightly when he realized that he even thought of the car by her name.

The conditions were clear, and Blake hoped to spot the truck's taillights ahead of him.

***

The wind rushing by the cars was the only noise Destiny heard as the police convoy sped up highway forty-nine to Hattiesburg. They had their lights on and their sirens off, and there was little chatter on the radio to break the silence at this hour of the morning. The police were focused on returning to their station and paid no attention to anything they passed on the road.

Destiny sat quietly in the back seat. The horrible dizziness was fading away. She was relieved to have her mind back, but she still didn't know what had caused the weakness. She closed her eyes and once again slipped into the void to search out her friend Marvalaine. When she opened her eyes, she was standing on a balcony looking over a river and a broad green field. Merchants crossed a bridge over the river, some with oxen and others with asses pulling carts full of their wares.

"Beautiful morning," Marvalaine said standing next to her. "Wouldn't you say?"

"Yes," she replied, "very striking, and quite the opposite of my life at the moment."

"Oh, I guess I shan't ask you how you are doing then."

"I'm sorry," she said, "and what of you? How are the children and that great beast that watches over them?"

"What was that?" he asked. "Did you just call Nimisen a beast?"

"Nimisen? No! His name was Chauncey and he..."

"Chauncey? That little pup?"

"Prepare yourself," she warned him. "He will grow to be as big as an ox and about half as graceful. You may need to add a wing on to your castle for him."

Marvalaine laughed and said, "Chauncey and the children are well. How may I help you?"

"Have you ever heard of a place that makes one of us sick? We went to my grandpa Zeb's farm, and I started getting light-headed all the time. But when the police took me away from the farm, I started to feel better."

"What is a police?"

"Oh," she said, "I'm sorry. A police is a law keeper; a constable; a sheriff. I'm not sure what you call them here."

"We have sheriffs, although I suspect that some realms only have their executioners to keep the peace."

Destiny winced at the thought.

"I know of no place that has such an effect upon us, but I can ask and get back to you."

"Would you?"

Marvalaine looked puzzled and replied, "I just said I would."

"Sorry," Destiny shrugged. "It's a phrase from my time."

***

The highway made a wide sweeping turn to the left and Blake could see the truck tail lights ahead in the darkness. Honey was itching to surge ahead and catch it, but they were boxed in by a semi-truck trying to pass another semi-truck. The truck in the left lane inched forward until it was ahead of the other semi, but it wasn't rushing to pull over.

In a mad impulsive gesture that Blake would have loved to blame on the car, he jerked it over to the right lane and rocketed ahead of the semi before it pulled over. He zipped past and back into the left lane. The engine roared as the throttle opened and the super chargers gulped in more air. There was little traffic between himself and the truck, allowing him to close the gap quickly, but it was the wrong truck. He knew it before he had even reached it. He could feel that it was the wrong truck because the further away he got from Destiny, the more he could feel the amulet ahead of him.

He pulled around the pickup and followed the amulet.

Abilene passed the cloverleaf at I-10 and forty-nine changed from a raised divided highway to a street highway. She hadn't really planned out what she would do when she reached Gulfport, but she figured she would just get a room and lay low while she contacted Frank for help.

The truck stalled then surged forward waking Honey.

"Shit," Abilene said.

"What was that?" Honey asked.

"Nothin'. We's just out of gas."

Honey pointed over to the right and said, "There's a gas station, let's just pull in there."

"I barely grabbed enough cash for a hotel room."

"There's a hotel," Honey said, pointing again, but Abilene didn't stop there. "Mama, you passed it."

"I want to ditch this old truck, anyway. Find me someplace that's busy lookin'."

The truck stalled and surged again.

"Quick," Abilene said. "Find me someplace with a lot of cars."

"There!" Honey exclaimed. "That looks like a club in that mall."

Abilene pulled into the mall lot and the truck died. She rolled it into a parking space in front of a hardware store. She would have preferred getting to where most of the cars were, but at least she got it away from the main street.

———

Laura Boutin-Macleon knew the way to Hattiesburg by heart and could drive it in her sleep. She had been through the police academy and even though she never finished; she knew the system of due process well enough to know nothing was going to happen to the kids tonight. Michelle had no such background to comfort her, and she fretted the whole drive up. Ashlin remained quiet in the middle seat, preferring to listen for signs of panic from her new sister.

"Unit 91, Unit 91..."

Laura picked up the mic and replied, "91 here."

"Be advised that your boy and that girl are being held under suspicion of murder."

"Murder?" Laura cried out. "Ralph only just met the girl!"

"The D.A. will probably sort that out before they see the judge in the morning. Justin says to call him if you need his help."

"10-4. Thank you, Katie."

"I'm sorry," Michelle said, "that we brung you all this trouble."

"I wish I could say don't worry about it," Laura replied. "I reckon I'm plenty worried, but when those men came to your property with machine guns, you was just defendin' yourselves."

"That's gonna be mighty hard to explain."

"You just has to tell the truth."

"The truth?" Michelle asked. "The house was burnt to the ground by sorcerer magic. How's that truth sound to you?"

"Okay," Laura admitted. "Maybe you needs to sugarcoat the truth a bit. It was still self-defense."

"Yeah you right," Michelle said, "and the funny truth is dey had Destiny and me tied to the chairs and that sorcerer fella was torturing Destiny. He was about to kill her when that boy she is sweet on stands up and burns him from the insides."

"From the insides?" Laura asked.

"Yeah," Michelle said quietly. "It was all horrible and kinda beautiful at the same time. I ain't never seen a worse man than dat one. He deserved him a hunert times worse death than dat."

"So," Laura said. "Your Destiny can say she didn't do it and be tellin' the truth."

"True dat," Michelle said.

Laura continued, "These guys is good at seeing when someone lies to them, and it's good to have some truth to tell them."

"Das good to know," Michelle said.

"Of course," Laura added, "that's only if they is lookin' for the truth and not already made up their minds."

Blake reached Gulfport and found cross streets everywhere. He was never going to spot the truck now. His only hope was to follow the amulet.

The street was lined with chain hotels and fast food. They could be anywhere. He pulled to a stop at a red light and tried to feel for Destiny. She was still ahead. The light changed, and he pulled forward, then, as he was passing a mall, he felt the amulet shift to his right and immediately slammed on the brakes and found an entrance into the mall.

The parking lot was largely empty, except for the cars that congregated around what looked like a nightclub. He drove directly towards the interior of the mall lot and felt the amulet to his right again. He hoped that meant they were in the parking lot. He turned to the right and slowly went down the aisle.

Abilene had more luggage than they could carry. She and Honey were repacking the essentials into two bags when Abilene heard Ralph's car drive by. She popped her head up and asked, "What the hell is he doing here?"

Honey looked up and recognized the car. "Thank heaven," she said. "He'll give us a ride and we can take all this shit with us."

"What makes you think he'll give us a ride?"

"Cause he's sweet on me."

"Like hell he is. You lost that boy long ago."

Honey checked her hair in the mirror and said, "That's ancient history. Once I tell him we need his help, he'll be happy to pitch in. I just has to ask him sweetly."

"You means, you just has to wiggle your butt and ask him to take us to a hotel. And I bet ya anything that you's expectin' me to wait outside."

"So?" Honey asked. "As long as it gets us there, what's the difference?"

Ralph's car turned down their isle and Abilene ducked her head down and said, "Shit! That ain't Ralph. It's that new boy."

"So? He wants the same thing Ralph wants, only he don't know it yet."

Abilene pulled Honey between the cars and said, "Get your tramp ass outa the street. That boy's with blondie and you knows it. We gots to hide. Run into the club."

"But we can't take this luggage into a club!"

"Just leave it behind and move your dumb ass!"

Blake slowed the car as he went down the parking isle. They were somewhere ahead of him when he started down this row, but now he could feel it tug to the left. He stopped the car. The amulet was moving, but slowly.

Blake pulled the car into a stall and parked it. He got out and just followed his senses. He closed his eyes and tried to pinpoint where it came from but was startled by a car horn.

"Get outa the road!"

Blake stepped out of the way and said, "Sorry." But the driver had already left down the aisle.

He turned back in the direction of the amulet. He crossed through a row of parked vehicles. He saw a truck across the aisle. He crossed over and saw their luggage inside the truck.

"Found you," he thought to himself with a smile. He opened the door and searched the luggage until he felt the amulet move again.

"Damn," he thought. "She still has it."

He looked past the parking lot towards the amulet and saw the club. He didn't think Honey was smart enough to hide in a crowd, but her mother might be.

And Honey was dumb enough to want a good time even in the middle of a chase.

———

Honey and Abilene entered the club and saw the bouncer carding a girl ahead of them. Honey flashed him a big smile and cozied up to him, brushing her breast against his arm and he passed her on though. Abilene just shook her head and muttered, "Skank."

Curtains were hung in the door keeping the light in the entryway from interfering with the performances. Abilene parted the curtains and stepped through. The scent of onions and garlic lingered from the dinner service. Squinting didn't help Abilene see in the dim light, but as her eyes adjusted, she spotted a table close to an exit but facing the entrance. She grabbed Honey's hand and led her through the back row to the table she spotted.

"We'll just wait here a bit," Abilene said. "If that boy don't show up, then we can go back to the truck, collect our clothes and hike it to the hotel."

Honey didn't really hear her. She was already watching the stage act.

A tall man in a tuxedo and top hat stood center stage and called out, "I need two volunteers for this next illusion." He stalked back and forth on the stage counting off the numerous patrons with their hands in the air until he finally pointed to a table on the right side of the audience and said, "You sir." Then he pointed to the other side of the room and said, "And you ma'am, if you would come up here, please."

Two attractive young girls went to the tables and escorted the volunteers up onto the stage. The tall man shook their hands as they were brought center stage to join him and asked, "Do either of you know me?"

They each shook their heads no, and he said, "Good. Last time I did this trick, the volunteers were from my ex-wife's family and they threw away the key."

He stepped forth on the stage and said, "Houdini was the greatest escape artist the world has ever known. Can I hear some applause for Harry Houdini?"

The crowd cheered and clapped.

"And now, can you give it up for Douglass the MagicMan?" He flapped his hands in the air to lead the clapping and pointed to himself, but received only a smattering of applause; much less cheering and clapping than he got for Houdini.

"Really?" he asked, "You're not my ex-wife's family too, are you?"

He turned to his volunteers and said, "What are your names?"

The man said, "Jim."

The woman said, "Candice."

He handed his coat to Candice and the handcuffs to Jim and said, "I want you to inspect these and make sure they are real and there are no lock picks, hidden keys, hand grenades or trapdoors."

The audience laughed while the volunteers inspected the items.

"Now," he said, "in honor of the great Harry Houdini, I would like to perform my famous handcuff escape, well, maybe it's not that famous, but my kids like it."

Honey snickered and said, "He's funny."

"Would you look at these people?" Abilene asked. "Do they really think that this is magic?"

"You want me to up there and show them the real thing?"

"No, just let them go on believing what they can see."

Destiny and Ralph arrived in Hattiesburg and were escorted into a brilliantly lit room for processing. Word of the two murder suspects had spread throughout the precinct and more than a handful of officers were present, watching them from the sidelines. It wasn't like Hattiesburg had never had a murder investigation before, but nobody remembered having one with a manhunt and extradition orders to another state.

The sergeant on the scene delivered Destiny to the booking desk herself. A couple of the onlookers ogled Destiny as she walked by and the patrolman who had witnessed Honey's brazen display joined them to share the story.

Destiny had seen her trial in her visions, but she hadn't seen any of this. It was brighter than she would have expected. She always pictured police departments and prisons were dark and gloomy places. This was bright like a hospital, and it even smelled like a hospital. She breathed in deeply and detected a hint of vomit and booze and understood why there was a strong odor of ammonia.

She wasn't overly worried about her situation. The trial had been revealed to her, even before those men tried to ambush them in their home. And she knew how the trial came out, assuming things in visions don't change. She was much more concerned about her mother and the visions she had of the world's destruction than she was of the trial.

Two officers from Lafayette waited patiently with their backs against the wall while the sergeant signed the necessary forms handing Destiny into the department's care. She glanced up at them and said, "You boys are mighty anxious, aren't you? How'd you know we'd have her already?"

They snickered and one of them said, "Interoffice cooperation and all that."

"Uh huh," she replied. "Are you boys sure about this girl? She doesn't seem the type."

"It'll all come out in the trial then, won't it?"

The processing clerk completed the paperwork and moved Destiny over to the finger printing station. Destiny looked around at all the people gathered in the room rather than watch the clerk roll her fingers on the pad and then again on the paper.

After finger printing, Destiny was taken into a private room and searched. She was spared the humiliation of an invasive body search, but she was patted down thoroughly by a matronly officer who sneered at her while she ran her hands up the insides of Destiny's thighs. After her search, she was taken to a detainment room and left alone.

Blake entered the club and the bouncer immediately said, "You can't come in here like that."

Blake looked at himself. His clothes were a mess. He pushed a new image into the bouncers mind and asked, "Why? What's wrong?"

The bouncer now saw a crisp Italian suit and froze for a second then said, "Look kid, no way you're getting in here at your age."

"My age?" Blake asked.

The bouncer now saw somebody complete different in his mid-thirties. He shook his head and rubbed his eyes saying, "I'm sorry sir, something must have been in my eye. Go on in."

Blake divided the curtains at the door and pushed through. The bartender eyed him suspiciously, so he expanded the range of his illusion. He stepped to the side and stood in the back of the room trying to sense the amulet. He felt it loud and clear to his right.

Douglass the MagicMan raised his hands in the air with the hand-cuffs dangling from his fingers and said, "Let's give a big round of applause for our two volunteers Candice and Jim."

The audience clapped appreciatively.

He then walked to the left side of the stage. The stage lights went black leaving only a spot on the magician. "Ladies and Gentlemen," he said. "It is every magician's dream to invent an illusion so big that it is named after him. Well, I think I have finally done it. A couple weeks ago, I was in the Orient looking at knives and food processors, when I was struck by the inspiration for this next illusion. It's true! I sense some disbelievers among you, but I swear to you that I was standing in the middle of the kitchen appliance department at Orient Imports at 55 and Lexington, when I had this idea for a new illusion. I call it the DOUGSU 5000 CHOP-O-MATIC."

A spot light opened on center stage revealing the medieval-looking guillotine with DOUGSU 5000 emblazoned across the top.

Blake saw Honey across the room. He started crossing the room to her table when Johnson grabbed him from behind and quickly said, "A mutual friend sent me here to help you."

Blake's first instinct was to fry the man. He whipped around and freed his arm but before he did anything, Johnson put his hands in the air and said, "Easy kid, I'm unarmed. I don't know what you guys are into, and I don't want to know. But this friend of yours keeps getting in my head and telling me to warn you not to do what you are thinking of doing."

"That's really vague," Blake said. "Who is this friend?"

Johnson just shrugged his shoulders and said, "I don't know, and I guess he didn't want to trust me with whatever it is you are into, but ask yourself this: How'd I know it was you when you don't look like yourself?"

Johnson was right. He couldn't have recognized Blake without some kind of help. He looked Johnson in the eye and asked, "Are you going to try to stop me? You remember what happened to your friends?"

Johnson shook his head vigorously. "I'm just a messenger. He wants me to warn you not to do it." Johnson did remember what happened to Hughes and Brian, although he never considered Brian to be a friend. Johnson was fully aware that he couldn't have stopped Blake by force. He would have to reason with him.

Blake was uncomfortable that Johnson knew his plan and claimed that he had a friend who apparently knew even more. He pretended to stand in the back and watch the show while keeping an eye on Honey. He inched over to his right, working his way around the tables and patrons lined along the back wall.

Johnson watched him slink away and disappear into the smoke.

Johnson just shrugged and shook his head, then headed down the aisle to the left side of the stage.

———

Abilene was getting nervous. She'd been watching the entrance, looking for Blake, but he never showed. Instead, some strange guy in a suit was watching them. She leaned over close to Honey and said, "Do you recognize that guy in the fancy suit across the room?"

Honey looked over through the crowd and said, "No, why?"

"He keeps looking at us."

Honey perked up and said, "He's not looking at us, he's looking at me. Guys do that."

"Come on," Abilene said. "Let's get out of here."

"Heck no, maybe he can help us."

"Look at him! He's staring at that damned thing you gots round your neck."

"That ain't what he's looking at," Honey said, "and guys like to look at them too, a lot. Besides, look at his suit. He looks like he gots money. We can get him to help us get a hotel room, easy."

But as he approached the table, Honey realized that her mother was right, and he was staring straight at the amulet. She jumped up from her seat and headed straight down the aisle towards the stage.

Abilene followed and said, "Where you going, the exit is the other way!"

Blake saw them take off and was not far behind.

Douglass the MagicMan scanned the crowd again and said, "I need a volunteer from the audience. Not just any volunteer. Our volunteer should be fearless with a good head on his or her shoulders with a neck size smaller than twenty-four inches and a shoe size no larger than fifteen. Okay, I don't know why we need the shoe size. The lawyers from my insurance company made me put that in. If you think you meet these qualifications, please see my lovely assistant and sign the release waiver in triplicate."

One of the magician's assistants intercepted Blake as he slipped down the aisle towards the backstage door. She turned him towards the audience and flashed a big friendly smile.

"You sir," the MagicMan said. "Come on up here and tell us your name."

Blake shook his head and said, "No thank you, not me." He tried following Honey but the other assistant joined them and tugged on his other arm, pulling him towards the stage.

The MagicMan clapped his hands and said, "I think he needs a little encouragement, ladies and gentlemen, let's all give him a nice hand."

The crowd put their hands together and Blake let the assistants lead him up the stairs to the stage.

Once Blake was in the magician's hands, the first assistant went offstage and met with Johnson who counted out two hundred dollars for her.

Honey stopped and hid behind a prop to watch the show.

"Hello sir," the magician said. "What's your name?"

"Bla-," Blake stopped himself from giving his real name and said, "Billy."

"Hello BluhBilly, where are you from?"

"Florida," Blake lied.

"Well, BluhBilly from Florida, let me introduce you to the DOUGSU 5000 CHOP-O-MATIC. It slices and dices and chops all your spices, but it won't cut you! Now if you would kindly put your head through that hole."

Abilene had already reached the stage door but had to return to find Honey. "Come on girl, we got to go."

"I want to watch," she whined. "Besides, that guy who was watching me is up there as a volunteer now."

Abilene peeked around a prop and saw the guy in the suit put his head into the guillotine. "Come on, baby, this is the perfect time to escape."

"What's your hurry? He's not going anywhere. I wonder if we can make the blade work for real."

Johnson stepped behind Honey and said, "Your mother's right. You need to go. He's not the only one following you."

Honey spun around with her hands in the air ready to fry Johnson. "Who the hell are you?"

Johnson raised his hands and showed his palms. He smiled and said, "I'm just a friend. I was sent here to help you out. You need a little money, don't you?"

Honey snarled at him, "I don't need nothin' and I don't like strangers messin' in my business."

Johnson pulled a few twenties out of his pocket and asked, "You sure?"

"And you don't want nothin' in return for this money?"

"Not a thing," he said.

"Cause it might be okay if you did."

Abilene grabbed the money and yelled, "Jesus girl! Stop jawin' and get your tramp ass out of here so we can go get that hotel room."

The apparatus smelled like a garage to Blake. He couldn't pinpoint a specific aroma like gas or oil, but it carried a musty storage smell that he equated to a garage. With his head in the blocks, all he could see was their feet, and with the magician at the front of the stage addressing the audience, only the assistant's feet were in view. The floor sparkled from the spot light reflecting off her sequined dress.

"Ladies and gentlemen," the magician said. "Are you ready? On the count of three, I will pull the cord releasing the blade at the top of the DOUGSU 5000 CHOP-O-MATIC."

He turned to Blake and said, "You may want to hold on to your head, just in case."

Returning his attention to the audience, he said, "Are you ready?"

"One..."

"Two days ago, I had a minor malfunction in my workshop." The magician took his hat off and held it over his heart and said, "Benny was a good assistant, but I assure you that I spent all night working out what I think was the final kink. Are you ready?"

"On the count of three..."

"One..."

"Two..."

Blake found himself staring at the assistant's feet. Her silver strapped heels sparkled as much as the floor. The magician's voice was fading from Blake's hearing as he felt the reflections on the floor taking him to a distant memory.

The scent of the apparatus was replaced with the fetid musk of smoke and burned flesh. He remembered the smell from the small island in the swamp where they fled the destruction of Destiny's home. The sky was blotted out by a thick blanket of smoke. It wasn't dark. It was still daytime, but a round orange circle in the smoke overhead was all he could see of the sun.

Blake walked through the streets. Everything wood was charred and broken. Some structures still burned as glowing coals that crackled and consumed any fuel remaining. Steel poles and girders rose from the concrete but were bent and twisted from the heat and destruction that had passed through here. Nothing was immune to the devastation.

Blake's host wept and asked, "Is there nothing we could have done to avoid this?"

A voice behind him responded, "Nothing is certain, but there are things we can try."

Blake turned around and faced the man in the grey robe. His face was hidden in by a hood that hung over his head. "I will try anything," Blake's host said. "Tell me."

The man pulled the grey hood back and let it hang from his shoulders. His face was burned beyond recognition on the left side. The burn swept back, taking most of his ear and all the hair on that side of his head. A tear fell from his right eye while he said, "I was there when the master was killed. I only overheard part of what he said, but what I heard was that all of this started when she got the amulet."

"She?" Blake asked. "Was he not more specific?"

"Alas, no. But, I believe it started even before that. I was there when we failed to prevent Destiny from reaching her mentor. I think that our attempts to prevent that meeting may have inadvertently led to her getting the amulet. It may be our fault."

Blake could feel tears on his host's cheeks as he asked, "Why were we so bent on preventing such a meeting?"

"Because our master said that her mentor would help her revive her mother, and that would have created a disaster of its own."

Blake climbed up some rubble and surveyed the destruction. "How did they become so powerful? Did we not hold them in check?"

The man in the grey robe replaced the hood over his face and sat down next to the rubble where Blake stood. "We held them in check, but their power radiated from the girl. Back to the moment she started it all. Their power grew as her fate faded. Even with them under our control, we were losing her."

"So it is our fault. All of it. And we have no hope of changing it."

"No hope of changing it?" his friend asked. "All we have done is change it. This is on us. Our only hope is to change it again and look around you now. What have we to lose?"

"What hope is that?"

"The mother. She may yet fix it."

Blake climbed down from the rubble and sat next to his friend. "Do we help her?"

"We must. But how much? I do not know."

Blake nodded and said, "If she asks, we will answer. Beyond that, we must tread carefully."

The vision popped from Blake's view as the magician said, "Three!"

The blade came crashing down from the top of the tower and into the chock below Blake's neck.

The magician removed the block and stood Blake up showing his fully intact head to the audience.

The M.C. yelled over the loudspeakers, "Let's hear it for Douglass the MagicMan!"

The audience roared with approval.

Honey clapped in the wings while Abilene mumbled, "Ninny," and pulled her out the stage door and led her back to the truck for their luggage.

Laura pulled the truck off the highway and into the amber glare of the Hattiesburg street lamps. Small trees lined the street at regular intervals with parking meters between them and a mostly empty street. The shops were closed and only dimly lit. The police station was only two blocks from the highway.

Laura drove slowly through the parking lot, but was unable to find an open space. She shook her head and said, "The parking lot shouldn't be this full this time of night." She piloted the truck back out of the lot and into an available spot on the street.

Michelle led Ashlin by the hand as she followed Laura to the front door and into the police station where they were met by a young nervous looking man.

He looked back and forth between the two women and finally extended his hand toward Laura and said, "Hello, my name is Avery Charles. Justin asked me to handle this case for him."

"You're a lawyer?" Laura asked.

"Yes, ma'am."

"But," Michelle said, "you're just a baby."

Avery blushed and said, "Yes, ma'am. I graduated young, but I assure you I'm fully qualified and licensed to practice in both Mississippi and Louisiana."

Michelle shook his hand, but worry distorted her expression.

Avery led them to the booking area and examined the warrants. "Are these all the warrants?" he asked.

"Yes sir," the booking clerk said.

"Did you even look at them?"

"Absolutely," the clerk replied. "Every 'i' was dotted and every 't' was crossed. The address of the location where they were intercepted is clearly indicated on the warrant along with names and descriptions of both suspects."

"Yes," Mr. Charles said. "They are very fine warrants and meticulously filled out, except for one thing."

This piqued the attention of the visiting officers from Lafayette as much as the clerk.

"The warrant is for a girl travelling in the company of a boy and an older woman."

Everyone looked over to Michelle.

Mr. Charles continued, "You have the wrong boy for sure. And seeing how you just picked up a boy and girl who were together in the same car, heaven knows if that's even the same girl in the warrant. Perhaps, and I suggest this only so you can avoid any embarrassment in front of a judge, perhaps you can simply remand them into my custody."

The officers from Lafayette stepped forward and scanned the documents, then looked at the suspects and scowled at the Hattiesburg officers.

Mr. Charles continued, "Right here, in the photocopy of the boy's license, his name is Ralph, not Blake." He paged through the girl's files.

The clerk said, "She didn't have any documentation."

"Is that what they do here in Hattiesburg?" Charles asked, "If you don't have documentation, you get thrown in jail under suspicion of whatever is handy? Is this Nazi Germany? Do you march around in your leather boots and demand, 'Show me your papers!'?"

One of the officers from Lafayette said, "If it's not her, then our eye witness won't pick her out of a lineup. But it's her. Just because she jumped into a car with another boy doesn't mean it's not her. For all we know, she'll jump into a car with any boy."

"Now just a minute," Michelle growled.

One of the arresting officers came forward and said, "There was another boy. He left in the car."

The Lafayette officer asked, "You let him go?"

"We only had the warrant for the girl. This boy was detained for resisting arrest."

"Resisting?" Charles asked. "Or was he just protesting his innocence?"

The arresting officer backed off a couple steps and the captain on duty came out of his office to weigh in, "You can have the boy, but the girl stays."

Laura hugged Avery and said, "Thank you Mr. Charles."

Michelle was terrified. Laura's contact sent a friend of his and he got her boy released. What would happen to her Destiny?

Charles saw the question in her eyes and said, "Don't you worry ma'am, I'm still on the case. I'll talk to your daughter and prepare a solid defense. She's in good hands."

Ashlin tugged on Michelle's sleeve and said, "I like him."

"Everything's going to be okay," Michelle thought to Destiny. "Mr. Charles here is going to take care of this for you."

"I know," Destiny thought back. "I've already seen Mr. Charles in my visions."

Blake left the theatre confused. He knew Destiny wanted the amulet back to save her mother. He also had seen the visions where her mother had to save Destiny. It was that circle thing he was told about. But he also knew Johnson. Someone with intimate knowledge about the future has gone to a lot of trouble to warn him about the amulet. Blake saw for himself how the world was being destroyed. Destiny had the same visions, and now there is someone else out there who claimed to know what he had planned to do and was there to stop him. It sure didn't come from Johnson. He had been in Johnson's mind before and he was no witch, but only a witch could have seen through his glamour. He should have invaded Johnson's mind to see who else was in there pulling the strings. They were a mystery, and he not only didn't know who they were, he didn't know why they didn't want Destiny to have the amulet. He trusted Destiny, and he trusted his own visions. If they were witches, and they appeared to be, he felt like he should trust them too, but didn't know who he trusted the most.

Black clouds collected around the moon darkening the small parking lot. A chill wind kicked up, and he tightened the collar of his coat, but the coat was an illusion and didn't keep the cold out. He dropped the glamour and was back in his t-shirt.

Blake returned to where he left the car. He probably should try to contact Destiny, but he wasn't sure, yet, how he would tell her the amulet got away. She could probably tell if he lied outright, especially if he tells her telepathically, and he didn't want to tell her he let them have it. He especially couldn't tell her about Johnson.

Michelle would freak if she ever learned that he met up with one of the mercenaries that had brought Blake to their home and then tried to kill them.

Chapter 8

Day three.

It has begun. Like a kettle of water on the fire: first one bubble forms; then another. The bubbles break free from the bonds that hold them to the bottom of the pot until the water is roiling with expanding bubbles fleeing to the surface and escaping into the air.

The world still didn't see the catastrophe that was just around the corner. Even those few who possessed the sight and were able to see a glimpse of what was coming couldn't understand what it meant. But little things will become known, and those little things will grow to big things until they escape their confines and explode upon the world.

Ashlin slept on Michelle's lap while Ralph drove the truck with his mother in the middle. It had been a long night in the police station and the sun was already lighting the sky in the East. The police station had been loud and tense, and Destiny's situation appeared dire, but she didn't seem to worry about it as much as Michelle. Michelle leaned her head against the window and succumbed to the dulling sensation of the road. She slept with Laura's dozing head on her shoulder.

Blake was already back at the farm when they arrived. He tossed the keys to Ralph and said, "Thanks."

"What happened?" Ralph asked. "Did you catch them?"

"Yeah, sort of. But they got away."

"They got away?" Michelle asked. "Did they put up a fight?"

Blake blushed and said, "Nah, I followed them into a club and was chasing them to an exit when I got picked as a volunteer for some magic show."

Michelle looked at him funny and said, "You're kidding me."

"Nope, it's the truth. He called himself Douglass the MagicMan."

"I heard of him," Ralph said, "Douglass the MagicMan. In fact, I saw him once in Baton Rouge. He's funny."

Michelle's voice dropped real low as she said, "So you let yourself be tricked into some magician's side show and let dem bitches escape? Is dat your story?"

"There's more to it than just that. I was warned to leave it alone. Twice. And you know, someone was trying real hard to prevent Destiny from getting that thing."

"Uhuh," Michelle said. "So when you says dey got away, you means you let 'em go."

Blake shrugged his shoulders, but nodded his head and said, "You had to be there."

"Well, I warn't there and I ain't gonna be. I gots to get back home to help get Destiny off of dem murder charges."

"She'll be okay," Blake said. "I saw it. She gets off."

"You seen it? Destiny's seen it! Who da hell be putting da curtain over my eyes?"

Blake shook his head and said, "I'll go get the car."

"Wait," Michelle said. "I dunno if we should be keepin' dat big ol' car. It tain't exactly ours."

"What?" Laura exclaimed. "You stole it? Wait, a minute! Don't answer that. I don't want to know."

"We didn't exactly steal it, I sorta used dat voice and made da driver give us his keys, asides, dey was shootin' guns at us."

"No problem," Ralph said. He tossed the keys for Honey over to Blake and continued, "I'll trade you. By the time I'm done with it, nobody will recognize it."

Laura covered her ears and left the conversation saying, "I definitely don't hear none of this."

The county clerk shook his head and said, "I don't know, this is all very irregular."

"Why?" Tangiers asked. "Don't you believe justice can be swift sometimes?"

The clerk looked at the paperwork and continued to shake his head.

"Is something wrong with the forms?" Tangiers asked.

"No," the clerk replied. "Everything appears to be in order, but there are no documents in here from either the coroner or any kind of crime tech and the alleged crime was only three days ago! That's hardly enough time for the police to complete their investigation."

"Well," Tangiers said smugly, "I understand your concerns and I realize that it's a little faster than usual, but as you yourself admitted, everything is in order."

The poor clerk was in over his head. He was just a law student working part time to supplement his scholarships and familiarize himself with how the administration side worked. He had no clout, but he knew enough to recognize when someone was being railroaded. "But," he said, "this is more than just fast, you've already arrested someone before the medical examiner has even declared this a murder yet. In fact, I don't even see any records at all from the M.E."

Tangiers smiled reassuringly and said, "She's there now looking at the remains. I've already seen them and the arson investigator has already said it looked suspicious."

The clerk was still shaking his head. "I don't have any records declaring arson, besides, you're trying to file charges of first degree murder! There's nothing here about arson."

The smile was starting to fade from Tangiers face. "Look son, you seem like a smart boy, but how long have you been here? I've been doing this a long time and I..."

"That's another thing," the clerk interrupted. "Who are you anyway? You don't work here. I don't know you. How can you file charges here?"

Tangiers pulled his wallet from his coat and opened it to his shield and slammed it against the thick glass that separated him from the clerk. "I was just transferred," he half yelled. "I'm sure the orders are working their way through the mail department. I'm really in no mood to debate this before a junior clerk.

I'd like to save my arguments for the jury. All you have to do is accept them, stamp them and log them in."

Ashlin was heartbroken. She gets a new sister and all the things in her head suddenly start to make sense, but after only one day, she loses her. She stood between Michelle and the car door pleading her case.

"You can't leave me behind," she cried to Michelle. "I'm her sister now, she needs me too."

"I'm sorry Ashlin, but your mama would miss you terrible. I knows how much I'm missin' Destiny already and I just cain't take you from her."

"You didn't even ask her!"

"I'm sorry Cherie, but I'm an old woman now and I don't know if I can watch you like you needs."

"MAMA!" Ashlin thought. "Please tell them I can go! Destiny is the big sister you never gave me and she needs me now!"

"Lordy girl," her mama thought back. "Wait right there while I come down to see them off."

Michelle sighed. Ashlin had the gifts, and at such a young age, like her own Tempest.

"Oh my God!" Ashlin exclaimed. "You can't leave her mama here! Savin' her mama is the most important thing in the world to her. If you leave her behind, Destiny will never forgive you."

"Yeah, you right," Michelle admitted, "but how in the world would I take care of her and help Destiny at the same time?"

Ashlin's mother burst out of the house behind Michelle and said, "Ashlin could help you care for your daughter."

Michelle turned around and saw that Ashlin's mother was carrying a medium-sized suitcase and a pink backpack with cartoons on it.

Ashlin hugged her mother exclaiming, "Thank you! Thank you! Thank you!"

Michelle looked perplexed and said, "But I ain't said yes yet."

Ashlin's mother shrugged and shook her head saying, "Dass okay, but there ain't no use fighting the inevitable. I'm Louise."

Louise handed the bags to Ashlin and Blake helped her heave the bigger bag into the trunk.

Michelle shook her hand and asked, "Is you sure 'bout this?"

Louise nodded and said, "You'd be doin' me a favor."

Michelle glanced at the precocious little redhead and said, "No doubt."

Word had spread that they were leaving already, and the family gathered around the car to say their goodbyes.

Angelica said, "I know that bitch Abilene said you was leaving in the morning, but I never believed it."

"Tain't how I planned it neither," Michelle replied. "Iffin it's alright with you folks, I'd sure like to come back when we gets this matter settled."

Agreement was expressed throughout the gathered family, then from the doorway to the main house, Zeb said, "You best come back, I ain't had my turn to visit with you yet. Besides, it seems like mebbe I kin use your help fendin' off Abilene if she ever slithers back here."

Michelle ran up to the porch and hugged Zeb, saying, "Dass a promise. But I spect the family mightn't be so easy for Abilene to run roughshod over no mores."

"You has a safe trip, cousin Michelle." Zeb waved as Michelle climbed into the car.

Blake pulled Honey out onto the drive. Ashlin waved at everybody from the back seat.

"Now," Zeb growled, "will someone please tell me how long I been asleep and what the hell's been goin' on in the meantime?"

Dr. Evelyn McMann was accustomed to examining remains long after the incident because they had been hidden from the public, but she wasn't happy about how long it took them to notify her department once the scene had been discovered. The arson investigator was on the scene a full day ahead of her. If it had been one of those discoveries of older remains hidden on some obscure trail, an extra day would not have made much difference, but this was a fresh crime scene. The remains were still warm yesterday. Who knows what details may have been lost by now?

She arrived on the island with an assistant, a photographer, and a local deputy escort. The scents of ash and sulphur were still heavy in the air. Clouds passed overhead threatening to drop intermittent showers which would only further contaminate her remains.

She led the team up the trail to the remains of the home. The photographer took pictures of the scene, the yard, and all the burning pits around the yard. She didn't expect to find any forensic significance in the yard photos, but she wouldn't mind having the pictures when she returned to her lab and wanted to remember where things were. She pointed to the fire pit outside the home. The pit was lined with stones and was obviously a feature of the home. It had an odd arrangement of different colored stones inside the circle with a peculiar odor coming from it. Though there was no evidence of remains in the pit, she took samples of the ash, anyway.

Inside the burned-out shell of the home, she found numerous piles of burning wood where the walls and furniture had once stood. A charred refrigerator and sink had tumbled over where the kitchen was and the metal coils from the bed mattresses and sofa helped her identify how the rooms were laid out.

There were two notable charred human remains between the kitchen and the dining room. She found dried leathery arms, legs and heads for two victims, but much of their abdomens were little more than ash and only a few rib bones remained. She took temperature readings while her assistant recorded her every note, and the photographer chronicled their movements. The remains were still warm. She directed her assistant to bag the remains, which in this case included a great deal of scooping and sweeping, while she sifted through the rest of the ash that covered the floor.

She found numerous bone fragments scattered across the floor. Some were obvious animal bones, while others may have been human and would require more lab work to identify. She had never seen so many bone fragments in a single crime scene and hadn't brought nearly enough bags. Her assistant got on the radio and requested more evidence bags. They should arrive this afternoon, and Evelyn had no doubt they would still be examining the site when the bags were delivered.

In the meantime, after she had used up all her bags and vials, she started setting flags at all the points where she would return to collect evidence once the delivery was made. She had no doubt that she would also run out of flags before too long. Her assistant and the deputy carried the first of the bagged remains down to the boat, but carried it back up to the yard when they saw a curious alligator near the boat.

They weren't concerned for their own safety. The gator would have surely left them alone, but it might have been tempted to taste the remains, so they kept them in the yard where the deputy could stand guard.

Tangiers had it all planned out in his head. The arson investigator had already examined the scene and the coroner should be there now. The suspect was in custody. Now he just had to get the case hustled up on the calendar and sped through the justice system.

He filed the necessary paperwork to have the trial moved to Cricket Bend instead of at the courthouse in Lafayette. He made a lot of excuses about the many witnesses who would be unable to attend a hearing in Lafayette, and he filled the petitions with a lot of legal bullshit to convince the judge that justice would be better served in Cricket Bend.

He not only wanted to convict the girl, but he wanted all those people that loved and supported her to see it. If she was 'The Chosen One', as Logan had suspected, he wanted to discredit her before they sentenced her to death.

The smoke blotted out the sun and shrouded the world in darkness. Ashlin tried fanning the acrid cloud away from her face. It burned her eyes and lungs. She could close her eyes. It was too dark to see anyway, but she couldn't avoid breathing. It dried her mouth and throat. The odor assaulted her nostrils, and she heaved, but she couldn't remember the last time she ate and had nothing to throw up. She kept low to the ground, crawling through the streets, hoping desperately to find a pocket of air. She knew it was morning, but she couldn't even see the round orange glow of the sun through the smoke and debris.

The sky flashed. It was the only light that was ever visible through the smoke, as if the smoke itself had flashed. She fell into a ditch and waited. Next came the searing heat as flames spread across the ground in waves. The heat was followed by the horrible wind that roared overhead and buffeted the pre-teen as she held her arms over her ears. The flames burned everything standing until it was crispy, and the wind tore it down and carried it away. The streets were littered with the charred remains of buildings and cars. The city blocks were like graveyards with corner stones and steel girders rising from the ground like gravestones, marking the locations where the buildings used to stand.

Ashlin crept forward along the ditch, but the ditch was littered with bodies. It was creepy and slow to traverse. When the winds passed, she climbed back to the street level and continued moving forward to the center of the destruction. The closer she got, the hotter it was. Eventually, as she neared the source of the fire, the ground burned with flames that would puff out in the wind, but spring back up like trick candles.

Ashlin was close enough now to hear her voice. She had arrived. It was closer than she ever wanted to be, yet she feared it might not be close enough. Only a small pile of bricks and stones stood between them now. She closed her eyes and took a deep breath and gagged on the poisonous air, but clenched her jaw to keep from coughing. When she was ready, she popped up from behind the stones and cast spells of regret and self-torment, but her target wasn't there and Ashlin's spells flew harmlessly across the glowing crater where her target had just stood moments ago.

Her spine went cold as she heard the girl's voice from behind her, "Now why would such a sweet innocent little girl like you want to do something nasty like that?"

Ashlin tried turning around to answer her, but her feet were stuck in the ground.

"What happened to you?" the voice asked. "Whatever turned you so mean?"

Ashlin thought she knew the voice. It was so familiar, but her mind reeled and her brain couldn't connect the voice to a face. She tried to answer, but all she managed was to cough and choke on the fumes.

"The truth is," said the voice, "that I never liked you. You were always little miss perfect. Everybody liked to call you sweetie pie and darling, but I saw the real you. You're just a conniving little con person who fooled everyone into thinking how nice you were."

Ashlin tried thinking her spells. If she could project them backwards, she could confine the girl in a binding spell until the others arrived to help, but she couldn't draw enough focus in her clouded mind. Her knees trembled and tears squeezed out of eyes that were too dry for tears. She wanted so badly to help Destiny, but she failed to muster even the tiniest of spells.

"You could have been such a beauty when you grew up," the voice continued, "with your long, flaming red hair and those sweet little dimples. You could have had all the boys wrapped around your fingers, but now you'll never know. Maybe I should show you! Would you like me to show you what it's like to be a real woman before you die?"

Ashlin heard the voice of pure evil. She closed her eyes and prepared for the end. Her whole body trembled now. The world spun around her and the ground shook, then she felt the power of the girl's spell rush through her fragile body and all at once, it was over, and she found herself bathed in a brilliant light. She opened her eyes and saw the sun streaming in through the car window.

"You, okay?" Michelle asked. "It sounded like you had you a whopper of a dream."

Ashlin closed her eyes and sighed. It was just a dream, but something deep inside told her that it wasn't just a dream.

The office was cold and empty when Mr. Charles visited early in the morning to pick up a few things and get some last-minute advice from some associates. The partners had already said that he should handle this, and he assured Michelle that he would continue to represent Destiny.

Laura was a member of the police force in Poplarville where Justin was an assistant D.A. and a personal friend of hers, but his office wouldn't allow him to handle a defense matter personally, so he convinced a local defense attorney to loan him an associate for this *pro bono*.

Avery was on the bottom of the associate totem pole, which is how he was sent to the police station in the middle of the night. He also lacked court experience, so his firm granted him time to see this through, even after he had already secured the release of Laura's son.

The office manager left him a list of instructions defining what expenses would be automatically approved, and which ones required review from the partners. Also included were detailed time sheets where he would record his hours to submit with his expenses.

An email from a junior partner was left in his in-box. It was intended as a pep talk, but without being delivered personally, it came across as cold and condescending. He was on his own, but he could call the office for research from the legal assistants as long as he kept it to a minimum. There would be no assistance from the partners until he reached trial, at which time he may or may not get someone to sit second chair. He would get a modest *per diem*, but he still had to use his own car and pay for his own room. He knew the partners would never travel like this. The firm supplied them with credit cards to record every expense, including a car, but at least the room was an expense item, and he would be paid back.

He wasn't letting any of this bother him. This was a big deal to him, even if not to his firm. He would have preferred a better send-off and more detailed advice from the partners, but it wouldn't affect how he approached the job. He made a promise, and he intended to keep it, even if he had to do it alone.

The drive from Poplarville to Lafayette wasn't far, but it was long enough for him to daydream and imagine a better goodbye from the partners. As long as he was daydreaming, he might as well imagine an investigator and a researcher to assist him.

Richard didn't suffer any of the kind of agony he felt now when he was working with Brian. While Brian was on the road hunting down the witches, Richard was busy measuring the power of the prophecy level events that Destiny kept generating and triangulating the epicenter. He even took it a step further and developed some hi-tech gear that was able to measure the witches' brainwaves during their extra normal activities. But now, he just sat in his office and waited for Logan to need something.

He had a little part to play yesterday in hiring the mercenaries, but they went quietly last night. Last night's fiasco was just another failure to add to his resume. He helped develop the backup plan, which was in full effect, but didn't require much effort on his part, so he was left with little to do now, except sit back at his desk facing the window, staring out into the world.

People still came and went, driving their little commuter cars, completely oblivious to the great changes that have taken place in the last couple of weeks. The world was going to be different. His people would come out of hiding and take their place once again at the top of the food chain.

Richard closed his eyes and shook his head. This marked two days since his mind had started its never-ending babbling, and he saw no sign that it would end anytime soon, until the phone rang. He jumped for the phone, eager for news or even just a distraction. "Hello? This is Dr. Schaefer."

"Oh, sorry," the woman said. "I musta dialed wrong."

"Who were you trying to reach?"

"Frank Logan. Does you know him?"

"Yes," Richard said. "Frank is out of the office. His phone must have been forwarded to me. Can I help you?"

"I don't know. My name is Abilene Boutin. Me and my daughter Honey was sorta workin' with Frank."

"Boutin?" Richard asked. "Any relation to Michelle or Destiny Boutin?"

"Dat no-account bitch Michelle is my half-sister, so you knows about me then?"

He didn't, but he wasn't going to admit that. "Yes, Frank and I are working on this project together and we're a little concerned about what went on last night. Perhaps you can tell me what you saw?"

"So you knows about what they was?" she asked coyly.

Richard could tell she wasn't too comfortable confiding in him yet. He had no idea how much she knew, but he felt safe enough asking, "You mean the witches?"

"Yes," she was relieved to say. "My cousin's little bastard whelp had something what gived her her powers. I never seen nothing like it before. That little witch made a storm brew in the sky and the ground shake both at the same time. You know, at dinner, she turned herself into a giant living fireball. Anyways, like I said, she had something around her neck, and we seen how it brung her power to her so my little girl took it from her and we ran."

"Tell me," Richard said, "did you see any men with guns?"

"Just the pohlice at the gate. They stopped us but my baby girl talked them into lettin' us go. Listen, we gots the necklace and all, but we is stuck at a hotel here in Gulfport and one of them chased us all the way here. I gave him the slip, but I ain't got enough money to stay long."

"Don't worry about that," Richard said. "We'll take good care of you. Give me the number for the hotel and I'll have someone come get you."

It was a relatively quiet drive to Lafayette. Once he was done pretending that this was a more prestigious assignment, Mr. Charles spent the remainder of the ride planning out his strategy. First, he would get his client released, then he would start scheduling depositions with witnesses until the pretrial hearing. If he hadn't been driving, he would have already filled out little cards of all the things he had to do. He still planned to do that and expected that he would probably spend the next few weeks rearranging them to fit people's schedules.

His first stop was to the clerk's office to get an official copy of the arrest record. He thought this would have been computerized, but the clerk took his request and excused himself for a few minutes. This left Charles staring at his own reflection in the thick bulletproof glass. He shifted from one foot to the other and fidgeted with his briefcase until the clerk finally returned.

"Sorry," the clerk said. "We just got these, and they haven't been entered into the computers yet." The clerk nervously slid two folders through the slot at the bottom of the window and said, "Good luck, counselor."

Charles had only expected a single folder, so instead of putting them away, he pinned his briefcase under his arm and started thumbing through the folders as he turned and walked away. He only took two steps before he turned back around and said, "Wait a minute, this first folder is the arrest report, but the second one is a trial docket. What's going on here?"

The clerk shrugged his shoulders and lowered his voice to say, "I don't know, but I have never seen anything like it. I even called my law professor this morning and asked him. It's all very peculiar."

"Where's the medical examiner's report?"

"I know!" the clerk exclaimed. "There is no report yet. She is at the scene looking at the bodies as we speak! Read the arson report. I don't know who this girl pissed off, but they aren't fooling around."

Charles opened his briefcase and put the folders inside. "Thanks, kid."

The clerk nodded and whispered, "Don't worry, man, I got your back."

Richard had a silly grin on his face. He sat at his desk, staring at his phone, and replayed his conversation with Abilene in his head. As newsworthy as the missing mercenaries were, the fact that this Honey girl discovered the source of the witch's power and stole it from her was phenomenal. That's what Brian was supposed to do.

He failed, but this girl did it! Richard dialed Logan's cell number, but it went directly to voice mail.

"Logan, it's Richard. We got a call from an Abilene Boutin. She says she's been working with you on the project at the Boutin farm. More importantly, she was there last night, and she says her daughter swiped some kind of amulet from the girl. She claims that the amulet is what gave the girl her power. She says the girl used it to make the earth quake or something. Did you hear that, Logan? We've done it! We've discovered the source of the girl's power and stolen it from her. It's ours now. Abilene and her daughter are stuck in a hotel in Gulfport. Since you are down there now, I thought you might want to go pick them up yourself."

Richard hung up the phone and realized that he would be tied to his desk for the rest of the day, or at least until Logan calls him back. He spun the chair around to face the window again and sighed. He still had the silly grin on his face. The world was going to change.

Destiny's holding cell was a small rectangular room with a high window and a skinny cot bolted to the floor. A small steel surface was hinged to the wall and folded down to be used as a table, with the only loose piece of furniture being a wooden chair that creaked when she sat in it. A sink with a metal mirror was on the wall opposite the bed with a toilet next to it positioned in a way that barely provided any privacy at all when viewed from the small window in the door.

Much of the morning had been spent being booked. She was fingerprinted and asked a myriad of questions, leaving her little time to sleep. Destiny lay on top of the thin bed, just waiting for what came next. She had no doubts that she could have escaped anytime she wanted. She could have been forceful and burned the hinges on the doors, or she could have simply placed thoughts into the custodians' minds to walk her out and let her go, but she had seen this phase of her life in her visions and the only way she could be acquitted was to ride it out to the end of the trial.

A much larger concern for her was her mother. She had already helped Zeb and couldn't suppress the desire to help her mother too, but she needed the amulet, and it was lost.

The door opened, and a guard stepped in and said, "You have a visitor."

Her hands were bound in metal handcuffs before escorting her out of the cell blocks to a room slightly larger than her cell with a larger window high on one wall and doors on each end. The sun streamed in through the window, but it would have been well lit in any case by the large fluorescent fixtures that were sunk flush with the ceiling. A large table sat in the center with Mr. Charles and her nana seated on one side with the window to their backs. Destiny was directed to sit opposite them. Mr. Charles nodded to the two guards, and they stationed themselves just outside each of the doors.

The room was quiet while he took a good look at his client.

Michelle's chair squeaked as she shifted her weight. She glanced at Destiny, then at Mr. Charles and back to her granddaughter. The silence was unnerving.

Avery shook his head slightly. She was obviously a teenager. She didn't look emo or punk. Her hair was blond, with no streaks or roots that he could see. She had no gang marks or tattoos. She was just a normal-looking girl who was a bit calmer than he would have expected given her situation, but he wasn't a shrink and didn't know how to judge that. He wondered what made her such a menace. Why was she being rushed to trial with so much vigor?

"Is something wrong?" Destiny asked while swiping her hands across her cheeks in case they were smudged.

"No," he replied. "I was just trying to figure out why someone wants to lock you up and throw away the key."

Destiny and Michelle both knew why, and even though Destiny knew they would eventually devise a defense around the prosecution's innuendo that she was a witch, something deep insider Destiny told her that she couldn't tell him about it just yet.

He smiled and tried looking confident and comforting. "My name is Avery Charles."

"I know," she said. "I've been expecting you."

"Oh?" he asked. "How did you know?" He glanced over at Michelle, then shook it off. "Never mind, it doesn't matter. I wish I could give you better news, but considering the gusto the prosecution is throwing behind your incarceration, I don't think we are going to have much luck with bail." He looked over to Michelle and continued, "Forgive me for being blunt, but my understanding is that you don't have any money for a deposit. Do you own a home?"

Michelle grimaced and said, "We did, but it was burnt down by them guys they say my Destiny killt."

Avery wrote some notes in his book and said, "Well, considering they caught you in another state, the prosecutor will certainly claim you are a flight risk."

"But," Destiny said, "we didn't even know they were looking for us."

"Dass right," Michelle added, "and with our house burnt to the ground, we had nowhere to stay, so we went to my kin in Mississippi. It tain't all that far away anyhow."

Avery took down some more notes and said, "Well, maybe the judge will take that into consideration."

"Course he will," Michelle said. "Just cause da prosecutor's got a bug up his ass don't mean the judge do."

"Well," Avery said, "we'll see. The first step will be the arraignment where the prosecutor will formally read the charges, which, as of now, appear to be two counts of first degree murder."

"How is they gonna say my little girl murdered those guys when dey's da ones dat come to kill us with guns and fire?"

"Guns?"

"Big guns!" Michelle said. "They burst in on our property like G.I. Joe shootin' daer rifles at us. One of them nearly burnt the whole island to the ground."

"The thing is," Avery said, "we won't be getting into that kind of testimony at this point."

"Why nots? How else is we gonna prove Destiny be innocent? And why is they puttin' all this on her anyways? She warn't the only one there. I was there and so was dat boy. Why ain't we in jail?"

Destiny protested, "Nana! Don't give them no ideas."

"Please, Mrs. Boutin, calm down. Like I was saying, the prosecutor will read the charges and the judge will ask you if you are guilty or not guilty. If you think we can prove not guilty, then you say that, and I will do everything I can to help you prove it."

"Of course she's not guilty. Look at her!"

"Lastly," Avery said, "we'll have to convince the judge that you aren't going to run away again. I can ask him to release you on your own recognizance, but I doubt he'll entertain such a request in a capital case."

"You go ahead and ax him," Michelle said. "We can be pretty persuasive when we has to be."

Destiny knew what she meant and gave her a cockeyed look.

Mr. Charles looked Destiny straight in the eye and asked, "Are you sure you want to plead not guilty? I'll represent you whether you did it or not, but if you say you're not guilty and the prosecutor wins the case, the judge will go a lot worse on you than with a guilty plea."

Destiny nodded her head and said, "Not guilty. I have a feeling about you. I know you're going to win."

Avery frowned and said, "I need to be honest with you. This will be my very first court trial. Are you sure?"

Destiny smiled widely and said, "Absolutely."

The phone hadn't even completed its first ring when Richard anxiously swiped the handset from the cradle. "Hello? Logan?"

"No, this is...well, I guess we never gave you our names."

"Who is this?" Richard asked.

"We're the guys you hired for a job down in New Orleans."

"Where the hell have you been? We expected to hear from you last night, then the whole operation was blown, and we had to rely on contingencies."

"Yeah?" the merc asked. "Well, you guys never told us there would be opposing forces. We could have been prepared for them if we had known. You told us it was just a bunch of hicks down on a farm."

"What are you talking about?" Richard asked. "You knew perfectly well that they were armed."

"It wasn't anyone from the farm," the merc said. "A team of professionals came in from behind and took us out one by one. They left us tied up in our transport. Two of our guys are still missing and may have been part of their team."

"Any casualties?"

"Not that we know of, just the two missing guys."

"Very well. Can you debrief the team and send us a report? We'll call you if we need anything more."

"Yes, sir."

The Honorable Harold Jamison knew what was on his docket. The clerks were tittering about it all morning and he listened to his law clerks. It was only an arraignment, but he wished he could be miles away from this one. It was next on his docket and his prayers for a bus or plane crashing into the building had not been answered.

He looked back at his current case and announced, "The defendant is released on his own recognizance. Call the next case."

A sharply dressed woman seated before the judge stood and called out in a clear steady voice, "Case number three one two six seven, the state versus Destiny Boutin."

A uniformed officer escorted Destiny into the courtroom. She was clad in a bright orange jumpsuit and her hands were cuffed in front of her. Michelle's knees shook as she stood up in the audience. Mr. Charles stood and joined Destiny in front of the judge on his right-hand side while Mr. Tangiers took his place on the prosecution side.

The judge scowled at Mr. Tangiers and said, "I don't know you. Who are you and do you represent the state here?"

"I'm new here," Tangiers said. "My name is Simon Tangiers and yes, I represent the great state of Louisiana, sir."

Harold looked over the paperwork on the case. It was the same he had scanned over earlier that morning. He then looked over at the defense and said, "We certainly do have a lot of fresh new faces here today."

Mr. Charles' voice shook while he said, "Yes sir, I am Avery Charles and I'll be representing Miss Boutin."

Harold leaned over as if a few inches would give him a better look and said, "May I presume that you are licensed to practice law in the state of Louisiana? Or maybe I should ask if you have passed the bar? In fact, I'll just come right out and ask, are you old enough to even vote?"

Mr. Charles blushed and said, "Yes sir, to all three counts."

Harold sat up and asked, "So, Mr. Charles, does the defendant waive the reading of the charges?"

"No, sir. It is the defense's position that the prosecution has exercised undo haste in going to trial, and we'd request they take the time to read the charges formally."

"Yes," Harold replied. "What do you have to say to that Mr. Tangiers? Why such haste?"

"Haste?" Simon asked. "The prosecution would like to commend the fine work of both the Lafayette and the Hattiesburg police departments. Their dedication and inter department cooperation led to a very quick apprehension of the suspect. And as far as this case is concerned, as you have already noted, I am new and this is my only case so far."

Harold was sorry he asked. "What are the charges?"

"Your honor, the defendant is charged with two counts of first degree murder."

Harold didn't want to be here for this one. The prosecution's commendations for the police effort aside, it all seemed like a shoddy investigation to him. "Mr. Charles, how does the defense plea?"

"Miss Boutin pleads not guilty."

Harold's clerk took down the plea. "Okay," Harold said. "Mr. Charles, do we have any motions?"

Charles was nervously thumbing through his paperwork.

"Mr. Charles? We're waiting. Any motions? This is where you tell me about the evidence you want excluded from my bail judgment."

"I'm sorry," Charles said, "but I'm looking through the prosecution's case, and I don't see any evidence to be excluded. They don't seem to have any."

The audience laughed and even Harold had to swallow a chuckle. "Nicely played," Harold said, "but let's save that for pretrial."

Harold turned back to Simon and said, "I suppose you are going to oppose bail?"

Simon already felt the balance of the court going against him. "If it please the court..."

"Mr. Tangiers," Harold scolded, "this is an arraignment hearing. I don't need any long-winded speeches here. You are not running for office in my court."

"Yes your honor," Simon cleared his throat and continued. "Miss Boutin fled the scene and was apprehended in another state. Since this is a capital case and she has already proven herself to be a flight risk, the state requests that her bail be denied."

Harold counted the words on his fingers. It was almost exactly what he had expected. "Mr. Charles, what do you say."

"Your honor, Miss Boutin is only sixteen years old. She didn't flee the scene as Mr. Tangiers put it. She, and her grandmother, were the victims of a terrible tragedy. The Boutin home was burned to the ground and with nowhere else to live, her grandmother took her to stay with their nearest living relatives, which are in Mississippi. I would like to add that these relatives, where they were staying, are only a few hours away. Their home was all they had. Michelle Boutin home schooled young Destiny and sold homeopathic remedies at the local general store. They are both well known and loved by their community. She had no knowledge that she was wanted for questioning, and when apprehended, there was no resistance."

"Objection!" Tangiers exclaimed. "The young man she was with did indeed resist arrest!"

Charles yelled back, "He only proclaimed his innocence and was later released because, get this, HE WAS INNOCENT! The officer who arrested him has been reprimanded for making such an outrageous accusation."

Harold banged his gavel and yelled out, "Order! Order! Mr. Charles, you will direct all statements to ME. And you, Mr. Tangiers, this is an arraignment hearing. Please conduct yourself appropriately."

"Yes, sir."

"Now," Harold said in a fatherly voice. "Mr. Charles, do you have any more to say before I pronounce bail?"

"Sir, the Boutin's have nothing to post for bail. Their home and the small plot of land in the middle of the swamp was their only asset. Miss Boutin has no priors, and she has no means with which to flee. The defense requests that she be released on her own recognizance."

"The court agrees. Release the defendant." Harold rapped his gavel, glad to get it off his desk. "Next case."

Logan's secretary entered Richard's office and handed him some reports from Lafayette. They each looked at the other expectantly.

Richard broke the silence and asked, "Still haven't heard from him?"

She shook her head and said, "I was hoping you had."

This was too familiar to Richard. When the witch had first gained her powers and unleashed her waves of energy on the world, Richard's boss Brian went to investigate and was never heard from again. Now Logan was taking the lead, and he was specifically upset at the way Brian had gone in solo and disappeared, but now it seems that Logan was missing too.

Richard looked up at the secretary who was still waiting for some kind of hope from him and said, "Okay. Book me a flight to Gulfport. I'll go talk to this girl myself. Maybe she's seen him. She did say she was working for him."

Tangiers stormed out of the courtroom muttering, "You can never trust those God damned witches."

Blake and Ashlin were hidden in the back of the audience during the arraignment. He had to push one of the guards to let her in and now he took her by the hand to lead her out. They found seats in the hallway where they could wait for Destiny to be released.

Blake saw Tangiers down the hall flailing his arms around and pacing back and forth. He couldn't hear what he was saying, so he entered Simon's mind to eavesdrop.

"Well," Tangiers growled, "how do you explain it?"

Polin looked around to be sure he wouldn't be overheard, then calmly said, "You're pushing too hard. The judge felt it and reacted by protecting the girl. That's all."

"That's all, my ass," Tangiers yelled back. "That witch has him under her spell."

A nearby court reporter couldn't help overhear Simon's remark. Blake was surprised he couldn't actually hear it. "What was that?" the reporter asked.

"Nothing," Simon said. "It was nothing."

The reporter pressed, "Did you just call her a witch?"

Simon collected himself and said calmly, "No, I was just ranting. She's an attractive young lady, and I inappropriately said, 'that bitch has him under her spell.' I shouldn't have said that."

"So," the reporter pressed further, "you're suggesting that the judge has a thing for young girls?"

"No! I never said that. Don't put words in my mouth."

Polin pressed himself between the reporter and Simon saying, "Let's go talk somewhere more private."

Blake dropped out of Simon's mind. There was no question about what Tangiers actually said. Blake not only heard it, he was in his mind and felt the full meaning behind it. Simon was one of them. Blake recalled the premonitions he had about the trial and it all made sense to him. And if he was talking so openly to the arson investigator, Blake was willing to bet he was one of them too.

Destiny was given her clothing and a place to change, then she was escorted to a multi-purpose room in the court building while the paperwork was completed. Unlike her cell, this room had a full size window facing out into a parking area. A thin patch of grass that lined the sidewalk was wet from sprinklers and a small bird had found a puddle of water to splash in. The tiny black and brown bird dipped his beak into the water then whipped his head up into the air spraying the water over his head and onto his back. Then he crouched down in the water and spread his wings which he flapped against the water while spinning around in a circle.

Destiny laughed at the little bird until he stopped playing and looked straight at her. He stared deeply into her eyes until he was all that she saw.

The bird cocked its head to the side and recited,

"The end is near, your mother still slumbers

It was in your grasp but now it is gone

Fear not, for you may yet find another

For you are still The Chosen One."

The bird jumped up and flew away. Destiny heard the door open behind her and she saw a guard with her Nana.

"You can go now," the guard said.

She aimed directly for her Nana's arms and hugged. "I still need to help my mother," she whispered.

Michelle held her warmly and replied, "Don't you think you're kind of busy now?"

They broke the hug and walked towards Mr. Charles who waited down the hall. Blake and Ashlin joined them midway down the hall. Before they reached Mr. Charles, Destiny whispered, "I know how the trial ends and it's not my biggest worry. Something bad is happening and I need my mama. The whole world needs my mama."

"Are you sure?" Michelle asked. "Maybe you're not interpreting the signs correctly. Was it another vision? What did you see?"

Destiny stopped a few paces short of Mr. Charles and crinkled her face before admitting, "A little birdy told me?"

Michelle scowled and said, "This be no time for making jokes."

"Sorry," Destiny said, "but that was my vision just now. A birdy actually told me, but I seen the future in other visions, and we are gonna need me mama."

"Yeah," Blake said. "I seen it too. It's like one of those movies where all civilization is destroyed. I swear, if we don't do something, we're all going to go back to living in caves."

"I seen it too," Ashlin said. She said it like a matter of fact, but everyone looked at her as if it were the most surprising revelation any of them had ever heard.

CHAPTER 9

P olin held his cell phone to his head as he followed Tangiers
into his new office. It was a cramped little office and wasn't
designed to entertain ex-football players. He pulled the small metal
chair back against the wall and seated himself.

Simon fumed as he paced behind his desk and slammed his briefcase down on the blotter. He growled like a bear and threw himself
into his chair. "Where the hell is McMann?" he asked. "We all need
to pow-wow before this gets any worse."

Polin pressed the speaker button on his cell phone and held it
up in the air between them. "You know I'm at the crime scene this
morning," Dr. McMann said. "Besides, you don't need me for an
arraignment. How'd it go?"

"Like shit," Simon said. "Those witches have the judge in their
pockets, but we want to proceed on this A.S.A.P. anyway. I want
your report this afternoon. I need to convict this bitch before she
gets any more of the court under her spell. Besides, how long does it
take to examine two extra crispy corpses? I figured you would have
bagged them and brought them here for an autopsy. We'd really like

identities on our two victims, especially since one of them may have been one of our people."

"I bagged the corpses alright," she said, "but there are literally hundreds, maybe thousands, of other bone material on the site. I need to bag them too."

"I don't see how those are germane to the case."

"Not germane?" she asked. "We have an explosion, a fire, and hundreds of forensic specimens that the defense could use to claim someone else was present, and you think they aren't germane?"

"So," Simon said, "we don't tell them. Just grab a few of the bones and make up a plausible story. We need you here creating some kind of explanation linking the girl to the corpses. That's all that matters."

"The defense will want to get to the truth."

"Screw the truth. You just make your story good enough to sound true. Bury the truth under a pile of scientific bullshit."

"We have a word, in our profession, for scientific bullshit," she said.

Simon glanced up at the ceiling and thought to himself, "Yeah, yeah, yeah. Here we go."

"Reasonable doubt," she continued. "We call scientific bullshit reasonable doubt."

"Can you give me some evidence to nail this girl or not? I don't give a shit about the truth. I just want to bury this girl and remove her from our future!"

Evelyn remained silent.

Simon shifted his gaze from the phone to Polin's eyes and asked, "What about you?"

Polin shrugged his shoulders and said, "You have no argument with me. We want the same things, but if we don't actually do our jobs the way they are supposed to be done, we start to look like idiots and then all of our conclusions are thrown out. Our people have spent centuries convincing the world that magic never really existed. That makes the evidence in this case pretty unbelievable and may make fools of us no matter how we spin it. If the defense asks questions about how all those little fire pits got started, I have no reasonable explanation. It will be a mystery, at best. By the way, do we know what really happened?"

"Let's not muddy your story with the truth. Just pin it on the girl. That's all."

Simon wasn't listening to them and no argument in the world was going to satisfy him. Polin sat quietly, looking at Simon and knowing it would not be as simple as he wanted.

Simon waved his hands to shoo Polin away.

"Okay," Polin said as he got up and left the office. On his way out he said into the phone, "Nice talking to you Evelyn."

Michelle led the group out of the courthouse. It was hot and muggy and she had to shield her eyes from the sun. Her Destiny was free and nothing was going to spoil her mood, but she just wasn't sure where they would go with their freedom.

"I just don't know," she said, "why it is that I be the only one who cain't see this horrible future? Even Ashlin seen it and she's only ten years old!"

"Twelve and a half," Ashlin was quick to correct.

"Twelve then," Michelle said, "but you is still too young. You ain't even old enough to been..."

"Nana!" Destiny snapped. "Let's not discuss that in public. Okay?"

"I'm sorry, but I just don't know why I be da only one who cain't see this bleak future y'all been seein'."

"Maybe," Destiny postulated, "it's like the stories you used to tell me about my mama when she was a little girl. You couldn't see her future neither."

Ashlin hugged Michelle and said, "We're not just family, we're a team. We protect each other. In my vision, I did a heck of a lot worse than just seeing what was happening."

Again, everyone looked at the young prodigy wondering exactly what role lay before her.

Mr. Charles came running down the stairs yelling, "Ms. Boutin! Ms. Boutin!"

All three girls turned around and asked, "What?"

"You're not going to believe this. I can't believe it. I swear, if they could, they would hold the trial this very afternoon before we can prepare a defense."

"Why?" Michelle asked. "What did they do?"

"They got the pretrial hearing moved up to tomorrow!"

"Wait a minute," Blake said. "I seen enough TV to know they can't do that."

"No," Charles said, "they can't, but they did it anyway."

Michelle frowned and asked, "What do you need us to do?"

"Normally, I'd want to prep you for questioning, but I need to get copies of the crime reports and that will probably take me all day. Just don't go anywhere and give me a number where I can reach you in case I have questions."

Michelle blushed and said, "We don't atchally have no place to go. We might just as well stay here with you."

Charles looked constipated and said, "Fffff... screw it. Here's my key. It's room 315 in that hotel down the street. I'll call them and arrange a room for you later."

Ashlin hugged Mr. Charles and said very enthusiastically, "Thank you!"

Michelle shrugged and winked saying, "She's a very grateful little girl."

———

Richard didn't go home to pack. If he needed anything on the road, he would just go buy it. Logan's secretary should have his tickets ready for him any minute now. He checked his email but there was nothing new.

She knocked on the door and let herself in without waiting for his invitation. "Here," she said. "Two tickets to Gulfport."

"Two?" Richard asked. He read the two tickets she handed him and asked, "Dorris?"

"I was just hoping I could help."

The idea wasn't entirely unpleasant to him until he realized it wasn't *his* company she wanted. "What if he calls? We might need you here."

As if on cue, the phone rang.

Dorris sucked in her breath and Richard sprang for the receiver. "Hello? Logan?"

She ran around the desk and put the phone on speaker.

"No, it's not Logan. But, I'd sure like to know what Logan is doing these days because this was a disaster."

Richard looked at her and they each shrugged. "Who is this?" he asked.

"This is Simon Tangiers. Can someone tell me how we can get this whole thing set up, the arrest, the arraignment, the trial, and yet we have probably the ONLY judge who isn't one of us?"

Richard motioned for her to close the door and said, "I know we planned to capture and prosecute the girl, but I don't know the details. Are you saying you've already held the trial? How is that possible?"

"No, we haven't had the trial. But the arraignment wasn't in one of our courts and the judge let her go! And now, guess what? We got the same judge for the pretrial hearing. This judge is going to expect a REAL trial!"

Dorris said, "I'm Logan's secretary. He's tied up right now, but I know who to call about this. I'll get right on it."

"Would you?" Tangiers growled sarcastically. "Please?"

Tangiers slammed the phone and Dorris said, "You're right. I'm needed here. Let me know as soon as you learn anything."

<hr>

Honey slunk down in the hotel chair playing with balls of fire in her hands. She expanded them and tried shaping them into people's faces, but she didn't have the artistic skill.

"Stop that," Abilene said. "You're going to burn the place down."

"So?" Honey shot back. "At least that wouldn't be boring. It's just so dark in here, I can't stand it."

"Maybe I wouldn't have to keep the curtains pulled over the windows if you weren't constantly playing with your fire!"

"Who cares? Let people see me. Let's go out and be bad ass. I have never felt so alive in my life and this place feels like a coffin."

"Jesus!" Abilene cursed. "One moment you're the slut of the world, and the next you're some crazed pyromaniac!"

"Let's do both!" Honey cheered. "We can go get laid and then torch the sorry bastard."

Abilene checked her phone again. Where the hell was Frank?

Charles entered the courthouse again and walked past the court-room and around the corner down a hallway to the judges' private chambers. Unlike the hallways that lined the courtrooms and were always bustling with people, this hall was eerily barren and quiet. The rubber heels of his shoes squeaked against the highly polished marble floors. He felt like he was in a mausoleum and was disturbing the dead. He tried walking on the balls of his feet, but the leather soles of his shoes slipped against the marbles slick waxed surface. He resigned himself to squeaking and walked past the various judges' doors until he came upon the one that read, "The Honorable Harold Jamison."

He knocked lightly on the door.

"Come in."

He opened the door a crack and just poked his head in at first. "Your Honor do you have a moment?"

"Mr. Charles," Harold said, "come in. Sit down."

Charles entered and accepted the chair he was offered. "Sir, have you seen the docket for tomorrow?"

"No, I usually check that after the second session concludes."

"Well, sir, you might want to look."

Harold scrunched his eyebrows and reached for his computer keyboard. He struck a few keys and scrolled down a few lines then arched his eyebrows and said, "Well, if you knew this, then you also know you shouldn't be speaking to me."

"I appreciate that, but I don't have time for formalities. You just arraigned the girl and now she's on tomorrow's docket for the pretri-al hearing with you presiding. I haven't even been given the medical examiner's report or the arson report yet. I need more time, but petitions for a change of venue or date are only accepted within twenty-four hours of the hearing, so it's already too late."

"Don't worry," Harold said. "This must be a clerical error. I'll get it straightened out."

"And," Charles added, "did you notice the venue? It's not being held here."

Harold looked again and frowned. "It's got to be a mistake," he said. "Thank you for bringing it to my attention."

———

Harold had his clerk look up the filing for the hearing. His findings were disturbing. It wasn't a clerical error. It was pushed through by Judge Maude Rawlings. The only thing that his clerk found odd was that she was supposed to preside over the case. Getting assigned to Harold seemed to be the only mistake. Harold didn't like her and scowled as he dialed her number.

"Harold," she answered on the phone, "I don't believe you've ever called me before. To what do I owe this pleasure?"

"I was just wondering," he said, "why you arranged this hearing tomorrow with such haste?"

"What hearing would that be?" she asked in an obviously vain attempt to sound innocent.

"How many hearings do you push through with extreme haste, Maude?"

She dropped the sweetness from her voice and said, "The girl deserves a speedy trial, and her victims deserve a quick verdict."

"This is nonsense," Harold said. "I'm going to have it postponed."

"Too late for that," she said. "You know the twenty-four-hour rule is in effect. If you don't want to do it, I'll trade with you."

"No, that's okay," he said. "I'll take care of this."

"Have a nice trip Harold."

This did not make him happy. He hated abuse of power and this smelled of the worst kind of abuse. He yelled out through the door, "Get that new prosecutor Tangiers on the phone."

His clerk yelled back, "It's ringing, line two."

Harold clicked line two in time to hear, "Simon Tangiers."

"Mr. Tangiers," he growled, "this is Judge Jamison. That little girl you tried railroading in my court today has a hearing scheduled for tomorrow. I'm giving you just two hours to get the medical examiner's reports and the arson report in the hands of that nice young attorney or else I'm charging you with contempt. Do you hear me? And if I learn that you have ANY other evidence that was withheld from them, it will be contempt. Are you getting this?"

"Yes," Simon said meekly. "I hear you, sir."

Harold slammed the receiver down and his clerk applauded from the doorway.

Honey lay on top of the bed leaning against a stack of pillows. She absentmindedly twirled a fireball in her left hand while watching TV. She twiddled the fingers of her right hand and changed the channel on the TV. She smiled and sang out, "Someone's got a new trick. Na na na na na na."

Abilene looked up and saw her changing channels and said flatly, "Woo. You can double as a remote control."

"You're just jealous," she cried. "Why can't you ever just be happy for me? Maybe even proud of me?"

Abilene sat up in her chair and yelled, "Proud of you? Look at yourself. You're a Goddamned slut and you whore yourself out to anyone with a lump in his pants."

"That's not true mama!" Honey smiled wickedly and said, "I don't restrict myself to only men." She jumped up off the bed and went to the mirror. "I'm bored here. I'm going out now."

Abilene jumped up out of her chair and screamed, "No you are not! I forbid it!"

"Really Mama? Did you just forbid it?" Honey shoved her hand in the air towards her mother and sent an invisible force to push her back and knock her into her chair. "Are you going to stop me?"

Abilene remained in her chair. Her body shook and every inch of her face expressed raw fear.

Honey returned her attention to the mirror. She ran a brush through her hair then reached in through the top of her low cut top to pull her breasts higher in their bra. She cupped her breasts from the outside and pushed them together and generally perked them up, then left the mirror for the door.

"Don't worry Mama, I'll be back, eventually."

It was bright outside, especially after being cooped up in the darkened room all day. She saw a bar across the street and stepped out to the sidewalk, then, paying no heed to the lights, stepped out into the street. An approaching car stood on its horn as it approached. Honey didn't stop until she was directly in front of the approaching car. She turned to face it and struck a pose with her hands on her hips. The car never slowed and veered to its left with the horn blowing the whole time.

Honey waited for the car to pass then she reached out with her mind and pressed the car down onto the ground. The rear axles broke and pointed the wheels up unnaturally to the sky while the back of the car scraped along the ground in a huge shower of sparks. The rear end fishtailed then went into a full spin until it slammed into a parked semi-truck.

Honey stood in the middle of the street and laughed, then returned her attention to the bar and the men she hoped to find inside.

Tangiers wasn't happy at all. The merits of the case were supposed to be mere formalities, but someone screwed up big time. Now he would be facing a judge who already didn't like him and had ordered him to provide the technical reports to the defense and he had never asked them to provide real reports.

He sent over what he had, which was just a hodgepodge collection of notes whose conclusions were written before the analysis, but it would be better to send the wrong reports than to miss the judge's deadline. The medical examiner hadn't even finished examining all the evidence yet, but she didn't need to as far as he was concerned. She only had to find enough evidence to support a murder charge. He hadn't thought the real autopsy report would have been required, but now he wasn't so sure.

He sealed the package around the two reports and couriered them to Mr. Charles. With the reports on their way, he dialed her number.

"McMann," she answered.

"Evelyn, have you completed the autopsy yet?"

"Doing it now," she said, "but the lab reports will take time."

"We don't have any time. The judge is breathing down my neck already. The preliminary hearing is tomorrow. Send what you can. Make up what you must. I need a copy A.S.A.P. and we need to send a copy to Mr. Charles too. I don't need to antagonize the judge any more than he already is."

"Okay," she replied, "if you say so."

"Wow," Ashlin said. "I ain't never been in no rich man's home before."

Michelle chuckled and said, "It tain't his home, it just be his hotel."

"Well, still," she said while twirling around the spacious room.

Destiny was on the balcony looking at the pool.

Ashlin joined Destiny and said, "Let's go swimming."

"I can't," Destiny said. "I don't got my cutoffs here, but if I did...Look at this Nana. Have you ever seen water that was blue before?"

Ashlin couldn't contain her enthusiasm or energy and ran off to explore another part of the room.

Michelle joined Destiny on the balcony and said, "It tain't the water that's blue, it be the pool that's painted that color."

"Well, it sure is pretty."

"Yes," Michelle agreed. "It certainly is."

The ripples on the water glittered. The children laughing and splashing in it sounded far away. Dark clouds gathered and blocked the sun but the water still sparkled. The darkness grew around them as the clouds blotted out the sky, yet the water still reflected a hundred points of light.

Michelle was mesmerized by the ripples in the pool. They started in the center and flowed outward in concentric circles. The ripples grew and lapped over the edge of the pool until they covered the deck surrounding the pool. The hypnotic rings continued expanding beyond the pool yard until everything in view was covered in the expanding loops.

The dark clouds descended and doused the lights that had been riding the ripples. The world was dark with smoke. Michelle waved her hands in front of her face to see through the thick dark fog, but it was everywhere. The balcony was gone; the hotel was gone; she felt the rubble crunch beneath her feet as she stared out into the inky blackness.

A light flickered in the distance before her. She stepped gingerly through the rough terrain. The light flashed and then went out again. She followed the light when she could see it and stepped through the darkness when she could not. She was getting closer. As she neared the flickering light, she could see a greater light in the distance.

She stopped for a moment staring at the great light. She couldn't go forward any more. She feared the great light and was frozen in place. The flickering light came to her and said, "You shouldn't be here. I can't protect you."

Michelle looked down and saw Ashlin standing between her and the great light in the distance. Her fiery red hair was short, burned off and matted against her head. She held out her hand and grew a flaming ball in her palm, then spun her hand around in quick circles and the ball grew into a flaming spike. She reared back and launched the flaming spike into the air towards the great light Michelle saw on the horizon. The spike flew into the air like a rocket and roared out of sight.

An ear-splitting siren filled the air, and the skies parted to reveal a giant blue ball of flame coming their way. Ashlin turned around and struck Michelle in the chest with both palms, screaming, "You shouldn't be here!"

The giant blue flame enveloped Michelle until it was all she could see, but it didn't burn her. It shrunk around her and receded away until all she saw was a blue ball in the distance.

All she saw was the glittering blue pool.

Abilene was glad that Honey left. She was tired of seeing her showoff her powers like they were nothing. Abilene held out her hands and tried arcing a spark between them, but nothing happened. She scowled and reached towards the TV hoping she could change the channels, but again she was powerless and only felt worse.

Someone knocked on the door and she yelled out, "What's the matter? Your new abilities can't open the damned door?"

Three more knocks.

Abilene pulled her brooding form up off the bed and went to the door. She opened it a crack and peeked outside.

Richard stood outside and said, "Are you Abilene? I'm Richard. We spoke on the phone. I work with Frank."

"Where the hell is Frank?"

"I don't know. May I come in?"

Abilene opened the door and went to the chair thinking of ways that she might get rid of him so she could continue sulking.

Richard entered the room and closed the door behind him. He scanned the room. The door to the bathroom was wide open and they were alone. "Where's your daughter?"

"She said she was bored and she left."

Richard sat in the other chair and said, "A lot has happened since you left the farm. The girl was arrested and taken back to Louisiana."

"What about the boy?" Abilene asked. "He followed us here and almost caught us."

"He took Michelle back to Louisiana for the trial."

Abilene sat up straight and smiled. "Then, I kin go back to the farm?"

"Why would you want to go back there?"

"Cause that's where my power is. Ever' time I leaves there, I lose it all." She slapped her hands together and rubbed them. When she pulled them apart, there was barely any sparks between them. "You see? Nothing."

Richard pointed at her hands and said, "What were you expecting? That looked normal to me."

"Sure it's normal, but I ain't normal. I don't want to be normal. On the farm I can make lightning come from my hands. I can make it dance all around me and do whatever I want. Here I got nothing."

If it weren't for the fact that Logan was invested in her, Richard might have thought she was crazy. He knew his people used to control lightning this way, but nobody has been able to do that in centuries, until a few weeks ago when Brian claimed he could.

"How long have you been able to do that?"

"I always done that," she lied. Then she remembered that Logan knew the truth and said, "No, that ain't true. It's only been a couple weeks."

"And what about Honey?" Richard asked. "Can she make electricity too?"

Abilene shook her head and slouched in her chair. Why did he have to ask about Honey? "No," she said. "Honey ain't never done that. She was better with fire, but now she can twiddle her fingers and change the channels on the TV. Since she got that damned charm around her neck, who knows what she might be able to do?"

"The charm?" Richard asked. "Is that the thing you said you took from the witches?"

"Yeah. And now she's makin' fire easier than spit. She can move things too, that's new."

"Does she have the charm with her now?"

"She had it when she left here, but she likes to strip off her clothes around men, so who knows?"

Richard jumped up from the chair and said, "We should go find her."

Abilene was less enthusiastic, but she followed him all the same.

The prosecution's package arrived in Mr. Charles' office, but it was much lighter than he anticipated. He thanked the courier and returned to his desk to open the envelope. There were only two slim folders inside.

The medical examiner's report had only the preliminary findings. There were no autopsy reports, and the preliminary findings barely said anything more than the bodies were burned to crisps. The reports included neither chemical analysis nor cause of death.

The arson report might as well have read, 'there was a fire.' It included a map showing hotspots and fires that littered the property. The map also indicated the location of the home and where the corpses were found within the structure. Avery turned the page and found that it had more detail than the M.E. report. It included some rudimentary conclusions: the fire was not caused by lightning; no known accelerants were found on the scene; sulfur was found all over the property, but it neither caused nor accelerated the fire.

The cause was inconclusive. It only detailed the common things that did NOT cause the fire.

He tossed the reports on the desk. He wasn't sure what to do now. He asked for the reports, no, he demanded that they send him the reports. Now he has them and he is no better off than he was before, except, neither is the prosecutor. Why then, are they proceeding without a case?

He was going to call the hotel and arrange for private rooms for Michelle and Destiny, but it looked like he would be spending all night pouring over case books looking for cases that were thrown out for lack of evidence.

He dialed the number to his hotel and asked for room three fifteen.

Michelle stared at the phone. It wasn't their room, and she didn't know if she should answer it. Blake had no such compunction and picked it up. "Hello?"

"This is Mr. Charles. May I speak to Mrs. Boutin please?"

Blake handed the phone to Michelle and said, "It's the lawyer. He wants to talk to you."

"Hello?"

"I'm going to be working on my notes all night. I want you to make yourselves comfortable. Go ahead and order room service for dinner and breakfast, and charge it to the room. I'll have the desk send up some more room keys for sleeping."

Michelle looked directly at Blake thinking she would very much like him sleeping in his own room, but Destiny shot her a knowing look and Michelle said, "That won't be necessary. This place is so big, and it already has two beds and a big couch. We'll be just fine."

"As you wish," he replied. "Try to get plenty of sleep, but be ready to leave by half-past six in the morning."

"We be ready for you. Thank you, Mr. Charles."

Destiny had overheard enough of the conversation to know what was going on, but Blake looked at Michelle expectantly.

"Mr. Charles says we is to have dinner here. He won't be coming. The girls will share the beds."

Blake frowned and said, "And I guess I get the sofa. I suppose it never occurred to him that I should have my own room."

Half a smile appeared on Michelle as she continued, "We needs to be ready to go at six thirty."

Michelle and Destiny were accustomed to rising early, but Blake grimaced at the notion. "Great," he thought to himself. "I sleep on the couch and I have to get up early."

As soon as they hit the street, Abilene saw the bar and said, "I know where that little tramp went."

Richard followed her across the street and into the bar. It looked pretty much like any other. The interior was a little dark with most of the ambience originating from neon lights of different beer distributors behind the bar. There were plenty of tables and bar stools, but they were empty. A crowd gathered at the end of the bar, whooping and hollering.

Richard and Abilene entered the crowd so he could see.

"Is that her?" Richard asked pointing to the girl at the pool table.

"Yup," Abilene said snidely, "although it's a little hard to recognize her with her shirt still on."

Honey raised her hands in the air. In one hand she held the pool stick and in the other she held a fistful of money. The crowd roared and applauded.

One angry man with a pool cue said, "One more game."

"Nope," Honey said. "Let someone else have a turn."

"I want my money back!" the man roared. He pulled out a wad of money and said, "Here's five hundred dollars." He placed the money on the edge of the pool table and growled, "We play again."

Honey looked at the money in her hand and said, "But I only have three hundred. You want to put your five hundred up against my three hundred?"

Someone in the back yelled, "Throw in your top."

The crowd chanted, "Shirt! Shirt! Shirt!"

Honey quickly pulled her shirt over her head and tossed it next to his money along with her three hundred dollars, then, without being prompted, she removed her bra and added it to the pile.

"Yep," Abilene said. "That's my Honey for sure."

"Rack 'em up," Honey said.

She placed her cue hand on the table and pulled back her stick. The amulet glowed slightly as she hammered the cue into the rack of balls. They scattered all around the table with three balls finding pockets. "Three ball in the corner," she said. She popped the cue ball and zipped the three ball into the corner pocket, but the cue ball spun around to the side and chipped the nine ball into the side pocket. "Five ball, off the rail and into the far corner." She sent the cue ball into the five which rebounded off the cushion to the far corner while the cue ball found both the eleven and seven hanging around the corner and sunk both of them. "Combination," Honey said, "six ball in that corner, twelve in that one, and the fifteen all the way down here."

"That's impossible," her opponent growled.

Honey stood up and sneered at him. "What are you driving?" she asked.

"A black half ton," he answered. "Why?"

"Put your keys on the table with your money, if you think this shot is impossible."

"And if you miss?" he asked.

"If I miss," she said while striking a pose, "I'll take off all the rest of my clothes."

"Do it!" a friend of his urged.

"No way!" he said. "My truck against seeing her naked? She ain't worth that much."

Honey ran her finger in a line starting between her naked breasts, past the amulet straight down past her belly until it toyed with the top of her jeans and said, "But I thought you said the shot was impossible. Besides, maybe I let you do more than just look?"

He put his keys on the table and Honey lined up the shot. Just as she called it, the cue ball rebounded off the six ball which fell in one corner, then hit the twelve ball into the next corner, and while Honey played with the amulet that hung between her bare breasts, the cue ball masse'd around the eight ball and put the fifteen into the far corner.

"You little bitch! That's impossible!"

"You saw it," she said. "Everybody saw it." She went to the bar and said, "Coffee!"

The bartender poured a fresh cup. She took it to her opponent, heating it up to boiling in her hands. "Here," she said. "In case you don't have enough left for coffee."

She grabbed the loot and smelled the money while swinging the keys on her finger. Her opponent's friend was the only thing keeping him at bay, but she wasn't worried. He tore free from his friend and lunged for her. She saw it like it was slow motion. She side stepped and pushed him in the direction he was already lunging. She also slipped a jolt of electricity into his body leaving him dazed as he crashed into the floor.

"What's wrong?" she crowed over him. "Did you want an ass whooping too?"

Abilene went to Honey and said, "Let's not make a scene here. This man I brung with me is from our people, and he is real interested in what you can do now. Let's get back to the hotel before you start a riot."

Honey took a good look at Richard and smiled saying, "Sure." She took his arm and started walking him to the exit.

Abilene grabbed Honey's shirt and bra from the pool table and shouted, "You might want to put this on!" Then she mumbled under her breath, "Tramp!"

The first librarian entered their meditation room looking shaken and pale. Sweat covered his face and his hands shook as he took his place in the circle.

"What's the matter brother," the second librarian asked.

"I've never seen him so upset," replied the first librarian. "We never should have let her have the amulet."

"But," the third librarian said, "we didn't let her have the amulet."

"Not her," the first said. "The other girl. She has the amulet now, and he is very angry."

"How can we fix it?" asked the second.

The third answered, "I think we have done enough. If he wants more done, he can tell us what he wants done, and he had better be more explicit with his instructions."

The first librarian pointed at the third and said, "I'll let you tell him that."

The third put both palms up and said, "No thanks. Not me!"

"Besides," the first admitted, "I don't think he can be more specific. Communication is difficult at best."

"So?" the second asked. "What is to be done?"

The first replied, "The chosen one will still want to revive her mother. We must not allow that. We need her to focus on stopping the other girl."

"But," the second asked, "what if the chosen one believes she needs her mother to stop the other girl?"

The first librarian bowed his head and shook it slowly. "It would be a tragedy," he said, "if all three of them ever get together in the same place, the world may cease to exist."

"Have you been outside?" the third asked. "How do we know they haven't already been together?"

"Perhaps they have," the first replied, "and it remains our duty to go back and prevent it."

The second librarian asked, "And what do we do with our two mercenary friends? Is it time to release them?"

"No," the first said. "Let's use them to set a trap for the girl. We know she is driving. Find a spot on their route and have them lie in wait."

"And," the third asked, "what of their hostage?"

"Take him with them. He may yet prove useful to us. I must meditate and observe the mother. If the girl tries again to revive her, we must intercede."

Richard took Honey by the arm and guided her and Abilene back towards the crosswalk leading to the hotel, but Honey stopped him and said, "Hey sugar, did you forget about these?" She twirled the truck's key ring around her finger then deftly swung the electronic fob into the palm of her hand and pressed the alarm button. When nothing happened, she turned and pointed it in different directions until a black pickup responded. "Well, looky there," she said. "We got us a ride."

She clung to his arm and pulled it against her breast while they walked the few paces to the truck.

Being seduced by a young nymphomaniac would have been a lot more tempting to Richard if she weren't both crazy and potentially dangerous. He could live with her being unbalanced if he didn't think she might accidently kill him in a moment of passion.

Honey guided him to the driver's door, opened it and pushed him up, refusing to let go of his arm. She continued shoving, forcing Richard to climb awkwardly over the center console into the passenger seat. Honey then reached across to pull down his seat belt and dropped the keys in his lap. "Ooops," she said as her hand quickly dove down into his crotch to fish out the keys.

Richard flinched and Abilene said, "Damn it, tramp, don't you know there is a time and a place?"

"No Mama, I don't believe there is a time or a place for me anymore. The whole world is mine. I'm the God damned queen of the world and I'll do whatever I God damned want to do to whoever I God damned please and any damned place I want!"

"Who the hell do you think you are?" Abilene screamed back. "I gave birth to you, you little bitch, and you is gonna show me some God damned respect. I don't..."

Honey held her hand up and closed her fingers together, clamping her mother's mouth shut. Abilene's eyes opened wide as she reached her hands up to her mouth and started crying uncontrollably. Honey released her grip and cried, "I'm sorry, Mama. I didn't mean to hurt you. I just wanted to shut you up. I just cain't take any more of your damned lectures. You should be more careful what you say to me because I might just lose control and it would be all your fault."

Abilene tested her jaw. It wasn't broken, but she had no more to say.

Honey turned around, no longer interested in playing with Richard, and said, "You kin put your pecker away. I lost the mood."

She didn't bother with the keys and put her finger to the ignition and started the truck with a zap from her finger.

"Where's our people?" she asked. "It's time they meet their queen."

Richard pointed in the general direction of the hotel and asked, "Don't you want to stop at the hotel to get your clothes?"

"Why?" she yelled at Richard. "Are you gonna start ragging on me about wearing clothes now?"

"No," Richard tried calming her down. "I just thought you might want your things."

"Ain't nothing there that my people can't replace for me. Where do I go?"

The truck was equipped with GPS, so Richard leaned forward and entered their destination and said, "There you go. Just follow its directions."

Johnson kept his distance when he followed Honey from the magic theater to the hotel and on to the bar across the street. He waited outside for her, but when she emerged with a strange man and climbed into a pickup truck, he could only jot down the make and license, then hightail it across the street to his own vehicle.

This would have been a good time for him to report to his friends, but they popped in and out of his mind on their own schedule. Keeping an eye on the truck proved to be impossible, even as he ran across the street and lost sight of it as it entered traffic. His best hope might have been to wait for them to return to the hotel, but then reacquired the truck when it squealed its tires, heading towards the interstate.

He started his car and headed in that general direction, but they were out of sight. It was a long, lonely road for a while, so he just headed in that direction, hoping it would keep him close until his friends eventually contacted him.

Chapter 10

Day four.

The beginning of the end can never truly be identified until one admits that they have reached the end. When the end in question is the end of ALL things, then that beginning would only be recognized when seen in hindsight, unless, of course, one is gifted with foresight.

The great evil that was to come may already have been unbridled, but it had yet to be unleashed.

Mr. Charles knocked on the door to his hotel room at a quarter past six.

Michelle opened the door and let him in. "I hope we looks okay," she said. "Our Sunday clothes got burnt in the fire."

"You look fine," Charles said. He didn't say that looking impoverished might help their case, especially after the fire.

They followed him to the car and filed in with Michelle in the front and Tempest in the back, leaning on the left door. Destiny sat next to her mother and Ashlin climbed in between Destiny and Blake, who sat next to the other door. Charles started the car and pulled it out of the hotel lot and turned left.

Destiny twisted her head around and pointed her finger the other way, saying, "I thought the courthouse was that direction."

"It is," Charles replied, "but for some reason, they wanted the hearing held in Cricket Bend."

"Ugh," Blake moaned. "It seems like all we do any more is go on long drives."

Michelle smiled and said, "Well, at least you ain't drivin' no more."

"Yeah," Destiny teased. "At least we got a driver with some real driving experience this time."

"And a actual license," Michelle added.

Ashlin didn't care. She had never been anywhere before and wished she could see out the window.

"Here Ashlin," Blake said. "Why don't you switch places with me?"

Michelle gave Blake an evil eye, and he said, "...or not."

Michelle saw the disappointment in Ashlin's expression and said, "Why don't you come up here and sit on my lap if you wants to see."

"I'm too big for laps," she whined. "I'm not a baby."

Michelle frowned and said, "Okay then. You go ahead and switch with him, but you keep an eye on him. You make sure there don't be no funny stuff between him and your cousin."

Destiny blushed beet red and leaned her head against her mother, wishing she were asleep already.

───────────

The sun shone through the window, landing on Destiny's eyelids and flooding her eyes with the color red. The warmth on her face spread slowly through her body until she felt a slight breeze in her hair.

"Aunt Destiny is here!"

She was surrounded with the screams and laughter of young children while their great beast Chauncey put his head on her shoulder and slathered her face with slobber.

Nimisen pulled Chauncey off of her and said, "Go on, you big mutt! Go find yourself a bone."

"Thank you," Destiny said.

Nimisen pulled Destiny to her feet and said, "You've really gotten yourself in a pickle. We should go find my husband at once."

"What are you talking about? I know how the trial comes out. I'm not worried."

Nimisen took Destiny by the hand and guided her up a long staircase to one of the castle towers. "Not the trial," she said, "the amulet."

"The amulet?" Destiny asked. "Oh yeah, that thing. You know, I think maybe it was the thing that was making me sick."

"Of course it was. It was feeding off of your energy, storing part of your energy in its reserves."

They reached the top of the stairs and ran into Marvalaine, who was on his way down.

"How could you?" he bellowed. "I mean, I don't blame you. I'm sure my wife didn't fully educate you in the care and safeguarding of such a trinket. But of all people, how could you let her have it?"

"Nice to see you too," Destiny said, "and I didn't let anyone have anything. She ripped it right off my neck and took off. We chased her and almost caught her too, until the police stopped me and charged me with murder."

Marvalaine went to the open window and looked out over the valley and the river. "This is terrible," he said. "She has it and with it, she has grown very powerful and has even been able to borrow some of your powers."

"My powers?"

"Yes," Nimisen said. "You stored some of your powers in the amulet, and now she has them."

"Can she use my own powers against me?"

Marvalaine shrugged and said, "We don't really know very much about how the amulet works."

"Why not?" Destiny asked. "Didn't you make it?"

Marvalaine shook his head and said, "Alas, no. They did. We stole it from them and used it against them, but we know little of what else it can do."

"I don't believe this!" Destiny shouted. "All this time, I've looked up to you as my mentor. I thought you were the one with the answers when I got in trouble. Now I learn that the sorcerers create an amulet that is able to store our powers in it, then they let you steal it, and it never occurs to you that maybe they wanted to use it to steal your powers all along?"

Marvalaine closed his eyes and hung his head.

"Now what?" Destiny asked. "How powerful does this make her? Can she defeat me now?"

Marvalaine shook his head and said, "I don't know. Perhaps."

"Then I'll just have to get it back," Destiny said, "somehow."

"Or," Nimisen added, "get another one."

The hairs stood up on the back of Destiny's head. "There are more of these?"

"Just one," Nimisen said.

"No!" Marvalaine barked. "She's not ready."

"Ready or not," Destiny said, "here she comes, and she's packing some power with her."

"It's too powerful," Marvalaine said.

"But," Destiny asked, "could I defeat her with it?"

Marvalaine nodded his head and said, "But you could destroy yourself in the process."

"Show it to me!"

Nimisen said, "You've already seen it."

"You should go now," Marvalaine said. "Concentrate on your trial before you worry about this."

Harold also set out early for Cricket Bend. This case will undoubtedly end up in his memoirs. He may even make some entries in the law journals if he can prove abuse of power and identify who the abuser was.

It was a fine morning for a drive. He turned the music up and let the music clear the peculiar circumstances from his mind for the next two hours. To keep his mind clear, he amused himself by counting bird species and out of state license plates. He offered to bring his wife with him for a mini vacation, but she knew he would not be in the best of humors and declined. His staff went down yesterday to oversee some of the preparations, so he was left to make the drive alone.

He could have requested a driver for a trip this long, but he liked to be more fiscally responsible than that and just reminded himself again that it was a nice morning for a drive, even if he was all alone.

Honey never cared for driving much before, but then she never had anything that made driving fun, either. Ralph's car was a hot piece of machinery, but then that asshole had to name it Honey because it was so fast and loose. No question in her mind. She would have to pay him a visit and use some new spells on him.

The night had been quiet and uneventful as the miles sped by on the nearly empty highway. There was little for Honey to do on the mostly straight road. All she could do was hold the wheel and press on the accelerator.

Abilene fell asleep quickly, if not easily, and once asleep, her mind was filled with terrifying images of Honey and her fire. She didn't have visions, but she had nightmares of her very unstable daughter getting everything she ever wanted with little regard to who she fried in the process. She didn't understand how she could have given birth to such a psychopath, but the truth was that the sorcerer clan was littered with psychopaths, and those that weren't were almost surely sociopathic.

Richard managed to stay awake a little longer than Abilene, but he eventually fell asleep with his head against the window.

Honey wasn't even tired. She should be, and she knew it, but she was filled with energy and simply drove through the night. The road was boring, and the headlights displayed a never-ending line of striped white paint, but she never even nodded off. The sun was brightening the horizon in the rear-view mirror. It was time to wake her minions.

"So," she said loudly. "You awake?"

Richard snorted and shook his head. He hadn't wanted to fall asleep, but apparently did. "What?" he asked.

"I asked if you was awake yet."

He rubbed his eyes and said, "I am now. How long was I asleep?"

"All night. Look! It's morning already."

He yawned and asked, "Are you okay? Do you need me to drive for a bit?"

"Nah," she said. "I'm fine. But I has some questions. I was wondering something. When you talks about our people, how many people do we have, exactly?"

"Exactly?" Richard asked. "I don't know exactly, but all around the world, we must have a couple hundred thousand that know who they are and maybe another million bastards around the world."

"Cool," she said. "I spect that's enough to start our own country. Are all them people in hiding?"

"No," Richard had to stifle a laugh. "Our people aren't hiding. Most of our people are important people like doctors, and scientists, and government leaders."

"And," Abilene thought to herself, "one dumb ass slutty hick from Mississippi."

"I like that," Honey said. "This is gonna be awesome."

She turned up the radio and started rocking side to side in her seat while nodding her head in time with the music. An old Impala came racing up behind her and rode her bumper, flashing his high beams. She rolled down the window and stuck her arm out the window and flipped him off. The Impala blared its horn as it raced around her and cut in front of her purposely close.

She flipped him off again and yelled, "Get off the road, asshole!"

As soon as the words were out of her mouth, the Impala swerved into the concrete barrier that divided the highway in the center and bounced back into the roadway sliding sideways leaving wide black marks on the highway surface before it spun around backwards and slid across the roadway and up the embankment until it finally came to rest under an overpass.

Richard saw it and had no doubt that she had caused it. His plan had always been for their people to resume their rightful place atop society. Their people were rich with the very best minds the world had to offer. This girl thought she was going to meet their people and be proclaimed queen. That was not the kind of world he foresaw. Unfortunately, he knew nobody capable of stopping her, except maybe for the witch girl.

As the car approached Cricket Bend, Michelle pointed ahead and said, "Them lights up there is the gas station and the diner. Next to it be the general sto where we come every week or two. Across from that is the bayou where we lived.

Charles paused the car on the side of the road by the dock and scanned the swamp before pulling the car into the diner's parking lot, where one of the prosecutor's assistants directed him to the community center building. He parked the car in front of the large barn they used for traveling revivals and occasional holiday pageants. He wondered if this would be the first trial held here.

Inside, they found a raised platform with a skirt hanging to the floor and a small desk atop the platform for the judge. Velvet ropes suspended from brass stands marked the jurors' box, which contained office chairs for the jurors. The prosecutor's table and defendant's table were also separated from the gallery by the same velvet ropes. Inexpensive folding chairs were set up for the audience.

Destiny and Charles took their places at the defendant's table while Michelle, Blake, Tempest, and Ashlin found seats behind them. Michelle leaned forward and said, "Mr. Charles, I thought you said there wouldn't be a jury for the preliminary hearing."

"There won't," he replied. "The prosecutor must be supremely confident that he will not only go to trial, but that it will be held immediately."

Julia and Carl Pinet entered the building with their daughter Danielle, Mrs. Thibodeaux and her son Gilbert. Carl and Julia were dressed like Sunday church and sat directly behind Michelle. Julia put her hand on Michelle's shoulder and said, "We're here for you." Danielle and Gilbert ran around to see Destiny.

"Hey," Gilbert said.

"Hey you," Destiny replied.

"We's all here," Danielle said.

"Yeah," Gilbert said. "We all think the pohlice is idiots to think you done this."

The kids ran back and took their seats with their parents.

Several more town folk entered the building and sat in the audience behind Destiny. Only Dr. McMann and Captain Polin sat behind the prosecutor.

The bailiff stood up and recited, "All rise, the Louisiana Criminal Court is now in session, the Honorable Judge Harold Jamison now presiding."

Harold came in and took his seat. He rapped his gavel on the desk and said, "Attorney's approach."

Mr. Charles and Mr. Tangiers both rose from their seats. Tangiers glanced over at Charles to see if he knew what this was about as they came forward to stand before his desk.

Harold looked directly at Tangiers and asked privately, "Why isn't this hearing in the juvenile courts?"

"Your honor," Tangiers said. "There was nothing juvenile about the crime. I intend to prove that not only should she stand trial for the brutal murders, but she should stand trial as an adult and receive an adult's sentence. The prosecution will be requesting the death penalty."

Harold turned to Mr. Charles and asked, "Are you prepared to defend a capital case?"

"Your honor," Charles said. "The prosecution's pursuit of an adult trial and capital punishment are just two more cases of flagrant abuse of power. They have been railroading my client from the beginning, pushing for an arraignment even before completing the police investigation and now this hearing..."

"But," Harold interrupted, "are you ready to proceed?"

"Yes, your honor, the defense is prepared."

"Very well then," Harold said for all to hear. "You may return to your seats. Mr. Prosecutor, please make your opening statement."

"Thank you, your honor, the prosecution will introduce medical and forensic evidence that shows that not only was Miss Boutin present when the two decedents were killed, but that there is sufficient evidence that she caused their deaths to warrant us proceeding to trial."

Tangiers sat down and Charles stood to say, "Your honor, the defense has copies of the forensic reports, and not only do they fail to implicate Miss Boutin, they fail to prove that a crime ever took place. The defense moves that these proceedings be thrown out for lack of evidence."

Harold glanced back and forth between Tangiers and Charles, then said, "The court will hear the medical examiner and the arson investigator accounts before ruling on the dismissal."

"Well then," Tangiers said, "the prosecution calls Captain Gerald Polin to the stand."

The captain's chair squeaked as his tall frame rose. He strolled up to the witness stand and placed his hand on the bible and replied, "I do".

Tangiers approached the witness stand and asked, "Captain Polin, please state your occupation for the record."

"I am an arson investigator for the Lafayette fire department."

"And did you personally examine the crime scene?"

Charles popped up and said, "Objection. Your honor, the court has not ruled that a crime exists yet, therefore there can be no crime scene."

Harold smiled and said, "Sustained."

"Alleged," Tangiers corrected himself, "have you examined the alleged crime scene?"

Harold nodded and Polin said, "I have."

"And did you find evidence that the fire was caused deliberately?"

Polin leaned over to speak into the microphone. "I did. I found evidence that someone in the household brewed a variety of home-opathic potions and concoctions, and various different flammable accelerants were used as ingredients."

Tangiers asked, "And which of these ingredients, in your professional opinion, caused the fire?"

"Well," Polin responded. "There were dozens of fires all over the property. I believe these were caused by throwing containers of alcohol and kerosine, like a Molotov cocktail. The fire in the house destroyed most of the evidence, but I found rope fibers which appeared to be used as a fuse. I gave the fibers to the medical examiner for DNA analysis."

"Thank you, Captain Polin. Your witness."

Charles was frantically turning pages in his copies of the arson report and asked, "Captain, I don't see any mention in your reports about Molotov cocktails or rope fuses."

"May I see those?" Polin asked.

Charles approached the witness and showed him the reports.

"Oh, those are the preliminary findings. You have my old reports."

"Your honor," Charles said. "The prosecution has not only rushed to hold this hearing, but they failed to provide full disclosure to their evidence."

"Noted," Harold said, "but I'll still hear the coroner."

Charles returned to his seat and said, "No more questions."

Tangiers said, "The prosecution calls Dr. McMann to the stand."

McMann pushed her black-rimmed glasses on to the bridge of her nose and walked to the witness box.

"Dr. McMann, have you examined the two decedents?"

"I have."

"And what conclusion have you drawn?"

"The bodies exhibited the worst burns I have ever seen. They were still alive when they were soaked with kerosene and lit on fire."

"And," Tangiers asked, "what about the rope Captain Polin mentioned? Did you examine that?"

"Yes, and it had skin cells embedded in it where the knot was tied. The skin cells were a DNA match to the Defendant."

"Thank you, Dr. McMann. No more questions."

Again, Mr. Charles was thumbing through the M.E. reports. He rose from his seat and showed his copy of the report to her. "Is this," he asked, "also an old copy of your report?"

She looked at it and said, "Why, yes, it is. I can't imagine how you ended up with that."

Charles looked pleadingly at the judge and asked, "Your honor?"

"Noted," was all Harold would say.

Charles froze for a few seconds, then turned to the witness and asked, "What knot?"

McMann looked confused.

"In the rope. You said you found skin cells in the knot of the rope. What knot?"

"Like you said," McMann replied. "I found skin cells where the rope was tied into a knot."

"That's odd," Charles said. "I never heard of a fuse that was tied with a knot. No more questions."

Tangiers stood and said, "The prosecution rests."

Harold said, "In light of the professional testimony, the court finds sufficient evidence to be held over for trial. This hearing is concluded. We will reconvene tomorrow at nine, however, if the prosecution fails to provide the defense with complete current copies of both the medical examiner's report and the arson report within thirty minutes from now, I will reverse my decision and dismiss the case with prejudice. The clock is ticking, Mr. Tangiers."

Blake followed Mr. Charles out of the hall and said, "Put me on the stand."

"To say what?" Charles asked while he continued walking back to his car.

"To tell them why these men were there. They came here to hunt Destiny down and kill her."

"And how are you going to tell them that?" Charles asked. "I don't need you getting up there and lying to the court."

"It won't be a lie."

Charles stopped walking and asked, "How? Where did you get your information?"

"I know what they were up to because I was one of them. I came here with them."

"You came here to murder Destiny? If you testify to that, one of two things will happen. You'll be arrested for perjury, or you'll be arrested for attempted murder."

"I didn't know what their plans were," Blake said. "I was only hired to track her."

"You?" Charles asked incredulously. "A sixteen-year-old kid was asked to track down a girl in the swamps?"

"I'm good at finding things," Blake said.

"Show me. Let's go to the edge of this lot and find some tracks, and you tell me something about them."

Blake had never tried anything like that before, but why not? He followed Charles to a spot behind the meeting hall where they found a small trail of footprints. He looked at the trail and tried to imagine it had a life that he could peer into, then he wound the image backwards.

"Two boys," he said, "they left their canoe on the banks instead of using the dock, then they snuck around this way to the back of the diner where they peeked into the back window and caught Marie getting ready for a bath."

Charles was only caught up by the story for a moment before he said, "Bah, you're just making that up."

"Why don't you ask Marie? She caught them and her mother ran the boys off."

Charles shook his head and said, "You're wasting my time."

Blake peeked into Mr. Charles memory and said, "Like the time you followed Mary Albright all around town and your friend Jimmy said you were wasting your time?"

"How could you possibly know about that?" Charles asked.

Blake shrugged and said, "I know things. I can see stuff."

"You're a psychic?"

"I've been called that."

Charles had to think about that a moment, but then he shook his head and said, "I can't put you on the stand and tell them you are a psychic, and you just know stuff."

"You don't have to. I was hired by these guys to find this girl. I came with them. That wasn't a vision. It was me in the car with them.

We had a room above the store. You can ask the old coot if he knows me."

Charles shook his head again and said, "Not if I can't explain why grown men would hire a boy to do their tracking."

Blake watched him walk away towards his car and said, "Just think about it. You don't know where this trial will go. I'll still be here if you change your mind."

Blake returned to the courtroom to find Destiny while a pang in Charles' gut made him wonder if Blake really was for real. He had to be. He couldn't know about Mary otherwise. What if he can see the trial and already knows he'll be called? Charles turned back to the courtroom to find Destiny. He would have to make a new plan.

The bright shining sun outside was the direct opposite of the murky clouds brewing inside Michelle's heart. Why didn't the hearing did not go the way it was supposed to? The prosecution had no evidence linking Destiny to the events, and the judge was supposed to let her go, but instead, the witnesses had entirely new stories and now they were going to trial. Something was wrong.

She left the makeshift courtroom in stunned silence, leaving Mr. Charles behind in the courtroom with Destiny. Michelle joined an equally stunned Ashlin in the parking lot.

"What happened?" Ashlin asked.

"I don't know," Michelle said, "but those people lied."

Blake and Destiny joined them, and Destiny cheerily said, "Hey guys, Mr. Charles says we can have lunch on him."

Ashlin wrapped her arms around Destiny, rubbing her tears into Destiny's blouse.

Michelle still had a blank expression on her face while she asked, "Is you crazy? How is it dat you be so unaffected by what just happened in there?"

"Because," Destiny said, "that was just the pretrial hearing. I knew I would lose it because I had already foreseen the real trial. Blake saw the trial too. He knows it doesn't end here."

"Maybe," Blake said, "but I don't remember them claiming those things about your DNA evidence or the alcohol and kerosene."

"Yeah," Destiny admitted. "I don't remember none of them, neither. Let's eat, I'm starving. Don't worry so much, it all works out."

They crossed the filling station, which stood directly between the barn and the diner. Marie saw them approaching and met them at the door. "Madam," she said, "mademoiselle, monsieur, et petite mademoiselle, I save a table for you. Come in."

They followed Marie to a corner booth. Destiny slid into the booth and eagerly looked over the menu. Blake slid in next to her and shared the menu with her. Michelle hesitated. She bristled when she saw Dr. McMann and Captain Polin laughing and smiling at a nearby table.

"Oui," Marie said to her. "Zey are here too. I hear what zey say inside and I don't believe."

"No," Michelle said. "You shouldn't believe them. They be bad liars."

Michelle approached their table. Ashlin blindly followed her. The smiles faded some from Dr. McMann's face as she saw them approach.

"How could you?" Michelle asked. "You swore to tell the truth, but you told a pack of lies. I was there. None of that happened the way you said. Did you lie in them reports too? Why?"

Dr. McMann said, "You know, you really shouldn't be talking to us. It could be construed as witness tampering, and it's illegal."

"So is lying on the witness stand." Michelle summoned up the voice and said, "You is going to fix this. Tomorrow when you gets on the stand, you gonna tell the real truth. You is goin' to take your oath seriously and tell the whole real truth."

Ashlin was mesmerized by Michelle's voice. Michelle returned to their table, but Ashlin lingered long enough to summon her own voice and add, "Tonight, you will fix the reports you wrote so they have the truth in them also. Fix the reports. Tell the truth."

Ashlin rejoined the group. Marie sat with them and summoned her mother to wait the table.

Honey felt like she had unlimited energy. She had already piloted the truck effortlessly across Mississippi, then northwest through Shreveport. Miles melted away, and she never tired. She left the Deep South behind and entered Texas, which in her mind was still the Wild West. She crossed through Dallas and Amarillo, expecting to see gun toting cowboys on horses any minute.

For the first time in her life, she felt like she was really in her element. This is what her whole life was leading up to. She already considered herself queen of her people and pictured herself surrounded with men commanded to please her, but her daydreamed image of the future was interrupted by bright lights and a siren.

Looking behind her in the rear-view mirror, she saw the flashing lights of a highway patrol car. She considered crushing the car and moving on, but thought it might be more fun to handle them differently. She pulled the truck over to the shoulder and stopped. The patrol car pulled up behind her and kept the lights on while another patrol car pulled in front.

"Ooh," she thought. "I got two of them."

Richard sat quietly in the passenger seat, watching her expression. He didn't know what to expect, but he was pretty sure he wasn't going to like it.

The patrolman approached the car with one hand on his holstered gun while the other pointed a flashlight in her face.

She smiled and asked, "Is there a problem, officer?"

He kept the flashlight in her eyes and said, "Can I see your license and registration, please?"

She patted her breasts, then squeezed them seductively and said, "Oops, I was sure I left it in there. Would you like to help me search?"

"Can you get out of the car, Miss?"

"Good idea," she said. "You might find some other places to search."

"Turn around and place your hands on the hood."

She turned around, placed her hands on the hood, spread her legs, and arched her back to accentuate her butt.

"Is this your vehicle, Miss?"

"Sure is. I just got it."

The driver of the second patrol car joined the first officer and said, "I confirmed the plates to the stolen truck."

"Stolen?" she screamed. "Why that little boy bitch. I won it fair and square playing pool."

The second officer pulled out some handcuffs.

"What do you plan to do with those?" she asked. "Cause it might be fun, but you just don't look like you want to have any fun."

As she spoke, the handcuffs became very hot. The officer dropped them on the ground where they sizzled and turned a brilliant red.

The first officer removed the clasp holding his gun in his holster, but his gun began to burn very hot. It was too hot for him to grip and began to burn his hip until he unclasped his belt and dropped the holster to the ground. The leather around the red-hot gun burst into flame. He kicked the holster away from them before the shells started exploding.

Honey turned around to face the confused cops. She shook her head and said, "Now, boys. This could have been a whole different kind of hot. It would have been a lot more pleasant, but you had to be all businesslike."

Their boots hissed and smoked as they heated up. One officer started stomping his feet on the ground while the other one was already kicking off his boots, which quickly erupted into flames. The first officer fell to the ground and kicked off his boots, only to have his pants start to sear his legs. Both officers quickly disrobed as everything they wore began to smolder against their skin.

"I'm sorry, boys. I'm glad to see that you wants to have some fun now, but I'm afraid that it's too late for that. Too bad too. I mighta liked a couple of upstanding boys like yourselves, but now I think I'm just gonna have to burn those things right off of you."

She pointed to their exposed crotches with one hand and formed a fireball in the palm of the other. They turned and ran naked down the highway. She wondered how far they would run before feeling safe.

She looked at their vehicles and reached out her hands, letting the energy flow out to wrap around the cars. The cars shook under the weight of her hands, then on a whim, she flipped her hands over and the cars rolled over. She pressed down again and crushed the upside-down cars into the ground.

She smiled while she clapped her palms together, then climbed back into the truck and said, "That was fun, but time to get back to work. My people await me."

Abilene scowled and said, "You don't think that was a bit much?"

"No, Mama. The more I do this, the more right it feels. I think I was born to do this, and I don't think nothin' is too much for me!"

Mr. Charles was just leaving the barn when Tangiers caught him and said, "You're not leaving without these, are you?"

Charles turned around and saw him waving some folders over his head.

"Here," Simon said, "these are my copies of the reports. I don't know how my staff could have given you those old copies. I take full responsibility and I apologize for the whole stupid mess."

Charles didn't believe it for a second, but he accepted the reports and looked them over to see if they matched the witnesses' testimony.

"Those are the real deal," Simon said. "Like I said, they were my personal copies."

Charles remembered that the other copies were also Tangiers' personal copies, but these at least matched the testimony. He jerked his head in a quick nod, which was as close as he wanted to get to an actual 'thank you', then turned in the direction of the diner to join his client.

Johnson kept a steady pace down the highway. He had seen several cops on the road and didn't want to be pulled over for speeding. He checked his speedometer again as he saw some flashing lights ahead of him. His heart raced as he passed them and saw the black truck with Honey draped over the hood.

He couldn't stop. There was nothing that he could either help her or the police. He would just have to pull over up the road and observe. With the hummer pulled well over on the shoulder and, he retrieved a pair of binoculars.

His heart thundered in his ears. He had to lean against the side of the hummer to steady his shaking hands. He saw more than he wanted to see. Honey held a ball of flame in her hand while she laughed at the patrolmen. She had stripped them naked and now she was toying with them. It was like the small island in the swamp, and she was just like the girl he was protecting. No, that wasn't quite true. The girl he watched in the field glasses wore a maniacal expression. There was a meanness about her that the other girl never displayed. She was more like the man that had hired him in the first place, and he was dead.

When she flipped the patrol cars over on their tops, he wished that he had been spying on her through a gun sight instead of binoculars. Something inside told him this girl should be put down. He wished more than ever that his friends would contact him now and tell him what to do, and maybe how to do it.

He put the glasses away and got back in the car, where he hunkered down so nobody would see him and waited for them to pass. He would keep following her, but at a much safer distance after what he had just seen.

Mr. Charles didn't stay at the diner. He got his food to go and drove the group to the nearby hotel he had arranged for them to stay while he sat alone in his room nibbling on his dinner, comparing the details of the false reports originally delivered to him from Tangiers with the new ones he got outside the court. He compared the old report with the new report and he compared the arson report with the M.E. report. There wasn't much in common between any of them. He got up to get a cold water from the mini fridge when Dr. McMann knocked on his door and personally delivered an authentic copy of her true findings. She gave him no explanation. She put it in his hands and left. Charles hadn't even closed the door when Polin arrived with his.

Charles stood in the door scratching his head, then returned to his desk and put the new reports next to the others. They all looked authentic. He had no way of knowing if this was a trick. He was going to have to compare all of them and be prepared to counter each of them, or even a mixture of them all.

CHAPTER 11

Day Five.

The Dinosaurs. The Passenger Pigeon. The Dodo bird.

All of them are extinct and gone forever. Like the loss of a species, questions of belief can be lost to the echoes of time, or they can be answered and never asked again. Educated people no longer ask if the world is round anymore.

This day marked the end of the question, "Do you believe in magic?"

The trial was the furthest thing from Destiny's mind while she paddled the old pirogue through the familiar bayou. The cypress trees held the sun at bay keeping the water crystal clear. The small boat sliced silently across the water until she came upon the familiar old dock on their family island. She tied the boat to the pontoon which held the wooden platform atop the water and stepped onto the small piece of land which had been her home since she was born.

The island was as she remembered it before the fire, without the tainted odor of charred wood or sulfur. She climbed the short path up to the plateau where the plot of land flattened out and the home was built. Everything was perfect. The home stood strong and sturdy and the chicken coop next to the smokehouse was fresh and new without the aged grey splinters she remembered.

She crossed the yard and saw her nana's garden with all the odd herbs she used for her potions. Further up, past the yard, was the hollowed out cypress tree where she liked to play as a child. She wanted to see inside the cypress. She couldn't explain why, but she had an uncontrollable urge to see inside the hollowed out tree and started to sprint, but skidded to a stop when a small dark-haired girl came out from inside and took one look at her, and then ran in the other direction.

"Wait," Destiny yelled. "What's your name?"

She ran after the girl. Destiny was older and faster, but as she closed the gap between them the dark-haired girl covered her ears with her hands and flung herself into the swamp. Destiny ran up to the edge of the shore and peered into the water. Other than the ripples on the surface of the water, there was no sign of the little girl. She strained to see into the water and spread her search outward expecting to see the little girl swimming away, but she was gone.

Destiny turned and headed back to the main house, shuffling her feet as she went. As she passed the old Cypress she heard a voice from the house yell out, "Tempy?"

She ran to the house and yelled, "Nana?" but it wasn't her grand-mother. The woman on the porch was as old as her nana, but she was thinner and had flaming red hair. Destiny stood at the edge of the yard and watched her great grandmother on the porch call out again, "Tempy?"

A clap of thunder exploded overhead, and the vision popped from her view. She was back in the hotel room staring at Ashlin's face. Neither of them said a word. Ashlin ran her finger across Destiny's forehead putting a stray hair back in place then left, apparently satisfied that she was okay.

With Amarillo and the cops behind her, Honey continued west out of Texas and into New Mexico, then turned North at Albuquerque. She crossed the south-west corner of Colorado then turned North West again at Durango. One out of every three towns she passed through sounded familiar to her, but the roads were all the same. They were all surrounded with sand and cacti. Buttes and pinnacles surrounded the desert and decorated the horizon where taller mountains loomed off in the distance. Some of the buttes sported colorful striations painted horizontally across their surface and provided a welcome break to the monotony, but the roads never varied much. A tumble weed rolled across the highway before her and was swept up in her wake after she roared by. She felt like she had driven through a dozen cowboy movies.

Utah was flat and dusty. Gone were the familiar cowboy towns, but the tumbleweed never left. Everyplace she had driven in the last three hours seemed like the middle of nowhere. When the GPS told her to get off the highway, she was still in the middle of nowhere and said, "The first thing I'm going to do when I take over is to upgrade our locations."

Richard winced. Their locations were meant to be secluded and secret. This girl didn't fit the profile. Their leaders were well organized and intellectual, but she was everything else.

A half mile off the highway, Honey pulled the truck onto a secluded road and slammed on the brakes when a bullet punctured the windshield and lodged into her seat just inches from her shoulder. She threw the door open and began scanning the area. The amulet throbbed between her breasts. She wrapped her fingers around the amulet and felt more than just its power. The amulet knew something she didn't know. She wiped her arm in the air in front of her and the amulet showed her how to create a protective shield.

A flash behind a short broken wall down the street immediately preceded a bullet smashing into her shield. She fired off a fireball that arced through the air and landed just in front of the wall. More bullets smashed against her shield in rapid succession. She set her jaw and fired off volleys of fire balls one after the other. The fireballs descended on the wall and created a massive fire surrounding the wall. More bullets impacted her shield.

Honey sucked in her breath and closed her eyes. Then she thrust both arms out in front of her launching fireballs so rapidly that they created a single solid arc of fire that landed on the wall. The arc of fire hit the ground and spread outwards engulfing the entire area around the wall as it grew. The bullets ceased flying.

Librarians two and three retreated back to the room of meditation. The two mercs that they had controlled were gone.

Johnson stood outside his vehicle watching through field glasses. He had recognized one of the gunmen as one of the orange bandana mercs and assumed the other was his partner, but they were toast now. This girl was way worse than the first one. He didn't know if she was any more powerful than the first, but she was way more mean and probably crazy and that made her very dangerous.

She ended the onslaught and held up her fingers like they were guns and blew on her fingertips like a gunfighter blowing smoke from his gun barrels. She laughed and climbed back in the truck and took off. The massive fire blocked her view of the Humvee.

Abilene rolled her eyes but kept quiet. She turned her head to look out the window, but couldn't look at her daughter anymore. She wasn't even sure that Honey was still the daughter she raised. Her daughter had changed into someone she didn't recognize.

Honey slipped her hand between Richard's legs and said, "I might just need you to take care of me tonight. Lettin' loose that much fire is a rush like you wouldn't believe."

Abilene closed her eyes and shook her head but kept her opinion to herself.

Johnson got back in his vehicle and drove down to those poor souls car and found a prisoner inside. He closed his eyes and thought, "Oh shit. Where the hell are those guys when I need them?"

He transferred the prisoner to his vehicle and continued his pursuit.

Mr. Charles spent much of the night studying and comparing the various crime scene reports. He eventually found time to sleep, but still rose early enough to get everyone back to the makeshift courtroom. He knocked on their door in the morning and said it was time to go. Ashlin let him in the room, but lingered a bit with Tempest who was still in bed. The precocious little redhead didn't feel comfortable leaving her behind and thought she would try to take her with them until another knock on the door brought a welcome visitor.

Charles opened the door and said, "Dr. Weinhart, how good of you to come."

"Not at all," she said. "I'm glad to help."

Charles left Tempest in Dr. Weinhart's care and took the rest of them to the diner to discuss their strategy. Marie gave them a table in the far corner and made sure to seat all their other customers as far away as possible.

"We've had a new development," Charles said. "The prosecutor gave me his copies of the forensic reports as we left the hearing. They pretty much said the same things his witnesses said in court. But then, the coroner and arson investigator each gave me entirely new reports which supported what you've been telling me. That bastard has been lying to the court and we're going to nail him and get you off."

"So," Michelle said. "If everyone tells the truth now, they'll have to let my Destiny go free?"

Charles nodded and said, "That just about sums it up."

Destiny glanced over at Blake then back to Mr. Charles and said, "I don't think it will be quite that easy. I don't think the prosecutor knows they gave you the real reports. If they start telling the truth on the stand, the prosecution will know something has gone wrong with his plans, and he'll improvise."

"He'll be caught in a lie," Charles said. "If he starts making stuff up in court, he'll just get more tangled up in his own lies."

Marie brought breakfast to the table. Ashlin still had a faraway look, thinking about Tempest, while everyone else scarfed down their food.

Dr. Weinhart opened the motel room's curtains and setup a chair looking out the window. She thought Tempest was doing surprisingly well considering the diagnoses in her charts. Tempest was admitted to the hospital long before Weinhart started working there, and she had never taken her off her medications long enough to gauge how she might react. Maybe her little girl had reached her and had done something to improve her condition, or maybe the charts overstated her illness. Dr. Weinhart was glad that she wasn't suffering any withdrawal effects, especially the vomiting.

Tempest saw Dr. Weinhart setup the chair and walked herself from the bed to the chair. She could see the pool through the fences. It wasn't as good a view of the pool as a second-floor room might have been, but she could still imagine the voices of the children playing in the water and smiled. It was too early for any children to be in the pool, but if she had learned anything during her time in the hospital, it was patience.

The GPS directed Honey into the parking lot of a modern-looking building and announced, "You have arrived at your destination."

She pulled the truck into the nearest slot to the door she could find. It said it was reserved, but she didn't care. As far as she was concerned, it belonged to her.

"Well," she said. "It might be out in the middle of nowhere, but it ain't half bad looking at least. Let's go inside and make us some introductions."

Richard hesitated a moment and said, "I haven't quite figured out how I'm going to do that yet."

"You mean that after all this time of you dudes having no real power, you ain't got a name for the person who arrives at your door with the real thing? I thought you said you had a lot of smart pencil pushers who could figure this shit out!"

Richard sighed and said, "There is a prophecy that says there would be a chosen one who would be the first to return magic to the world and she..."

"Well there you go," Honey said. "The Chosen One. I like it. It has a kind of God like sound to it."

"Except," Richard said, "that you are not The Chosen One, your cousin Destiny is. She's the one that brought back the magic. Frankly, I don't know how you got so powerful."

"Well I do," Abilene said, "and it's right there bouncing between her tits. She stole it from that bitch you calls 'The Chosen One.'"

"It's mine now," Honey said sternly. "Your prophets must have a name for the one who come and kicked The Chosen One's ass, don't they?"

"Well," Richard admitted, "we don't have any prophets. Only the witches do, and you haven't kicked her ass yet..."

"You saw what I can do."

"Yes," Richard said, "and it was very impressive. Very reminiscent of what is recorded in the ancient scrolls."

"So," Honey said. "Let's go in there and tell everyone that the ancient power has returned to our side and after we kick some Chosen One's ass, we plan to take over the whole God damned world."

Anything going on around Cricket Bend was cause for excitement. Turning the community building into a courtroom for a murder trial was the biggest thing that ever came this way. News had spread rapidly throughout the swamp of the trial at Cricket Bend. Friends and enemies alike gathered to witness the event, and assembled in the gallery. Many arrived early so they wouldn't miss anything.

Destiny and Mr. Charles found their places at the defendant's table followed by Mr. Tangiers and his assistant at the prosecution's table. Michelle sat directly behind Destiny in the front of the gallery with Blake and Ashlin behind Mr. Charles. Ashlin stuck her tongue out whenever Tangiers glanced over at them.

Most of the locals filled the seats behind Destiny. Zeline, who thought herself to be a witch, chose to sit up front on the prosecution's side. Marie's mother, much to Marie's displeasure, sat in the back of the room on the prosecution's side.

The jurors were escorted in and the bailiff took his place in front of the central desk and cried out, "All rise. The twenty-third district court of Louisiana is now in session. The Honorable Harold Jamison presiding."

Harold entered the court swiftly and stepped up onto the makeshift riser and stood behind the desk while he banged the gavel on the desk then motioned for everyone to take their seats while he sat himself down.

"Mr. Charles," Harold said. "My clerk informs me that the forensic reports were delivered to you within the thirty-minute deadline I imposed yesterday. I trust you have had time to review them?"

"Yes, I have," Charles said, "but..."

"But what?" Harold asked. "Are you requesting more time to review them?" Harold was expecting an extension and was prepared to grant one.

"No, your honor," Charles hesitated a moment while he looked over at the prosecutor's table, then continued, "The defense motions the court to dismiss this case with prejudice."

Harold was prepared to dole out leniency and grant the continuance, but he wasn't in the mood for grand standing. "On what grounds?" he asked.

"After receiving the prosecution's personal copies of the forensic reports, the defense received these other reports which not only contradict both of the first reports, but supports the defense's positions that Ms. Boutin was not responsible."

Mr. Tangiers stood and exclaimed, "Your honor, this is outrageous. The defense can't come in here and produce false evidence..."

Harold banged his gavel and yelled, "Approach!"

"Your honor," Tangiers continued privately with Harold and Mr. Charles, "the defense can produce their own witnesses to argue the merits of the forensic evidence, but they cannot produce falsified documents and claim them as authentic."

"Let me see them. Where did you get these?" Harold asked.

Charles handed Harold the documents and said, "They were delivered personally by both the medical examiner and the arson investigator, Mr. Tangiers' own witnesses.

"That's not true!" Tangiers argued. "They produced the documents I provided. The defense is lying!"

Harold held up his hand to stop Tangiers tirade and said, "Careful Mr. Tangiers. They look authentic enough to me. Your witnesses will have to testify to which document is authentic."

"Well then," Tangiers said, "the prosecution requests a recess to examine these new documents."

"Denied."

Tangiers tried a different tactic, "The defense never disclosed the existence of these new documents. The prosecution needs time to review them."

Harold shook his head and said, "Denied. They were from your own witnesses. The defense has no reason to suspect you are unaware of their existence."

Tangiers took a step back and said, "You aren't suggesting that I knew of their existence, are you?"

Harold leaned forward over the desk and said, "I am suggesting that you take your place and carry on with this trial."

Harold gave the new reports to his clerk and said, "Take these documents and the prosecutor's lovely assistant to my temporary office and make copies of them. Give the copy to Mr. Tangiers' assistant and return the originals to Mr. Charles."

He then sat up straight again and announced to the court, "The motion to dismiss is denied. The prosecution will proceed with their opening remarks."

Tangiers wasn't sure what to say. The opening remarks he planned to make might make no sense in light of the new evidence he hasn't had time to review, but he wasn't given time to write a new opening speech, so he stuck with the script.

"Ladies and gentlemen of the jury. The prosecution intends to prove that the fire on June the 3rd was not only intentional, but it was caused with the specific purpose of killing the two decedents whose charred remains were found in the home. The prosecution will show that this heinous act was both intentional and premeditated. It sickens me to say this, but burning to death like they did must be the most horrific way to die of all. Don't let the defendant's sweet girl next door appearance fool you. She is a calculating, cold-blooded murderer of the most cruel kind. Thank you."

Richard led Honey into the facility. The corridors were empty with only a single receptionist in sight. The receptionist saw Richard enter the building and called Dorris.

"Where is everyone?" Honey asked. "Why is it so empty?"

"Because," Richard said, "we don't do our work in public, so if the public enters this building, they don't see anything."

"I see," Honey replied. "Well, all this hiding from the public stuff is gonna stop."

"Maybe we should take that slowly," Richard said. "We wouldn't want to learn if you have any limitations while the public was watching."

"I ain't got no limitations."

"Oh, my God!" Abilene exclaimed. "Don't you never listen to no one? You only just become powerful since you stole that rock. You don't rightly know *IF* you has limitations. You knows that my limitation seems to be leavin' the farm. You might have limitations just waitin' to spring on you. Even superman had his kryptonite. What if you was out in the street doin' your ass kickin' when all of a sudden you come up dry? Maybe just because a puppy dog walked by and you cain't do magic around puppy dogs? Wouldn't you want to know that before you shows it to the world? If they sees it, then everyone will by gettin' themselves puppy dogs."

"Oh God, Mama! Is you saying I cain't do magic around puppy dogs? I like puppy dogs! That's terrible!"

Abilene just closed her eyes and shook her head.

Richard was about to ask the receptionist if anyone had heard from Logan yet when Dorris emerged from the elevator.

"Richard!" she screamed. "I was worried about you! I was afraid you might have disappeared, too."

"I ran into something interesting," Richard said. "It sounds like you haven't heard from Logan yet."

"Not a peep," she said.

"Well," Richard said, "let me introduce you to Logan's friends. This is Abilene, one of his special projects, and that is her daughter, Honey. Abilene here has some of the old magic, sort of, but Honey there seems to have it all."

Honey shook her hand weakly and said, "I'm gonna need an office here; someplace to set up while I take over."

"Take over?" Dorris asked.

"I'll explain later," Richard said. "Let's give her Logan's office for now."

Dorris was confused, but she nodded and led them to the elevator.

***

Mr. Charles stood up and walked to the jury box. He slowly stepped down the full length of the box, looking each juror directly in the eye. When he reached the other end of the box, he turned towards the center of the jurors and said, "The prosecutor called her 'a calculating, cold-blooded murderer.' Well, I hate to disappoint you, but the only cold-blooded calculating going on here is from the prosecutor himself."

"This little girl lost her home and everything in it. Imagine it: one day you're home, safe and sound, then the next day all of your possessions are burned to nothing. The walls and roof of your home are gone. Your bed is gone. All you have left are the clothes on your back, and thankfully, your grandmother, who also survived the horrific tragedy. What are you going to do? If you're only sixteen, you'll probably just follow your grandmother. If she takes you to a nearby relative, then that's where you'll go. But our prosecutor tried to construe that into evading prosecution. Calculating and cold-blooded, if you ask me."

"She was arrested three days after the fire. That's before the arson investigator finished writing his findings. It's before the coroner concluded her investigation. Calculating and cold-blooded. And now we are at trial only two days later! What is the rush I ask you? Calculating and cold-blooded."

"Ladies and gentlemen of the jury. I will prove to you that this rush to injustice was not only unnecessary, but it was misguided. I will prove that there is no way this little girl could have committed this crime. When we are done, you will agree with me that the only criminal in this courtroom is sitting at the head of the other table. Thank you."

Mr. Tangiers blushed dark red while he stewed in his seat. Defenses are allowed too much latitude in their opening statements, in his opinion.

Johnson stopped the hummer just outside the parking lot and watched Honey enter the building. He still hadn't heard from the librarians and he had no idea why the two mercs had taken a prisoner, but they had been working on the same side as him, so he kept the prisoner's hands strapped together.

Johnson reached behind him to pull the field glasses from the back seat when something in the prisoner's eyes prompted him to ask, "Do you know this place?"

Logan nodded his head and mumbled, "mmmph bmmph."

Johnson reached over and removed the gag and Logan said, "This facility is operated by my company."

"You own the company?"

"No," Logan said, "but I'm a regional director. I have a temporary office here to work on a new project."

"How did you end up those guy's prisoner?"

Logan shrugged and said, "I can only guess. I covered my tracks pretty good, but it was like they knew what I planned. They were waiting for me when I got off the plane."

"Do you know why they wanted you?"

"I only know what I overheard, but it sounded like they wanted to detain me long enough to miss meeting up with one of my subordinates."

Johnson nodded his head towards the building and asked, "What about that girl? Do you know her?"

Logan said, "No," but Johnson could tell that he knew something.

"What aren't you telling me? Do you know that girl?"

"No. I've never seen her before."

"What about the other one?" Bingo. Johnson saw the recognition in Logan's eyes.

"No," Logan lied. "I never saw either of them."

"You're lying," Johnson said. He reached for the gag that still hung around Logan's neck and said, "I might as well keep you gagged, so I don't have to listen to your lies."

Logan shook his head around violently so Johnson couldn't put the gag in place and said, "Alright. I know the mother. She was the subordinate I was going to meet."

"Have you ever seen shit like that girl did before?"

"No," Logan lied, and Johnson reached for the gag again.

"The other one," Logan said. "She used to do stuff like that, only not so big."

"Well," Johnson said, "I *have* seen someone else do shit like that and just as big, too. She reminded me of him. She had the same crazy expression and, just like him, she enjoyed doing it too damned much."

"Was he a friend of yours?"

"No," Johnson said. "He was no friend of mine. He hired me to do a job, only when he started pulling fire out of the thin air, I wished I hadn't taken the job."

"What was his name?"

"What do you mean, 'what was his name?' Why do you care?"

Logan stammered, "Nothing. Just curious."

"You're lying to me again. You know something. Did you know this dude?"

Logan shrugged.

"Brian," Johnson blurted out. "His name was Brian. Did you know him?"

Logan's expression was all Johnson needed to see.

"Well," Johnson said, "your friend Brian thought he was king of the world, just like this girl, and he got himself fried. He met his match and burned for it."

Logan closed his eyes. He already knew as much.

He didn't know who this girl was yet, but as terrible and powerful as she seemed, there was someone worse out there, only she wasn't one of theirs.

***

Harold waited for Mr. Charles to return to his seat, then he gave the court a few moments for the opening remarks to sink in and a few more for the whispered remarks that followed to die down. With calm peacefully restored, he turned to Mr. Tangiers and said, "Call your first witness."

Mr. Tangiers took a quick breath, then stood up and called out, "The prosecution calls Dr. Evelyn McMann to the stand."

A bailiff in the back of the room repeated, "Dr. Evelyn Mc-Mann?"

Dr. McMann stood up and pushed her dark-rimmed glasses up onto the bridge of her nose. She wore a tight pencil thin skirt that forced her feet on a straight line as she walked from the back of the court to the witness stand. The crisp suit together with the glasses and the bun her hair was rolled in gave the impression of a very professional woman. The jury already viewed her as a very credible witness before she even repeated the oath and took her seat in the witness stand.

Mr. Tangiers picked up the two versions of her report and approached the stand. "Dr. McMann, would you please state your name and tell the court what you do?"

"My name is Dr. Evelyn McMann, and I am a medical examiner from Lafayette."

Simon held up a copy of the report that he had given to Mr. Charles and asked, "Dr. McMann, is this a copy of the OFFICIAL medical report that you gave to me?"

Dr. McMann held out her hand, asking to see the report, and when handed to her, she looked it over and said, "Yes. This is the report that I gave you."

Simon turned to the jury with a great smile on his face and said, "So, you would say that this report in my other hand is a fraud?"

Dr. McMann shrugged and held her hand out to see the other report. The smile faded slightly from Simon's face as he handed it to her. After reviewing the other report, she said, "No. I would not call this report a fraud."

Simon took a step back. The smile was completely gone from his face. "What do you mean?" he asked. "Did you create that report?"

"Yes," she said. "I did."

"But," Simon replied, "I've never seen that report before."

Mr. Charles stood up and said, "Objection. Counsel is testifying."

Harold smiled and said, "Sustained. Please question the witness."

Simon nodded and asked, "To your knowledge, have I ever seen this other report before?"

"No."

"Why not?"

"Because," Dr. McMann said, "you never asked for it. I gave you the report you asked me to make."

"Objection!" Simon exclaimed.

"Objection?" Harold asked. "She's your witness, and it was your question."

"Your honor," Simon stammered. "The prosecution has only just learned of this report and has not had time to depose this witness regarding its contents. The prosecution requests a continuance to address this matter."

Harold rapped his gavel and said, "Motion denied. Move along."

***

Dorris led Richard and Honey to Logan's office. She loathed doing anything that in any way removed Logan's presence, but it was only his temporary office, and now it would be her temporary office. "This," she said, "was my boss's office, but now it can be yours."

Richard watched for any expression on Honey's face as to whether it would be acceptable, then he turned to Dorris and said, "Have security make a complete set of photo I.D.'s and badges for her."

"Oh," Honey said. "I don't think I'll need none of that. Everyone here will get to know who I am soon enough."

"But," Dorris said, "the badges work on the doors and stuff, and they make you look official and more important."

Honey doubted she actually needed the badges to open doors, but she liked looking official and nodded her head. "Dorris? What's the biggest room we got? I want everyone here to learn who I am. Do we have someplace with a stage?"

"A stage?" Dorris asked. "No. Just some conference rooms, but no place big enough to fit everyone."

"Outside then. I want you to get everyone outside for me. No exceptions, you hear? I want everyone outside in front of the building. I'll say what I have to say from the top of the steps."

***

Destiny knew the jurors were looking at her. They had to. She certainly would if she were one of them. They split their attention between watching the witness, judging how honestly they felt he or she delivered their testimony, and they watched Destiny to see how she reacted, but one of them was different.

Destiny would have thought that a jury of her peers held right here in Cricket Bend would have been people she knew, but she didn't recognize any of their faces. None of them had ever been to one of Mrs. Planchette's shin digs and she always thought the whole parish had attended. She didn't recall ever seeing any of them in the travelling revivals where she again thought all of Cricket Bend attended. They were complete strangers to her, except for one boy. She had never seen him before in her life, but somehow, he wasn't a total stranger to her.

He was the youngest juror. He didn't even look old enough to serve on a jury. Maybe he just had a birthday. His face was completely unfamiliar to her, so why did she think she knew him?

She couldn't help staring at him. Her pupils widened and her face relaxed into a blank zombie-like expression. The court room melted away, and she saw a group of five boys standing at the base of some steps to arough-lookingg wooden building.

The boys watched the jeep come in and saw a boy in the passenger seat. One of the boys had binoculars and said, "He's just a kid. Way younger than any of us were when they brought us here."

"Let me see," another boy said while yanking the binoculars away. "Aww, he ain't nothin'. Just another dumb kid."

"Well," a third boy said, "I'm just glad it's not a girl. I hate it when they bring girls here."

"Why?" the first boy asked. "We get rid of them pretty easy. I kinda like it."

The third boy preferred not to admit that he didn't like what they did to the girls.

"Come on," the first boy said. "Let's go wait in the barracks. We can meet him there and explain to him how things work around here."

But, the new kid wasn't brought to the barracks. They saw him go into the commandant's office, where everyone was taken first, but then he was escorted to the VIP quarters.

"Well, how do you like that?" the second boy said. "He must be someone special."

"He don't look special," the first boy said. "Maybe he still wets the bed."

The other boys laughed, and the first boy said, "Follow me. I'm gonna go meet this new kid." But before they reached the VIP cabin, the bell rang, signaling the end of recess. They had to return to class. This wasn't the kind of school where you cut class. Even the toughest of the boys, and they all thought they were tough, were always present. It was a privilege to be here. Even though it was like a crappy summer camp and sometimes even more like a prison, it was still prestigious to be invited. Screwing up around here meant expulsion, and that was bad for the whole family.

The boys assembled in class. The instructor stood up at the head of the class and began his lecture, but the first of the boys raised his hand.

"What is it?" the instructor asked.

"Aren't we going to wait for the new kid? Maybe he doesn't know his way here. You want me to go get him?"

The instructor looked upset. He walked down one of the aisles between the desks and said, "The new boy is none of your concern. He won't be joining us in this class, and you would be best to forget you even saw him."

The boys looked at each other and shrugged.

"Now if you don't mind," the instructor said, "I would like to continue my lecture."

The image faded and Destiny found herself staring blankly at the jury, particularly at the young boy in the jury. Several of the jurors were watching her. She suddenly felt very self-conscious and wondered what she looked like when she had her visions.

"Dr. McMann," Tangiers said. "You said that you found dozens of bone fragments…"

"Hundreds," she corrected him, "maybe thousands."

"I'm sorry," Tangiers said. "You found a lot of bone fragments in the ashes. Can you tell the court how many victims you identified among all those bones?"

"Objection," Mr. Charles said. "The prosecutor has not established that there were victims."

"This is a murder trial," Tangiers responded.

"A murder trial where the cause of death only states they were burned, not that a crime was committed."

"Counsellors," Harold interrupted. "As entertaining as this is, I'd like to remind you to direct your comments to me and not to each other. The objection is sustained."

Tangiers regrouped his thoughts and continued, "Dr. McMann, the defendant is charged with the murder of two specific decedents. Did you examine the two remains?"

"I did."

"And are you telling the court that there were more remains than just the two decedents?"

McMann adjusted herself in the chair and said, "There were certainly more bones."

"How many?" Tangiers asked.

"Thousands, I'd estimate. Although, I identified some cases where many of the bone fragments originated from the same bone."

"Fragments?" Tangiers asked. "Why were they fragmented?"

"Some probably broke from the heat of the fire; others may have been cut apart."

"Cut apart? Are you telling the court that some of the remains were mutilated? Did this fact make it into your coroner's report? I'm sorry, into EITHER of your reports?"

"No," she said. "I did not include the cut bones in my report."

"And why not?" Tangiers demanded. "The defense is begging for a bona fide statement that a crime was committed, and you left this out?"

"Yes, I left it out. They seemed unrelated to the alleged crime."

"Unrelated? What did you learn? What else did you find on the bones?"

"Well," McMann said, "there were numerous scrape marks and teeth marks on the bones."

Tangiers was stunned. "Teeth marks?" he asked. "Are you telling us the defendants are cannibals? Why wouldn't you include that in your report?"

"Because they didn't do it. It wasn't their teeth marks, and they didn't make the scraping marks."

"You're sure of this?"

McMann was losing her cool and raised her voice as she replied, "Of course I'm sure. If the defendants were to have made the teeth marks, then I would have included it in my report! Most of these bones were around twenty-five thousand years old and the defendant is only sixteen. She didn't do it."

"Twenty-five thousand years old?"

"Yes. I don't have all the results back yet, but I have enough. The bones appear to be some kind of ancient religious artifacts."

"But you're still examining the bones?"

"I think I said that."

Tangiers had no reply and turned to the judge. "Your honor, may we approach?"

Harold was annoyed but waved him up. Tangiers waited for Mr. Charles to join them and said, "Your honor, the coroner hasn't even concluded her investigation and I don't want to appear 'calculating and cold-blooded' to the jury as Mr. Charles so eloquently put it. Perhaps we should recess so she can complete her lab work."

Harold turned to the witness and asked, "Dr. McMann, how long do you think it would take to complete your examination of the evidence?"

"Well," she said, "there are a lot of bone fragments. It could easily take many months, even years, to DNA and carbon test all of them. Frankly, DNA testing is rather expensive, and the county could exhaust its funds before the results are all in."

"In your expert opinion, do you think the remaining test results would alter your findings in this case?"

"No sir," she said. "I think it highly unlikely that the bone fragments would have any bearing on the case."

"Just highly unlikely?"

"No sir," she said with more confidence. "In my expert opinion, I would say there is no possibility that the remaining bone fragments would alter my finding. Impossible."

"Thank you, Dr. McMann. I suspect that Mr. Tangiers may still have some more questions for you before you may step down."

The judge turned his attention back to the prosecutor. "Mr. Tangiers, I find it ironic that you manipulated the system to rush this case to trial and now you want a continuance. You see those twelve people sitting over there? I think they all have lives waiting for them. I know I do. And how about that little girl over there? I think she would like to return home with her nana. Now, as the lovely Dr. McMann has so eloquently stated, there is nothing to be gained from delaying this trial any further just to examine the remaining evidence. Do you think we could continue this questioning and finish up this trial?" His voice was sweet and lyrical, but his eyes were threatening. He dropped the sweetness from his voice as he proclaimed, "Motion denied!"

The two attorneys left the bench, Mr. Charles returned to his seat, and Tangiers returned to the witness.

Tangiers was clearly frustrated with his witness. Forensic reports are always slanted to favor the prosecution, and his did until these new reports showed up out of nowhere. There was something wrong here, and he suspected supernatural influence. He wasn't especially surprised. If he were in the witch's position, he would tamper with the minds of the witnesses, too. "Dr. McMann, can you please confirm that we still do have two corpses from the ashes?"

"Yes."

"What can you tell us about them?"

Dr. McMann sat up a little taller and turned to the jury. She crossed her legs and said, "Two male remains were found in the home."

Tangiers waited for more, but getting nothing prodded further, "And were you able to determine their ages?"

"We estimate their ages are between twenty-five and thirty-five."

Tangiers nodded and asked, "Did you carbon date the remains? They weren't holy relics too, were they?"

Charles stood up timidly and said, "Your honor, the prosecutor is badgering his own witness."

Harold asked, "Is that an objection, Mr. Charles?"

"Not really, sir. I just felt bad for the witness."

The judge rapped his gavel. "Noted. Mr. Tangiers, get to the point, and do it quickly, and try to tone down the sarcasm."

"I'm through with this witness."

The morning nip still hung in the air as the front of the facility began filling with various employees and associates. All assembled were descendants of the sorcerer clan. All of them knew at least some of their heritage. None of them, except for Richard, had a clue what was coming.

"What's this?" Johnson asked as he nudged Logan, who was napping in the passenger seat.

Logan winced, but followed Johnson's pointing finger to see the gathering in the parking lot. "What's going on?" he asked.

Johnson shrugged and said, "That's what I was asking you."

Logan sat up a bit and watched the proceedings. "Beats me. Let me see those."

Logan reached for the binoculars, but Johnson yanked them away and pointed to another pair in the back seat. Logan couldn't reach back there with his hands strapped together, so Johnson pulled out his knife and said, "Don't make me regret this."

Freed from his bonds, Logan retrieved the other glasses and got a better look. "I've never seen them do that before," he said. "Maybe that little bitch started a fire and they're evacuating?"

"That makes sense," Johnson said, "but I don't see or smell any smoke."

"Me either," Logan admitted, "and I don't hear any alarms."

The crowd grew thicker, and as they gathered, they too asked each other what was going on.

"Do you think we should go in?" Johnson asked. "You could introduce me as one of your associates."

Logan looked at Johnson like was crazy. He didn't know who the hell Johnson was, only that he was hired by Brian, but they did have one thing in common: a healthy dose of not wanting to be around Honey.

Honey came out on the top of the steps and the crowd was as puzzled as ever. "Hey y'all," she said. "I bet you're wondering what we are all doing out here. My name is Honey Boutin, and I'm going to be making some changes around here."

Richard was the general manager for the facility, and all the other managers in the crowd glanced over at him, hoping he would confirm her statement.

"Hey!" Honey shouted. "I'm right here. You keep your eyes on me and don't be worrying about what Rick thinks. I'm in charge now."

One of the same managers glanced back at Richard again and Honey barked, "Was I not clear enough? He works for me! All y'all work for me."

The same manager looked back at her and asked, "What kind of shit is this? I'm not reporting to some dip shit little hick like you. Just who the hell do you think you are? Richard? What the hell..."

Honey stepped down two steps and reached out in the direction of the loud-mouthed manager. Richard didn't want to see what would follow and closed his eyes. Honey mimed picking the man up and dragged him to the stairs. Like a rag doll, she lifted him off the ground and tossed him onto the steps.

He looked up at her with wild eyes and said, "What the..."

She mimed grabbing him again and, like a rag doll, she tossed him to the step below her, where he landed on all fours.

"Kiss my feet toad."

He started to get up, saying, "I will not!"

She didn't even use her hands this time. She just looked at him and squashed him down on the ground with his head at her feet. "Kiss my feet!" she repeated. "Use your tongue! I want you to french my shoes, maggot."

He had no control. His tongue came out of his mouth involuntarily and thoroughly licked her shoes. He fought to resist, but was unable.

"Damn," she said. "You're good at this. I think you like it. Is that right maggot? Do you like this? Does it turn you on? Are you getting all hot?"

"No!" he shouted, and she glared at the back of his head, slamming his jaw shut, severing his tongue.

"Now look what you did, maggot! You got blood all over my shoes." She nodded her head and flung him down two steps, then he burst into flames. "You see?" she said. "You was all hot for me after all."

She flicked her wrist, and the burning corpse was flung to burn out on the side of the steps. "Here's how it is," she said. "I'm the queen around here and y'all are gonna work with me so I can be queen of the whole damned world, unless someone else out there wants to object like maggot did?"

Nobody came forth.

Johnson and Logan were unable to speak. Shivers ran up and down their spines while they sat in the car and observed the spectacle.

This wasn't the vision Logan had seen in the laptop, but then, he reminded himself, his people don't have visions. Whatever he saw must have been placed in his head, and it didn't show a girl taking over. That was supposed to be his power. He was educated enough to control it without becoming a wild animal like this girl. He needed her out of the way before it would ever be his power. Logan took a deep breath and forced himself to say, "I don't know who you work for, but I sure hope they know some way to stop her."

"I only know one person who can stop her," Johnson said. "I seen her stop Brian, but I'm not all that sure she is strong enough to handle this girl."

Mr. Charles approached the witness stand and said, "Dr. McMann, I'll try to be brief. Can you tell us how the victims died?"

"They burned to death."

"In the fire?"

"Yes, and no," she said. "There is no doubt that they were in the fire, but it didn't kill them. I've never seen anything like this before, and my office is unable to determine the exact cause, but according to my findings, they burned from the inside out."

"Can you speculate on what kinds of things could cause this type of burning?"

Mr. Tangiers sprang up and shouted, "Objection! Calls for speculation."

Harold waved his hands at Simon, motioning for him to remain seated, and said, "Sit down, Mr. Tangiers. I'll allow it. I'd like to hear what she has to say."

Simon sat down timidly, stunned by the flow of events.

Dr. McMann continued, "Well, it's almost too hideous to consider, but I suppose if someone ingested a powerful incendiary substance and ignited it, they would burn from the inside out."

"Are you aware of any such substance that could be ingested by accident?"

"None. I don't believe you could hide it in food. The taste would be far too unpleasant."

The young attorney knew what he was going to ask, but pretended to think about it anyway, for the jury's sake. "So, a person would have to ingest it on purpose."

"Yes, or be forced to ingest it somehow."

Mr. Charles paused for a moment, letting that answer settle in with the jury, then asked, "Dr. McMann, were you able to measure the deceased's weight for us?"

"Adjusting for fluid and tissue mass lost in the burning, we estimate their weights to be two hundred twenty-five pounds for the smaller one, and two forty for the big guy. They may have weighed an additional five or ten pounds. They both appeared to be very fit."

"And have you also measured the weight of our defendant?"

"She's about one hundred and fifteen pounds."

"Hmmm. So, each of the victims was approximately twice here weight, and there were two of them."

Dr. McMann nodded her head and said, "Yes. That's about right."

"Could you detect any drugs or chemicals in the remains that could have been used to incapacitate them?"

"None. We checked for both drugs and poisons. They were spotlessly clean."

Mr. Charles walked over to the gallery behind the defense table and pointed to two men. "Could you two please stand up?"

Mr. Tangiers started to object, but a quick glance from the judge stopped him.

Mr. Charles faced the jury and pointed to the two men with his left hand, and the defendant with his right. "Dr. McMann, can you think of any way a small one hundred and fifteen-pound girl could force two fit men, both over two hundred and twenty pounds, to ingest a deadly incendiary chemical?"

"No way," she said. "Besides, I said an incendiary substance could be used, but we detected no such chemical in their remains. How they burned is a complete mystery. We only know that they did, and we are estimating their internal temperature was over two thousand degrees."

"Dr. McMann, your report indicates that you gathered additional evidence besides the medical evidence. Can you tell us about that?"

"Certainly," she said. "In addition to the bones and the remains, I collected fifty-eight bullets scattered throughout the home, plus another eight outside the home."

"What can you tell us about these bullets?" Charles asked. "Were they sitting in a box that exploded in the fire?"

"No," she said. "They were most definitely fired into the home. They were military rounds consistent with the calibers fired by the M16 and M4 assault weapons."

"Did you find any such weapons among the remains?"

"No, sir."

"Did the bullets you found indicate what direction they came from?"

"I found several bullets still embedded in the timbers of the home that indicated several different positions surrounding the home."

Mr. Charles walked the length of the jury looking each of them in the eye while he nodded his head and said, "So, there could have been many more intruders present that day."

Dr. McMann shrugged and said, "Or it could have been one man circling the home."

"Thank you, doctor. No more questions."

Ashlin watched Dr. McMann exit the witness stand. She didn't look like a doctor at all to the young girl. She was slender and very elegant looking. Her tight-fitting skirt and suit coat made her look more like a model than a doctor. She certainly walked like a model.

As she walked past the defense table, Dr. McMann pulled her glasses off her face, smiled weakly, and nodded to Destiny. She had beautiful eyes, and Ashlin wanted to look like her when she was older. Her mother wouldn't let her use makeup, even though she insisted she was old enough. She stared into Dr. McMann's eyes and saw her own with the smoky dark eye shadow and dark but delicate mascara. She imagined looking at her own face in the mirror, applying a fine edge to her lips with a dark red pencil.

A raven-haired woman behind her said, "This is no time for daydreams."

Ashlin looked at the woman's reflection in the mirror and said, "I just want to look my best."

"One day," the woman said, "if we survive today. A great evil threatens to erase all the beauty from the world, and it is our job to stop it."

Ashlin walked to the bed where the raven-haired woman lay and said, "Don't you mean it is her job? We support her, but she must be the one."

"You know better than that," the raven-haired woman said. "You are not a little girl anymore."

Ashlin returned to the mirror and said, "This is much better than being twelve."

"Is that all you plan to do? Play with your face in the mirror while the world collapses around you?"

Ashlin applied another coat of mascara and said, "She's doing fine. The world will be fine. Let me enjoy this while I can."

"Stop focusing on yourself," the raven-haired woman said. "That's what they do. Your time will come. Trust me."

Ashlin turned away from the mirror and saw the raven-haired woman floating over the bed. Her image was wisps of light and smoke.

"Why are you so concerned when everything is going so well?"

The raven-haired apparition said, "Because the evil does not wait for us. It grows now and before she can face it, she will need your help."

"How can I help when you wish me to return to being twelve again?"

The apparition morphed into the woman again, standing on the ground before Ashlin and said, "She can't face the evil alone, and when the time comes, you will help her get it."

"Get what?"

"You will know when the time is right."

The vision faded and Ashlin saw Dr. McMann sit in an empty seat behind her instead of taking her previous seat behind the prosecution.

Honey stood at the top of the steps, staring at her people. They stood silently in their places, afraid to move or say anything. She shook her head and said, "I thought I was being brought to my people. MY people. I was expecting other people like ME. The world out there is going to learn that there is just THEM and US. Now I'm not so sure there is an US. Because if you're not with me, you're with them." She pointed to the smoldering corpse and said, "Maggot wasn't with me. He must have been with them. That is their fate. They either serve us or they die."

She still received no movement from the crowd. Honey had an urge to consume the entire group in flames and move on. The urge moved to the pit of her stomach and nearly emerged as a massive ball of flame when a faintness came over her and she turned to Abilene and Richard. "I'm hungry. Please tell me y'all got a cafeteria in this place."

"Yes!" Richard said, happy to diffuse the situation. "Right this way! Follow me."

Abilene looked critically at her daughter's face and asked, "Is you okay? You look a bit pale."

"I'm fine mama. I said I was hungry, didn't I?"

Mr. Tangiers turned to face the gallery and said, "The prosecution calls Captain Gerald Polin."

The bailiff echoed through the court and out into the makeshift hallway, "Captain Gerald Polin?"

Polin stood up from behind the prosecution and walked to the witness booth, where he raised his right hand to take the oath. There was no Bible present.

The Bailiff asked, "Do you swear to tell the truth, the whole truth, and nothing but the truth?"

Polin nodded his head and said, "Yes, I do." He sat down and adjusted the microphone in front of him.

Simon took his place in front of the witness and said, "Please state your name."

"My name is Gerald Polin, captain, Lafayette Fire Department."

"Lafayette is pretty far from the location of the fire. Why would you be involved?"

"We don't respond to fires here; they have local volunteer firemen for that. I am the regional arson investigator, so my involvement is purely after the fact."

"Have you concluded your investigation of the fire?"

Captain Polin both nodded and shook his head, saying, "I have concluded my investigation, but I have not closed the file."

"Why is that?"

"The cause of the fire is still unknown. We exhausted all the evidence, and further investigation was not warranted."

"Have you been able to rule out any common causes for the fire?"

"It was not caused by a gas leak. There was no evidence of gasoline or kerosene or any other kind of accelerant. We ruled out every known cause of arson."

Mr. Tangiers nodded his head and made eye contact with the jury. He wanted them to follow along. "What about natural causes? Did you rule out the weather?"

"The temperature was around eighty-six degrees, with over seventy percent humidity. There were no lightning strikes that evening. I can't attest to the whereabouts of fire ants or lightning bugs."

The courtroom laughed at the last remark, but quickly quieted before the judge had to go to his gavel.

"Were you at least able to identify the location where the fire started?"

"Yes. I have a map of the property, if you would like to see. I identified twenty-seven sources where the fire started."

"And you are quite certain that there was no lightning?"

"Absolutely certain."

"Twenty-seven sources where the fire started. My, my. Doesn't that suggest foul play to you?"

"Sure, it suggests foul play, but I deal in evidence, and there was absolutely no evidence of foul play."

"Thank you, captain, no further questions."

Mr. Charles stood for his turn and said, "Captain, I have just a couple of questions for you. How large an area did these twenty-seven hotspots ignite?"

"They were all over the entire property, over three thousand square feet."

"Were there any signs that a remote-control device was used to ignite these fires?"

"None. I found no evidence of any kind of electronic devices, or even of any accelerants."

"Could you determine when the fires started, and in what order?"

Polin's face grimaced slightly. "I can't give you an exact time, but I can tell you which ones had been burning longer, which should give us the approximate order in which they ignited. They did not start up in a straight line that we usually see when an arsonist lights a fire. One would ignite on one side of the property, then another a hundred feet away, then another seventy feet away from that one, all within about three seconds."

"Wow," Mr. Charles mused. "One hundred feet, then another seventy feet in three seconds. That would be one really fast arsonist. I think maybe the NFL would like to recruit him."

More laughter ensued. This time, even the judge succumbed and snickered.

"No more questions."

Polin stepped down.

Mr. Charles turned to the judge and said, "Your honor, the defense fails to see any evidence that links any loss of life to my client. I respectfully request that the charges be dropped so we can all go home and let this poor young girl get on with her life."

Mr. Tangiers sprang to his feet and yelled, "I object!"

Harold coolly replied, "I knew you would."

Simon elaborated, "The prosecution is allowed to present its full case before the defense can make such a motion!"

Harold nodded and said, "I'm fully aware of the procedure, Mr. Tangiers, so if you'll just settle down a bit, I'll explain it to young Mr. Charles." The judge turned to the defendant's table and said, "Son, I know this is your first jury trial. I also know this is a pretty important case for a young man who just passed the bar. You did pass the bar, didn't you?"

"Uh, yes ... yes, sir," he stammered.

"That's good. And you are doing just fine, under the circumstances. But right now, we're just gonna let the prosecution finish up all their talking and ballyhooin'. Then after he rests his case, that's when we can entertain motions to throw this case out of the courts. Okay?"

"Yes sir, thank you, sir."

Tempest turned on the TV and tuned it to an empty station that played static out of the speakers. Dr. Weinhart thought she just needed help finding a show, so she cycled through the channels and left it on a soap opera hoping the many characters would make her feel at home, but when Dr. Weinhart returned to her reading, Tempest changed it back to snow.

Dr. Weinhart glanced up and saw that Tempest had returned to staring out the window, but she rocked her head slightly now and listened to the static from the TV, so Dr. Weinhart continued reading.

The weather outside warmed and the pool finally filled with children. The air conditioning kept the room comfortable and added to the soothing background noise of the TV and the splashing from the pool. Dr. Weinhart turned the page of her novel and noticed that Tempest was gone, and the door was ajar.

She sprinted to the door and saw Tempest crossing the street and heading down the highway towards Cricket Bend. She quickly grabbed her purse and ran across the lot after Tempest. As she reached the far edge of the lot, she saw a cab pull up alongside Tempest.

"Wait for me!" she yelled out.

Tempest turned toward her voice, then slid into the cab, but the door remained open. Dr. Weinhart ran across the road and stood outside the cab, breathing heavily.

"I'm sorry," she said between gasps, "but she's not supposed to be going anywhere."

The cab driver looked at her like she was crazy.

"I'm her doctor. She doesn't know what she's doing. She doesn't even have any money to pay you."

"What?" the driver asked, but when he turned to see her, Tempest held out her hands with a small wad of money.

Dr. Weinhart was surprised and asked, "Where did you get that?"

Tempest glanced at her purse and shrugged.

"Come on Tempest, you've used up enough of this nice man's time. He has a job to do."

Tempest shook her head and said, "She needs me. I must go to her."

Dr. Weinhart was surprised by her clarity and her use of full sentences. They were short, but they were complete. Then, in a move that made no sense, she slid into the seat next to Tempest and closed the door. "Why should this make any sense?" she thought to herself, "when nothing else does either?"

"You'll be okay," she thought to herself, but in her head, she heard her thought in Tempest's voice.

Harold waited for Captain Polin to take his seat before he asked, "Mr. Tangiers, do you have any further witnesses? Perhaps someone who actually witnessed a crime?"

"Yes sir," Simon said, "well I mean, sort of, your honor. At this time, we would like to enter this video tape into evidence."

"You are aware, Mr. Tangiers, that in capital cases, the court prefers to have real live witnesses instead of recorded depositions."

"Of course, your honor, but this is not a deposition. This is a security tape. Really, sir, it would be much easier for me to explain while viewing the tape."

"Very well." Harold motioned for a clerk to bring in a video player, which was all done very quickly, and the tape inserted.

The screen came on, showing a handful of people sitting in a room wearing robes and pajamas.

"Where was this shot, Mr. Tangiers?"

"Your honor, this is from the St. Austin Mercy Hospital. It is a home for extremely troubled mental patients. Can we increase the audio, please?"

A man in uniform approached the video stand and pressed the volume button.

"Thank you. Now please watch the woman sitting on the couch. She becomes very agitated and starts to speak. Just listen to what she says."

Harold motioned to have the tape stopped, the same uniformed man pressed pause on the tape player.

"Mr. Tangiers, I asked for relevant evidence about this case. What can a security video from a mental hospital possibly have to do with this case?"

"Please bear with me, your honor, just a few moments, I promise you."

Harold snarled and frowned, but motioned to have the tape played.

On the screen, the woman on the couch started to rock back and forth. "Watch out baby! Look behind you! Duck!" She got up from the couch and moved to the window. "Yes! Burn him baby, burn him! That's my baby, my little girl! Make him pay. Watch out for the other one! Duck! Burn him! Light him up! Go baby go!"

Mr. Tangiers paused the tape. "Your honor, please look at the date and time on the tape. It matches exactly with the time of the fires and the death of those two men."

The judge rolled his eyes. "Mr. Tangiers, how does the babbling of a crazy woman have anything to do with our case?"

"Your honor, can it be a coincidence that this woman accurately described the death of two men at the same exact time it occurred? How can a woman hundreds of miles away know about these things as they happened? This woman was admitted to the hospital with symptoms that included hearing voices in her head. I submit that she does hear voices because she is psychic. And she witnessed the events that occurred in Cricket Bend just as clearly as if she were there herself. What's more, I think you should know that there is a connection between this woman and the defendant." Simon approached the television himself and pressed play on the tape player.

The woman in the window raised her hands to her mouth and shouted as loud as she could, "I love you, Destiny! I love you!"

In the back of the room, Tempest stood up with a tear in her eye, but said nothing.

Destiny felt her mama crying and stood up herself and said, "Momma?"

The crowd clicked and clucked over the turn of events.

Harold banged his gavel and shouted, "Lunch!" He turned to both attorneys and growled, "In my chambers!"

Harold waited for Mr. Charles and Mr. Tangiers to enter the small dressing room which had been set up as his temporary office before slamming the door and yelling, "What the hell are you doing out their Tangiers? If you turn my court into a circus, I'll charge you with contempt so fast your head will still be spinning even after you've been locked away in the deepest, darkest dungeon with the key tossed into the swamps for safekeeping by the gators! Am I making myself clear?"

Tangiers shrunk back against the wall and shrugged his shoulders. "I'm not making this stuff up," he said. "It happened just like you saw it on the tape."

"Did it?" Harold asked. "After the fiasco surrounding the crime scene reports, how am I supposed to believe you?"

Mr. Charles struggled to suppress a smirk and remained quiet.

Tangiers shrugged again and said, "I don't know what it was that we witnessed on the tape, but seeing is believing."

"Like hell it is!" Harold growled. "I've seen teddy bears dance and sing on a strange moon circling a faraway planet, but that doesn't mean I believe it! You had better walk on eggshells from now on, Mr. Tangiers. Do you read me?"

Tangiers nodded and said, "Yes sir, your honor, sir."

Harold turned to Mr. Charles and said, "I'm inclined to give you a bit of leeway should you feel the need to argue Mr. Tangiers' so-called evidence. Do not take too much advantage of my generosity, or you'll be sharing his dungeon cell."

Mr. Charles nodded and said, "Thank you, your honor."

CHAPTER 12

"Mama?" Destiny asked. "What are you doing here?"

Tempest opened her mouth to speak but said nothing and instead wrapped her arms around her daughter in a warm hug, then returned to her semi-vegetative state.

Dr. Weinhart said, "In all the years I have cared for Tempest, I have never known her to get up and go somewhere on her own."

"She's coming back to us," Destiny said wistfully.

"Maybe so," Weinhart admitted, "but let's not forget that it won't be without consequences. She's going to need a lot of therapy to learn to deal with the voices she hears."

"Maybe," Destiny said, "and maybe not."

Dr. Weinhart remembered who she was talking to and said, "Well, she'll need something. I saw you in my office the other day. I'd sure like to learn more about what you were doing. Is it something you could teach me?"

"You have to be born with it before you can learn it."

Dr. Weinhart frowned but nodded her head.

"Don't fret," Michelle said. "I seen the books in your office, and I seen how easily you accepted what Destiny done, maybe you be born with it and just don't know it."

Dr. Weinhart felt a glimmer of hope and smiled while they all walked Tempest across the lot to the diner.

———

Honey sat in her new office staring at a map of the United States, which covered her desk. She held a fat felt-tip pen over the map and closed her eyes while circling the pen blindly over the map.

Richard entered the office and watched her. She circled the pen over the map, then frowned and opened her eyes.

"What's wrong?" he asked.

"I was just trying to pick a good place to start," she said, "but I wanted to surprise myself. Even though I close my eyes, it seems like I know where the pen is going."

"And what was it that you wanted to start?"

"You know," she said, "taking over the world. I guess I have to start somewhere."

"Ahh," Richard said. "You know, we have lots of really smart people who are really good at planning this kind of stuff. They would know the best place to start."

"At first," she said, "I thought I wanted to start with Washington. I thought maybe I could start by burning it down or blowing it up."

She traced a finger from Utah to Seattle, Washington and said, "But then I seen it was too far away and I don't want to wait that long."

Richard swallowed hard to keep from laughing at the ignorant girl, thankful that she didn't have the witches' ability to see what was in his mind. "Something else you should know," he said, "is that we have people in office around the country. We have infiltrated just about every facet of government. I think they hold the key to overthrowing the system. We can use them to facilitate your rise in power."

"That's good," she said. "I won't have to worry about being locked out."

"And you might not want to burn the whole place to the ground because our people are in it."

"Yeah," she said. "That too."

"Good," Richard said. He stood up and started to leave.

"Wait," she said. "When can I get these people to make my attack plan for me?"

"I'll get right on it. But the plan may call for a little patience. Sometimes we like to slip in when people are looking the other way."

Honey bit her lip. She didn't like patience. She sat down in the desk chair and spun it around.

Tangiers was leaving the courtroom when a small angry looking woman with wild hair approached him in the hallway. "You cain't beat them regular," she said. "Dey uses magic to make dem people like 'em."

"Excuse me," Simon said, walking away from her, "but I need to get my lunch."

"Oh," she said dramatically. "Your lunch be more important dan winning."

Simon stopped and turned. "What," he asked, "does a crazy old woman know about winning court cases?"

"I don't know nothin' about winning in da court. But I knows a ting or two about da magic dey uses."

Simon wondered if Logan had sent her, but he had never told him he was sending anyone. "Magic?" he asked. "Are you crazy? Why in the world would I care about magic?"

"Oh, you be carin' on da inside. I hears it in your thoughts, and I feels it in my guts. I knows what you is and you be carin' alright."

Simon had a bad feeling about involving this woman, but he couldn't risk missing an opportunity if she was on the level. "Okay," he said. "What's your name?"

"I be Zeline."

"And you know something about magic?"

"Of course I does. I be a witch and I been knowin' about Michelle and her brood since before dat girl was a teet baby."

"Are you hungry?" Simon asked as he continued to the diner.

"I could eat," Zeline said, "but I tink dey be eatin' in the diner and maybe dey don't need to be seein' me wit' you."

"Oh," he said. "Have you some reason to be afraid of them?"

Zeline stiffened and said, "I ain't afraid of nobody, especially not dem!"

"You don't like them much, do you?"

"I doesn't like dem at all. Dat's why I come to help you."

"Well, Zeline, I don't think it will do any harm at all if they see you having lunch with me. It will certainly let them know that they can't do any magic of their own without me knowing about it."

"But I can'st be a secret if dey sees me. Dey is gonna know I be doin' somet'ing."

"And then I will catch them red-handed when they try to stop you."

Simon held the door for her and led her outside towards the diner. While they crossed the gas station, he asked her, "Can you do anything to make that little girl appear guilty to the jury when they look at her?"

Zeline smiled and said, "I tink she be looking guilty already, but I hear what you be sayin'. I kin sure open up da jury's eyes to see what I sees."

"Right zis way," Marie said to Michelle, "I save ze table for you all morning. I hope you has ze good appétit."

"Oh," Michelle said, "can you join us? I don't believe you has met my daughter Tempest. She be Destiny's mother."

"Of course," Marie said. "Just let me tell ma mere I will have ze dinner now."

Michelle slid into the round corner booth, followed by Tempest and Destiny. Ashlin was curious about Tempest and wanted to sit next to her, but she was too late, so not wanting to be between Destiny and Blake, she sat next to Michelle. Mr. Charles would have preferred a better opportunity to speak to Destiny in private but accepted a seat next to Dr. Weinhart who was next to Ashlin which at least put him across the table from Destiny.

"Mother agrees," Marie said. She started to take the end seat next to Blake when a voice in her head suggested sitting next to Mr. Charles instead.

"Well," Charles said, "that was certainly an interesting morning. I had absolutely no idea they were going to pull up a tape of your mother and start claiming some supernatural hocus pocus. I wonder if the jury noticed your mother there in the back of the courtroom."

"I don't think so," Blake said. "They were all watching the tape and Destiny, and I was watching them pretty closely."

Mr. Charles assessed Tempest. She sat quietly across from him. She wasn't as withdrawn as she was when she was catatonic, but there was something different about her. "I wonder," he said, "what they will pull next. If the prosecution noticed that your mother was there in the court, do you think they will call her to the witness stand?"

"And say what?" Destiny asked. "Do you think they would ask her if she actually saw the incident from the hospital? They might as well come right out and ask her if she is a witch."

Mr. Charles frowned as he chewed on that thought.

Ashlin thought to Tempest, "This is all really boring, and I've been trying to meet you since yesterday."

"I'm sorry," Tempest thought back, "but who are you?"

Ashlin smiled and thought back, "My name is Ashlin. I'm really a kind of cousin, but Destiny and I have become like sisters."

"You said a witch," Charles said. "If they try painting your mother as a witch who is able to see things from miles away, what would stop them from claiming you are also a witch able to burn healthy young men from the inside out?"

Marie laughed and said, "Can you hear how ridiculous that sounds?"

"It's genius," Blake said. "It's so crazy sounding that if YOU said it first, the prosecution could never go there."

"Yes," Charles said, half lost in his thoughts.

Destiny thought to Blake, "Something's different. This ain't how I remembered the trial in my visions."

"How so?" Blake thought.

"Well, for one thing, my mama was still in the hospital when I first saw the trial."

Blake scowled and thought, "Yeah, that's how I remember it too. What does it mean?"

"It means things can change. It means maybe I don't get off like we remember it."

"Hmmm," Blake thought, "but if that's true, then it also means that we can change all these awful things we've been seeing for the future."

***

"We need to stop her," Johnson said.

Logan searched the face of his rescuer for some clue that Johnson knew how to stop her, but saw none. "By we," he said, "I guess you mean me. I'm the man in charge. I need to go in there and take charge."

"Are you crazy?"

"No," Logan said. "I'm not crazy, but I'm out of options. I don't know what to do with her, and I'm damned sure that those people in there won't know what to do with her. I need to go in and try to neutralize the situation until we can learn what we can do about her."

Logan opened the door to leave the car, but Johnson said, "Wait. That girl is clearly crazy. Maybe she was already nuts before she could do this shit, but now she is completely bat shit crazy with power. There's only one person who can stop her and it's not you or me."

"You mean the other girl?"

"Picture this girl with all that power, but none of the crazy."

Logan closed the door and said, "But she's not one of us."

"Us?" Johnson asked. "Do you think that hot head in there is one of you? Hell, I'm not one of you, but that don't mean we can't work together to stop her."

"You mean, the enemy of my enemy?"

Johnson nodded and replied, "Something like that."

Logan thought about it for a moment, then shook his head saying, "But I can't go to her for help. It's impossible."

"I don't think you have to ask her," Johnson said. "All we have to do is get them in the same room together and the rest will take care of itself."

"What if your girl loses?"

Johnson closed his eyes and shook his head. "I don't even want to think about that."

After lunch, Dr. Weinhart took Tempest aside and asked her, "Well, do we go back to court? Or do we go back to the hotel room to wait for them?"

Tempest nodded to the community center and walked with Weinhart back to the makeshift courtroom.

Dr. Weinhart wondered how much effort it had taken for Tempest to speak those two sentences in the cab. They were the only ones she has uttered so far, but it was still pretty early in the process of weening her off her medications. She found herself increasingly fascinated by Tempest and her family. She couldn't help thinking that she wished she could continue to care for her even if it meant quitting her job, but she didn't know how she could support herself.

"You could write a book," she thought, but like before, the thought sounded like Tempest's voice. She glanced over at Tempest, who was smiling at her. A half smile appeared on her own face as she nodded her head and thought to herself, "Yeah, I could write a book."

Tempest's smile grew wider, and she hugged Dr. Weinhart, whose head was now racing with unusual and unbelievable thoughts.

Dr. Weinhart took Tempest up to the front of the court instead of the back row and sat with Ashlin and Michelle.

Honey was bored. She slouched in her new office chair, creating fireballs in one hand and making them jump in an arc to the other hand. She found that if she twisted her fingers like she was spinning a ball, the arc had a pretty corkscrew tail that stretched behind it like a comet.

Richard came into the office with a couple of advisers in tow. "Honey, I'd like you to meet Howard and Sven. Sven is visiting from one of our European offices, and I thought they could give you some idea of the infrastructure we've been setting up around the world."

Howard and Sven sat down in the guest chairs while Richard leaned against a side table.

Howard said, "First of all..."

Honey held up her hand to stop him and said, "Wait a minute. What's a infrascripture?"

Richard replied, "An infrastructure is all the people we've placed in government positions. These are people who can move supplies or help us get laws passed. When you make an order, they are the people that see to it that it gets done."

"Oh," she said. "I like the sound of that." She turned the palm of her hand up and produced a perfectly round ball of fire. "Can you do this?"

Howard stammered, "I, uh, that is, no, I can't."

"And all them people in your infrastructure? Can they do this?"

Howard swallowed and said, "No. None of us can."

"Then," she said, "I don't see how anything you have planned so far has anything to do with me. You need to be thinking up new plans, like, how can your infrastructure get me in to see the governor this afternoon?"

"The governor?" Howard asked. "We always thought we would start small, at the bottom and work our way up. We can get you in to see the mayor this afternoon."

Honey slammed her fire ball onto the top of the desk, sending sparks and cinders in all directions. "You think small because you ARE small. I'm not small! I don't need to start with some lame ass mayor. Get the car and let's all go see the governor. You can alert your infrastructure on the way."

The gallery and the jury reassembled. The bailiff waited a moment for the creaking chairs to settle down before he sang out, "All rise. The twenty-third district court of Louisiana is now in session. The Honorable Harold Jamison presiding."

Harold entered the room and took his place behind the desk. He hoped it would be a short trial and wondered briefly how many times he would have to hear the bailiff recite the same phrase in this particular place before he could return to his home and family. He took his seat and rapped his gavel, then pointed the gavel over to Mr. Charles and said, "Mr. Charles, it is now your turn to make your case. Are you ready?"

"Yes sir," Charles said. He turned to face the jury and recited, "The defense would like to call Ms. Destiny Boutin to the stand."

Destiny stood and tried walking calmly to the witness box, but she was intensely aware that everybody was watching her and found that her knees shook slightly in spite of her confidence.

The bailiff stood before her and said, "Raise your right hand. Do you solemnly swear to tell the truth, the whole truth, and nothing but the truth?"

Destiny swallowed hard but squeaked out a nervous, "I do."

The bailiff backed away from the witness box and said, "Sit down and state your name, please."

She sat down and brushed a few stray hairs out of her face. "Destiny Faith Boutin," she said a bit faster than she had intended.

Mr. Charles approached the witness box and asked, "Where do you live, Miss Boutin?"

Destiny remembered her visions of the trial and found it impossible to repeat the exact same words which left her wondering just what her visions really were. "I was being held at the Lafayette Parish Correctional Facility until they let me out on my own recognition. Since coming back here to Cricket Bend, I've been staying at a hotel down the interstate with my nana."

Mr. Charles turned to the jury and feigned exasperation. "I meant before you were arrested, Miss Boutin."

"Well," she replied, "my nana took me to her daddy's farm in Mississippi, but I was only there a day or so. I guess you'd say I'm between homes at the moment."

"Well then, Miss Boutin, perhaps you can tell us," he spread his arms dramatically, indicating the jury and the audience, "tell us where you used to live, before you were between homes."

"I grew up right here in Cricket Bend, Louisiana."

"Can you narrow it down a bit from all of Cricket Bend?"

Destiny turned towards the jury and explained, "Cricket Bend doesn't have any streets, except for Main Street, and I don't live on Main Street. We never had no address to speak of, so I guess I can't really narrow it down much more than Cricket Bend."

"Did you have a home, Miss Boutin, in Cricket Bend?"

"Of course I had a home. I lived with my nana, in the house you been talking about all morning. That's the one that burned down, as if you didn't know."

Mr. Charles exhaled a deep breath and said, "Thank you, Miss Boutin. Can you tell us, please, how long you lived there?"

"Since I was a baby, I guess, pretty much since I was born."

"And during all that time, your nana has raised you?"

Destiny looked over at her nana and her mother in the gallery and smiled. "Yes sir," she said. "My mama was in the hospital all that time and couldn't raise me."

Mr. Charles turned the pages in his tablet, going over his notes. "How old are you, Miss Boutin?"

"I just turned sixteen."

"Where do you go to school?"

"My nana gives me my lessons."

"So," he said. "You don't really go to school? You're home schooled?"

"Yes sir, but I take the tests at the end of the year to prove that I've had the right lessons."

"I guess that means that you've been with your nana pretty much all the time for the last sixteen years?"

"Yes sir, pretty much."

Mr. Charles backed away from Destiny, keeping his back to the gallery. He held out his left hand indicating Michelle and asked, "And you would know more things about your nana than anybody else?"

"Yes sir, I suppose so."

He stepped slowly towards the jury, nodding his head as he walked. Before reaching them, he turned back to Destiny and started to say something, then stopped and laughed to himself. He looked at the jury and grinned, then turned back towards Destiny and asked, "Is your nana a witch?"

"Excuse me?" she asked.

"I'm sorry," he said. "I'll rephrase. Does your nana believe she is a witch? Does she practice secret rituals?"

Destiny laughed. "A witch? Well, she doesn't fly around on a broom, if that's what you mean. I suppose you could say my nana taught me about many different religions. I think maybe she respects most all of them, and even though she doesn't go to church on Sundays, she's a Christian, like most everybody in these parts. At least, that's how she raised me. As far as secret rituals are concerned, they wouldn't be very secret if I knew about them, would they?"

He smiled and nodded his head. "That's a very clever answer, only you never really answered my question. Does your nana believe herself to be a witch?"

Mr. Tangiers had heard enough and wanted to end this ridiculous line of questioning, but the judge was completely enthralled with her answers, so he kept mum. Those damned witches did something to the judge. He was sure of it!

Destiny raised a curious eyebrow and asked, "Are you asking me if I know something that she believes?"

"I am asking you, since you know her better than anyone else in this courtroom, probably better than anyone else alive, if you can share with us whether or not she believes she is a witch."

"Of course she does! She is a witch. I am a witch. My mother is a witch. We come from a long line of witches. Excuse me a second, I'll read her mind." Destiny waved her hands around her head and rolled her eyes backwards. "You know something? She does believe she is a witch."

The audience roared with laughter, nearly rolling in the aisles.

"Order! Order!" Harold rapped his gavel until the din died down.

Mr. Charles continued, "Miss Boutin, did your nana kill those men?"

"What? You think she chanted some incantations, and those men burst into flames? Or maybe she brewed a magical potion and teleported it into their tummies?"

"Did she?"

"Of course not. She doesn't have those kinds of powers."

"What kind of powers does she have?"

"She's pretty good with local herbs and homemade remedies."

Mr. Tangiers could stand it no longer. He stood up and meekly asked, "Your honor, how long must we endure this magical carpet ride to nowhere?"

Mr. Charles was frankly surprised that Tangiers had lasted this long. He turned to the prosecutor and showed him his palms in surrender, then turned back to the judge and said, "I'm through, your honor."

Tangiers approached the stand and asked, "Miss Boutin, where is your mother?"

Destiny pointed behind the defense table and said, "She's right there."

Tangiers nodded politely towards Tempest and asked, "Where was she on the day of the fire?"

"She was in St. Austin Mercy Asylum that day. She was the woman on the tape you showed us, remember?"

"Why was she there?"

"I'm probably not the best one to ask, but I believe she was diagnosed with schizophrenia and paranoia, but you can ask her doctor if you want. She's sitting with my mama."

He approached the witness stand, pretending to study the medical charts in his hand. "So, she hears voices?"

"Of course she does. She's not deaf."

"But she hears voices that aren't really there."

"Well, I guess we don't really know that, do we? She might just hear voices that others don't hear."

He dropped his arm with the papers to his side with a half-smile on his face. "Miss Boutin, how do you suppose your mother had prior knowledge to the events of June 3rd?"

Destiny shrugged and said, "Maybe the voices in her head told her what was going on."

"So," Tangiers said with a hint of authority, "you believe the voices are real and not imaginary. We've already heard testimony about whether or not your grandmother believed herself to be a witch. You made a very clever joke that you were all witches. But I wonder, was it really a joke? We've seen your mother on tape, as if she were watching what was happening from clear across the county. How do you explain that?"

"My mama was in a crazy hospital. She probably has been saying the same thing every day for the last 15 years. You know what I think? I think maybe you might be crazier than my mama is."

Mr. Charles stood up and asked, "Your honor, where is the prosecution going with this? If he is suggesting that this crime is truly of supernatural origin, then I wonder if it is out of this court's and his jurisdiction."

Harold rapped his gavel and growled, "Approach!"

Honey sat in the back of the limo with Richard and Abilene while Howard and Sven sat in the rear facing seats. Richard poured himself a drink and offered one to Howard, who eagerly nodded his head.

Sweat was becoming a permanent feature of Howard's temples, as was the worried curl of his brow. He sat nervously in his seat, afraid to speak, and hoped the bourbon would help calm his shaking hands.

Richard took the phone from the center console and speed dialed the facility they had just left. "Dorris," he said. "I want you to call the

Salt Lake facility and tell them to prepare a reception for us. Don't tell them who is coming; just tell them we're bringing a VIP to see the governor."

"Anything else?" she asked.

"Just a sec," he said. He covered the mouthpiece and asked, "Would you like me to have our people pick out something fresh for you to wear? If you prefer, we could take you shopping, but..."

"No," Honey said. "A change of clothes sounds good, and I'd like to go shopping, but not this time. We're in a hurry."

Richard nodded and asked, "How do you want to play this, then? Do you want them to get you a business power suit? Do you want a fancy cocktail dress? Or would you prefer to keep the innocent girl from the sticks look?"

"Power suit is a cool sounding name," she said, "but I don't want to look like no stuffy old ambassador lady. Get me something sexy. You know, something short and sassy that says I just blew into town right out of the pages of Cosmo, and I look bitchin' because I am."

"Dorris? Make it a..."

"I heard," Dorris said. "Ask her what color she likes."

"What color?"

"Red like fire."

"Did you hear that, Dorris?"

"And shoes too!" Honey shouted. "Make them match! I want heels!"

"Shoes too," Richard repeated. "She wants heels. Tell them to hurry. We'll be there in under three hours."

"Wait!" Dorris shouted. "What size is she?"

"Dorris needs to know what size you wear."

Honey reached out and said, "Gimme the damned phone." She took the phone and turned to face the back corner of the cab. "Dorris? I can't say my size in front of all these men!"

Abilene just shook her head and wondered how she could raise a girl that would run around naked but not want to say her dress size publicly.

Dorris whispered into the phone, "Two?"

"No."

"Four?"

"Sometimes."

"So," Dorris whispered, "Something in a four or a six then?"

"Yeah," Honey said, "and make sure it's a girl who does the shopping, okay?"

"Sure," Dorris said. "Now what about shoes? Seven?"

"No."

"Eight?"

Honey said, "Almost."

"So, seven and a half heels then?"

"Yep. Thanks, Dorris."

Honey gave the phone back to Richard and said, "That was a good idea. I'm glad someone around here knows how to make a good plan."

Howard's hands started trembling again, so Richard freshened his drink for him.

Sven remained as quiet and invisible as possible.

Johnson saw Honey get in a limo with her entourage and said, "Here we go. We get to play follow the leader again."

Logan frowned when he saw who they were following. "Remind me. Why are we following her?"

"We need to know where she is going before we can set the other girl on her. I don't even know where the other girl is yet."

Logan frowned and said, "I think I know where she is."

"Great," Johnson said. "That will save us time looking for her."

"Maybe," Logan said, "but she might not be available."

"How so?"

"She's on trial for murder and I pretty much have a lock on a conviction."

"You what?"

"She killed one of mine," Logan said. "I'm putting her away for murder."

"No wonder you can't ask her for help."

"Hey," Logan said, "I'm open to new ideas, if you got any."

"I got nothing," Johnson replied, "but I have some friends. Maybe they can cook up some way to get these girls together."

Johnson kept a comfortable distance behind Honey's limo. They headed out on the highway and kept at a constant speed. A highway sign said Salt Lake was ahead, but it was a long way ahead.

Logan saw it too, and if that was their destination, this would be another long ride. He settled back in his seat to close his eyes for a bit.

Tempest was thrilled to be back with her family. She watched intently while Destiny testified. She laughed and cried and thought her daughter made the prosecutor look like a fool. She concentrated on Destiny, but found it increasingly difficult to remain focused on her.

The constant chatter from the guests in the gallery was annoying. She held and squeezed Dr. Weinhart's hand to help her refrain from slapping the woman behind her, who had nothing kind to say about Destiny. Maybe this was normal. She expected the judge to bang his gavel and settle the crowd down, but he just ignored it. She decided that he must have real good concentration.

She narrowed her eyes and focused on Destiny's lips, but three women behind her kept going on and on about how evil Destiny's eyes looked. Tempest didn't see anything evil in her daughter's eyes, but she found it impossible to focus on her lips when they kept drawing her attention to her eyes.

Dr. Weinhart winced as Tempest's grip squeezed harder.

Ashlin took Tempest's other hand and held it softly, thinking to her, "It's okay. We're all here with you."

Tempest turned her head to look at the young girl. Her voice wasn't irritating like the others.

Ashlin looked deeply into Tempest's eyes and thought, "I hear it too, but you don't have to let it bother you. I'll help you through this, but you might want to let your doctor have her hand back."

Tempest jerked her head around and saw the pain on Dr. Weinhart's face. She released her hand and thought, "I'm sorry."

Dr. Weinhart rubbed her hand and thought back, "It's okay."

"You see?" Ashlin thought. "We're all here with you. You just listen to us and don't let all those other people bother you."

Tempest looked back at the young redhead. Her wild red hair framed her young face and fell on her narrow shoulders, but deep inside, Tempest saw something entirely different. She looked into the girl's soul and thought, "Why are you pretending to be a little girl?"

"But I am a little girl," she thought back. "I am what I am, what you see."

"Why are you here?"

Ashlin smiled impishly and thought, "I came to help support my new sister, Destiny. But now I think I also have a new mother, too."

"No," Tempest thought. "You are older and wiser than I. I am not your mother. You have that backwards."

"But *your* mother is sitting right there," Ashlin thought, "behind your daughter. I can't be your mother."

"It's okay," Tempest smiled and thought, "I'm just glad you're here with us."

She hadn't even noticed it at first, but all the chatter from the gallery had faded away. Tempest was able to follow the proceedings again.

Dr. Weinhart was speechless. It was clear, as she sat there watching, that there was some interaction between Tempest and Ashlin, but not a word was spoken, yet Dr. Weinhart's mind filled in all the spaces between their glances with dialog. She imagined an entire conversation between the two of them, and even imagined she saw an older woman within the young girl. She returned her attention to Destiny's testimony and concluded that she was overly tired.

Harold put his hand over the mike and said, "Mr. Tangiers, it does indeed sound like you are suggesting that the defendant used real magic as a murder method, so let me be clear: This court does not recognize magical powers as either fact or evidence."

"But, your honor," Tangiers argued. "The defense already opened this door by suggesting the defendant was a witch. I only..."

"Mr. Tangiers," Harold said while shaking his head. "Get a grip. The defense was poking fun at the notion that there was anything unnatural about these events. Given the mysterious nature of the deaths, the court appreciates the defense's efforts to keep the jury grounded in reality. If you wish to introduce potions or herbs into evidence as poisons related to the crime, the court will consider them."

Harold turned his attention to Mr. Charles and said, "Now, as for you, Mr. Charles, this court will not tolerate any more shenanigans like claiming we do not have jurisdiction over the events, no matter how witty or amusing your words may be."

Tangiers and Charles both nodded and mumbled, "Yes sir," before Harold waved them away. Mr. Charles returned to the defense table while Mr. Tangiers stepped over to the witness stand.

The limo rolled smoothly and quietly down the road. Trees and rural communities flew by, each one looking pretty much the same as the other.

Richard turned to Honey and said, "You've never really been taught the history of our people, have you?"

Honey didn't know if she had or hadn't.

"It's okay," Richard said. "We have some time. Let me tell you a bit about us. We've always been around. Our people have existed since prehistoric times. There were always the regular people and us, but we were never alone. There are two families of magical people. Our people were usually called wizards or sorcerers. We could do physical things..."

"You mean like fireballs?" Honey interrupted, excited that the story turned to her.

"Yes," Richard replied. "Fireballs, lightning, moving things, all that stuff. The other magical race was the witches. They could see the future and the past. They could also get into our heads and make us see or do things. The farm you grew up on was a family of witches, or at least their descendants. After we lost the power of magic, we never really considered ourselves witches and sorcerers anymore, but those were the clans we came from."

Honey shuddered and said, "I always hated them goody goodies."

"Our people have always hated the witches. We had a war with them. In fact, we have had many wars against the witches, but the last war was the one that ended everything."

"Oh my god," Honey exclaimed. "You mean we lost to them? Is that why our people been hiding?"

"No," Richard said. "We nearly wiped them off the face of the Earth, but they had a prophecy. Only they can have prophecies. They said that if we killed all of them, we would lose our powers. They also said that one day, a chosen one would come to return magic to the world."

"Me! Me!" Honey exclaimed. "I'm the chosen one!"

"No," Richard said calmly. "We think your cousin Destiny is the chosen one."

"That hooker!" Honey spat. "I shoulda killed her."

"And perhaps you shall," Richard said. "We've been trying to figure out how to deal with her. We sent a team in to kill her, but they never returned. Frankly, we never expected you. Only one of our people got his powers back, and he is dead now. We don't know how or why you got your powers and nobody else has gotten theirs."

"She stole them," Abilene said.

"Mama! I did not!"

"We always had our own powers when we was on the farm," Abilene explained, "but when we left the farm, mine went away but you kept yours cause you stole that locket from her."

Richard reached out and asked, "Can I see it?"

Honey instinctively covered the locket with her hand.

"It's okay," Richard said, withdrawing his hand. "I just want a look."

Honey pulled the neckline of her shirt down, revealing the locket between her breasts. It glowed and pulsated.

"Can you feel it?" Richard asked.

"Sometimes," Honey said. "Sometimes it feels like it's feeding me, but other times, it feels like it is sucking my energy out of me."

Richard glanced over to Howard and Sven, who were still staring at the locket.

"That's enough," Abilene said as she reached over and pulled Honey's neckline back up.

Howard shrugged his shoulders and said, "I never heard of anything like that."

Mr. Tangiers stood quietly in front of Destiny for a moment. The judge had warned him to stick with the facts and stay away from suggesting anything supernatural, but nothing could stop him from touching any subjects that were opened up during direct questioning by her own counsel.

The jury grew restless as Simon stood there. Harold prompted him, "Counsellor? Mr. Tangiers? Did you have any further questions for this witness?"

Simon glanced at the judge and nodded. "Ms. Boutin, did you know those men that died in your home?"

"No sir, I had never seen either of them before."

"Did they have guns?"

"Yes sir," Destiny nodded. "They sure did."

"Is that why you killed them? Was it self-defense?"

Destiny shook her head and said, "I didn't kill them."

Tangiers' case had disintegrated to nothing. His only hope was for his witch to make her look evil, but he had to help. "Did you see what happened when they died?"

Destiny shrugged and said, "I don't remember much details."

Tangiers found a crack. She was hiding something. "You don't remember any details? Why not? You were there, weren't you?"

"I was there all right. I remember being tied to a chair."

"You were tied up? Was this before or after all the bullets were being fired into the house?"

"After," she said. "The fighting was all over."

"Fighting?" Tangiers asked. "It wasn't just them shooting up your house?"

Destiny felt trapped, and her face looked guilty.

Tangiers pressed, "Who were you fighting, Ms. Boutin?"

"They said they were government men, but we knew they were lying."

"How could you tell they were lying?"

"Because," Destiny said, "this is America, and the government doesn't order you out of your home for no reason."

"So, you fought with them?"

"I argued with them. I told them we weren't coming out, but that they could come to the porch and talk to us like civilized human beings."

"You told them this?" Tangiers asked. "Where was your nana?"

"She was hiding in the corner."

Simon paced back and forth in front of the jury while he said, "So, let me get this straight. You were the one talking to these men while your nana was hiding in the corner? Why is that? Why were you the one in charge? Why was your nana hiding in the corner while you dealt with these men?"

"Because I answered the door first. I saw they were bad men and told my nana to hide in the corner because I love her."

"And you fought with these men?"

"I don't remember."

"Your counsel has already shown this court how big they were and how small you are! Do you actually want us to believe that you would fight two armed intruders empty handed?"

"It wasn't my finest moment," Destiny said. "And it didn't end well. They tied me to a chair and tortured me."

"They tortured you? Why? What did they want to know?"

"They didn't want anything. The guy in charge was a sadistic pig, and he enjoyed it."

"So," Simon exclaimed. "You do remember!"

"Bits and pieces," she said. "He would wake me up after I passed out."

"How did he torture you?" Simon asked. "Your face looks remarkably good for someone who has been tortured."

Destiny didn't want to go there. Tears welled up in her eyes as the incident bubbled up in her memory.

"Ms. Boutin," Tangiers repeated. "How did he torture you?"

"He used electricity. I can still taste it in my mouth."

"How long did this go on?"

"I don't know."

"And how did this man end up dead?"

"I don't know."

"Did he deserve to die?"

"Yes! He said he was going to kill me!"

"You're glad he's dead!"

"Yes!"

"How did you kill him?"

"I don't remember!" A gasp flowed through the gallery.

"I mean," Destiny stammered, "I didn't kill him! I don't remember what happened."

"Ms. Boutin, do you really expect this court to believe that this man had you tied to a chair and tortured you, but then spontaneously erupted in flames?"

She couldn't stop the tears now. They pushed from her eyes and streaked down her cheeks. "I don't remember," she sobbed. "He was torturing me. He said it was time for me to die and I blacked out. Maybe my guardian angel came to my rescue."

"Your guardian angel burned your home to the ground?" Simon asked. "Between the fire and the sulphur found all across the scene, I just don't think this sounds like the work of angels."

Simon returned to his table and said, "No more questions."

Salt Lake wasn't dominated by downtown skyscrapers at the point where the limo crossed the border. They entered a rural suburb with nothing but a large blue sign informing them that they had just crossed into Salt Lake City.

"Really?" Honey asked. "This is it? It's as unimpressive as the office building you showed me this morning."

Richard said, "That's not by accident. We've had to remain invisible for centuries."

"Yeah, you have," Honey said, "and you done a dang good job of it too."

"We've done a lot more than just hiding," Richard continued. "We've learned a lot about manipulating the system from the inside without being detected."

"Why bother? If you're gonna remain invisible, then what's the point of controlling things?"

"We believed the prophecy. We didn't know which clan would get the chosen one, but if it was the witches, we wanted to be in control so we could snuff her out. If it was us, we figured it would be all that much easier to rule the world."

Honey smiled and said, "Ain't y'all just like little boy scouts being all prepared? And look now, it's like both clans got a chosen one."

Richard hadn't really considered that angle. They had always believed the chosen one was the first one to bring back magic, but why couldn't it be both of them? He looked at Honey in a new light but still came back to the thought that they had better candidates for their chosen one.

Richard's people in Salt Lake told them to go to the Royal Argus hotel to meet. The limo pulled up out front and the doorman opened the door. The bellboy was unnecessary as no luggage was delivered, but that wasn't so unusual for a prestigious hotel with excellent banquet facilities. What was unusual was Honey, whose looks were very out of place, but the hotel staff was professional and treated her like a VIP anyway, assuming she must be some kind of rock star.

The bellboy left the luggage cart by the door and showed them to their suite. In the room, Honey met Margaret, who had helped select her dresses. Margaret took her to the bedroom and showed her three dresses on the bed. Two of them were a dark red, one with sequins, while the third was black with a red piping on exaggerated lapels and a bright red belt.

Honey had asked for red, but she loved the black dress, which brought smiles to Margaret, who matched it up with red heels. Margaret then cracked open a gift box on the bed to reveal some stockings and a small selection of red and black unmentionables for Honey.

"You've had a long trip," Margaret said. "Why don't you go ahead and shower before I bring in Maurice? He's a bit flamboyant, if you know what I mean, but he performs miracles with hair. You'll find a robe in the closet."

"Finally," Honey thought, "someone knows how to treat a girl."

———

Johnson pulled over across the street while Honey and her entourage emptied out of the limo and entered the hotel.

"Do we follow them in?" Logan asked.

Johnson shook his head and said, "Let's stay with the limo. If the driver leaves the car, we can go look for them. I don't think she will be very hard to find."

———

Mr. Charles looked at his notes and shook his head. He couldn't believe he was about to do this, but he also would not have believed the course that the trial would have taken. He glanced back at Destiny and Michelle, then back at the judge and said, "The defense calls Blake Winters to the stand."

Destiny gasped. She never saw that in her visions, and neither Blake nor Mr. Charles had told her that he would be called upon. She thought she knew how the trial went, but she had never even seen him present in the courtroom.

Blake stood and walked to the witness stand. He was a little concerned that he would implicate himself in the crime, but he reminded himself that the prosecution didn't even have solid evidence that a crime actually existed. This whole trial had been a fishing expedition aimed at getting Destiny out of the way. He could put an end to that, assuming he doesn't look untruthful when he leaves out the part that he is the one who magically burned those men from the inside out.

He raised his right hand and listened to the oath, then responded, "I do."

Tangiers was furiously pouring through his notes and finally stood up and said, "Your honor, the prosecution was not informed about this witness."

Harold turned his head towards Mr. Charles and raised an eyebrow.

Charles nodded and said, "My apologies to the prosecution, but this witness only recently came forward."

"What?" Tangiers shouted. "This young man has been with the defendant since the pretrial hearing."

"This is true," Charles said, "but he only recently came forward with evidence regarding his firsthand knowledge of the incident in question."

"Your honor," Tangiers whined. "He's her boyfriend. How can we trust his testimony will be the truth?"

"He took the oath," Charles said.

"That's right Mr. Tangiers," Harold repeated. "He took the oath."

"But," Tangiers argued, "we haven't had an opportunity to depose him!"

"Again, with that argument?" Harold scolded. "After the nonsense you pulled with the crime scene evidence, you are actually going to call foul over a surprise witness?"

Simon's jaw dropped. That wasn't very judicial. He had stacked the deck in his favor from the start and now it was clearly against him. He stood speechless for a moment, then sat back down.

Harold smiled thinly and said to Mr. Charles, "You may proceed."

"Mr. Winters," Charles said. "Would you please share with the court what you confided with me just yesterday?"

"Yesterday?" Tangiers thought. He jerked slightly as his instinct was to argue that the defense did indeed have time to inform him, but regained control and remained in his seat.

"I was there," Blake said. "I not only saw everything, but I knew the men who died. That's why I was afraid to tell anyone."

"How did you come to know those men?" Charles asked.

"They hired me to help them track down Destiny. I came with them, but I didn't know what they wanted. I mean, I thought I knew why we were there, but I didn't know what they really wanted to do."

"What did they tell you they wanted?"

"They told me that her long-lost grandfather had left her some money, and they were hired to track her down."

"With assault rifles?" Charles asked.

"They said that was to protect us against alligators, and I sure seen plenty of them."

"Mr. Winters, the defendant testified that she was being tortured by one of the men. Were you present for that?"

Blake nodded and said, "I sure was. It was awful. I don't know how he did it or what you call those things, but I saw sparks coming from his hand. I guess he was holding something."

"Like a tazer?" Charles prompted.

"I dunno, maybe. I just know he used it to electrocute her. She froze up and couldn't even scream all the way. Then she would pass out and he'd slap her cheeks to wake her up."

"Was he asking her anything during the torture?"

"Nah. It was sick. He'd wake her up and say he didn't want her to miss any of this. Then he said she was going to die."

"Why?" Charles asked.

"Man," Blake said. "I been asking myself that every day, but I got no clue. He was one sick, crazy bastard. Then I guess he blew himself up. I expect he thought that would kill us all."

"And the other man?" Charles asked. "Did he blow himself up too?"

"I got the feeling that he was just following orders. He seemed like a cool dude on the trip."

"Thank you, Mr. Winters." Charles returned to his table and said, "Your witness."

Johnson followed Honey's limo from the garage back to the front of the hotel. A whistle escaped his lips as Honey emerged from the hotel and slid back into the car. It wasn't just the dress. He hadn't really noticed how smudged her skin had always been until he saw a clean Honey in a new dress and new hair.

"Is that really her?" Logan asked. "She cleans up pretty good."

"Yeah," Johnson agreed, "but I doubt it changes her mood any."

He followed the limo back to the highway and then off again into a residential area. They quickly pulled into an affluent neighborhood with tree-lined streets and manicured lawns and parked in front of a nice brick building.

"Okay," Johnson said, "where the hell is this?"

Logan played with the GPS to identify where they might be. "I'll be damned," he said. "You know where that is?"

Johnson pulled the hummer into a parking spot with a view of the parked limo and said, "Not a clue. If you had asked me twenty minutes ago, I would have guessed capitol hill."

"You're close," Logan said, pointing to the GPS. "This is the governor's private office. Capitol hill is only about seven minutes away."

"So, our girl is going to visit the governor?"

Logan's face creased with worry as he thought of the repercussions of her visit.

"What's wrong?" Johnson asked.

"I think she's going to go public."

"What do you mean?"

"We've kept our kind secret for centuries. Most people don't even believe we ever existed."

"I had to see it myself," Johnson admitted.

"But we were public once. We ruled the world, either behind a king offering advice, or just by show of might. There were thousands of us, and we all had power."

"What happened?"

"We had enemies. The other clan opposed us, and mankind hated us."

"Yeah," Johnson said. "I can see that. If you come down on us like lords, we tend to rebel."

"Well," Logan continued, "this time there's only one of her. We should be training the rest of us and cultivating the power instead of it being in the hands of one unstable little girl."

Johnson nodded his head like he was sympathetic and said, "She's not so little anymore, but I know what you mean." The truth was too disturbing for him to show his true feelings. This guy was as crazy as the girl was, only craftier. His whole clan is probably mad with power. Johnson hoped his friends and the little blond girl could contain them.

"I'm sorry," the receptionist said when she saw Honey and her entourage approaching, "but the governor is busy."

"This is a rather delicate situation," Richard said to the young lady. "The governor is not going to want to put this off."

The receptionist looked over the governor's calendar and said, "I can squeeze you in at three."

Honey stepped forward and demanded, "Where is he?"

The receptionist's eyes inadvertently glanced to her left.

"Thank you," Honey said. "I'll see myself in."

The receptionist frantically pushed buttons on the intercom to warn the governor, but Honey was already barging through the large closed doors.

"What's the meaning of this?" he barked.

"I needed to see you," Honey said, "and when I need to see you, you make yourself damned available to me."

The governor looked at the chic woman before him, but her identity escaped him. "Just who the hell do you think you are?" he demanded. "I'm a very busy man and I have a very tight schedule to maintain."

"My name is Honey, and you should thank me. I'm going to simplify your schedule and relieve you of all your busy obligations."

His face darkened and his brows furrowed. He yelled, "You what? Get out of here before I have you thrown out!"

Honey smiled coyly and said, "Aww, now that's not very nice. Do you like riddles? I have a riddle for you. What did St. Peter say to the politician when he showed up at the pearly gates?"

The governor looked at her blankly and said, "I don't have time for this."

"No, silly!" Honey exclaimed. "He said, 'What the hell are you doing here?' and the politician said, 'I don't know. The last thing I remember was telling a pretty young girl that I didn't want to meet with her.' and St. Peter said, 'That's too bad, but you're in the wrong place.' Now, governor, are you sure you want to blow me off like that? I think you'll find that you'll be in the wrong place, too."

The governor growled, "Get her out of here."

Two large men approached Honey.

"Are these your bodyguards?" she asked. "Are they like secret service? They're cute, but you might be better protected by firemen."

The governor had no idea what the crazy girl was talking about, but as soon as his guard detail grabbed her arms, their sleeves erupted in flames. She pushed them off of her while they flailed around, trying to get their jackets off. Another guard at the door pulled his revolver, but she wagged her finger at him, and the gun became red hot and fell from his sizzling hand.

The governor backed away behind his desk and pressed the intercom. "Vicky, call the po..."

Honey pointed at the phone and shot a long jolt of electricity into it, leaving it a fried and melted pile of plastic and glass.

The governor was helpless. He stood behind his desk wide eyed and asked, "What do you want?"

"Like I told you," Honey said. "I'm relieving you of all your duties. I'm taking over and then I'm marching to the very top. What do you think I should do with you? Are you going to be on my team supporting me, or are you one of those sad guys that I step on and leave behind?"

The governor glanced at his guard detail, but they had no answer for him.

Honey looked at the guards and said, "Same question for you boys."

The guards looked at each other quizzically until one stepped forward and nervously said, "I'm with you."

Honey smiled and stepped up to the volunteer seductively. "Good boy," she said. "I won't be needing you to guard my body, but I do have other positions you can fill."

Abilene repeated what was becoming an overly familiar scene as she closed her eyes and mouthed the word, "Slut!"

Logan leaned his head against the door window and closed his eyes. He just wanted some rest, but his mind kept returning to the maelstrom that had engulfed his captors, and then again, when Honey had burned the man at the facility. Nothing he did could erase those images from his mind until he finally drifted off and returned to the vision handed to him by the librarians.

The scent of sulphur was unmistakable. He saw the familiar grey robes walk, unscathed, out of the fire and up to him. He mimed the motions he had seen the girl do and doused them with fire. It didn't affect them. He pointed his finger at one of them and lifted him off the ground like a rag doll, then slammed him to the ground, but he landed on his feet, unaffected.

Logan couldn't harm them, but that didn't dampen the exhilaration he felt when he marshaled the power in his own hands. This was his destiny. He didn't care what kinds of warnings they had for him; he was supposed to own this power and he would do anything he had to in order to get it.

———

Tangiers approached the witness stand with some hastily scribbled notes. He flipped his notes over a couple times to organize his questions in his mind, then said, "Mr. Winters, why haven't you come forward before now?"

"At first," Blake said, "it was because I didn't want to be associated with them at all. Once I learned what they were up to, I stopped helping them, but they were scary dudes, and I didn't want the guys that hired them to know about me."

"The guys that hired them?" Tangiers asked. "You don't think they worked alone?"

"No. One of them was in contact with someone over the phone who was also helping to track her down."

Tangiers scratched his head and asked, "Why would they even hire a kid like you? Ms. Boutin does not seem like a girl who spends a lot of time on the internet. What exactly are your skills?"

Blake knew the question would come up, and he knew it would be hard to skirt around. "I'm just good at finding stuff. You might say that I have good instincts."

"Mr. Winters, I don't think good instincts count as a job qualification. You might as well tell the court you're just lucky, so people hire you."

"You could say that too," Blake replied.

"What could I say?" Tangiers asked.

"Like you said. I'm lucky. I'm lucky and I find stuff."

"What are you holding back, Mr. Winters? Let me remind you that you are under oath. Explain to the court how you find stuff."

"I'm not sure that I can," Blake replied.

"Why should this jury believe anything you have to say if you're unwilling to explain how you operate?"

"I didn't say I was unwilling. I said I didn't know if I can. The truth is that I don't know if I'm allowed to say how I operate."

"You're under oath to answer my questions," Tangiers said. "What more permission do you need?"

Harold leaned over and softly said, "Answer the question, son."

"But your honor..." Blake stammered.

"Answer the question," Harold repeated.

"Okay," Blake said, "but does the court recognize psychic ability, or is that like magic and inadmissible?"

Harold smirked and said, "You're correct. The court does not recognize psychic abilities."

"That's what I thought," Blake said.

"Unless," Harold continued, "those abilities can be proven to this court's satisfaction."

"The prosecution moves that this witness's testimony be stricken from the record as unreliable."

Harold was about to agree when Blake said, "Would the court be satisfied if I told you that your honor only ate three of the blueberries on his pancakes because the rest weren't plump enough?"

Harold raised his eyebrows, but Tangiers said, "We all ate at the same diner. Anybody could have witnessed that."

"Or," Blake continued, "that you thought the milk was too warm and the orange juice was sour?"

"Again," Tangiers said, "we all had the same milk and orange juice."

"Or that your cat, Mrs. Pippins, carried her newborn kittens up to the top bunk so you could help keep them warm and protect them?"

Harold's jaw dropped as he asked, "How did you..."

"How about juror number six?" Blake continued. "He was supposed to go fishing today, and he's worried about what his brother-in-law might do to his boat. Juror number three is afraid she left the lights on, but in a couple hours, she's going to worry about the iron... oops, now that I said it, she's already worried."

Harold put his hand up and said, "That's all very entertaining, son, but the court would like a more practical proof."

"Okay," Blake said. "How about the seventy-eight cents you have in your pockets? I'm only counting the U.S. coins and not the Canadian dime."

Harold fished the coins out of his pocket and counted them, then proclaimed, "This court will accept this young man's psychic ability as fact, but will not accept any eyewitness testimony that was received through these abilities. Fair enough counselors?"

Tangiers was flummoxed. He couldn't introduce the mother's vision as testimony, and now he couldn't impeach Blake's abilities.

"Mr. Winters," he said. "If you were sent here with those men to kill Ms. Boutin..."

"I was only sent here to find her."

"Yes, of course," Tangiers said, "but how is it that you have become such intimate friends with her in such a short time?"

Blake blushed and said, "I don't think I would call it intimate. People might get the wrong idea, but being able to see into people as I can makes it a lot easier to get to know them and trust them."

"And do they trust you?"

Blake looked over at Michelle and said, "No sir, not one hundred percent."

"Why not?" Tangiers asked.

"Because Destiny is a pretty girl and I'm a boy," Blake said. "Why else?"

Tangiers started the interrogation believing he could pull out a win, but now just surrendered and said, "No more questions."

Johnson followed honey back to town again. The sun had risen high in the sky and the temperatures were rising as well. He parked on the street as the limo pulled up in front of another nice hotel and let the passengers out.

Logan put the window down and the aroma of boiled hotdogs wafted into the car. "You think we got time for a couple of dogs?"

"Yeah, sure," Johnson said. "I'm starving."

"You keep your eye on them," Logan said. "I got this. What do you want?"

"Relish, onions and mustard. If he has polish, I'd like one with mustard and sauerkraut, otherwise two dogs."

"You got it. Yellow or brown?"

"Brown."

Logan hopped out of the car and stretched his legs. The vendor had a line of customers, and Logan didn't feel any need to rush the few steps to his cart. He wished he had a better idea of what Richard's involvement was with the girl. Logan didn't want Richard getting the girl's powers before he could steal them for himself. He also needed some way to get rid of the girl and he didn't relish getting in bed with the enemy, but the witch might be the only person able to control her. Then there was the trial, which he might have to do something about, but decided that if she couldn't get herself out of trouble, then maybe she wouldn't be good enough to handle this new girl. He hoped he wouldn't have to go up against any more of his own people, but Richard hadn't proven himself to be a valuable asset since the Brian fiasco, anyway.

The governor's hands shook as he took Honey by the arm and guided her into the swanky restaurant. The host was all smiles as the governor came in. The governor's voice cracked as he said, "We're going to need a few extra seats for lunch."

The host counted guests and asked, "Will there be more?"

"God, I hope not," the governor replied.

The host motioned for a waiter and told him to set six more places. The waiter ran ahead to assemble the extra tables while the host guided them leisurely to their table.

Margaret whispered to Abilene, "I wish I had been told you would be joining us. I could have selected something for you to wear, too."

Abilene felt the eyes on her. She couldn't have been more shabbily dressed. "Thank you," she said. "Part of me wishes I weren't even here. In fact, what would be the farthest place from here? China maybe? I think I'd rather be in China for my remaining days."

Margaret didn't quite understand. She wasn't in the governor's office and didn't know what Honey could do, but Honey thought Margaret was the only one who knew how to treat her right and insisted she come to lunch. They were going to be new best friends, but Margaret had no idea what she was getting into.

They arrived at the newly lengthened table and their host tried sitting the governor at the head of the table with Honey to his right, but she shoved him over and took the head for herself. The young host looked at them blankly for a moment, then shrugged it off and returned to his post. The governor's guests, supporters, and contributors had not arrived yet. With the governor shoved over to her left, Honey insisted that Margaret be on her other side with Richard and her mother. Howard and Sven, who she was convinced would prove themselves to be absolutely useless, could sit next to the governor.

"So," Honey said. "Are we early, or are our guests late?"

"It's their money," the governor said, "and we allow them their eccentricities like arriving fashionably late. It makes them feel like they have the power."

With his words still on her ears, two older men and one sharply dressed man still in his thirties joined them. The younger of the three sat opposite Honey and asked, "Who is this ravishing creature you have brought before us?"

The governor sat dumbly, unsure what to say. Honey kicked him under the table, and he said, "Gentlemen, I'd like you to...t hat is, this is... her name is Honey, and she is..."

Honey kicked him again and said, "Honey. My name is Honey, and I'm going to be taking over for the governor."

The young man opposite her looked to his left, then his right, and started laughing. "Please tell me," he said. "Exactly what duties you will be taking over for our dear Percy?"

"All of them," Honey said, "Starting right now, I'm your new governor."

He tried to keep laughing, but there just wasn't enough humor to fuel any more chuckles. The three new guests watched Honey's expressions, which seemed strangely and insanely serious. The elder man to his left said, "You don't seem to be too concerned about the line of succession that will take over his job should he step down or otherwise fail."

"No," she said. "Do you think I should be concerned?"

"Yes," the other elder man said. "If anything happens to the governor, the laws state precisely who takes over."

"And if something happens to them?" Honey asked.

"Then," the same man said, "the law tells us exactly who would be next to take over."

"That's not a problem," Honey said. "I'm going to rewrite the laws."

"You're going to what?" both elder men exclaimed.

"You heard me. I'm throwing out everything you think you know about the rules around here. We're going back to a Queendom, and you can start right now by calling me 'Your Highness.'"

"Well, Your Highness," the younger man said, "we control over a billion dollars, and you won't be able to do anything without our money. The laws are the laws because we put them there. Our money buys the laws, and our money buys the men that run them."

Honey stretched her lips into a wicked smile and asked, "Do you really think your money is the greatest power in the world?"

"It is," the younger man said flatly.

Honey shook her head and said, "Your money isn't even the greatest power at this table." She stood up and placed her hands on the table. The tablecloth around her hands erupted into small flames. The flames traced a path from each of her hands and joined up in front of her between her plate and the candles, then created a track of flame down the table like a burning fuse until it surrounded the young man's plate. "Does your money have that kind of power? Can your money even buy that kind of power?"

All eyes in the restaurant were on Honey and their table. "Look around you. Do you think all these people fear your money more than they fear me?"

The young man didn't know how she did it, but he refused to show fear and clapped his hands instead. "That's a very fine trick. Do you plan to burn down all of Salt Lake?"

Honey nodded yes.

"And then," he continued, "all of Utah?"

"Pretty much," she said.

"When does it stop?" he asked. "Do you burn down the whole country then the whole world?"

"If I have to."

"Then, even if this were real, who would be left to follow you?"

"You see it," she said, "but you still don't believe it?"

"Miss Honey," he said. "You're certainly a smoking hot babe with a smoking hot pyrotechnics act, but I don't have a clue what you're trying to sell me. The only thing I'm buying right now is that you are one seriously crazy chick."

"You really think this is a trick?" she asked. "Is that burning cigar in your pocket a trick, too?"

"Oh, shit!" he exclaimed as he removed the lit cigar from his jacket pocket.

"Or is your glass of water supposed to be boiling like that?"

Three people at a nearby table got up to quietly leave and Honey pointed to the exit and shot flames out of her hand to engulf the exit door. "Did I say anybody could leave?" The three patrons quickly returned to their booth and huddled behind the table.

The young man needed no more convincing and said, "It seems you have us at a serious disadvantage. It also would appear that you have no need of our funding. What exactly do you want?"

"I already told you. You can start by calling me 'Your Highness'. Beyond that, we'll think of something. I always wanted to do it with a billionaire."

One of the elder men chuckled, quietly saying, "It'll probably burn off inside of her!"

The other elder man laughed and added, "Not anymore. It just shriveled up and became no use to her."

The young man saw no escape, but he also saw an opportunity. He stood and bowed at the waist, saying, "My lady, would you like to accompany me somewhere where we might privately discuss how your power and my wealth might work together for both of our advantage?"

Honey giggled and nodded her head.

Once again, Abilene whispered the word, "Tramp!"

CHAPTER 13

C harles stood behind the defense table and checked his notes to see if he had missed anything. He glanced over at the prosecution, took a deep breath and said, "Your honor, the defense rests."

Harold nodded to the defense and said, "Thank you Mr. Charles, at this time the court will hear your summations before turning it over to the jury. Is the prosecution ready?"

Mr. Tangiers stood up and said, "I am, sir." He stepped out from behind his table and approached the Jury. "Ladies and gentlemen of the jury, this has been an unexpected ride. We have a stack of mysterious facts, and we have a family of mysterious people. Two men are dead, and that is for certain. We know that they were burned to death in the most horrific manner possible, but we don't know how they were burned. We've heard testimony about a party held just days before the tragic crime in which the defendant's own grandmother predicted that a stranger would come to town and somebody near the defendant would die. How did she do that? Another mystery. The witnesses said she read the bones and saw the future. She didn't see the future for anyone else in this community except the defendant."

"She reads the bones. Let's let that sink in a moment. She spills bones out onto a table and sees the future in them. She also brews potions and tonics that she sells at the general store. Residents in these parts go to her for homeopathic remedies. She sees the future, and she does things to heal people. A man mysteriously erupts in flames in *her* home. She certainly has an interesting lifestyle, but she's not the one on trial. Her granddaughter is."

"Does she really see the future? Or is she one of those con artists who knows how to read people and tell them what they want to hear? Has she been lying to these people when she reads the bones? Has she been lying to these people when she cures their pains? Is she lying to us now when she tells us that the man mysteriously and spontaneously burst into flames from the inside out, or does she really have these powers? And if she really has these powers, and she really is telling the truth that these two men simply caught fire, then what other powers does she have? What powers has she passed on to her daughter and her granddaughter?"

"And what about the daughter? She hears voices. We lock her up in a hospital for patients with incurable mental conditions because she hears voices. Of course we do. What sane person would believe she could really hear voices? I know I couldn't. At least, I couldn't until I saw the video with my own two eyes. You saw it too. It was like she was watching her daughter, the defendant, burn those two men. It gives me goose bumps just to think about it."

Her grandmother reads the bones and sees the future. The mother hears voices and sees a supernatural battle from miles away. The daughter, our defendant, fights armed men with her bare hands and, as a result, we have little fire pits all over the property that our own arson investigator can't quite explain. A professional athlete couldn't run fast enough to start them all. Then, that same daughter is captured and tied to a chair and tortured. She is tortured mercilessly by a man who says he is going to kill her, only he spontaneously erupts into flames from the inside out. I can't believe what I am thinking. I look at the evidence and add it up and just can't believe what it adds up to."

"I certainly don't envy your decision, ladies and gentlemen of the jury. You must decide if this family is lying to us about how these men burst into flames, or worse, does the defendant actually have the power to make them burn? Just look at her. Go ahead and look at her. She's young and pretty and totally unafraid. That is the face of someone who doesn't care what you decide. Look at her eyes. Those are the eyes of someone who already sees past you. Those are the eyes of a stone-cold psychopath. We may not know how or may not want to believe how she did it, but she killed those men. I see it in her eyes, and you can too. I urge you to find her guilty, or I promise you, she will do this again."

"Thank you."

Tempest's mind grew clearer with every moment as she rapidly returned to a level of awareness. She listened to the prosecutor's summation and wished she could burn him from the inside out. How could he even suggest that her Destiny looked guilty? But the jury heard him, and she could feel his words sweep them away into a bizarre world of paranoia and suspicion. Their thoughts crept into her head, layered on top of each other, one louder than the next.

The jury's thoughts mingled in her mind, jumbled and out of sequence at first, but slowly merging together into a single unified thought, "Her eyes. Her eyes. Guilty eyes." The voices in her head were chanting. She heard a menagerie of thoughts from the gallery that picked up the chant, "Her eyes. Guilty eyes."

Tempest's head swooned with the voices. She felt another voice that wasn't caught up in the chanting but was guiding the jury's voices. Someone was planting the words in their heads. The voices were overpowering. The cacophony of sound was pushing Tempest into a bad place where she couldn't cope with the noise, but as they joined in unison and began chanting together, she found it easier to join with them than fight against them.

"No," Ashlin thought to her. "Don't let the voices sway you. You have your own voice. Listen to my voice as I guide you to your own. You have to concentrate. You should have learned this years ago."

Tempest listened to Ashlin's voice and as she listened, she could hear her grandmother saying, "The voices you hear are just people who can't keep quiet. They are like children in a playground or crickets in a field. Focus on your own voice and they are like laughter in the wind. Calm your heart and your mind."

The panic passed. She could still hear the jury and the gallery chanting, but she wasn't caught up in the wave of chants.

She looked over at Ashlin and saw the child smiling at her. A single tear gathered in the corner of Ashlin's eye and Tempest thought she had never felt so much love before.

Johnson licked the last morsel of mustard from his finger and promised himself he would get back to a normal life. The limo didn't stay in front of the hotel. It moved across the street and parked behind another limo. The drivers of both vehicles relaxed on a bench under a small awning and talked gossip with each other.

"I could never be a private investigator," Logan said. "This is boring."

"Yeah," Johnson agreed. "You mind if I close my eyes for a few minutes?"

"Not as long as I get my turn, too."

"Just a catnap," Johnson said. He leaned his seat back a little and closed his eyes. It felt good just not looking at anything. He took a couple of deep breaths and was ready to drift off.

"Johnson? Are you with me?"

"What did you say?" he asked. "I was almost asleep."

Logan shrugged and said, "I didn't say anything."

"Johnson?"

It was them. "Where the hell have you guys been?" Johnson thought. "I been calling for you for hours."

"But you don't know how to call for us," the librarian replied.

"No shit. I just thought you might eavesdrop once in a while."

"We need you to go to Salt Lake as fast as you can."

Johnson struggled to control his thoughts and not give away that he was already there. "Why?" he thought. "What's happening in Salt Lake?"

"We have a problem brewing there," the librarian thought, "and we need you to put an end to it."

"Stop being so cagey," Johnson thought back, "and tell me plainly what you know and what you want."

Logan watched Johnson's expressions. It wasn't the face of someone getting a catnap. His face contorted and grimaced like he was having a nightmare, or worse, a flashback to a war. It was obvious to Logan that Johnson was some kind of veteran, and he had seen the news and movies about post-traumatic stress. It was bad enough that they were tailing a crazy chick with a mean temper who could single-handedly bring the world to an end, but now he was sitting next to a soldier who might, at any moment, turn to face him and see a Taliban terrorist.

"It's the girl who took the amulet," the librarian continued. "We don't want her to have it anymore. If she learns how it works, she could cause a lot of trouble with it."

"A lot of trouble?" Johnson thought back. "Is that really how you want to say it? The girl is a terror. She's as bad as the other girl! Maybe worse! You're too late to stop her, bub. I don't think there's a damn thing I can do about it. So why don't you tell me just exactly how bad things can get?"

Silence followed. Librarian number three consulted with numbers one and two before he returned to Johnson. "Very well," he thought. "We shall tell you. Our world is done. She has managed to turn the entire planet into an uninhabitable lump of coal. Smoke covers the planet, preventing the sun from warming the oceans. There is no rainfall. The air is unbreathable. What few refugees remain have no food and some have resorted to feeding upon each other. Need I go on?"

"No," Johnson replied, "but you need to figure out a better plan. I can't stop her. She's as bad as the blonde girl, only she's meaner, and I'm pretty sure she is completely insane. The other girl could stop bullets and I have no reason to think this girl can't as well. If I try to approach her, she'll fry me before my knife reaches her throat."

"You're right," the librarian said. "I know I ask too much, but the world depends on us stopping her."

"What do you mean by us?" Johnson complained. "You're the ones who are able to contact me. You seem to have some powers of your own, but I'm the only one you are asking to stop her! That's not us! Show me how to stop her. Give me a plan. Tell me this has happened before and there is some way to end it! From where I'm sitting, it's going to take fire to fight fire and there's only one person who can do that: the blond girl."

"He'll never allow that. This whole mess was to keep her out of..."

The librarian was cut off for a minute.

"Hello?" Johnson asked. "Hello? Are you there?"

"I am here," the librarian said, "but I said too much. What matters is for you to know that normal men like yourself have stopped her kind before. But you are correct when you say you cannot face her alone. You must meet her with overwhelming numbers and force her to exhaust herself, but it won't be easy."

"Great," Johnson said aloud. "Thanks for the newsflash."

"What was that?" Logan asked.

"Nothing," Johnson said. "I was just given orders to stop her, but they admitted that I can't do it alone."

Logan had been watching Johnson. He wasn't on the phone or the radio. Logan had wondered if he could work with a witch when he considered enlisting Destiny for help, but it would seem he was already working with them.

"We knew that we couldn't do it alone," Logan said. "That's why we need the girl."

"They don't want us to use the girl."

"Why not?"

Johnson shrugged and said, "He wouldn't say, but I got the impression that we weren't supposed to know that they didn't want to use the blond girl. He said that we could overpower the girl with overwhelming numbers. I think maybe it's been done before."

Logan pulled out his phone and selected a number from his contact list. He waited for someone to answer and said, "Eddie? It's Logan."

"Logan? Aren't you missing?"

"Let's just say I'm undercover. I need a favor. Something is going down at the Brewster Hotel and I need swat, homeland security, the National Guard, anyone you can get to come down here. Tell them it's terrorists and bomb threats. The governor is inside with some wealthy businessmen. I need this all to happen within minutes."

"Are you sure about this?"

"Yes," Logan said, "and for now, let's keep my name out of it."

Honey followed the younger investor from the restaurant to the elevator in the hotel lobby. She knew he was much thinner than his chubby older friends, but she hadn't noticed from the far end of the dining table that his hair was long and flowed down just below his shoulders. "So," she said. "Do you have a name, or am I gonna have to call you money bags?"

"Thomas," he replied. His dark locks swung low around his neck while he bowed deeply at the waist. "Thomas Perceval Eldridge the third, at your service."

"The third?" she asked. "Hasn't your family got it right yet? Maybe I should hold out for the fourth."

"No need, my lady. We finally got it right."

"Good to know," she said. "So, what was wrong with Thomas Eldridge the second?"

Thomas hemmed and hawed but was saved by the elevator door and said, "Your carriage awaits."

She entered the elevator and said, "You didn't answer my question."

"About that, there is no second or third. I made that up, so it sounded like old money."

"You lied to me?"

He held up his thumb and finger and said, "Just a little lie. I was only trying to impress you."

"Still," she said. "I don't know if I like you anymore."

"But does that mean you like me any less?"

The elevator door opened, and she pushed him out and followed him into the hallway. "Did you really think lying to me was going to work for you?"

He took her hand and walked backwards, leading her down the hallway. "Why not? That's how I made my money. It's worked for me for a long time now."

"Do you even really have any money?" she asked.

"Oh yes, a great deal more than I need, but still less than I want."

"And you lied and cheated to get it?"

He pushed his key card in the lock and opened the door for her. "A little larceny can go a long way."

She entered the suite and swept her gaze around the luxurious room, nodding her head and smiling at its opulence. "I like how you live. Now, how do you intend to get into my pants?"

He took her in his arms and pressed his lips against hers. Her lips were warm and inviting. He abruptly pulled away and asked, "You're not going to suddenly catch fire if I kiss you, are you?"

"No," she said coyly, "not if you kiss me."

He walked her backwards through the suite to the bedroom and gently sat her on the edge of the bed. He dropped to his knees and removed one of her heels. "And what if I do this?" He squeezed her foot warmly and massaged the joints around her toes. "Will you catch fire if I do this?"

"No," she said, "I don't think so."

He raised her foot to his face and kissed the top of her toes. "And what about this?"

"No," she panted. "I'm not going to burst into flame."

He removed the shoe from the other foot and proceeded to massage it. "The fire on the lunch table was real, wasn't it? I mean, it wasn't some kind of trick, was it?"

"Yes," she said. "It was real. Now concentrate on what you're doing."

He pulled her off the bed and stood her up, then pulled her face to his again and kissed her. Pushing the thought of her erupting in flames out of his mind, he swore that her lips and her whole body were getting hotter. He pulled back gently and asked, "How long have you been able to make fire like that?"

"I don't know," she said. "Since puberty I expect. Now are you gonna take that shirt off or am I gonna have to burn it off?"

He ripped his shirt off and dropped it to the floor.

"Wow," she said as she gently ran her hands down his chest. "You got more ripples than a freshly plowed field."

"You're kidding me," he said. "You're a farm girl?"

"Hell no," she replied. "I was raised on grandpa Zeb's farm, but I ain't one of them. You?"

"I grew up on a Nebraska ranch."

"Why is we talking about farms?" she asked.

He shrugged and gently raised her dress over her head. "How much control do you have on the fire?"

"I swear," she said, "if you don't get your head in the game, you're gonna find out how much control I have when I try to burn your pants off you. I never tried it before, but I feel it coming."

He quickly unbuckled his belt and dropped his pants while she swiftly shimmied out of her panties.

"No more talking," she said, "or I might just burst into flames!"

"But you said you..."

She put her finger to his lips and waved her arm over the bed. The blankets and covers landed in a pile on the floor.

She leapt onto the bed and said, "Well, farm-boy, you gonna plow my fields or what?"

Johnson returned to his catnap, and Logan scanned the streets. It was a quiet day. Joggers and dog walkers came and went. There were taxicabs, but Logan couldn't recall seeing a bus the whole time. The taste of the hotdog lingered, and he wished he had another, but then decided that he was more bored than hungry. The food-high came and went, leaving him slightly drowsy as he stared at the serene streets of Salt Lake.

His cell phone played a cheerful melody. "Hello? This is Logan."

"Eddie here. Mission accomplished."

"Thanks, I owe you one."

"No, you don't," Eddie said. "I placed the call, but someone had already alerted the authorities. Swat and FBI should be on the way already."

Johnson had opened his eyes when the phone rang. Now he watched Logan's eyebrows fold into a scowl. "What's wrong?"

Logan glanced over at him and said, "My friend says that the police have already been called."

"By who?" Johnson asked.

"By who?" Logan repeated into the phone.

"That wasn't clear, but it sounded like the governor's people may have made the call."

"Thanks Eddie."

Logan ended the call and said, "It sounds like the governor's staff called them."

Mr. Charles walked before the jury and said, "Wow. That was some story, but it was just that. A story. Ladies and gentlemen of the jury, you just heard the wild ramblings of a very vivid imagination. Two men die of mysterious causes; therefore, it must be witchcraft. Did I just wake up in the seventeenth century? What's next? You predicted the winner of the super bowl, therefore you must be a witch! And to top it off, the prosecutor described the defendant's grandmother in great detail and expects you to conclude that this sweet young girl is guilty because her grandmother sells lotions at the general store. I don't believe I have ever heard anyone say, 'The grandmother is a witch, therefore the granddaughter is a murderer.' It's absolute nonsense."

"And who were these men? They storm into these women's peaceful home intent on killing the young girl for reasons unknown. Maybe they probably saw it in the stars. They're not just any random men. They bring all manner of high-tech weaponry, and they end up getting killed themselves in a mysterious fire. It was them who brought the weapons, but let's all blame the low-tech country girl. She doesn't even have a TV, and we are to believe that she can kill two much larger armed intruders with some weapon so high-tech that the coroner doesn't even know what it is? Oh yeah, the prosecutor wants us to believe that it's witchcraft."

"Even if we believed in witchcraft and knew beyond a doubt that it was actually witchcraft, it would have been self-defense. And if it wasn't witchcraft, if she actually had done it and we just didn't know how, it would still be self-defense. But she didn't do it. She's just a sixteen-year-old girl raised by her grandmother in the bayou. Tell the prosecutor to go find the real killers and leave this nice young girl alone."

Johnson climbed over the seat and into the back, then slouched low in his seat as the street started to fill up with police vehicles.

Logan had been watching the hotel's front door through the field glasses, but he had seen Johnson's movement from the corner of his eye and said, "Don't you think they'll be too focused on the hotel to notice the two of us parked way back here in a Humvee?"

"I think," Johnson replied, "that they've been warned about a possible terrorist attack on the governor that possibly involved a bomb threat. Standard operating procedure would probably include surveying the area for additional combatants, and two guys in a Humvee with field glass might look a bit suspicious."

Logan quickly put the large field glasses down and climbed over the seat to join Johnson in the back seat and slouched down himself.

The street rapidly filled with police cruisers, various vans with bomb disposal squads and swat teams. Fire and rescue lined up on the perimeter with an assortment of ambulances.

Johnson put his finger to his lips and said, "Shhh." An armed officer walked the length of the street, looking into the parked cars. The super dark tinted windows would hide them in the back, and the seat backs would hide them from the front window.

They saw the spot of the flashlight through the front windshield, but they weren't detected and he moved on.

Harold took a deep breath and exhaled. Both sides have rested and given their summations. He could see the light at the end of the tunnel. He smiled and said, "Thank you, Mr. Charles. Ladies and gentlemen, that concludes the testimony portion of our trial today, and now it is up to the members of the jury to weigh what they have seen and heard and decide the fate of our young defendant." He turned to speak directly to the jury and said, "The charge brought before you is murder. Your task is a serious one. I need you to come to a unanimous decision. If even one of you doesn't agree, then you must continue to deliberate until all parties come to the same conclusion. Should you need clarification on any points of law, ask the bailiff and he will bring your questions to me. Thank you and good luck."

Harold stood, and the bailiff sang out, "All Rise."

Harold left the bench and was followed by the jury, who were led to a secluded room.

Destiny joined Michelle and started towards the exit, but a burley officer blocked her way. Simon grinned in the background as the officer said, "We'd prefer to keep you in custody while the jury is out."

Charles objected and said, "Where is she going to go?"

The officer just shrugged and said, "I have my orders."

Destiny said, "It's okay, Mr. Charles. Like you said, where would I go anyway?"

Destiny followed the officer to the exit. Michelle followed behind and was blocked by another guard.

"What?" she demanded with the voice. "Are you going to stop me?"

The guard was visibly shaken and stepped out of the way. Michelle and the whole gang followed behind. The room only had two chairs. Michelle glanced back at the already shaken guard and without saying a word, he fetched more chairs, then seeing the room was too small, he moved them to a larger room with a table in the center.

When everyone had found seats, the guard stepped inside and closed the door, but a glance from Michelle was all it took for him to open the door and say, "I'll just wait outside."

Honey returned shamelessly back to the governor's luncheon. Her hair was mussed, and she didn't know how to fix it without Maurice. She left her panties in Thomas's breast pocket in place of his hankie, but otherwise assembled her dress and shoes reasonably well.

Richard and the two strategists, whom she had come to think of as the two idiots, were still at their end of the table talking amongst themselves. The two elder money bags sat like peacocks at their end of the table. They smirked as their eyes followed Honey's return to their table. The governor sat alone between the two ends of the table, with fear written across his face.

The rest of the restaurant was strangely quiet. Honey was too lost in her thoughts to notice, but Thomas saw immediately that the entire establishment was empty.

Richard stood in the old-fashioned way as she joined them. He smiled and shook his head.

Thomas followed her instead of joining his cronies and asked, "What's going on here? Where is everybody?"

Richard replied, "Some people just never learn. Your friends aren't ready to believe what they saw and will require further demonstrations."

Thomas turned toward his friends and asked, "What have you idiots done?"

They pointed at Honey and said in unison, "That's her."

Swat teams appeared as if from thin air. The restaurant was filled with armed men focused on Honey. Some held both hands on assault weapons trained on her, while others held shields and batons. They circled around her.

The glow on Honey's face morphed into anger. She looked around her and frowned at the fools who had just ruined a beautiful moment for her.

Richard took Thomas's elbow in one hand and offered his other arm to Abilene. "I think we should wait outside."

Margaret and the two strategists followed them to the lobby.

Honey turned in a circle so everyone could see and hear her. "Anybody who doesn't want to die should leave now."

The men of the swat team chuckled and wondered why so many of them were there. Those with the shields stepped forward to apprehend the obviously crazy young girl.

A glow between her breasts shone through the dress. The temperature surrounding her rose dramatically. The rising heat raised her hair into a dramatic halo around her head. Honey clenched her fists and was surrounded by an aura of flame. Her lips curled into a smile because she was doing what she had seen Destiny do at dinner.

The men with the shields stopped approaching. The smiles evaporated from their faces.

"Last chance," Honey said. "Anybody who doesn't leave is going to be a pile of ash in just a few seconds."

"It's a trick," one man with a shield said as he stepped forward.

Honey pointed to his feet and flames rose up from the floor to consume him. He cried piteously until she turned the flame white and crushed him into a tall column of cinders that fell harmlessly to the floor.

"Who's next?" Honey asked.

The men closest to her tried getting away, but the men further away only saw a flash of light and blocked their escape.

"Ok then," Honey said. A searing white ring of heat spread slowly and terrifyingly from her body. It was a cylindrical ring that stretched from floor to ceiling and incinerated everyone as it touched them. Now the other rows of men in the back saw it, too. Some started firing their weapons, but their munitions could not survive the heat of the white ring. The ring expanded. Some men tried retreating, but the chaos led to trampling over other men with nobody escaping the carnage.

As the circle approached the end of the table, a split opened around the two elder gentlemen, saving them to watch the massacre. When the room was cleared, and only the three of them were left, Honey walked down the table to them. They tried getting up to leave, but she held them in their chairs.

"So much death," she said. "You two killed all these men. With all the money you have, I guess you don't figure their lives are worth two cents. How much value do you put on your own lives now? Your money means nothing to me. I sure don't need you. This country is going to be mine. I don't spect I really need anyone to help me get that, but I might need people who can keep everyone else under control for me. Now, do either of you have any value for me?"

Both men nodded their heads vigorously and said, "I can help you."

She looked at the two of them and said, "I don't need two fat assholes in my organization. One is enough. Which of you is more valuable than the other?"

"I am!"

"No, I am!"

"Then get rid of him! I only need one of you."

Their jaws dropped open. They stared at her, then at each other, then back to her again.

"Jesus!" she exclaimed. "Do I have to spell it out for you? You got steak knives! Use them!"

They each grabbed their knives and then stared hesitantly at each other.

"If you don't have the balls to prove your value to me, then I don't have much use for either of you."

One of them swallowed hard, then swung his arm, penetrating the other's shoulder with his blade. She released them from their chairs and they both got up onto their feet and started stabbing each other like pin cushions.

Honey stood back and laughed at them. "You are some seriously dumb assholes. How the hell did you ever get your fortunes?"

One of the men fell to the ground, and the other stepped forward. He bled profusely and still held the knife as he announced, "There, it is done."

"No, it's not," she said. She wrapped her mind around his arm and forced him to stab the knife into his own throat. He stared vacantly at her as the blood stopped coursing through his brain. He fell to his knees and said, "But..."

"But nothing," she said. "Now it really is done."

The dead silence of the court's waiting room was only occasionally broken by a cough or sneeze, or the squeak of a folding chair when someone crossed their legs the other way. The sun cast a slender beam through a hole in the blinds that created a shaft of light in the dust suspended in the room. As the sun traced its arc across the sky, the beam slid across the table until it landed on Tempest's face and the room exploded with the sound of squeaking metal.

Tempest rocked in her chair. Her face was crowded with grief. New voices invaded her brain. Some cried out in pain. She felt a searing heat wash over them, and their voices were extinguished. Others had not yet cried out, but Tempest could hear the silenced voices of their spirits call out in anguish.

Dr. Weinhart stroked her hair and asked, "What's the matter?"

Ashlin was on the other side, holding Tempest's hand. She said, "Something bad is happening. We can feel it."

Michelle was horrified. She didn't feel anything and had to ask, "With the jury?"

"No," Ashlin replied. "Something much worse is happening."

Ashlin stroked Tempest's hand and said, "It's okay. You can hear the voices. I hear them too, but they are far away. Hear how far away they are. My voice is very close to you. Your own voice is in your head. We are much louder than those far away voices."

The pain melted away from Tempest's face, but not the concern. Something was wrong and she could feel it. She stopped rocking and leaned her head against Ashlin's, but she still whimpered over what she heard.

***

Honey left through the doors to the lobby and went straight to Thomas. "Your friends were stupid," she said.

"Idiots," he agreed.

Richard was looking out of the hotel's front door with Sven and said, "I don't think it's over yet."

Honey joined Richard and saw a very anxious swat commander frantically trying to reach someone on the radio. Up and down the street, patrolmen stood behind their vehicles with their side arms trained on the hotel door. Honey pushed out the door and yelled, "Oh my God! Are those your men in there? Somebody call the National Guard! The police are in there molesting and raping innocent little girls!"

The crowd that had gathered around the police gasped. Several of the police retrained their guns on Honey.

Honey jumped up on the commander's squad car and reached for the megaphone that was hanging from his belt. It flew off his belt and snapped into her hands. "Can everybody hear me? The cops are in there right now, showing their teeny, little peckers to your children! And not just the girls, either! Are we going to take that kind of shit from the police? I'm certainly not! From this day forward, I am taking over around here! Your governor has resigned from his office and, as of right now, I am your new governor. Very soon I will take over the whole damned country and then the world."

The crowd which had reacted to her first statement now discounted her as an obviously mentally disturbed young lady. Half the police weren't sure where to aim their pistols anymore.

One of the commander's lieutenants said, "That's enough. You can get down now."

"No!" she yelled. "Didn't you hear me? I'm in charge. You do what I say!"

He reached up to grab her wrist, but she stood her ground and said, "You see this? They think they can manhandle you and me."

More of the guns swung around to Honey.

The lieutenant pulled on her wrist to force her down, but she pointed her finger at him and lifted him up into the air and said, "I told you 'No' already. I'm in charge."

The man floundered in the air, unable to touch anything solid. He reached for his gun and Honey said, "Really? Is that all you assholes can ever think of? Your guns?" She pushed the gun back into the holster and pushed the belt and his pants down around his ankles.

Half the guns pointing at Honey began to tremble.

"You bitch!" the lieutenant spat at her. "I'm going to tear you apart when I get my hands on you!"

"No, you're not," she said, "and if you say one more nasty comment, I'm going to turn you into a firework display."

"You crazy piece of..."

She flicked her finger to the sky, and the lieutenant flew up into the sky and burst into a shower of glowing embers.

At the back of the gathering crowd, a little girl said, "Oooh, pretty!"

All the guns trained on Honey trembled now, but several of the officers had the presence to begin firing their weapons. Most of the fired rounds simply missed her, but those that were on target stopped and hung frozen in the air when they reached her, then slowly slipped to the ground. A dusty cloud formed around her, carrying with it the obnoxious scent of sulphur and gunpowder. A pile of lead collected around her as bullets impacted on her shield and slowly fell off.

Honey's expression went from crazed to furious. The amulet glowed hot beneath her dress. She lashed out at the nearest man who had fired upon her. He stood behind his vehicle in the open door with his gun still pointed at her. She slammed the car door shut, snapping his shin bones, ribs and his spine. Then she shoved his remains into the car and flattened it to the ground.

More bullets were fired. A wicked smile appeared on her face. This was fun. She reached out to two men who were firing their weapons at her. Like the first, they were stationed in the open doors of their cars. She slammed the doors shut, snapping them into pieces, then slammed the two cars together and created a giant fireball out of the heap. The fireball spread across the ground and took out another ring of frightened cops who were pointlessly emptying their clips into her.

She turned around and saw car after car lined up down the street, all firing at her. Some of these cars had assault rifles. Instead of attacking them directly, she reached out and sent heat waves to a skyscraper that stood down the block. The ground floor burst into flames that spread upwards through the lower floors. The fake stonework on the outside of the building rained down upon the street, which was already filling with smoke and the stench of sulphur that permeated everywhere.

Johnson climbed back into the driver's seat and started the car. He smoked the tires as he backed out of the parking space, then slammed it into drive and crossed the sidewalk, guiding the hummer across a corner plaza and through a fence into a park that led them away.

Logan lusted for her power, but he couldn't take it away from her without help. He couldn't believe that the only way for him to take it would be to align himself with a witch. He closed his eyes and gritted his teeth. She wasn't just any witch. She was a witch with his people's powers. There was something very unfair about that. He opened his eyes and said, "Good idea. Get us away from this crazy bitch."

Johnson wound his way through the park, trying to find an exit that would lead them back onto the streets. They could hear the mayhem continue behind them, but he couldn't just leave. He slammed the car into a left-hand turn and climbed a hill with a view of the street. He skidded to a stop and stood on the running board, watching the chaos through the field glasses.

A screeching sound filled the streets as the iron and steel girders of the burning skyscraper twisted and bent. The tall building bent at the third floor and leaned over the street, falling and crushing police vehicles and bystanders alike. Fire and rescue was lost under the rubble. Clouds of dust and debris filled the street and spread outwards then pushed upwards when it reached the buildings that lined the street. Stones and rubble bounced in every direction and rained down around Honey, bouncing harmlessly off her invisible shield.

Honey smiled broadly, then turned to the swat commander who had managed to get a call through to the National Guard. He had no protection against the pelting and held his arms over his head as she asked, "Did you see that? I brought the whole friggin' building down on all of them, and I'm just warming up. You got any last words?"

"Plea..."

She didn't let him finish. He twisted like a taffy until he was long and thin, then she lit him like a fuse and tossed him away to burn out in the street. She turned to the other half of the block away from the skyscraper and waved her arm across the street to clear all the cars and debris out of the street leaving a clear path from the hotel to the limo, and a clear road for the limo to get out of here.

She turned to the hotel and spread her arms wide. "Gentlemen?" she asked. "Are we ready to go?"

Richard and Thomas guided the shaken governor from the hotel. Howard and Sven followed nervously behind. Margaret and Abilene followed Sven. They crossed the street to the limo, but the driver was gone.

"Look at that," Honey said. "It would appear that our ex-governor is not out of a job after all!"

Margaret giggled.

Honey sidled up to Margaret and put her arm around her waist and whispered in her ear, "Did you like that, girlfriend?"

Margaret could only say, "Wow."

"Stick with me," Honey said, "and we're gonna have us some fun."

They walked up to Thomas and Honey added, "Don't look so dejected, sweetie, I still got room for you. We're all gonna have some fun together!"

Abilene pursed her lips to say something, then decided not to.

***

Destiny went into the trial, confident that she had seen the outcome in a vision and had nothing to worry about. Blake had seen it too, but things had changed. There were subtle differences in this trial which left her wondering whether the future she saw in her visions was really true, or just maybe true.

Blake felt the concern emanate from within her and quietly said, "It's okay. I'm sure they'll rule in your favor."

Michelle was wringing her hands and thought to herself, "Why in the world did I leave it in their hands to decide for themselves, anyway?"

Destiny, Blake, and Ashlin all gasped.

"Oh Lord," Michelle said. "Did I say that out loud?"

"Not exactly," Destiny said.

"But close enough," Ashlin added.

"I'm sorry," Michelle said. "I shouldn't be thinkin' that way. It tain't right."

"Why not?" Blake asked. "If it's a gift and you shun it, isn't that being ungrateful?"

Michelle didn't know how to answer that. She'd been riding Blake since the beginning about his willingness to push people to do what he wanted.

Tempest began moaning and rocking again. Ashlin still held her hand and Dr. Weinhart tried stroking her hair, but she rocked too violently.

"What's wrong?" Michelle cried. "Is it the jury this time?"

"No," Ashlin said, "but it's real, real bad."

Michelle was frantic. "What's real bad?"

Destiny closed her eyes and answered, "You remember the sorcerer who came to kill us?"

Michelle moved her lips to say yes, but nothing came out.

"Well," Destiny said. "It's like that. Another one of them is acting like him, only a hundred times worse."

"Who?" Michelle asked, "Who?"

"I don't know who it is," Destiny said.

"I do," Ashlin added. "It's..."

The door burst open, and the bailiff said, "Time to go. The jury's back."

"Okay gov," Honey said. "It's time for you to prove your value to me. Get us out of here."

The governor fired up the engine and stepped on the gas.

All the power rushing through Honey's body had pushed her already aggressive libido into overdrive. She sat in the back seat with her arm around Margaret and looked hungrily into her eyes. Margaret was enamored with Honey's power and presence. She wished she had Honey's power, but at least she could have Honey and be close to her power. Margaret steadied her heart, tilted her head and leaned forward slightly.

The governor slammed on the brakes and ended the tender moment that almost passed between Honey and Margaret.

"What the hell are you doing up there?" Honey screamed.

The governor stammered from the front seat, "The road is blocked."

"So?" Honey asked. "Drive around it."

"I can't," the governor said. "It's blocked with tanks and they're pointing right at us!"

"Oh hell," Honey said. "I guess it's up to me then." She gave Margaret a quick peck on the lips that made Thomas wince. Honey rubbed his thigh and said, "Don't worry, sugar. You just keep your pecker warmed up till I get back to you."

She climbed out of the car and faced the tanks.

An amplified voice from the tanks proclaimed, "This is the national guard. Hold where you are."

Honey turned around coyly and pretended there must be someone behind them, then turned back and asked in her most sugary sweet voice, "Are you talking to lil old me?"

"Put your hands in the air."

Honey laughed and said, "Why sure, sugar. Why don't you come out here so I can see who I am talkin' to?" She raised her hands and arched her back to thrust her breasts against the thin material of the slinky dress. "Surely, you ain't afraid of me?" she asked.

A dozen armored infantrymen came out from behind the tank and surrounded Honey. One on each side grabbed her wrists and brought them down behind her, binding them with zip ties.

"So many of you," she moaned. "I can't take all of you at once! Three or four at a time, maybe, but the rest will have to take turns."

One of the infantrymen said into his radio, "Are you sure this is the right girl? This chick is nuts, or maybe she's high on something."

Honey smiled and fried the tie straps, freeing her hands. She wrapped her arms around the man who had just asked the question and kissed him full on the lips. Then she swept her arms from around him, in a circle, to behind her own back and the five men nearest them all turned to ash and fell to the ground. The man before her shook violently as she grabbed his head again and brought his ear to her lips. "I'm the right one," she said, "and I'm getting pretty good at this."

The remaining men were still processing what had just happened when she swept her arms around again and six more of them fell to earth in a pile of ashes.

The tank turrets turned as they refocused their barrels from the limo to her.

"Aw, that's not very nice," she said. She turned the man in her arms around to face the tanks and said, "Tell them. Tell them it's not very nice to point those big guns at us."

The poor man was unable to speak.

Honey closed her eyes and bowed her head. She reached up with one hand and pulled the amulet out of the plunging neckline of her dress. She squeezed the amulet in her hand and looked at the tanks again. One of the turrets jerked back and forth. Two men inside began screaming as they tried opening the hatch to get out, then their screaming ended as a flash could be seen just as they pushed the hatch open a crack.

The scene became eerily quiet. Only the sound of the other latches opening on the other hatches was heard. A red glow started in the bottom of the first tank and spread throughout the structure as it spread to the other tanks. Their screams were brief and quickly ended as their hosts were incinerated.

Margaret exited the limo and ran up behind Honey. She wrapped her arms around Honey's waist and said, "That was incredible. I gotta have you!"

Honey released the soldier and said, "Sorry lover boy, I guess I don't need you. You go tell your bosses that I'm in charge now. They have only one choice and it's really quite simple. They can bow to me or die."

She waved her arm and pushed the center tank out of the way and shoved the soldier toward the opening. Then she took Margaret by the hand and returned to the limo.

"Oh my god," Johnson said as he watched from the hill. "That is one sick chick."

"It's not just her," Logan said as he watched from the other running board. "It's our people. We're built that way. It's the whole absolute power thing." Logan paused for a moment, then said, "I can't believe I just admitted that."

"What about you?" Johnson asked. "Would you be like her?"

"I don't know. I'd like to think I'd be more civilized than that."

"But you want to be her."

"I can't help it," Logan admitted. "It's what I am. I lust for her power, but I don't want to be like her. At least part of me is rational enough to want to keep that in check. She's like a wild beast."

"I guess I'm kind of amazed that this didn't happen long ago, when your people had their power."

"There are stories of wizards trying to take control by force, but bitter feuding between our people prevented any one of them from becoming too powerful. So, our people tried working together to conquer the world, but it was the witches that kept us in check. Without them, we all would have been like this girl."

"Let's hope we can find this other girl so she can keep this one in check."

Logan agreed. "You remember where Brian took you?" he asked. "The girl is there now, but I don't know how much longer she'll be there."

"Geez," Johnson said. "It would take a whole day to drive there. Better buckle up."

Logan flipped out a credit card and said, "Maybe it will take less time if we fly?"

The makeshift courtroom wasn't any different from before, but something about it seemed different. Destiny's heart fluttered as she passed through the door. The air felt thicker and harder to breathe to her, though she knew it was the same.

Tangiers and his assistant were already seated at their table. Simon grinned smugly, like he knew something nobody else knew, as he watched Destiny and Mr. Charles return to their table.

Somewhere outside, someone was yelling that the verdict was in, and throngs of people were hastily leaving their tables at the diner and rushing across the service station to file back into the court. The room bustled with the sound of feet scraping across the dirt floor as the room swelled with the cacophony of everybody gossiping at once. An orchestra of squeaking chairs flooded the senses and grated on the nerves like raw, out of tune violins.

Destiny was surrounded with noise and tension, but nothing she felt came close to the calamity that was coursing through her mother's brain. Ashlin was steadily calming Tempest, but her brain was practically dialed into the carnage that was fifteen hundred miles away.

"You're doing fine," Ashlin said. "Look how well you are focused on the faraway voices. You hardly even hear those around you anymore."

Tempest heard her and placed her other hand over the Ashlin's. Focus was returning to her, but she didn't want to see this. She had never visited the memories. She had never seen the ancient wars.

This was too disturbing for her. Some instinct in her youth had told her that she never wanted to see the future, but here it was.

Michelle watched the young redhead with her daughter and wondered how anyone could be so composed at such a young age. Ashlin's mother must have been a wonderful teacher. Michelle heard Ashlin instruct Tempest, and it was as if she could hear her own mother teaching her when she was younger.

"All rise. The twenty-third district court of Louisiana is now in session. The Honorable Harold Jamison presiding."

Harold strolled into the room, confident that he wouldn't need to hear that cry again anytime soon, or at least not in this venue. He climbed up on the riser, lowered his gavel, and sat down. He waited for the jury and gallery to seat themselves, then asked, "Has the jury reached a decision?"

A serious-looking man in the jury stood and said, "We have, your honor." He held out a piece of paper with their decision written on it. The bailiff took the paper to Harold, who read it and nodded his head. He looked up from the paper and asked, "What say you?"

Simon puffed out his chest, confident that the decision was a foregone conclusion.

Destiny and Blake held their breath, less confident than they were when the trial began.

The foreman turned to the gallery and announced, "We find the defendant..." he paused for a moment, relishing in his fifteen seconds of attention, "...not guilty."

"What?" Simon exclaimed.

"So say you all?" Harold asked.

"Poll the jury!" Simon demanded.

"So say us all," the foreman declared.

Simon turned and glared at Michelle, shouting, "You did this!"

"Thank you," Harold said to the jury, "for your time and your service. You are excused."

"What did I do?" she asked, using the voice.

Harold stood and hustled for the exit.

"You tampered with the jury!" he involuntarily blurted out. "You used your witchcraft to sway the vote!"

"What do you know?" Michelle demanded.

"I had the jury in my pocket!" Simon yelled uncontrollably.

Harold didn't make it out the door. He had already heard too much.

"I arranged everything," Simon continued. "I even had my own witch and you..." Simon stopped ranting when he realized the judge was listening to every word.

Michelle smirked and left with her family.

The National Guard commander was screaming into his headset, "Shore up the center! Retreat the command post!" He ran and jumped into a Hummer and lit out in the opposite direction. He covered the headset mic with his hand and yelled at his aide, "Do you have General Hammond on the phone yet? GET ME SOMEONE!"

The governor guided the limo between the tanks, but the soldier Honey let free was blocking the way.

Honey had returned her attention to the attractive Margaret, but looked up to see why they were moving so slowly. "Oh hell," she said. "Honk twice and if he don't move his ass, run him over." She turned her attention briefly back to Margaret.

He did eventually move. Soldiers surrounded him and guided him away while other infantrymen filled the road in front of the limo. The limo stopped and Honey had to distract her attention from her playmate again.

"Shit! Must I do everything?"

"Gimme that necklace," Abilene said. "You play with your friends, and I'll take care of it."

Honey glared at her mother and opened the car door. As she stepped out of the car, she said, "Thomas, keep Margaret's motor running while I'm gone."

She walked out front and approached the soldiers. They hadn't seen what she had done and were looking for some kind of machinery. They didn't know that she was their target and thought that she might be a survivor of the massacre, so they surrounded her to guide her away.

"Well, howdy boys," she said to them. "You seem like a friendly lot, but my dance card is full up and I would really appreciate it if y'all would just get the hell outa my way."

The soldiers didn't understand and reached to take her arm to guide her away, but her skin burned their hands.

"I asked you nicely," she said, "but if y'all want me to be more forceful, I can surely oblige."

Margaret had her in a playful mood at the moment, and she gently pushed a force field against them and shoved them backwards.

"Sir," the commander's aide said as he handed him a phone. "It's General Hammond."

"General?" the commander said. "What the hell kind of weapon do they have? They just neutralized a whole row of tanks. The crews can't be reached and are presumed dead. They shoved one of the tanks out of position like it was a toy. We need regular army and air support here."

"Air support?" the general asked. "Are you crazy? I can't order air support on our own soil!"

"Get us some surveillance at least!" the commander pleaded. "They've already brought down one building and..."

"Sir," the aide interrupted. "The men are being pushed back and want to know if they can return fire."

"They want what?" the commander asked incredulously. "Of course they can open fire! Tell them to throw everything they have, including missiles and artillery!"

"What was that?" the general asked. "This is supposed to be a police action, not a full scale war!"

"Then get some eyes in the sky," the commander suggested, "and see for yourself."

Johnson was grateful that the signs pointing to the airport headed away from the mayhem Honey was creating. He could hear the battle behind him as he sped the vehicle away. It went in bursts, starting with rapid fire assault weapons followed by the roar of a fire, sometimes accompanied with screeching metal which could have been crushed vehicles or more buildings pulled down on their heads.

As the battle faded behind them, they heard the distinct sound of explosions.

Logan spun around to see out the rear window and said, "That was different. Do you think she learned something new?"

Johnson shook his head and said, "No. I think that was desperation. I'd guess that she's generating enough heat for them to try aiming some heat-seeking missiles at her."

"Stingers?"

"Maybe, but stingers are designed to take down aircraft."

Logan turned to face forward again and said, "Great. She can fly now?"

Johnson almost chuckled and said, "Not necessarily. If I were desperate enough and she were hot enough, I would aim some stingers at her even if she were on the ground."

Johnson sped into the airport and left the car in the departure zone. He didn't care if they towed it.

Logan headed toward the nearest airline, but Johnson said, "Not them. They don't have a direct flight. Go down one. They have hourly flights."

Logan did as Johnson suggested and started negotiating with the ticket agent. They were in luck. The next hourly flight was in twenty minutes.

Logan took the tickets and led Johnson to security.

"Let's hope," Johnson said, "that we can get out of here before she closes down the airport."

CHAPTER 14

Destiny wasted no time leaving the makeshift courtroom, but she stopped just outside to grab Mr. Charles' hands and say, "Thank you so much, Mr. Charles. You did really good in there, but I gotta go now."

Something was going on and she needed to go handle it, but she couldn't go anywhere. She was immediately surrounded by old friends and neighbors congratulating her and patting her on the back.

"You ain't goin' nowhere," said Mrs. Planchette. "You already left us once without so much as a goodbye. Tonight, you be headed to my place and we gonna celebrate that you is free."

"Thank you," Destiny said, "but I really can't. Something even more important than this trial has come up, and I gotta go take care of it."

"No!" Tempest said. "We can't leave yet. Someone is coming."

A shiver ran up Destiny's spine. The last time they had a party at the Planchette's was just a few weeks ago, and her nana had used those very same words. She had read the bones and said, "Someone is coming and someone near you is going to die."

Destiny shouted back. "No! We can't let them come here! Maybe if I go away, they'll follow me away from here."

"Someone is coming," Tempest repeated, "and he is going to ask for your help."

The National Guard was decimated. Not in the Roman sense where one out of ten men are killed in a show of power, but in the modern usage where they are nearly annihilated. Air reconnaissance was coming, but it was too late. Honey walked across the scorched ground and surveyed the grisly scene, stepping over the bones and ashes of fallen soldiers. Burnt bodies and rubble covered the ground. The air was thick with the scent of burning flesh and none of it bothered her.

She turned to find her car, which was following slowly, and said, "I'm hungry! I feel like a steak. I bet they got good steaks in Wyoming!"

She climbed in the car and smiled wickedly toward her two new friends.

"How long till we get to Wyoming?"

"About an hour to the border," answered the governor.

"Then step on it!" she said, "And Mama? You may want to avert your eyes for an hour or so."

Mrs. Planchette led them to the dock, where they met up with the Pinets.

Destiny took Blake's hand and led him to her friend Danielle. "Danielle, this is Blake."

She looked at him approvingly and asked, "Is he the reason you run away?"

Destiny and Blake left the question unanswered and followed Danielle and her parents onto their boat.

Michelle, Tempest and Ashlin also followed Mrs. Planchette but stopped when they saw Zeline standing off to the side watching them.

Michelle glared at her and said, "I'm gonna go give her a piece of my mind."

"No," Tempest said. "I'll talk to her."

Michelle and Dr. Weinhart looked at each other and shrugged their shoulders. They weren't accustomed to Tempest saying so much.

"Don't worry," Mrs. Planchette said. "She warn't invited to the social."

Tempest walked off with Ashlin while Dr. Weinhart waited with Michelle.

"Who is you?" Zeline growled as they approached.

Tempest mustered a smile and said, "I'm Destiny's mother."

"She be yonder," Zeline spat. "What you doin' here?"

"I come for you," Tempest said.

"What you want?"

"I want what you want."

"Bah," Zeline said as she turned away. "I ain't gots time for no riddles."

"They don't understand," Tempest said. "You're one of us. We're family. You should come with us."

"You doesn't want me, I..."

"I know it was you," Tempest said. "I know what you did. That's how I know you're one of us."

Zeline was seldom lost for words, but she stood awkwardly, unable to respond. Tempest smiled and gestured politely for her to follow. Zeline hesitated, but eventually followed Tempest back to the boat. She walked haltingly, unsure if she was even the one in control of her legs. Mrs. Planchette started to argue but Michelle surprised herself by shaking her head no.

As soon as Destiny and Blake were in the boat, Mr. Pinet fired up the motor and guided them up the bayou.

Mrs. Planchette opened a basket and handed out ice-filled glasses, then pulled the plastic lid off a pitcher of amber liquid and poured it for everyone. "It's just sweet tea, folks, but don't worry yourselves. We be havin' somethin' a bit stronger at mah place."

Mr. Pinet's boat was fast, and he pushed the throttle forward, cutting through the bayou and sending a spray of water on each side of the boat. Danielle stretched her neck and pointed her face into the wind and spray, letting her hair fly behind her. She loved it when her father went fast. She also loved it when they went to the Planchette's for a party. Everyone loved the Planchette's parties. She glanced over at Destiny with a big grin on her face, but did not sense the same exhilaration from her best friend. Destiny didn't even look a little bit happy.

"What's wrong? You look more like you lost than you won."

Destiny shrugged and said, "It's hard to explain."

"So?" Danielle said. "That don't mean you cain't try."

Destiny just shrugged.

Danielle put her arm around Destiny and said, "It be like that night when your nana said someone was gonna come here and someone was gonna die. We was afraid it might be you, but it wasn't. Maybe Mr. Wizard can't explain how your nana knowed what was coming, but all us around these parts know it pretty good. I know your nana's different. I know you probably is too. Your mama shore is different, I mean, she's just different, but at least she ain't in no crazy hospital no more."

Destiny looked back at the other boat. Something was going on with her mother. She was coming back to them, but something more was happening in her head.

Danielle continued, "It's okay if you don't want to talk about it. But you just don't have to be using the 'we won't understand' excuse. I think we understands pretty good."

The spray thickened behind the boat until it was a fog that blotted the other boat from her view entirely. The sun lit the fog and blinded Destiny's eyes. She rubbed her eyes until she could see through the fog.

But she didn't see the other boat. She saw her mother standing next to her holding her hand. Destiny tried to speak, but she was frozen in bed. She rose up from the bed only to realize, she was floating above the scene watching her mother sing Hush Little Baby while she still lay motionless in the bed.

Destiny couldn't speak, so she tried thinking to her mother, but this was more like a regular vision where she was only watching, except she wasn't some ancestor in the room. She was a spirit floating above them all.

The lights in the room flashed and were followed by the sounds of explosions. Destiny realized it was war just outside the window. Tempest glanced at the window but immediately returned her attention to Destiny and cried out, "Don't leave me now, baby. Stay with us! Stay with us!"

Blake burst into the room. He was covered in ash and blood.

Tempest turned to him and shouted, "Did you get it? Tell me you got it!"

Blake handed her a leather bag. She took the bag and turned back to Destiny. She held the bag to her head and closed her eyes, saying, "Please let this work."

Blake walked around to the other side of the bed and took Destiny's other hand. "She's cold!" he blurted out. "Why is she so cold?"

Tempest opened the bag and pulled a trinket from inside. Destiny recognized the object. It was the jewel that Nimisen tried stealing from Marvalaine. He called it the Orb of Destiny.

Tempest held the orb over Destiny and began chanting something, but Destiny couldn't hear the words. Her mind spun inside, and the vision blacked out of view.

"Are you listening to me?" Danielle asked.

"I'm sorry," Destiny said. "If you really think you can understand what's going on and that I can tell you anything, then I should be able to tell you that I just had a vision."

"A vision?" Danielle squealed. "What did you see?"

"I think it was the end of the world. Something really bad was happening, and I was supposed to stop it, only I couldn't because I think I was dead."

Danielle's jaw dropped. There was nothing she could say in response to that.

***

Mr. Pinet pulled the boat up to the Planchette's private dock and tied off the bow line, while Mrs. Planchette brought her boat in. A few pirogues were already pulled up onto the shore, but most of the invitees were present at the trial and were yet to arrive. The shoreline and the dock will be crowded with a variety of watercraft before the night was through.

Mrs. Planchette's staff had everything in place. She had either put a lot of faith in Destiny's acquittal, or she planned to have a gathering in either case, but the win in court would certainly prove more festive than the alternative.

Destiny waited on the dock with Danielle while Mr. Pinet tied Mrs. Planchette's bow line to one of the cleats and helped the women out of the boat. Danielle saw Zeline and whispered in Destiny's ear, "What's Zeline doing here?"

Destiny replied, "She always comes to these shindigs."

"Maybe so," Danielle said, "but she been seen with the prosecutor fella, and I got the feeling she wasn't invited to this party."

"I dunno about that, but I'm kinda wonderin' why my mama is sittin' with her and talkin' to her like they's old friends."

Michelle walked with Mrs. Planchette and said, "Oh, Arlene, you should'n a gone to so much trouble."

"What trouble?" she asked, "You an' dem tain't never been no trouble. You be a breath of fresh air in dis parish. I be remiss if I doesn't celebrate such a historic occasion."

"I'd hardly call it historic," Michelle said.

"Dat man called you a witch in da public an' he meant it like he was fixin' to burn ya at da stake. He woulda too, ceptin dey let you go 'n' now. You 'n' miss Destiny be walkin' free. I'd say dat be history. An' wouldcha look at Miss Destiny? She got herself a man child, I see. Mah po boy Anton be without his dance pardner tonight."

One of the servants came to Mrs. Planchette with a problem, and she excused herself. Michelle waited under the string of colored lights that surrounded the patio area and watched Tempest walk up to the patio with Zeline. Ashlin saw the look on Michelle's face and could only shrug.

The band struck up a lively tune and old Rene snuck up behind Michelle and wrapped his arm around her waist. "I has ya now," he said. "It be dat time we kin shuffle our feet across the floor agin."

"Oh, Rene, does you never give up?"

"Not ever."

Michelle was too kind to turn him down. He always had his way of catching her at these affairs and she always had her way of allowing him a dance and slipping off when he wasn't looking.

Ashlin wandered off to the desserts while Zeline pointed to the picnic tables off to the side of the patio and told Tempest, "I usually hangs out daer and does da readings and stuff until your mama comes and spoils tings for me. Den dey all calls me a fake and gathers round Michelle. I don't know why I keep coming to dese tings."

"Well," Tempest said, "I know you has the gift, but my mama has it real strong, much stronger than even she knows, and ma baby is real special."

"What about you?" Zeline asked. "You must got it strong enough."

"Sure," Tempest replied, "but my gifts landed me in the crazy hospital. It warn't the gifts' fault I went crazy. I know that now. The gifts need to be learned and practiced. I'm practically a beginner now."

Tempest and Zeline took seats at the table. Ashlin joined them with a bowl of ice cream.

Zeline took one look at the ice cream mustache on Ashlin's lip and started laughing. "Sometimes," she said, "I cain't tell if you is a little girl or a shrunken ol' lady."

Tempest laughed and said, "Neither can we."

The limo sped across the border to Wyoming. The air force arrived too late in Salt Lake to even know what to look for. There was nobody left of the National Guard to follow them and even if there were survivors, they would have needed a combination of stupid and exaggerated balls to go after her.

A sign on the highway indicated a restaurant with the word ranch in its name, so the governor pulled the limo down the off ramp and to the right. The parking lot was full, which was a good sign. He pulled the limo to the entrance and let the guests out. Abilene was quick to leave the vehicle, as were Sven and Howard.

"I thought you was hungry," Abilene yelled sarcastically into the sweaty car.

Richard climbed out and went inside to arrange a table.

"I am," Honey yelled back. "Just let me throw my clothes back on."

Abilene turned away from the car and stretched her back, muttering, "Well, that's gotta be a first."

Sven and Howard found a quiet outdoor bench as far from the car as they could.

"We gotta get away from this bitch," Howard said. "She's completely crazy."

"I know," Sven agreed, "but I don't see any way for us to leave that doesn't end with us both burned to crisps like those soldiers."

Howard hung his head and looked at his shoes. He was afraid to stay by her side, but he was maybe just a bit more afraid of leaving her. "I wonder how they did it in the old days? How did we ever survive for so long?"

Honey and Margaret finally climbed out of the limo. They spent a moment rearranging their dresses, so they hung properly from their bodies. Margaret licked her thumb and wiped off some lipstick that had smeared around Honey's mouth.

Richard came out and said, "We came at a bad time. They said it would be about forty minutes."

"No, it won't," Honey said as she started marching inside.

"Wait a second," Richard said. "How are you going to enjoy your steak if you end up torching the place?"

Honey stopped for a moment and bit her lip, then her face brightened up as she smiled and said, "I don't need to torch it. I just need to convince forty minutes worth of people to leave."

"If you did that," Richard said, "someone would call the cops and eventually they'll call the National Guard again until someone decides to send in some serious troops."

Honey frowned and asked in a little girl voice, "Is Ricky afraid that I can't handle whatever they send our way?"

"No," he said. "I'm afraid we won't get dinner and I'm getting hungry, too."

"Oh," she said, smiling brightly again. "Not a problem. Let's get everyone inside."

She entered through the heavy wood and iron doors and waited while Richard ushered her entourage inside. Margaret and Thomas stood on either side of her with their arms around her waist while everyone came inside. Howard and Sven were the last to enter, and neither of them looked too happy to be there.

She waited for them to close the doors and said, "Can I have everyone's attention, please?"

A few heads turned her way, but most of the patrons in the waiting area ignored her.

The hostess called out, "Jones? Party of four? Jones?"

"Everyone?" she asked. "Stop talking and pay attention."

"What is she up to now?" Sven whispered to Howard.

Howard just shrugged his shoulders.

"Damn it!" she yelled. "You're gonna pay attention to me or I'm gonna do this to you!"

She reached out and wrapped a force field around Sven, then slammed him against the doors, where he burst into flames and was turned into a puddle of smoking ash barring the door.

"Now, do I have your attention? I'm the new queen of America and y'all are going to wait a little longer for your supper while I go inside with my friends to eat. You can sit back down now, Jones party of four. I just got moved to the top of the list."

The hostess could barely breathe and whispered, "Right this way."

Honey started following her, then turned and said, "Oh yeah, don't nobody leave, or nothin', or else you know what'll happen to ya."

Richard whispered to her, "They might call the police on their cell phones."

"Good point," she said. "Howie? Be a sweetie and collect all their cell phones. If they argue, kill them. If any of them resist and force me to handle it myself, I'll come and kill all of them."

Howard's knees shook as he followed her instructions. He was definitely more afraid of leaving her than staying, but he didn't think he had much chance of getting out of this alive either way.

The hairs stood up on the back of Johnson's neck. Logan had found them a flight to Lafayette and now they were driving back to Cricket

Bend. He ran like hell through the snake and alligator infested swamps to get away from there and now they were going back. At least Logan had hired a driver, so he didn't have to take them there himself, but that left him in the back seat, running the facts through his mind. They weren't just going back to visit; they were going to seek out a girl who could create fire from her hands; a girl who probably hated him as much as anybody.

Johnson shrunk down into his seat and said, "Tell me again why we're going back there on a suicide mission?"

"It's not a suicide mission," Logan said. "It's a rescue mission. We're trying to rescue the whole damned planet."

"She's going to kill me just like you watched that other girl kill so many others."

"You don't know that. Maybe she'll be reasonable."

Johnson didn't know what reasonable meant to Logan.

"You're thinking about this too much," Logan said. "Try to relax. Her kind are always more into love and peace than war. We'll be fine."

"You don't know that. I tried to kill her as much as the other guys did. I fired a modern assault rifle at her, and the bullets just bounced off her."

"That's ancient history," Logan said. "I tried convicting her of murder. I was going to have her executed if I could."

Johnson turned away and mumbled something about this so-called ancient history being just last week. He looked out the window and saw the light from the gas station and diner down the road.

"Relax," Logan repeated. "You're way too tense. You look guilty. Try looking sorry instead."

"Too late to relax," Johnson said. "We're here. Driver? Pull up to that diner on the left."

Johnson waited in the car while Logan went inside.

Marie was in the back stacking dishes under a counter when she heard him come in. She poked her head up from the counter and said, "I'm sorry, monsieur, but we're closed tonight."

"I understand," Logan said, "but perhaps you could tell me where we could find the girl who was on trial today?"

"Why do you look for her? Are you ze reporter?"

"Yes," Logan lied. "No. I'm not a reporter. I have a message for her."

Most of the locals were immediately suspicious of strangers, but Marie's job at the diner made them a regular occurrence. She didn't detect any deceit in his voice. "You don't look like a messenger."

"I'm not. The message is from me. I need her help. It's very important that I see her."

Marie's eyes narrowed. "She is my friend. She is everyone's friend around here except for the man who tried to put her in jail, and you, of course."

"I understand you don't know me, but she has a cousin. Her cousin is like her except she is crazy. The fire that burned down your friend's home was nothing compared to the fire her cousin just created in Utah."

News of Salt Lake was all over the radio. "They say that Salt Lake was terrorists."

Logan shook his head and said, "I was there. It was a girl like your friend. They're cousins, only this girl is crazy with power. I'm hoping your friend will know how to stop her before we have another disaster like Salt Lake on our hands. In fact, I'm afraid that Destiny might be the only one anywhere in the world who can stop this girl from destroying everything."

Marie believed him. "I'm going to see her after I close up. You can come with me."

"I have two people with me. I planned to leave one of us here at the diner but…"

"I only have a small boat with room for my mother, myself and one other."

"A boat?" Logan asked. "We can't drive there?"

"Oui," she said. "We can drive. It's a little farther, but still faster than rowing."

"Great," Logan said. "We'll drive then. I'll wait for you in the limo outside."

"I'll get my mother."

The diners seated in the restaurant weren't aware of what happened in the entrance. Some near the door may have heard a commotion, but they dismissed it and turned their attention back to their own guests and their meals. They couldn't, however, ignore the procession of patrons that entered the dining area. Abilene was hardly dressed for such a fine establishment and Honey's clothes, while elegant, were laced with soot and she reeked of smoke.

Honey was inclined to take the large center table in front of the fireplace. She didn't care that it was occupied and was about to suggest that the patrons find another table when Richard gently took her arm and pointed to another large table that was empty. She withdrew the temper that was broiling inside of her and nodded her head, then wrapped her arms around his and leaned her head on his shoulder wishing he had been her daddy instead of the womanizing drunk that knocked her mama up and stuck her in the Boutin farm.

They seated themselves around the thick wooden table. Honey looked around and saw various eyes on her. "What?" she sneered at them until they turned their attention back to their own tables.

The waiter's knees shook as he took their orders. The staff was told what had happened out front and the hostess had pointed Honey out to him before he had approached the table so he could address her first, "Good evening, Ma'am, what can we get for you tonight?"

"Ma'am?" Honey burst out. "Do I look like a Ma'am to you?"

"I'm sorry," the terrified waiter said. "They told me you were the queen. I wasn't sure what to call you. Should I say, 'Your Majesty'?"

"Oh," Honey said calming down. "I guess ma'am does sound kinda queen like. What do you got that's crunchy burnt on the outside and blood red on the inside?"

Sweat dripped from the waiter's temples. He took a calming breath and said, "We have a blackened prime rib with a crunchy tangy exterior that is slow roasted to perfection."

"I'll have that," she said. "Bring me a big juicy one and a baked potater fully loaded."

The young waiter's hands trembled as he wrote it down. "And would her highness like a salad?"

Honey looked around the room at the other patrons' salads and said, "Nah, not if it looks like weeds."

An older, more seasoned waiter came and said, "Why don't you go ahead and take her order to the chef while I get the rest of the orders?"

Logan's driver pulled the limo into the long, tree lined drive leading up to the Planchette home. Most guests came by boat, leaving the circular driveway at the end of the road nearly empty.

Johnson smelled the bayou as soon as he cracked open the door and said, "Yup. This is the place I swore I would never see again."

Logan climbed out of the car and said, "Nice place. I thought everyone here would be poor. I wasn't expecting a mansion."

Marie said, "Zis is ze Planchette mansion. Long ago, it was a sugar cane plantation. Mrs. Planchette likes to throw parties here for ze whole parish."

Marie had to coax her mother out of the car and lead her around the house. She turned and said, "Well? Are you boys coming?"

Johnson and Logan looked at each other and gestured that the other should go first.

Johnson shook his head and said, "She'll kill me on site. You should go first."

Logan was about to argue when Ashlin came around the corner. She grimaced and held her hand to her stomach while she said, "You better come with me."

Logan was astonished to see the little redhead was looking directly at him. There was no question her statement was directed to them. He nodded his head and followed her around the side of the house to the back.

Most of the partygoers were on the dance floor, gyrating in time to the music with large mugs of beer in their hands. Another group congregated around the bar, hitting the hard liqueur. Every couple of minutes, one of them would drink enough courage to go out on the dance floor and work up a thirst. As the night progressed, they would spend less time dancing and eventually find a table and a chair.

Logan followed Ashlin past the dance floor to the picnic area on the side. Blake was seated with Destiny while Michelle and Tempest were opposite them at the same table. Zeline couldn't look Destiny in the eye and wouldn't join them, but Tempest talked her into at least sitting at the next table, where she could hear what was said. Dr. Weinhart sat with her.

Ashlin plopped herself down next to Tempest and held her hand. She sensed that Tempest felt the same tension in her gut, too. "It's okay," she thought to Tempest. "I heard of this before. We get these cramps when we're around their kind, but I never felt it myself until now. It feels kind of like the cramps I used to get on the farm."

Johnson and Logan stood awkwardly at the end of the table, unsure how to start the conversation or even if they should be the ones to begin. Johnson kept his head down, but peeked up at Destiny and watched her expression. He could tell she recognized him. Blake certainly knew him.

Michelle's gut also twisted. She scowled and said, "You come a long ways just to stand there like that. My daughter says you come to see us, and now you sees us. Why is you here?"

"Yes ma'am," Logan said. "Our people…" He stopped abruptly and looked at all the faces that sat around the table and said, "I'm sorry, I was only expecting to speak to two of you. My name is Frank Logan. I'm…that is, I'm one of…excuse me, but can I speak freely in front of everyone here?"

Destiny remained focused on Johnson.

Tempest said, "We know what you are Mr. Logan, and we knew you were coming, but we won't accept what you want with us until we hear you say it."

Johnson's knees began to shake under Destiny's gaze.

"Oh Lordy," Michelle said, pointing to Johnson. "I remember who you is too. Now why don't you just set your bones down here by me before you pee yourself?"

Johnson did as instructed and said, "Thank you, ma'am, and I'm sorry."

"You is sorry that you has to sit down next to me?" Michelle asked.

"No ma'am. I'm sorry that I tried to kill you, both of you."

"Well, it is good that you is sorry," Michelle said. She pointed to Blake and continued, "But you see that boy over there? He come with you to kill us and we ain't killt him yet, so why don't you just settle down a bit?" She turned to Logan and said, "You may as well take a seat while we parlay, too. I think our hostess is bringin' us a tray of libations."

Johnson and Logan accepted seats across from each other, with Johnson next to Michelle, where Destiny could keep her eye on him.

Before Logan could clear his throat to speak again, Arlene arrived with a tray of sweet tea on one side and gin and gin fizzes on the other. She handed the teas to the kids and let the adults figure out the rest.

"Thank you, Arlene," Michelle said. "We'll send Ashlin if we need anything else."

With Mrs. Planchette gone and a gin to gird his resolve, Logan said, "We have a problem. One of our people has gone quite out of control." He sipped his gin and continued, "In fact, she's your cousin. I don't know how she became so powerful, but I don't have anyone who can control her, and I'm afraid she has gone completely insane with her new power."

"No," Destiny said. "I know exactly when and where she got her power, and I'm pretty sure she was already insane before that."

"Yeah," Blake agreed. "Even before she had the power, you did not want to get stuck alone with that crazy chick."

Destiny shot Blake a hard look. She did not need him to remind her of the image of Honey running topless from his room.

"So," Logan said. "You're aware of what she can do? Johnson here thinks you are the only ones who can stop her."

"Why do you think we have to stop her?" Blake scoffed. "She's your problem. You deal with her. So, she can start a few fires. Big deal! Can't you deal with that?"

Logan shook his head and said, "She wiped out a whole swat team like they were bugs. She defeated the National Guard's tanks and missiles. She brought down a high rise building and leveled three blocks! It looked like a nuclear blast zone! How do I deal with that?"

Ashlin sucked in her breath and said, "It's like my vision."

Blake nodded and said, "Yeah, I seen it too."

"It's the amulet," Destiny said. "It amplifies her power."

Logan looked around the table again. Fear registered in his eyes, and he asked, "Are you all getting your powers back?"

"Yes," Blake lied, "and you are right to be nervous around us. You should fear us." He whipped out a round ball of lightning and rolled it around in his hand.

Zeline's jaw dropped, and she was momentarily unable to breathe.

"But," Logan stammered. "Lightning? Fire? You're witches!"

Blake put the lightning away and said, "It's a new world, Mr. Logan. Our people tried to warn your people that your attempts to wipe us out would end in your losing your powers, but your people didn't want to listen."

Logan shook his head and said, "None of that matters. Can you band together and stop her? I don't care what you have to do to her."

The conversation paused as Mrs. Planchette arrived with two servants carrying a platter of pulled pork and buns, plus a large pot of jambalaya. "I know you be scheming and plotting over here, but dat ain't no cause for you to not have your eats too."

The sky had darkened around them and even with the strong aroma of barbecued pork, the air filled with a strong floral scent. Mrs. Planchette sucked in a deep draught of air and said, "Isn't that wonderful? That be my spring blooming Cerus. They only bloom once a year. This must be a good omen, don't you think?"

Michelle smiled weakly and said, "It's heavenly, Arlene." But she thought to her guests, most of whom could hear her, "Let's hope it gets to bloom again next year."

"There's something else you should know," Johnson said. "You're not the only other ones interested in this girl. There is another group that keeps getting in my head and telling me what to do. They really don't want you to go up against this girl and…"

"Johnson?" the librarian asked. "What are you doing, Johnson?"

"Oh shit," Johnson said. "They're listening now."

"You're hearing voices?" Dr. Weinhart asked. "And they are actually telling you to do stuff?" She suddenly wondered if modern psychiatry had the wrong idea about schizophrenia all along.

"I thought we had an understanding," the librarian said. "We don't want the girl involved."

"But," Johnson said out loud, "we can't stop her. If we don't get these witches involved, she'll destroy us all. Isn't that what you're afraid of? Unless you can come stop her yourselves, these are the only people who can."

"What are they saying?" Michelle asked.

Destiny wasn't waiting for an answer. She wanted to know who was pulling Johnson's strings, so she entered his mind and followed the link to the librarian. She raced through the librarian's memory and found an image she recognized. "You son of a bitch!" she blurted out for all to hear. "You're the people who sent Migul back in time to kill Mala? You should have said so in the first place, because I don't want to do anything to save your people!"

"We'll find another way!" the librarian yelled back. "Our master doesn't want you going in there! It's too risky for all of us. You could be dooming all our fates, including you and your family!"

Destiny dropped out of Johnson's mind and closed her eyes. She was furious. She hated Migul more than anyone in existence. He killed her mentor Mala, and he almost killed her. Mala sacrificed herself so Destiny could survive. She wanted to go back and save Mala, but she couldn't.

Johnson heard the anger in her thoughts when she yelled at the librarian, and he saw the fury in her eyes. His eyes widened as he saw her staring into him, but her anger wasn't aimed at him.

Destiny fought unsuccessfully to hold tears back as she remembered Mala dying at their hands. "This is a nightmare," she cried. "There is no reality on this Earth where I am going to work with those people to save their world. I'll save us and I'll save our world, but I'll do anything I can to make sure their world rots!"

"Oh shit," Johnson said. Everyone looked at him and he just shrugged and pointed to his head.

"Good!" Destiny shouted. "I'm glad they're worried! They should be."

"But they aren't the enemy," Blake said calmly. "At least, not the one we need to worry about now."

"How can you say that?" Destiny cried. "They tried to kill me and you're standing up for them?"

The tears flowed freely down Destiny's cheeks now. Michelle reached across the table and wrapped her hands around her granddaughter's and said, "Easy, Cherie. Ain't nobody here dat be against you. We just don't want to lose you."

Destiny pulled away from her grandmother. "You don't think I can do it, do you?"

"No Cherie, I didn't say dat." Michelle reached across to brush a stray strand of hair out of Destiny's face, but Destiny slapped her hand away and inadvertently administered a small shock.

"Maybe we should all take a moment to calm down," Ashlin said.

"What was dat?" Zeline asked. "Did you see dat flashy ting? And dat ting da boy did... How you people do dat?"

"Fine," Destiny cried. "If none of you believe in me, I know someone who does."

Michelle got up from the table and put her arms around Ashlin. "How about you and me go see what kind of ice cream be waiting for us at dis party?"

Ashlin shook her head and said, "I can't. Aunt Tempest needs me." She leaned close to Michelle and cupped her hands to whisper, "I'm helping to keep the voices out of her head. Besides, I already had my ice cream."

"But," Michelle said softly, "someone your age shouldn't have to get mixed up in this."

"My age?" Ashlin asked. "Just how old do you think I am?"

Michelle stood up, but still left her right hand on Ashlin's shoulder. "Oh, I thinks I knows just how old you be."

"If you did," Ashlin said, "you wouldn't be seeing a little girl anymore."

A tear crept out of Michelle's eye. She didn't mean to hurt Ashlin, and she sure didn't intend to cause another scene. She patted her shoulder and said, "I think I sees you for who you really be. I just wanted some time to spend with you before this is all over and it be too late."

"It's okay," Tempest said. "Go get some ice cream. Bring me something too."

"I think that's a good idea," Blake said. "I'll go with you."

Destiny closed her eyes and focused on her friend Marvalaine. The void zoomed past her and flung her into a room where he lay on his bed. He was a withered old man, much older than she had ever seen him before. Trinkets and mementos of his life surrounded his bed where he could see and sometimes touch them.

His eyes brightened under thick, bushy white eyebrows when he saw her standing there. "Ah, Nimisen my love, you have come for me at last."

Destiny looked for a mirror to see if she had somehow slipped into one of Nimisen's memories, but she saw only herself. "No, it's me, Destiny." She even heard her own voice. She was confused, but the old man before her was even more confused.

He wrinkled his already prune-like face and squinted his eyes. "Destiny?" he asked. "Do I know you? Wait, don't tell me. I'll remember. I always do."

"What's happened to you?" she asked.

"Why?" he asked. "Is something wrong with me?" He sat up slightly to examine himself and said, "I don't see anything wrong. What do you see?"

She might have found him amusing if she hadn't known him so well.

"Ah," he said. "I remember you. You're the girl from the future. I told you I'd remember."

"Yes!" she exclaimed. "That's me. I have a problem. You remember when I told you about the man that tried to kill Mala and me? It turns out that he's from the future, too. Have you ever heard of a group called the librarians? They're the ones that sent him to kill me and now they're the ones who are trying to stop me from fighting Honey, only they act like they're trying to protect me. Have you ever heard of them?"

"Just give me a second," he said. "Let me think. I got it...I remember you! You're the girl from the future! Why are you here? Where's Nimisen?"

"Think," she said. "Have you ever heard of the librarians?"

"The librarians?"

"Yes," she replied. "The librarians."

"No," he said sadly. "Nimisen is not at the library. She's gone. Who are you?"

Destiny couldn't stop the tears that collected in her eyes and streamed down her cheeks. He was her most vital ally and now he was reduced to this. She put her hands on his head and felt the familiar tingle in her hands as she released the healing powers.

"Thank you for trying," he said. "Nimisen tried often, but it never worked. In some ways, I was gone before her. I look forward to the next life where I will find her again. We always do find each other."

Destiny smiled at him through her tears and rubbed his beard covered cheek. "I know Nimisen loves you," she said, "because I love you too."

"You should go now," he said. "I'm sure you have more pressing matters to deal with."

She nodded her head and said, "I wish I had something to give you for your collection so you could remember me."

He pointed a crooked and shaky finger to the wall at the foot of the bed and said, "That is the dress I gave to my cousin Destine when she told off the snooty Vivian. And that hat next to it was my son's, who you never met, but you knew his mother."

"I remember," she said.

He patted her hand and said, "Thank you for visiting, but you should go now."

The dessert table was long and well stocked. It stood near the house on the far end of the patio from the picnic tables. Michelle held

Ashlin's hand while Blake led them across the patio, working their way around the dancing couples.

Two waiters manned the table, smiling and dishing out anything the partiers requested. Michelle and Ashlin went straight to the ice cream as they had said they would. They found the standard vanilla and strawberry, but also pecan praline and cherries jubilee. Michelle ordered a modest bowl of praline ice cream while Ashlin filled a waffle bowl with French vanilla and piled gummy bears and chocolate chips on top.

Blake gravitated away from the ice cream when he saw the bread pudding smothered in caramel sauce. He smiled as he closed his eyes and inhaled the sweet aroma. He turned his back on the desserts to return to the picnic area, but old Rene stopped dancing long enough to step in front of him. He was a wiry thin man holding a mug of beer, which had mostly sloshed out onto the dance floor. He walked directly in front of Blake and pointed a thin, bony finger directly at him. His tired old face sagged as he said, "Don't let her go. It's too dangerous and only you can stop her."

Blake opened his mouth to respond, but Rene had already returned to his dancing with no further acknowledgement that Blake was even there.

Blake watched Rene for a moment, then shook his head and returned in the direction of the picnic area again. Mrs. Planchette's sister, Margot, hooked her hand around Blake's arm. She was toasted, as usual, and asked him, "Hey sugar, you wanna dance?"

He shook his head and said, "No, thank you." He tried pulling away, but she hung on and said, "You can't let her go. Somethin' terrible is goin' to happen. She could die and you'll lose her forever. We'll all lose her forever."

Having said her piece, she let him slip out of her hand and returned to her drink as she stumbled across the dance floor.

Blake returned to the table and found Destiny huddled up with Johnson and Logan.

"I can get us close to her," Logan said, "but the rest will be up to you."

"I still don't think we should rush into this," Blake said. "What if we can't stand up against her head-to-head? What if we run in there on the attack and she squashes us?"

"I'll stop her!" Destiny said. "And if I can't stop her, then there's no one else who is going to either, so what difference would it make?"

"If we run in there and commit suicide, then the world is finished, but if we think of some way to go in and test her powers, maybe we can spot some weakness and learn how to fight her before she kills us."

"How do you plan to do that?" Destiny asked. "Are you going to walk up to her and wager her a dollar to see who has the biggest powers?"

"No," Blake said. "Someone is going to have to force her to use her powers. You're the one we need to defeat her, so that leaves me to go in alone to fight her. You watch from a distance, maybe even get in my head to see what she does."

"NO!" a librarian yelled in Johnson's head.

"NO!" Johnson repeated.

All eyes were on Johnson.

"Sorry," he said, "but they think that is a really TERRIBLE idea, though they like the part about not running in before you know what she can do."

"It *IS* a terrible idea," Destiny admitted. "I should just go in there and blast her when she's not looking."

"That's a huge gamble," Blake said. "If you fail, it's all over."

"No," Destiny replied. "If I fail, my mother will save us."

The confusion in the restaurant grew worse as the meal progressed and patrons that had finished their meals were not allowed to leave. Coffee cups were filled, and a dessert cart was rolled around the room. Nobody was told why they couldn't leave, but eventually, all suspicion fell upon the large table in the center of the room.

A minor argument broke out in the kitchen as the restaurant manager wanted someone to present the bill, but none of the waiters were willing. The bill was over three hundred dollars, and he wasn't paying for it himself, so he marched out to the table and placed the bill in front of Richard.

The meat had a lulling effect on everyone's senses, which probably saved the manager's life. Honey picked up the slip of paper, but it burst into flames like a magician's flash paper. "Oopsie," she said in a sweet, lyrical voice, but she looked at the manager with intense and intimidating eyes. His legs wobbled as he backed out of the room and stood with the waiters.

Honey stood and said, "Well, I think it's time the governor finds us some rooms for the night." All eyes were on her as she left the table and strutted out of the dining room. A few patrons started to ask why Honey was allowed to leave, but enough spouses and dates had the foresight to kick their shins and quiet them before they made a scene.

Honey strolled through the entrance and kicked Sven's ashes out of the way. "Jones, party of four? Your table should be ready soon."

She laughed and swung open the large doors and found half a dozen squad cars parked outside the door with flood lights trained on her. A single shot was fired. The sniper placed a bullet directly in Honey's chest. She fell backwards and banged her head on the floor. Richard knelt down to see how she was. It couldn't be this easy, but she was dead.

Paramedics rushed in and took her pulse, then pronounced that she was dead, and the sheriffs and deputies roared their approval. Richard pulled out his cell phone and started to re-call Frank's number when Honey opened her eyes. The amulet glowed brightly between her breasts as the bullet was expelled from her chest. She sat up and climbed to her feet.

The police were still congratulating themselves when she walked out into the parking lot. The air swirled around her as her fury built up inside. She scanned the scene until she could identify the one cop being congratulated by the others. He held a long rifle with a scope on it.

She started with the rifle. It quickly grew red hot and branded its shape in his hand as he flung it to the ground. It glowed red hot on the ground and naturally, all the cops circled around it, staring at it. She moved now to the sniper's service revolver, which glowed red on his hip. He tried removing the gun belt, but the buckle was red hot too. His pants smoked and caught fire. He frantically tried ripping away his clothing, but the heat from the fire was already searing his flesh. While he panicked, the cops around him watched in utter confusion. None of them had ever seen anything like this before. None of them had ever been trained for anything remotely similar.

The sniper fell to the ground and Honey lit him on fire. The flames roared up from his body as he finally stopped squirming and morphed into a smoldering pile of ash.

Honey yelled out at them, "You really is a bunch of dumb sons a bitches, ain't ya?"

In unison they pulled their revolvers and trained them on Honey, but this time she was ready. Multiple shots fired out and impacted on the invisible bubble that surrounded her. She laughed at them and reached out to pick a bullet off the bubble and play with it.

One of the deputies yelled, "Oh shit!" and jumped into his vehicle. He barely had time to start the engine before Honey sent an arc of flame from her hand to his car. It roared down the road, still engulfed in flames, until the tires burst, and it spun out of control and exploded.

More bullets were fired. That was all they knew to do. Honey walked out among them until she was surrounded with cops firing their weapons at her. A great pleasure filled her body as the rush of energy channeled through her and exploded out from her. The cops and all the cars within thirty feet of her were covered in flame. The men wilted and burned while the cars blackened and the windows cracked.

She walked out of the flame unscathed and said, "Governor? Get the car. I'm tired of this place."

She was tired. Her mind was completely buzzing. Nothing could compare with this feeling, not even sex, but even though she had just eaten, she felt her energy draining from her. A good night's sleep should fix that.

Richard joined her while the governor was fetching the limo and asked, "How did you do that?"

"What?" she asked. "You seen me make fire before."

"You were dead," he said. "They shot you in the heart and you had no pulse."

"Oh that," she said. She lifted the amulet that hung from her neck and said, "I think this thing did that. I dunno how or why, but I sure is glad I got it."

Abilene scowled behind Richard. She should have grabbed the amulet while Honey was still dead; then she could be the queen.

"We can't sit back and do nothing," Logan said. "And we can't keep bickering over who's going to do what. She's already a monster and from what we saw, she is just getting worse."

Everyone at the table was in agreement. Honey had to be stopped. Even Michelle and Zeline had shared a look and nodded their heads.

"Agreed," Blake said, "but we just can't send Destiny in until we know what Honey can do and how we can stop her. We need to know her weaknesses. Maybe we should contact the elders."

"The elders?" Logan asked.

"Yeah," Blake nodded. "They are from the ancient days. They usually have good advice on this stuff."

Logan shook his head with an amazed look on his face and said, "Damn. That's really awesome. I wish we could do that."

"I already tried," Destiny said. "They weren't any help."

Johnson started nodding and shaking his head. Something was going on.

"Are they talking to you again?" Weinhart asked. "What are they saying?"

"No," Johnson said. "It's not them. I don't want to die, and I was kinda talking to myself about it."

Destiny patted Johnson on the back and said, "Stop cringing. I'm not going to hurt you."

Johnson let out a low, "Thank you, but I was thinking you should send me in and watch what she can do."

"That's very brave of you," Destiny said, "but the only way to see what she can really do is to send someone in with magic against her."

"Can't you do that?" Johnson asked. "I mean, these guys get in my head all the time and I'm pretty sure they were controlling these two other dudes like puppets. Can't you get inside my head and make the magic go through me to see what she can do?"

Destiny and Blake looked at each other and shrugged.

"That's an interesting idea," Logan said, "but we still need to find her first." He dialed Richard's cell phone.

Richard looked at the caller id and answered the phone, "Frank? Is that you?"

Abilene's attention was instantly drawn to Richard. "Is that my Frank?" she asked.

Richard nodded his head and said, "Frank! Where the hell are you?"

"That's what I was going to ask you," Logan replied.

"I'm with your charges," Richard said. "The girl is real. She's the one. She's putting our people back on top, Frank. You should be here."

Logan closed his eyes and shook his head. Richard was lost. "I wish I was there," Logan said, "so I could see them again, but I've been tied up with that legal matter we were doing."

"You know," Richard said. "You didn't have to do that. In fact, I wish you hadn't."

Maybe Richard wasn't lost. Logan thought that maybe Richard was trying to talk in code. "Well," Logan said. "That whole legal thing didn't go the way we had planned."

"Ah, that's too bad," Richard said, "but don't worry about it. We should meet up and have a party. Bring everybody with you." He held the phone away from his head and asked, "Where's a good place for Frank to join up with us?"

"Where's the capital?" Honey asked.

"Cheyenne," the governor answered. "It's about five hours by car."

"Five hours?" Honey asked. "Let's get rooms and rest the night, then head up in the morning. We can meet him there around noon."

"Noon?" Richard asked. "You want to get up around six in the morning to leave?"

Honey shook her head and glanced over at Thomas and Margaret and said, "No, maybe around ten."

"Hey Frank, we can meet you in Cheyenne around four or five pm tomorrow."

Logan ended the call and turned to Destiny and asked, "Is there anything that you need to take with us?"

Destiny shrugged and said, "Just a plan, I suppose."

Everyone at the table was starkly quiet after Logan's call. Everything just got real. They knew where she was going to be, and they were going there to meet her. They just weren't quite sure what they were going to do when they found her.

Blake broke the silence when he asked, "Does anyone know how Honey became such a threat? Are we even sure she's the right girl? She showed us what she had our first night on the farm and it wasn't very impressive. We put her in her place without any kind of fight. She had nothing for us to be afraid of."

Destiny cocked an eyebrow and said, "You sure looked scared of her when she came running out of your room."

"What?" Blake argued. "I wasn't afraid of her, at least not from her magic."

"And maybe you can tell me why she didn't have her shirt on?"

Blake stammered, "I...uh..."

"Don't blame him," Ashlin said flatly. "Honey is a sexual predator."

Zeline's jaw fell open and Dr. Weinhart asked, "How old is she?"

"I didn't do anything," Blake protested. "She came after me and I turned her down. She probably goes after anybody with a Y chromosome."

"No," Ashlin said. "She casts her nets wider than just the male population. I feel confident saying that she has daddy issues, and I wouldn't be surprised if repeated rejection during her adolescent years and her failure to find the love that she so deeply craves has led her over active libido to build up her inner power and manifest itself as magical energy in the form of an uncontrollable rage."

"Really," Dr. Weinhart repeated. "How old is this girl?"

Zeline forgot her plan to remain quiet and asked, "Who be dis Honey girl y'all be talkin' about?"

"Is it my fault?" Blake asked. "You think maybe I shouldn't have turned her down?"

A sharp elbow from Destiny answered his question.

"What did you guys see?" Destiny asked Logan and Johnson. "What can she do now? How do we stop her?"

Johnson kept his head down, staring at the table while he said, "She's a walking incendiary device; a human weapon of mass destruction. I seen her do a hundred times worse than what I seen you do."

"I can do a lot more than what you saw," Destiny said.

Johnson looked up timidly and said, "I was hoping you would say that."

"She did more than just make fire," Logan added. "She pulled a friggin' building down onto the street. It must have been at least seven stories high, and she knocked it over like a kid pushing over a stack of blocks."

"And she just keeps getting worse," Johnson said. "Plus, I think there's something wrong with her in the head."

"What if we give her Thorazine?" Weinhart asked. "We know it worked for Tempest's voices."

Tempest nodded, but Logan asked, "How do you plan to administer it? She's protected by an invisible shield that bullets can't penetrate."

"Yeah," Johnson said. He looked straight at Destiny and continued, "Her shield looked a lot like yours."

"You have a shield, too?" Logan asked. "If you know how the shield works, do you know how to counter it?"

Destiny shrugged, but Blake said, "If you can distract her so she loses her concentration, the shield can fail."

"She's not very smart," Ashlin said. "It probably takes a lot of concentration for her to maintain her shield."

"Nah," Blake said. "I've been in the mind of a brute who could hardly put a sentence together, but his magic was very powerful, and it didn't come from his mind."

"If I can enter her mind," Destiny said, "I know how to compartmentalize her brain to change it and modify what she thinks and remembers."

"Yeah," Blake agreed. "I've seen that done in a memory. You can change her into someone harmless."

"If," Destiny added, "I can get into her head without her blowing up the whole damned world."

Blake suggested, "Maybe we can lure her into a dream world and use the illusion to our advantage? She can think she's blowing up the world, but she only blows up the dream world."

It was a good idea, and Mala could have done it. A tear collected in Destiny's eye as she remembered her fallen mentor.

There was so much remaining for Mala to share with her.

Honey couldn't see much of the dark Wyoming landscape through the limo's tinted windows. Streetlamps and building signs would occasionally fly by, but beyond that, the dark evening countryside was a blur and even more boring than Utah.

"Hey gov," she said. "Where's that hotel? I'm tired."

"There's been nothing but cheap flea bag motels," he replied. "Just looking for something worthy of the queen."

"I like the way you think, but right now, I don't care. I just want a bed so I can sleep."

"Yes, ma'am."

The governor saw a motel sign up ahead and pulled the limo into the parking lot. It wasn't even a common chain, and it looked like crap, but it would have beds.

Richard went to the office and arranged rooms for everyone. He took Honey to her room with Margaret and Thomas close behind, but when she entered the room, she looked at them and shook her head no. Richard gave them his key and said, "I'll get myself another room."

Before Honey could close the door, Richard entered her room and said, "You really look exhausted. Maybe you're taking on too much by yourself."

In an uncharacteristically vulnerable moment, she shrugged her shoulders and leaned her head against his chest, as any other daughter might have done if she were with her father.

Richard spoke softly into her ear, "Have you ever considered teaching others of our kind how to do the magic? You could build up an army and send them out to fight your wars for you."

"That won't work," she said, "unless you got a stash of these necklaces lying around in storage."

"But you could already do your magic before you got that thing. You and your mother could. If our people were empowered again, our numbers together could work in our favor. You don't think your cousin will be doing the same thing with the witches?"

"It won't do her no good without this neither."

Richard walked her to the bed and pulled the covers down for her. "I hope you're right," he said, "but our archives are full of stories teaching us that the witches often found clever ways to band together and either escape us or sometimes to even defeat us."

She climbed into bed and mumbled, "Mmmf hrmff," as she drifted off to sleep.

Blake slid into the limo first, but when Destiny climbed in after him, she stayed on the opposite side of the seat, forcing Johnson to sit awkwardly between them.

Ashlin held Tempest's hand and said, "I still wish we were going with them. She's going to need us. I've seen it."

"She will need us," Tempest said, "but not today."

Ashlin didn't understand. She held Tempest's hand as they turned around and walked back to the party and said, "We know something bad is going to happen, and we know that Destiny is going to need our help. If that's not today, then why are they going? If they are not going to stop Cousin Honey, then what's the point?"

Tempest looked up at the stars while she answered, "The world's a complicated place. We've seen something from the future, but Destiny and Blake are going to try to change the things that led up to that future. We don't know which way it will turn out."

"Well, we know one thing for sure," Ashlin said. "There's another family of witches in the future and they don't want Honey to destroy the world either."

Tempest found a chair and sat down. "They are from the future," she said, "and they are probably afraid that something we do might prevent them from existing."

"Well, they should have thought of that before they started meddling in the past. Destiny said they killed someone she knew."

Michelle joined them at the table and said, "Things be so crazy around here, we ain't been to see each other just to visit a spell. How you be?"

Tempest smiled and said, "I'm fine, Mama."

"But how it be dat you is not crazy?"

Tempest shrugged and said, "I don't know. It's like someone was helpin'..."

Ashlin blurted out, "Hey Zeline! Over here!"

Zeline joined them at the table. Michelle smiled politely, though it mostly looked like a grimace.

"Hey," Zeline said.

Ashlin raised Tempest's hand in the air and declared, "We're gonna teach Zeline about being witches like us."

"Whazat?" Zeline argued, "You talkin' like I ain't no witch like you! I'z da real ting. Y'all cain't be teachin' me what I already is. My mama already done teached me what I is."

"But did your mama teach you this?" Ashlin thought directly into Zeline's head.

Zeline was looking straight at the little girl, and she knew that she hadn't spoken out loud. "No," she replied meekly.

"And I bet your mama taught you stuff we don't know about," Ashlin said.

"Mebbe," Zeline said. "Ma mere taught me da voodoo."

"Bah," Michelle scoffed. "Witch doctors and medicine men."

Ashlin scrunched up her face and asked, "Wasn't Destiny's mentor a medicine woman?"

Michelle opened her mouth to respond, but said nothing.

"Don't worry about my mother," Tempest said. "Just give her some time and she'll come around."

Chapter 15

Day Six.

The world heard, but it didn't listen. It saw, but it didn't understand. News of the massacre in Utah and the horrific events in Wyoming spread rapidly over the news wires. Video of the events went viral across the internet. The world saw the images and heard the descriptions, but found the most obvious conclusions too hard to believe. Those who believed what they saw were branded as crazy, but those who didn't believe were doomed to die in ignorance.

For the first time in twenty-four hours, the world around Honey was eerily quiet. Even while the rest of the world was buzzing with the news of what trailed in her wake, she slept peacefully; unconcerned about what the rest of the world thought of her, or what they might plot against her.

Eyewitnesses couldn't comprehend what they saw and coached their admissions with vague suggestions that it was all a trick. Law enforcement was eager to accept that the witnesses had seen an illusion, but the fire and destruction were very real. There was no lack of evidence. A skyscraper littered the streets in Salt Lake. They had hundreds of casualties that were burned beyond identifying. Experts combed through the video accounts and could not explain what they saw.

Every agency was involved. The event had already crossed state lines, and a governor had been kidnapped. The president's secret service detail was on high alert, but they were watching for terrorist attacks. Homeland security tried to assume control, but they couldn't link the events to any radical extremist group, and nobody came forward to claim responsibility.

Agency cooperation was at an all-time low. The army scoffed at the National Guard's description of the events in Salt Lake, just as the FBI did at the deputy sheriff's descriptions from the restaurant in Wyoming.

The FBI had a description of the limo and knew what direction they had taken. They would be in pursuit already if homeland security hadn't ordered them to stand down and wait for the army to take over. Then the lawyers came out like ants at a picnic.

Claims were made by one side that military action had to be committed by the national guard, but other lawyers asserted that the multi-state nature of the events superseded the state controlled national guard and required the federal army under the control of the president. State politicians went on the record and on the televised news, claiming support for one group or another, but nobody moved in on Honey, and if they had, they wouldn't have known what to do.

So, Honey slept and recouped. The amulet nestled comfortably between her breasts and pulsated with a dim glow that synced with the beating of her heart. While the rest of the world talked only of the horror of the incidents she had caused, she only dreamed of the future where she was in charge, and she was the only one with the power. A voice in the back of her head echoed Richard's words that maybe she should try to teach it to her followers, but she didn't see that in her vision of the world.

The road from the Planchette plantation took them back to the main highway and Cricket Bend. The lights of the gas station disappeared in the rear window as the limo roared down the highway towards Lafayette.

Logan smiled uncomfortably at Destiny, who sat directly across from him. Johnson sat next to her and tried to smile, but it looked more like a grimace. Blake scowled and looked out the window. Nothing he said could lessen her resolve. Destiny saw Logan's glances at her and knew he had something to say, but resisted the temptation to pull it directly from his mind. The tension in the car only grew worse.

Logan coughed nervously as he looked around the occupants of the limo. He looked like he would speak, but instead just kept averting his eyes and said nothing.

Destiny couldn't stand the tension, but she wasn't about to make peace with Blake. She forced a thin smile and said, "I never been in a car this nice before. It's a whole lot smoother than the bus. It's even a nicer ride than our other limousine."

Logan recognized the sound of a youth trying to make small talk. He smiled, but couldn't muster a better response.

Destiny pressed her face to the glass, but it was too dark outside to see anything. "It feels like we're going a lot faster than when we took the bus, and I know it's a lot farther than just Lafayette. How long before we get there?"

"We'll be there before they are," Logan replied, grateful to have something to add. "We'll catch a plane at the airport and be in Cheyenne before noon."

Destiny's eyes widened as she asked, "An airplane?"

Logan smiled and nodded his head. "You'll probably have to take little catnaps on the plane. We want you two to be fresh and rested tomorrow."

Destiny couldn't imagine how she would ever sleep on a plane. It was just too exciting. She closed her eyes and leaned her head against the window.

Blake still wanted to talk her out of it, but if he couldn't do that, he wished he could at least hold her hand to reassure her. He couldn't shake the bad feeling he had about tomorrow.

Honey stood off to the side near the front of a small auditorium with Richard. The room was filling with assorted members of her people. Most of them were high ranking and had arranged to be included here, while others were deemed worthy based on how high their parents ranked. Some paid for the privilege to be here, but in a very real sense, most of those with rank had already paid to have that rank, so everyone in attendance had paid to be here. There was a lot of money seating themselves to be the first of Honey's students. They sat and talked amongst themselves while waiting for the lesson to commence.

When the seats were full and the procession had ended, she stood up and walked to the podium at center stage. She wished she could tell who among them had the aptitude to be the better students, but all she could judge by looking at them was who was hot and who was not. Most of them were not. The room was full of mostly older gentlemen, many of whom she would prefer to dismiss. A couple of the old guys were kind of cute, but not cute enough. She was struck by the fact that there were no women in their ranks at all.

She walked backed to the side and asked Richard, "Are these really the best of the best? Why aren't there any women here?"

"Most of our women aren't like you," he replied. "Even in our historical documents, most of our women only battled to protect their children. We don't usually send them to war."

"Uh huh," she said blandly, "but you send a bunch of old farts to war? Look at them."

She returned to the center of the room and said loudly, "So, I guess you all want to learn how to do this." She held her hands out and formed a fireball in her right hand, then tossed it in the air to her left hand. The crowd erupted in applause.

She created another fireball in front of her and spun it around with her finger like she was stirring a coffee. She stirred it into a funnel cloud that extended down to the floor. "Not just anybody can do this," she said. "Some of our people might only be able to generate a little spark. That's why I asked for the best. I want our best people to learn this. Are you my best people?"

Every man in the audience sat a little taller and nodded his head in a small jerk.

"It's not enough to learn this," she said. "We're going to war. Are you ready to go to war?"

All heads nodded.

"Cause, from where I stand, you don't look like the kinds of boys I would have picked to go to war. I want ten volunteers to come up here and show me how strong you are."

Ten men from the front row jumped up in front of everyone, but two gentlemen from the middle rows also joined them and directed two of the other men back to their seats.

"Well, well, well," Honey said with a fake smile. "So, you are the first of my new army. Let me get a good look at you. Show me how you stand at attention."

They put their feet together, but not one of them stood with the crispness of a man at attention.

She reached out and squeezed her hand in the air. One of the men in front grimaced as he suddenly stood tall and straight. The others followed suit.

"That's better," she said. "So, are you prepared to go decimate my enemies?"

Their voices rang out with a haphazard cadence, "Yeah, sure," and "Yep, we're ready."

Honey's face grew stern as she asked, "Is that how you answer your queen?"

The audience grew concerned and the ten volunteers even more so.

"I asked you if you are prepared to go decimate my enemies!"

"Yes, yes," answered the group, this time a little louder and almost in unison.

"Are you prepared to die for your queen?"

No answer.

"Because I am going to teach you about fire now, but only those who survive will learn how to make it."

All eyes on the stage widened. Before they could either object or inquire what she meant, Honey engulfed them in flames. They screamed mercilessly and fell to the floor in ten little smoldering heaps.

A man in the audience yelled out, "Those were some of our most important people!"

Honey reached out in front of her and grabbed the speaker from across the room. She plucked him out of his seat and dragged him through the audience, bouncing his feet off the heads of anyone between him and the stage. She lifted him up above the stage and pulled him through the air until he was in front of her, dumping him on the floor at her feet, and bellowed, "No, they aren't! I am your most important people. Only me! I asked you to send me the best of the best to build my army, and all I get is a bunch of old geezers who think they are in charge. Newsflash everyone. You either serve me or I turn you into kindling. Now get me my army! And I better see some tits in it, too!"

Honey stormed out of the room. She was pissed and had to burn something else, but when she exited the building, Destiny and Blake were standing on the steps with a hundred witches behind them. They all fired upon her at once. She was pelted with fire, lightning and some kind of cutting blades. She thought the cutting blades were pretty cool, but they sliced the amulet from around her neck and she felt the power draining away.

The flames shrunk in around her until the world faded away. When she came to, she was staring at the motel ceiling, still waiting to drive to Cheyenne.

It was a peaceful trip to the airport. Destiny napped while Logan arranged the airfare over the phone. There were no non-stop commercial flights to Cheyenne and the connecting flights took a minimum of nine hours. It would literally be faster to drive, but he found a charter service and used up the remaining balance on his charge card securing a private jet.

The airport reminded Destiny of the bus depot, but without the diesel smell. It was cleaner and less crowded, but it was late, and she was sure it held plenty of people during the day. They left the ticket counter and walked down corridors that were lined with closed shops that reminded her of the mall in Lafayette.

Logan needed directions to find the charter's terminal. It was independent of the main commercial terminals and as they followed the corridors, the shops and services degraded until even Logan thought it looked like a bus terminal.

The small jet had only five passenger seats and one of those had a sign on it telling them that it was being repaired.

The pilot stood in front of the cockpit and welcomed them aboard. "I was replacing a spring in this seat when you called, but the other four seats are in perfect condition."

Destiny boarded first, ducking her head while she walked down the aisle to the back of the plane, where two seats were set adjacent to each other without the aisle in-between. She had never been on a plane before, but she certainly hadn't expected the seats to be plush recliners like she had seen at the mall once. She sat down in one of the back seats. Blake sat down beside her and tried taking her hand in his. She jerked her hand away from his and got up to find another seat, but Logan and Johnson had already taken the remaining seats.

"Wow," Blake said. "This is way nicer than the plane they used to fly me out of Montana."

"Montana?" Johnson asked. "Is that where you're from?"

"Nah," he replied, "not really, but that's where they raised me. I'm not sure where I'm really from."

Destiny looked out the window of the plane. The airport was full of lights. It even had colored lights stuck into the ground. The pilot dimmed the cabin lights and taxied the small jet out onto the runway. Traffic was light and there were no delays. The pilot powered up the engines and pushed Destiny slightly into the back of her seat while it roared down the runway. The nose lifted up and the plane launched up into the sky.

The air was clear, and Destiny had a wonderful view of the city lights shrinking below them. At first, she could clearly make out the outlines of building lights and vehicles. Some streets were lit with orange-colored lights, but as they climbed, the lights shrunk and blended together until they finally faded from view. A blinking light on the wing flashed in her window. She closed her eyes and could still see the flash against her eyelids. The mesmerizing beat of the light turned into a chaotic flash that felt warm on her face.

She opened her eyes and saw a great column of fire rising into the heavens. A ring of fire spread across the ground, radiating from the rising column. It burned and cleansed the ground as it spread until it finally had reached its maximum size and just hung there like burning air.

Honey walked out of the flaming air and said, "Hey cousin. You just couldn't stay away, could you? I bet you thought this was going to be your show, didn't you? You thought you would be the one. Isn't that what they called you? The 'One'? No, it was 'The Chosen One'. I remember. Well, it looks like they was wrong about that. You ain't 'The Chosen One' after all."

While she talked, flames hung off her head like hair and draped over her body like a dress. She held her arms out wide and said, "How do you like the new me? I think I look HOT! What's the matter, cousin? Why ain't you laughing? Oh, that's right. You cain't laugh. All you can do is just lie there, stuck in your bed. You ain't dead yet, but you're not quite alive either. See what I mean? You're not really 'The Chosen One'. I is. You was just the lucky one with the key to unlock my powers."

The plane was rocked by turbulence and Destiny reached for Blake's hand.

"It's okay," Blake said. "There's nothing to be afraid of. It's just a little rough air."

She retracted her hand and was filled with regret, but she wasn't sure whether she regretted reaching for his hand or pulling it away.

***

Honey eyed Richard suspiciously as she boarded the Limo in the morning. He's the one that was pushing for her to share her powers and train an army, but she saw how that would turn out. He climbed aboard and smiled pleasantly. But now when she looked at him, she saw a man who lusted for her power. She started a mental list of people she had to watch more carefully.

Howard followed Richard meekly into the car. She never trusted him anyway. He was always huddling up with Sven, whispering things behind her back. Now that Sven was gone, he had nobody to whisper to, and he was even worse. He moped around and followed them, but behind his eyes he was dead to the world. She couldn't trust him before, and now she could trust him even less. He definitely belonged on her list of *untrustables*.

Margaret and Thomas were perky and playful as they boarded the Limo. Honey could tell that they must have had a good night without her. There's no loyalty in the world anymore. She added them to her list of people she was keeping an eye on.

Abilene was the last to board. If there was anyone Honey should be able to trust, it would have to be her mother, but as she leaned over to climb in, Abilene directed her glance to Honey's amulet and landed on the list with everyone else.

The governor climbed in and adjusted the mirrors. She took his job from him and demoted him to chauffeur. He should definitely be on her list, but somehow, he seemed to be the least of her worries.

He wasn't one of them. For one thing, he couldn't try to steal her powers from her. Maybe he was an ally.

Honey stared out the window. They were still about four hours from the capital, and she would have to spend the whole time in a car full of traitors. She reached between her breasts and fondled the amulet. It throbbed warmly in her hands. Maybe she should just fry them all and start over. She could hitchhike to Cheyenne and take over herself. It's not like any of these people helped her. She kept her head pointing out the window while she glanced sideways out of the corners of her eye. Richard had that same stupid smile on his face. He wanted to help her. He wanted to share her power so they could take over together, or maybe his plans didn't include her.

She looked back out the window and sulked. How did things ever get this bad? She could feel her mother's eyes staring into her cleavage at the amulet. Her thoughts drifted again to frying everybody and starting over.

Destiny pulled the shade down to block out the blinking light and closed her eyes, hoping she might catch one of those naps Logan suggested that she would need. She sucked in a deep, cleansing breath and tried to forget how much Blake was against her and that he was sitting right next to her.

She leaned her head against the shade and breathed in a slow shallow rhythm until her mind faded to black except for a dim spot of light far away. The world was inky black around her, erasing even her hands from right in front of her. She didn't dare walk in this blackness, but found herself drawn to the spot of light in spite of the danger. She glided towards the light, as if she were standing on the moving sidewalk she saw at the airport. The light grew larger and closer until she arrived upon the scene.

There were no colors. The world before her was rendered in black and white and shades of grey. Three figures stood in the center of the light wearing large, grey hooded robes that hung low over their faces. She sensed two other people hiding in the shadows. One of the hooded figures turned to face the shadows, and she saw his face. It was him. The bastard that killed Mala was standing right there in the shadows. She wanted to kill him, but she couldn't. It was one of those visions where she could only watch.

These were the librarians. She didn't know how she knew it, but it was clear to her now. They spoke to each other in muted tones too low for her to hear. It played before her like a silent movie. She saw their mouths move, but she heard no sound. She heard nothing. No wind, no rustling of their robes. She felt an emptiness in the silence and imagined the clicking of sprockets pulling some ancient celluloid film through a projector as the surreal scene unfolded before her.

The three librarians turned suddenly to face the other shadowy figure. He was yelling at them. She still couldn't hear anything, but he lit a great fireball and threatened to loose it on the librarians. It was Blake. She saw his anger and wished that she could hear what was said. How did they capture him? What held him back now? She saw the fear in their faces and felt the fear in Blake's heart.

One of the librarians walked fearlessly up to Blake and calmly took the fireball from his hand. He held it and played with it, then looked him straight in the face, eye to eye.

Destiny wished again that she could hear what was said. She wished she could help save Blake. He could not end like this.

She squeezed her eyes shut to stifle a tear, and when she opened them, she was on the plane once more.

Honey stared out into the bland expanse of Wyoming as the limo followed the Lincoln Highway through the eastern Rocky Mountains. They passed through occasional settlements, but no real population. She wondered why she would bother taking over such a deserted state.

They eventually dropped out of the mountains and entered the vast Great Plains, but she still yawned at the overwhelming waste. There was nothing to see. She should have driven all night and slept in the car. This was utterly boring.

She may not have been so bored if she had seen the predator drone following the limo from high in the sky. The army still didn't know what they were dealing with. But they had seen the video and while they didn't want to be foolish enough to believe what they saw, they damned sure weren't going to make fools of themselves by blindly storming in on her.

"Good morning, everyone." Even in the jet's small private cabin, the captain used his mic to feed his voice through the overhead speakers. "I'm starting our descent into Cheyenne now. The sun is up, and it looks like it's going to be a splendid day. Please check that your seat belts are buckled. We'll be on the ground momentarily."

Destiny lifted the shade on the window. She squinted her eyes against the brilliant sun outside, but remained focused outside the window. She could feel Blake's eyes staring into the back of her head. He wanted to talk her out of going, but she couldn't allow that. She had her own vision of the future, and she wasn't going to let him fall into the librarian's hands.

"Destiny?"

She kept her head locked out the window and ignored his plea.

"Destiny? Can we talk?"

She squeezed her eyes shut and kept her head pointed out the window so he wouldn't see the moisture in her eyes, then shook her blond locks and said, "There's nothing more to say. I can't allow you to go in my place. You heard Johnson. Even *THEY* don't want you to go in for me."

"Maybe so," Blake replied, "but they don't want you going in either. I know you've seen the same visions that I've seen. It's going to take both of us to see this through."

"No," she said. "I saw something different, something you haven't seen."

"I don't want to lose you."

She turned to face him. Against her wishes, her eyes were still wet with tears straining to find her cheeks. "And I don't want to lose you."

"Then let's find another way," he said as he turned to face Johnson.

Johnson saw them look at him. He remembered his offer to go in their place and already regretted saying it.

"No," she said. "I'm not going to be responsible for someone's death like that."

"We don't know he would die."

"Don't we?" Destiny leaned back in her chair and wiped her arm across her eyes before they leaked out. "You know perfectly well that it would be a suicide mission."

"But what about the needs of the many?" Blake asked.

Destiny didn't know the reference. She simply shook her head and said, "I don't want to talk about this right now."

The phone in the limo's center console rang. Richard and Honey each shared a look and shrugged.

"Hey gov?" Honey yelled. "Are you expecting a call?"

"No, but I suppose somebody could be looking for me. I am missing, as far as the world knows."

Richard reached for the phone and Honey held out her hand, expecting him to hand it to her.

She didn't say anything as she held the phone to her head; neither did the caller, at first, but then, after a silent pause, a woman said, "Hello? Percy, is that you? The news said something terrible may have happened to you."

Honey cupped her hand over the phone and asked, "Hey gov, is your name really Percy?"

The governor shrugged and said, "Yeah. It's short for Percival."

"Oh," Honey replied. "I'm sorry." She put the phone back to her head and said, "No, this ain't the governor. He cain't come to the phone right now. Who can I say is callin'?"

"This is Ophelia. I'm the governor's wi..." The phone was yanked away before she could finish saying "wife".

"Hey gov? Is your wife's name Ophelia? Really? Percival and Ophelia? Sounds like one of those old Greek plays."

A gruff man's voice came on the phone and demanded, "Who the hell is this? Where's the governor?"

"What?" Honey asked. "Who the hell are you and just who the hell do you think you are?" Honey thought it was funny, but only she heard it and she laughed alone.

"This is Major Flinch."

Honey thought his name was funny and laughed again.

"Put the governor on the phone," he demanded.

"I don't think so," she said. "He's busy, and I don't like your tone. Let me talk to Ophelia now."

Honey heard the man growl and slam the phone on a table. Another man picked up the phone and said, "Hello? This is Captain Saunders. Please let me apologize for Major Flinch. He's had a bad morning. To whom am I speaking?"

"Well, Cap'n Saunders, you're much more pleasant sounding than Major Buttcramps, I mean Major Flinch, oh heck, sounds the same to me. Could I possibly speak to Ophelia again for a moment, then, maybe, we can continue our conversation?"

"This is Ophelia."

"Ophelia, I want you to know that your husband is fine. He's been a big help to me, and his assistance has guaranteed both of you a place in my ministration. I'd let you talk to him now, but he's driving, and we all know it's not safe to talk on the phone while we are driving."

"He's driving?" Ophelia asked. "What happened to Roger?"

"Sadly," Honey said. "Roger did not want to be part of my ministration. So, your husband saw an opening and jumped at the chance to work for me."

Honey heard the phone change hands again and Captain Saunders asked, "Now, may we have a name that we can use to call you?"

"Oh yeah, sure. My name is Honey."

"Honey? Is that your legitimate name?"

Honey glared over at her mother and said, "Well sweetie, I don't rightly know that I actually am legitimate, but it be my real name."

"Okay," the captain said. "We'll just go with Honey then. Where are you from, Honey?"

"Mississippi. Somewhere between Gulf Port and Hattiesburg."

"No," the captain said. "I mean, where are you from *originally*?"

"Oh, I guess you might say that I was from Gulfport originally, but I 'spect it was really somewheres between Gulfport and Biloxi."

"Gulfport?" he asked. "Biloxi? So, you started out in Mississippi?"

"Only till my daddy moved me and my mama to live on his farm up north."

"Your mother and father?" he asked. "Are they with you now?"

"My mama is, but I don't see how that matters none."

"And you all come from Mississippi? I mean, you were born and raised right here in Mississippi?"

"That's what I said, ain't it? Why? Wait a minute. Did you..." Honey began laughing hysterically. She laughed and laughed until tears streamed from her eyes. She wiped her arm across her face and took a calming breath before returning to the phone. "Cap'n? Are you still there? Was you thinkin' that I was from Mars or somethin'?"

Several seconds passed with no reply.

"Cap'n? Tell the truth. Did you government boys in the army think I was some kind of advanced alien invasion?"

Several more seconds passed before Captain Saunders said, "Let's move on. Maybe you can tell us a little about yourself?"

"Really? You want to know more about me? Why don't you stop pussy footin' around, Cap'n. Just ask what you really wants to ask. How the hell do I make the friggin' fire? Ain't that what you boys want to know?"

"Well, actually, we'd like to know why. What do you want?"

"Ain't it obvious? I ain't makin' no secret about it, and I sure said it enough. I'm takin' over. I'm the new queen of the world and I'm just gettin' started. Today I own Utah. Tomorrow I'll own Wyoming, though now that I seen it, I'm not quite sure why I wanted it. I think that the sooner you gets use to it, the better."

Honey could hear some commotion on the other end, but Saunders offered no reply.

"That's where I'm goin' Cap'n. Cheyenne, Wyoming. You can meet me there and surrender if you want. You might save thousands of lives that way, and maybe I'll even offer you a job on my staff."

More activity could be heard on the other end, then Captain Saunders said, "Sure. Sure. We'll have someone meet you in Cheyenne to negotiate the terms of a surrender."

"Uhuh," Honey said. "You don't sound convinced. That's okay. I like convincing people. It's a real rush. Sometimes it's even better than sex. Speaking of which, how much time before we reach Cheyenne?"

Honey looked over to Richard for an answer, but Captain Saunders was quick to reply, "Two hours and eighteen minutes."

"Damn, Cap'n. Is you watchin' me or somethin'? I don't mind. It don't make no never mind to me at all. In fact, if you can see me through the window, y'all might just get a real good show for the next hour or so. Gotta go, now. See y'all in Cheyenne."

Honey ended the call and said, "Okay, everybody. Time for musical chairs. I want my Maggie and Tommy back here with me for a while."

Abilene rolled her eyes as she switched to the front seat and tried looking out the window.

Destiny wished she could create a dream world to keep everybody occupied, but Mala was the expert at crafting dream worlds. She had never trained Destiny how to do it, but Destiny's gift had always been her uncanny ability to learn new magic just by being touched by it, and Mala had certainly taken her through a few dream worlds.

Destiny wanted to laugh it off and ask, *"How hard could it be?"* But she knew better. She had seen how much Ishun and the other elders had respected Mala for her ability and knew it couldn't be easy. It even sounded difficult. She looked hard at her surroundings and tried replicating the airplane's cabin in her mind. The plane was descending, but she couldn't have it descend forever, so she leveled it out in her mind.

Then she visualized herself sitting in an empty airplane, flying level and going nowhere. The seat next to her was empty until she pictured Blake. She saw his form start to shimmer into view, but she didn't want to make a replica of him. She wanted to pull the real Blake into the dream.

As Blake's form materialized in the dream, he was looking into Destiny's eyes and never noticed the empty seats across from them. She stroked the side of his head and entered into his mind, pulling the dream world with her. He closed his eyes and savored the touch of her fingers. She pulled Johnson and Logan into the dream. They were preparing for landing. The overhead speakers sputtered, and everyone heard the captain say, "I've just been informed that there are a few planes ahead of us. We'll be circling until the pattern clears up. I'll get you down on the ground as soon as possible."

Destiny was pleased with how real it sounded and couldn't help but smile a little.

Blake smiled too and said, "I like it when you smile."

Destiny leaned back in her seat and said, "I know you don't want me to do this, and it's really unfair for me to not hear you out. Since we're stuck up here a while, I thought I'd give you your chance to say what you had to say."

Blake wasn't expecting this, but he wasn't going to let the moment slip away.

Destiny ducked out of the dream but left a decoy of herself leaning against the back of the seat, smiling and listening to Blake. The plane had landed already. Destiny waited for the captain to pull it to a full stop, then she walked up to the front while he was unlatching the door.

"That was a wonderful flight," she said. "I think my companions had a little too much to drink. Would you mind if they slept it off a while longer? Logan won't mind paying you for the time."

He looked at the three sleeping passengers and scratched his head. "Sure," he said. "I guess it's alright. I'll just see if I can finish up this seat I was working on."

Destiny's heart raced as she took one last look at Blake, then slipped off the plane.

As Honey neared Cheyenne, traffic coming out of the capital had tapered off significantly and ultimately stopped completely. When they reached the outskirts of Cheyenne, they could see tanks blocking both the off-ramps and on-ramps.

Honey was done playing with her playmates and scowled when she saw the tanks. She reached her hand out and the phone receiver jumped out of its cradle and into her hand. "How do I get that captain back on the phone?"

Richard shrugged and said, "I don't know if it's the same for every carrier."

"Hey gov! Pull up to the next tank."

The limo pulled up to the tank and Honey got out and tried knocking on the tank, but her knuckles didn't make any noise. "Hey you!" she shouted. "In the tank! I want to talk to your boss. Can you hear me?"

There was no reply, so she held her hands in the air and shook them. The tank rattled violently. Honey remembered that they were watching her and looked up in the sky for an airplane, and sure enough, there was the drone following them. She smiled broadly and waved at the drone, then mimed holding a phone to her head and mouthed the words, "Call me."

In the military HQ, Saunders and Flinch both shook their heads.

"She's got balls," Saunders said, "and she sure isn't afraid of us."

"Why should she be?" Flinch asked. "Did you see her shake the damned tank?"

The limo phone was ringing by the time Honey returned to her seat.

She picked up the phone and said, "I hope this is the cap'n. I already decided that I'm gonna make that Flinch dude my bitch."

"This is Saunders."

"Hey Cap'n, what's with the tanks? You're not under the impression that you are in control of anything, are you? Do you think your little toys will impress me even a little bit?"

"No, that's not it. We just..."

"How would you like it if I reached through the phone and plucked your balls right out of your pants? Then you can be my bitch like Flinch is gonna be."

There was no response.

"Let's get this through your head," Honey yelled. "Your tanks don't mean nothin' to me. I could crush them like ping-pong balls if I wanted. I'm the one who will decide when and where I get off this road. I'm going to the capital and there ain't nothin' you can do to stop me."

"Believe me," Saunders said. "They weren't there to stop you. We blocked the roads to keep civilians out of harm's way. We never set up a specific meeting place, so if you follow the tanks, you'll come directly to us."

"Maybe you wasn't listening," Honey said. "I'm going to the capital. If you're not there, then you're in the wrong place and your God damned tanks ain't doing nothin' to change that."

Destiny pushed the mind of a taxi driver to take her downtown. She didn't know where she should go to stop Honey, but she saw the tanks lining the roads and followed them to a place where they apparently planned to ambush her. The taxi dropped her off at the site and she released the driver. She pushed a few of the soldiers' minds to let her stay and wait with them, but all the tanks started to move.

She overheard some orders to move everyone to the Capitol building and hitched a ride with them to get there.

Tanks and armored personnel carriers lined the streets. Destiny's ride pulled up to a long row of vehicles that also lined the road in front of the state Capitol building. She jumped out and ran to the steps in front of the building. Sentries stopped her, but she planted the thought in their minds, "*You don't see me.*" She wasn't too concerned about the sins she might commit, especially if she was probably going to die stopping her cousin.

Honey's limo pulled up to the row of tanks that guarded the capital. The army didn't want to open fire until they secured the governor's release, but she was getting close now and the Major was getting really nervous.

She exited the limo and walked up to the tanks that were directly in front of the steps. The Major might not get a better chance, so he ordered the infantry to open fire and sent commandos in to secure the limo.

Bullets flew in from all directions and impacted on Honey's protective shield. This was the regular army, and they had dismissed the reports from the National Guard, but they couldn't ignore what they witnessed now.

Destiny sat patiently on the steps and watched. She saw the commandos push the governor aside and drive the limo away from Honey. She felt the heat when the tanks opened fire directly on Honey, but when the explosions and fire dissipated, Honey was still standing there.

Helicopters moved in next and fired missiles at her. Again, she was surrounded with a massive ball of fire and explosions, but she still stood there.

"Are you done playing?" she yelled out. She cocked her arm and flung her hands towards the first helicopter. A massive fireball shot from her hand and engulfed the chopper until it teetered over sideways and crashed to the ground. She spun around and instead of flinging a fireball, she reached out and grabbed the second chopper and simply crushed it in midair. It fell like a rock and she slapped her hands together as if wiping dirt off of them.

"Wheeee," she said. "That was fun."

More bullets flew and were equally ineffective.

"You can't beat me," Honey yelled. She reached her arms out and divided the tanks, shoving them sideways into each other and pushing all of them out of the way until she could see the capitol steps.

"Hey cousin," Destiny shouted at her. "Whatcha doin'?"

"Oh shit," Honey said. "What in the hell are you doing here?" Honey reached between her breasts and fondled the amulet to remind Destiny, who owned the power.

Destiny yelled back, "Did you really think that thing gave me my power? You got that backwards. I shared my power with it. All that power that's been goin' to your head is just a teeny part of my power. When it comes right down to it, you got nothin'.'"

"I don't think so," Honey said. She reared back and fired a giant fireball at Destiny.

Destiny caught the huge fireball in both hands, then squeezed it down to the size of a tennis ball and toyed with it. "Was that supposed to impress me?"

"Did you see that?" Flinch asked. "Who's that girl? Where did she come from? Why can she do that?"

Saunders could only shrug and watch.

Honey reached her hands out and wrapped her power around Destiny to crush her, but she couldn't crush Destiny's field.

Destiny just laughed. "Come on cousin. Don't you know who I am? They call me 'The Chosen One', as in number one. I'm the original. You can't come late to the party and steal my lines. You're just a cheap knock-off."

Honey was incensed by Destiny's taunts. She fired off lightning bolts and wrapped them around Destiny, but failed to penetrate her shielding.

"Fine then," Destiny yelled. "If that's how it's going to be."

Destiny spread her arms and cast fireballs out right and left. The fireballs arced in opposite curves that converged on Honey in the center. Destiny fired a giant fireball into the ground below Honey, a trick she learned when she was attacked by the sorcerer at her home. Honey was thrown off balance and tossed into the air. Her shields dropped as the fireballs converged on her. Her clothes and hair were singed, but she wasn't substantially harmed.

The army opened fire on her again, but she recovered enough to raise her shields again.

"Find out who she is," Flinch commanded.

"As long as she's on our side," Saunders said. "I don't really care right now."

Flinch agreed and kept the field glasses glued to his head and trained on the battle between the two girls.

Clouds gathered unnaturally overhead as Destiny called on thunder and lightning to rain down on Honey from the skies.

Honey's frustration was mounting. She screamed, "I hate you! I'm going to kill you with my bare hands if I have to."

She ran between the tanks and up the steps. The two girls locked in an embrace and rolled down the steps.

"Cease fire! Cease fire!" Saunders ordered the troops.

Honey and Destiny each released electric shocks directly into the other. Destiny's head started to feel faint as the amulet began to suck her energy directly from her and feed it to Honey. Destiny felt the amulet and knew it was her weakness. It was their amulet, after all. It was designed to steal her powers. She knew she would lose if she remained locked in battle with Honey. She had to act quickly. She entered Honey's brain and planted the weakness she felt into Honey. She added the fear of losing her powers if Honey continued attacking her.

Honey screamed, "You bitch! You're trying to steal my powers. I'm going to kill you!" But the feeling of weakness and the fear of losing her powers were too much. She backed off and yelled, "I'll be back. You're a dead woman, Destiny Boutin. You're dead!"

Honey created a blanket of fire and smoke all around and ran off under the cover of the smoke.

Destiny lay in a heap on the steps, drained, with not a drop of power left in her. Darkness enveloped her as she felt her life ebb away.

The army wasn't sure what to do, but they wanted her as an ally. Medics rushed in and checked her vitals. She was slipping away. The first responder shined a flashlight in her eyes, checking for pupil response.

Consciousness slipped away from Destiny, and with it, the real world. Darkness draped over her and blotted out the world, leaving only a single bright spot in the center. Destiny lay on her back, staring up into the bright light, which grew larger. Or maybe it came closer to her until the light covered her and she bathed in it. The inky blackness faded around her and revealed a forest around her and a bridge over her head.

She heard the distinct sound of hooves and wheels echoing in her ears as something crossed the bridge and rode away from her. Her companion tapped her on the shoulder and said, "Okay, let's go."

She sprang up and out from under the bridge and began sprinting through the forest. She felt light on her feet as she bounced up and out from under the bridge. The forest floor flew beneath her as she ran through the trees. She swung her left arm out at her side to balance her weight against the basket she carried in her right. She felt her companion watch her as her hips swayed seductively with each step.

They broke out of the forest and into a meadow. Across the meadow was a hill with a small settlement atop it. Beyond the thatch-roofed homes were the spires of a castle overlooking the community.

Destiny ran by instinct, but she was also guided by magic. She knew the blind spots where she could run through the town un-noticed, and she could feel the sorcerers that stood watch around the town and especially in the castle. Goats and cows roamed freely through the streets but paid her no mind as she swiftly and silently glided between them and turned the corner to the final street that led them to the castle ramparts that guarded the gate.

She couldn't believe they had reached this point undetected. It was their plan, but she hadn't expected it to work this well. Nobody noticed them until they arrived at the main gate. They could almost knock on the door before a guard finally barked out, "What are you doing here? Hold it now, what the hell are your kind doing here, anyway?"

Destiny fell prostate on the ground and held the basket up over her head, pleading, "We seek an audience."

She felt her companion fall prostate next to her and the guard asked, "Why should I let you in?"

"We come in peace and bear gifts."

The guard took the basket and poked about inside. "Don't mind if I do."

Destiny asked, "You don't think he minds if you do?"

The guard looked at her warily. He was inclined to keep the basket and dispatch the two witches like the vermin he thought they were. "And what makes you think he even knows you're here?"

Her companion asked, "You really think he doesn't know we are here?"

It was clear from the clatter originating inside that he did indeed know and had ordered someone to see what was going on this late at night. The gate swung open from the inside. "What's all the racket out here?"

The guard, whose back was conveniently turned to the gate, extracted his hands from the basket, and spun around to face the secretary at the gate. "They seek an audience." He thrust the basket towards the secretary. "They bring gifts."

"Who seeks an audience?" The secretary stepped out through the gateway and gasped, "My god, they're witches! Did you not notice they were witches?"

The guard stammered, "I did sire, I was just questioning them to learn their intention."

"Who cares about their intention?" the secretary bellowed. "We don't admit witches. We kill them!"

The guard bowed low and said, "They said they comes in peace. I thought it might be bad form to kill them that comes in the name of peace."

The secretary stepped around the guard and pointed to Destiny. "You there! Witch! Why do you bother us?"

Destiny raised her head. Her voice quavered as she said, "We have important news. We wish an audience to share what we have learned."

The secretary said, "I can't grant you an audience without knowing what you wish to discuss."

Her companion said, "We know why your people are losing their powers."

"What? That's preposterous," the secretary said. "We aren't losing our powers." He turned to the marshal of the guards who had arrived behind him. "Kill them. When you are through with them, discover their route and kill anyone they snuck past."

The marshal grunted and nodded his head.

Her companion raised his hand. In it, he held a rolled parchment. "Wait!" he shouted. "We bring a prophecy. You need us. Killing us will only hasten your own demise."

The secretary had not quite returned inside. He turned and saw the male witch pleading for his life. "Why aren't they dead yet?"

The guard went to do his duty, but the male witch continued, "What will your masters say when they learn you were presented with a prophecy to save magic for both our kinds, only you killed the messengers?"

The marshal was clearly hesitant to continue, but the secretary only grew more annoyed. "Why do you hesitate? Must I kill them myself?"

"No, your lordship."

"Then do it and give me that scroll and the basket."

"Wait!" The male witch raised his voice so all could hear. "The prophecy says that if you extinguish all the witches, you will be stripped of all your magic and will be doomed to live mundane lives with the simple folk."

The secretary turned his back on them and said, "Idle threats from two pathetic witches." He waved his hand in the air, dismissing them, and the marshal nodded to the guard, who took his blade and slit her companion's throat.

Destiny was frantic. "Magic will be lost for centuries," she cried out. "The first scroll tells of a chosen one who will return magic to the world." She raised her left hand to show them the other scroll, but her hand was empty. "Wait," she pleaded. "There's more." The guard placed the blade against her throat and sank it deeply into her larynx. "The other scroll," she tried to say, but all that came out was the sputtering of air and blood. She continued thinking, "The other scroll tells of one who will rise among us and covet all the power for herself." Her heart pounded against her ears, but she continued trying to share the final prophecy, "She will destroy everything. She won't stop until the whole world is a smoldering pile of ash. Hear me! We are all doomed." Destiny felt the world fading around her.

This wasn't the first time Destiny had experienced another witch's death in a memory, but it was the first time she didn't wake up from it. As life ebbed from her host's body, she felt the world grow dark and cold around her. She tried opening her eyes, but the completeness of the darkness had thoroughly enveloped her, leaving her lost in it. Her body felt neither cold nor warmth, nor any sensation of any kind. She cried softly, or maybe she only thought she did. No tears were felt, nor could she hear her own sobs, but she felt the regret growing within her, knowing that this was what Blake wanted to prevent all along.

The End

Jonni Jordyn was born in Oakland, California in 1957. She started writing at an early age, writing music, poetry, short stories, radio, film, and stage scripts. She didn't start writing novels until later in life, after she retired from playing music, and found herself travelling away from home for extended periods.

She currently lives in Denver, Colorado.